One
FATEFUL
Night

BLEEDING HEARTS BOOK 2

INTERNATIONAL BESTSELLING AUTHOR

MICHELLE B.

Editor: Raven Quill
Cover Designer: The Book Boutique (Opium House Creatives)
Formatting: AJ Wolf Graphics

Strong
women
aren't born,
they're forged
in the fires
they've had to
walk through.
They're warriors with
hearts of gold.

Silver Ravenwolf

Blurb

He was everything my mom neglected to warn me about, and I was everything he hated about his mother.

I spent one reckless, lust filled night in the back of a man's SUV in the alley behind my job on a whim. A revenge tryst in retaliation against my husband for his brutal sins against me turned into more as the hours passed between us. Months later, we met again. Only this time, my husband is at my side. Little did I know, through whispered words over the passing months, the best night of my life was with a very powerful and ruthless man known as The Fixer.

Giovanni Moretti is the brutal right-hand man and top caporegime to one of the most dangerous underbosses. He is feared by most but respected by all who have dared to mention his name.

He's the handsome devil in a suit I gave myself to.
The dangerous man I haven't stopped thinking about.
And he just walked right back into my dismal life, looking to do what he does best.
Fix it.

Note From The Author

One Fateful Night is a dark contemporary romance. Isabelle's and Giovanni's story contains verbal and physical violence in a marital setting that one may find disturbing. If you have been the victim of domestic abuse, please think twice before reading their story. Also, this book contains graphic sexual content and language some may find offensive. If you have any concerns with any of these elements, please do not read.

National Domestic Violence Hotline
1-800-799-7233

Giovanni
CHAPTER ONE

The wavering minutes between the break of morning light and the dark of night glimmer over the tops of the early summer blossoming forest trees. The unearthed dirt at my feet darkens with each drop of sweat my body releases from exertion. I grab a hold of my tie, loosening it from its constraints then pull it through the starched material. After tightly rolling the red, silky material around my hand, I slip it over my tattooed knuckles and slide it into my pocket. With the flick of the top two buttons, my dark dress shirt falls open. I pull the material wider to get more air. The slight breeze is damp from the thunderstorm still lingering from the night before. It adds to the moisture rolling down the back of my neck. The new season brings revived life to all that live and breathe, but for the dead guy at my feet, he will never get to smell the newly blossoming spring flowers or the strong fragrance of the mid-summer bloom. He didn't deserve that.

I rest the handle of the shovel on my hip and roll my sleeves to my elbows as I give my surroundings a piercing evaluation, checking security. I'm at the graveyard. Not your typical graveyard where loved ones lay their family to rest and grieve over small and large headstones. No, this is *my* graveyard. I can tell you where each body has been placed and covered with the earth I have become personally knowledgeable of. The land on the east side of the property has loose soil throughout most of the year whereas the soil on the north side takes until late spring to defrost fully. I can tell you where each body is laid to rot, how they died, and what month and year their life was snuffed. The details are important. In order for me to stay safe and keep myself out of prison, I have certain ways I deal with situations that arise. That's why I have held the title of The Fixer, because I fix everything.

The dead guy who's rolled in a cheap decorative area rug, laying at my feet, is a justified kill. I have no problem putting men in the ground if they deserve it.

He deserved it.

More than deserved it.

With each forceful stab of the earth I throw over my shoulder, it brings me some sort of peace. Each body I dispose of gives me a certain comfort that my family, nor I, will ever fall victim to that individual again. I could say that I have suffered in my lifetime, but then that would be an admittance of weakness. That is one thing I am not. I am far from being weak. Although, what I will admit, is that I have been a casualty at the hands of a man I should have been able to trust implicitly. Sadly, at too young of an age, I learned my lessons with each pound of his fist.

With a shovel full of dirt heaved over my shoulder, an image from back when I was six years old floods my thoughts. My jabs at the ground become angrier as each moment of the memory flashes. I was just a small boy with nothing but little boy dreams and unconditional love for his mother and father. It was the first time I knew the house I lived in wasn't like my best friend Kat's house. The vision of my mother's body lying on the cold floor halts my movements. The dirt beneath me morphs into a black and white projector of life. I squeeze the bridge of my nose, trying to shake it off, but my high-pitched childhood voice rings throughout my skull.

"Mommy, my tummy hurts."

"Here, baby." She hands me the half of a pickle from the refrigerator. "Your tummy will feel better as soon as Daddy gets home with our dinner."

"I don't like pickles, they taste yucky," I told her, pushing the green spear back in her direction, telling her she could eat it because her tummy was making noises too, but she said my belly was still growing and it needed food for me to grow big and strong. She says one day I will become someone important, someone people will look up to, so I needed to grow.

I ate the yucky pickle she gave me and then told her I was cold. We climbed under the big blanket on the couch so we could cuddle while she read my favorite book, Mommy Loves You.

"I love you with all my heart." She squeezed me to her side and kissed my hair.

She tells me that all the time. I asked her how big her heart is and she told me it was as big as the universe. I don't know what the universe is, but her eyes grew big, and her arms stretched wide and then she wiggled her fingers.

She pulled me into her side more and wrapped her arms around me, but her belly gets in the way. She has a big bump there. She told me my baby sister is growing inside her belly. I don't know if I liked her yet, because she kicked me in the head a few days ago when Mommy was laying in my bed because Daddy was mad. Mommy makes Daddy mad a lot. Mommy laughed

2

when my eyes grew big, and her eyes sparkled like she was going to cry, but she was laughing. She does cry a lot when Daddy yells though.

Mommy was reading my favorite part when I heard our squeaky front door. I heard Daddy's deep voice. He sounded funny, but I was excited for my dinner. I jumped off the ratty old couch that had holes in it and ran towards the front door.

When Daddy walked into the room, Mommy started to cry.

"Daddy, what did you bring for dinner?" I looked at his empty hands.

"Gio, go wash your hands, baby." She turned me towards the bathroom and shooed me along. "Go get ready to eat."

"But Mommy." I tugged on her hand. "My belly hurts."

"Go, Gio baby. I'll get your dinner ready for you."

"Yeah, you little shit. Go wash your hands. Your momma and I have something to discuss."

"Daddy, did you bring us dinner?"

"I ate your dinner, you little bastard. I'm a growing man. It was good too." He patted his belly.

"Gio, baby, go." Her hand held my shoulder then she leaned down and whispered in my ear. "Go hide and don't come out until I come find you." She shoved me toward the hallway.

I don't like my daddy. He is mean. Not like my sissy kicking me mean but mean to my mommy. One time, I kicked him in the leg when he was hurting her. He had her hair in his hand, and he was pulling on it. I like my mommy's hair. It's soft and yellow and she lets me play with it when I'm falling asleep. I twist it in my fingers, but not like my daddy. My daddy pulls on it and my mommy's head jerks really fast.

I was hiding behind the bathroom door, watching them through the crack. Mommy was crying and yelling for him to stop. I was hiding like Mommy told me to, but Daddy was calling me. I kept peeking through the crack because I was scared. Daddy says it's my fault that he hurts my mommy. One time, he said it was because I didn't pick up my G.I. Joe off the floor. Daddy broke it when he stepped on it and that made me sad. I only had five toys to play with and Daddy broke my favorite one. Mommy tried to put him back together with glue, but it kept falling apart.

Kinda like Mommy.

I heard Mommy yell while I was washing my hands like she told me to. If Daddy kept calling me and I didn't wash my hands, I couldn't eat. I was trying to be fast because I was so hungry, but I kept hearing my daddy yell for me. He was scaring me so bad that I didn't use soap. I hope Mommy doesn't get mad. I heard my mom yelling, but it didn't sound right. It scared me. I peeked around the corner. My mommy was fighting my daddy. He had her arms above her head. He was laying on top of her and he was trying to kiss her, but she kept turning her head. She lifted her leg and Daddy fell to the floor and curled into a ball. When Mommy got up and started to run towards me, he grabbed her legs and pulled her down with him. She cried out and held her belly.

That's the night my sister was born.

That's the night I only ate a half a pickle for dinner.

I hated that meal.

And even though I didn't know what the word or what it meant at the time; I loathed the man who claimed to be my father.

Satisfied with how deep this guy's new home is, I lower the shovel to the ground. With a now angry shove from my leather encased foot, the cold body is forced to tumble into the void I just excavated. I jump down into the hole and arrange him just so. When I am satisfied my job has been done perfectly, I raise my hand and wait for the other to clasp mine.

"We good?"

There are three people that know about this place: Mr. Heart, Antonio, and Demetri. I go down, they go down. The property might be listed under a dummy corporation, but I am the one that owns all five thousand acres, plus the two separated by miles of houses on the northeast side. It's my home away from home. The place I go when I need a moment.

My hand grips a hold of his. The clasp of loyalty radiates with the strength of his pull.

"I'm good." I grab the shovel, avoiding his inquisitive eyes. My boss may only be two years younger than me, but in this business, it's life or death, so our perception of situations better be spot on.

"You're not." He grabs the other shovel and starts to heave the dirt back in the hole.

"Let it go."

"This one's personal for you."

"They are all personal, Antonio."

"This one is different."

Giovanni
CHAPTER TWO

I rearrange the oranges for the second time this morning. The sink in the bathroom has been bleached and rinsed twice as well. The towel I hung over the warm towel rack was set just so. My gym clothes from my early morning workout are already on the spin cycle in the washing machine. I head back to the kitchen to make an egg white omelet with spinach. *Simple Man* plays quietly throughout the penthouse. The fresh orange juice I squeezed earlier sits waiting for me. My stomach growls for food then quickly turns nauseous from triggering memories. It's fight or flight inside my gut. At thirty-six years old, I still feel the hunger pangs from thirty years ago. Even at this age, knowing they are phantom aches, I always make sure my refrigerator is stocked.

My phone beeps from where it lays on the kitchen island just as the front door locks sound as they disengage, and the thick steel dead bolts electronically slide open. Even though I know who it is, my hand automatically reaches for the piece tucked under the countertop of the kitchen island.

My boss—Antonio Robert Heart, the underboss of the Heart syndicate—and I have targets on our backs. They are bloody daggers with severely pointed edges waiting in the dark with distorted confidence to pierce our skin and sheath the blade within our bones. We have undermined some big deals over the past few months; crippling organizations that thought they could stomp on our territory. Our segregation in ruling over certain physical land entities will always be challenged, and we will always accept the challenge with brutality if warranted, but instead of being like our ancestors and working the streets by foot, we have grown into something bigger, better, more lucrative. It is our dealings in the world beyond the streets that we now flourish in revenue.

I reach for my phone just as my sister walks in with a bag of groceries. I hold my finger up as my call connects with my boss.

"You just getting up?"

"No. Been up. Already hit the gym."

"Me too. Stop worrying."

"It's my job to worry, and Lilah doesn't count as a workout."

"It sure as shit does when you have the chemistry my wife and I have."

I knowingly chuckle at the accuracy of Antonio's statement. "I'll meet you at the club or are we debriefing?"

"Debriefing. Pick me up. We gotta be at Pop's house at 11:00."

"See you in a bit."

"Tell Hope I said good morning."

"Will do."

I watch my sister putting my groceries away. As she arranges my refrigerator the way I like it, I plate the food that was for me and slide it across the table with the glass of orange juice I squeezed earlier for myself. My sister will always eat before I do. I could simply buy a gallon of orange juice from the food store to make my morning easier, but I also know what it feels like to not be able to bite into fresh fruit and taste the natural juice that comes from it. I turn back to the oversized range and make my own omelet. I hear my sister moan behind me from food happiness. I internally smile at that. It gives me the slightest bit of peace knowing she won't go hungry today. I plate my own food and sit down across from her. She is holding the daily newspaper in her hand. At my request, she buys me one every morning. When breakfast is over, and our day begins, it is destroyed in the fireplace.

I live in an exclusive building just two blocks from Antonio. The owner of this building is also the owner of his as well. The security the owner has implemented is of the highest level. It is one of the reasons why I purchased this place and the apartment two floors below where my sister lives.

I notice the article she is reading. An explosion and subsequently the 5-alarm blazing fire took two massive warehouse buildings down at the docks last night. She lays the paper down, glances at me without saying a word, then finishes her eggs. She knows. She doesn't have to ask. I pull the paper over and study the misinformed article for any clues that I need to be aware of. I read it over three times, memorizing it. Then I walk to the fireplace and toss it into the flames.

"Antonio says good morning," I relay the message as I walk back over to the kitchen.

"Tell him I said hi."

"What's your day look like?" I grab my glass of juice and swallow it.

"I have five clients today."

"And after?"

Michelle B.

"Meeting up with Daniel for dinner."

Daniel, the boyfriend who isn't good enough for her. Because in the end, no one is good enough for my sister.

"Make sure you check in."

"I will. Thank you for breakfast." She pops a kiss on my cheek after dropping her dish in the sink then bounces out to begin her day.

Every morning, Hope thanks me for breakfast even though she knows she doesn't have to. I have taken care of my little sister since we were kids, and I have made provisions to make sure she will continue to be taken care of even in my afterlife.

Giovanni
CHAPTER THREE

I jump in the running SUV waiting for me at the curb and head towards my boss's estate. I reach down and grab for my pack of gum only to find the pack empty. Gum to me is like a cigarette to a smoker. After the first initial crushing blows, I no longer chew it. I hold it in my cheek. It brings me a certain kind of comfort. Two miles up the road, I whip the truck over and hop out at the corner bodega. I hit the candy aisle, grab my favorite cinnamon gum and head to the other side of the store to pour myself a coffee.

The steam rises as the continuous stream of black, velvet liquid fills my cup. I grab for the half and half and pour some in. Just as I'm setting the container back in its spot, I hear a commotion in the aisle behind me. I halt my movements, hone in on the energy of the raised voices, and decipher if the threat is for me or someone else. Then I slowly step in their direction. When I hear the distress in the female's voice again, a chill rips down my spine.

Flashbacks of what feels like another lifetime breeds deep in the loins of my soul.

I leave my coffee sitting on the counter and walk to the end of the aisle. There stands a girl I know but haven't seen in a few months. She has on a royal blue jogging outfit that has definitely seen better days. Her saturated red hair, that is usually well kept and up in a ponytail, is now a massive mess on top of her head. The dark circles under both her eyes tells me she hasn't slept soundly in what looks like forever. The small scattering of freckles across the bridge of her nose are dull in comparison to her fluorescent green eyes. In her trembling hand, she cups the small hand of a child with big, innocent, green eyes just like her momma. There is no denying it is her daughter.

"You got a problem?" a male's sharp misguided authority snaps at me.

My attention breaks from her to the arrogant asshole standing a foot away from her. My gaze slides back to her with no words spoken to him. "You okay?" I inquire, keeping my voice calm while watching her carefully.

With an embarrassed blush to her fair skinned cheeks, she nods at the same time she squeezes her baby girl's hand in reassurance. The gesture is one I know all too well. It's the lifeline of reassuring love from an abused mother to an innocent child.

"We got a problem here?" The guy steps in my direction, asking again.

"If you take another step in my direction, you will be the one with the problems," I warn.

"Clearly you don't know who I am."

"Clearly you missed the memo that I care."

"Okay. Okay." She raises her free hand and tries to calm the situation down.

"You know this guy?" The loudmouth grabs her upper arm and twist her to look at him.

"I–No. Tommy, no, I don't know him." She yanks her arm from his grip. My gaze drops directly to the spot he just had a hold of. I know underneath the thick material of her jacket there will be red marks blemishing her skin. Even without the confirmed visualization, I see red. "Can we just go, please? I have to be at work soon," her lifeless voice begs.

"Pay for your own shit. I'll be outside. Make it quick." He eyes me from head to toe with arrogance.

"Isabelle, what's going on?" I gruffly whisper when he is out of ear shot.

"Nothing," she hisses, glancing around.

"Momma, who da man?"

"No one, honey. You ready to go?" She wiggles her arm and smiles as best she can behind her embarrassment.

"Isabelle, are you in trouble?"

"It's none of your business." She deflects from looking me in the eyes by looking down at her daughter. "Come on, honey." She turns her back and walks towards the check out.

I contemplate whether I should stop her and ask more questions or let her go. I glance out the store front window. Whoever he is to her, he is now leaning against a truck, waiting. I take notice of the vehicle and memorize the make and model. With one more step around the shelves, I see his license plate number and memorize that too.

I head back to grab my cup of coffee and walk towards the front of the store. I stop when I see Isabelle counting change at the counter. The clerk shakes his head no. She reaches in her pockets and comes up empty. She glances out the window at the asshole who's still leaning against his car waiting, then she turns back to the clerk and shakes her head. She grabs what looks like a small toy and slides it to the side.

"But Momma!" her daughter cries out, pulling on her hand.

"I'm sorry, baby. I'll buy it for you tomorrow. I promise." Mother's guilt shines in her eyes.

"But Momma!" Her little girl cries with big, sad tears. Her red little curls bounce with the stomping of her foot.

"Abigail." She sighs heavily, then glances out the window. "I'm sorry, baby. I promise, tomorrow I will buy it for you." She grabs her stuff off the counter and walks out the door.

I step from around the corner and watch her walk to the truck. With a lift from his leaning spot on the front fender, he says something to her and walks to the driver's side.

I throw my coffee and gum on the counter and watch them pull out while the clerk rings me up. When I turn back, he's watching me, waiting. I throw a twenty on the counter and glance back out the window.

"You see them before?" I grab my stuff and wait for my change and his answer.

"They come in a few times a week."

"He always an asshole?" He stays quiet until I lift a demanding brow.

"I don't want to get involved." He shakes his head while hurrying through with ringing up my order.

"You already are. Answer my question." I throw another twenty on the counter and grab the toy Isabelle had to leave behind.

"Yes."

"They come in here again and she has to walk out without something because she doesn't have enough money, I will hold you personally responsible. We clear?" I reach over and grab a piece of paper and the pen next to it. "That's my number. Call me if she owes you anything. Don't try and rip me off either. And if you see him treating her that way again and you don't intervene because you 'don't want to be involved' then you and I are going to have a discussion, and I can promise you, you will not fare well in that conversation. Understood?"

"Yes, Mr. Moretti."

I hold his gaze. Damn right he knows who I am. "Good. I'm glad we came to an understanding."

I pull down the winding road that leads to a house I recognize as my home away from home. The camera at the last corner before the house, catches the image of my SUV. The gates are opening before I reach the stone wall that protects the occupants inside. Mr. and Mrs. Heart are like second parents to me. Mr. Heart took me under his wing when I was just a teenager. He was leaving a restaurant one night with some associates when he caught me in the alley working over a dealer who ripped off some street kid. On principle, I intervened. The street kid ran. I worked over the dealer pretty good before he had the chance to pull his gun. The problem, I had no weapon to counter with. I had two choices as I stood there in front of him. Die in the alley for what I believed in or run like hell. I don't run. Ever. I never have. Not even from the viciousness of my father's fists. And I never will. But I also had a little sister to look out for too. At the time, she was waiting for me to bring back food to the foreclosed abandoned house when crashed in. So, as I stood there, with the barrel of his gun pointed at my chest, I made the decision in a split second. The arm stretched wide pointing the gun at me was grabbed, twisted, and broken within three seconds. The gun was tossed to the side, and I beat that dealer to a bloody pulp before arms wrapped around me and pulled me off. A large frame held me tight. I fought against his restraint. I roared my demands. I cursed him with the promise of a vicious death. But I was no match for the man holding me.

What I got back from him was a calm but assertive voice that held so much confident control. *"Calm yourself, boy. Before you hurt yourself."*

I knew in that moment he wasn't going to hurt me.

I relaxed and stopped fighting. When I looked up, I unknowingly looked directly into my future. My boss, Mr. Robert Heart stood before me.

"Put him on his feet, Lorenzo."

I took a step to the side once I was released so I could face both men head on. I stood there heaving breath, eyeing the both of them while the dealer laid bloody and unmoving two feet away.

"See if he's dead."

"You going to rat me out? You don't look like the type of guy that would," I told the guy in the sharp suit before I knew who he was.

"First, do not ever use that word in my vicinity again unless there is one. Rats die. And I don't mean the ones scurrying through the alley. Second, what type of guy do I look like to you?"

"A wealthy one that doesn't worry much about his next meal and doesn't care if his enemy gets his last supper."

"Smart." He raised his brow, watching me. *"You hungry?"*

"Always."

"That's what I want to hear, Son. Lorenzo, make this go away." He nodded at the still body. *"Let's go. Inside. You can put a meal in that stomach of yours while we talk business."*

That's the day my life changed for the better. Anything would be better than the life I had lived up until that point. I was seventeen years old. I had been living on the streets for two years. The dealer I beat to a bloody pulp was never seen on his corner again and the very next day, I was dressed in a thousand-dollar tailored suit, running errands for Mr. Robert Heart, my boss, the Don, Mafia King of New York City.

It was also the same night I saved three quarters of my meal for my little sister.

I make the long drive down the paved driveway. Throw the car in park when I'm halfway round the circular driveway and shift to get out.

"Hey." Antonio grabs my arm, holding me back from going inside. "You good?"

"Yeah. What's up?"

"You didn't say a word the whole ride over."

"I'm good."

Mr. Heart taught me a few lessons that night. The first one was to always be in control in any situation I found myself in. It was a weird concept for me. Something I had to work on through the years. I had no control in my life up until that point. Food was scarce and shelter was something I looked for, for me and my sister every single day, until we found that abandoned house. The second lesson was to know your enemies. The third, know your family. Not your blood. The family that had your back. Mr. Heart bought that foreclosed house so my sister and I had a place to live.

His family always has my back.

And I will always have theirs.

"Give me the run down for last night?" Mr. Heart leans back in his leather chair and waits.

The man is intimidating as hell. Nineteen years later, I still respect him for what he stands for. He's a good husband. A great father. A stellar leader. But cross him and you will find yourself in a grave with either two bullets in your heart or your heart cut completely out of your chest. It is his calling card and the reason why he changed the spelling of his name from Hart to Heart. He wanted men on the streets to know that if you did him wrong, he took it personally. Business is not just business to him, it's fucking personal.

"It was easy," I explain. "Almost too easy." If those two warehouses were Senator Hunts, a rival no one saw coming until a couple of months ago, his lack of security was disappointing. Especially if one of our biggest buyers is his partner. Kazimir, a Russian arms dealer made a subtle threat against Mr. Heart a few months back. He's lucky Antonio controlled himself or Kazimir would be deteriorating in a fifty-five-gallon drum right now. If Senator Hunt and Kazimir are working together, I would expect some kind of retaliation in the near future. The buildings we set on fire was a warning. "I expected some bloodshed but there was none. Both buildings are simmering ashes as we speak," I inform him.

"You wiped the cameras?"

"I took care of it inside. Freddy took care of what I couldn't."

Freddy is our tech guy. What I can't do, he can, but I always double check.

"No worries then?"

"We're good," I assured him. My word is a good as my name, never being etched into a tombstone. It's a guarantee. Set my body on fire and let the flames take me to hell when death comes knocking for my soul.

Mr. Heart turns to Antonio and asks him some questions. I zone out while they discuss the events from the night before. I can't stop thinking about a certain freckled face girl. The sadness that held in her facial features captive. The tears in her daughter's eyes. The way the guy she was with spoke to her. I saw him, my father. I saw him in the guy's eyes, and I sensed the fear in her just as I did my mother. I was right back in my childhood house all over again, except I was standing in a bodega thirty years later.

"You ready?"

The tap to my shoulder snaps me out of my thoughts. I stand and respectfully shake my boss's hand then head for the door to start the day.

I double check with Antonio to make sure we are headed down to the warehouse since I missed the tail end of their conversation.

If the warehouse is owned by Senator Hunt, and Kazimir is his partner, that would mean Kazimir lost some valuable merchandise. The only thing is, we don't have concrete proof the warehouse is owned by him. Although the intel we received tells us it is. The deed to the warehouse has a dummy corporation listed. All standard practice in the world of crime. My guess is we will find out in the next few days.

"What's the plan?" I glance over at Antonio as I'm pulling out of the front gates.

"Head to the pier. I just shot a message off to Demetri and Luca to meet us there. We will set up security detail for the rest of the week and get ready to move the product tonight."

The rest of the morning and part of the afternoon went by quickly. Arrangements were made to stash our merchandise at a friend's safehouse up north. We have a meet with a new buyer two nights from now. Cillian McKittrick is the boss of the Irish mob. He is branching his way into the states. He reached out. We accepted the meeting. Skepticism weighs heavily in our thoughts. Why now? Why when we just wiped an entire organization out a few months back? Alvarez was a rival with a vendetta against Antonio and his then girlfriend, now wife, Lilah. It seems a little too coincidental that we demolished one organization, and another one steps up almost immediately. But then again, every organization is waiting for that step up. The Heart syndicate is one of the wealthiest most influential in the world of illegal activities. I have to wonder if Cillian McKittrick and Angel Alvarez had business together.

I drop Antonio off at Temptations. It's our home base when we are not required at the main house. Prior to Antonio opening the night club, we would meet at his penthouse in the morning. Now that he has his club, all business is conducted there in his office. I call Hope and check up on her, pop another piece of cinnamon gum in my mouth, and make my way across town. There is a certain little furry stuffed lion that needs to be delivered.

I pull up in front of O'Brien's Pub and head inside. Pat, the owner, greets me with a smile. Most don't know this, but Pat is Mrs. Heart's best friend from childhood. That bit of information is kept under wraps. Pat and the bar are under our protection, but Boss wants the relationship kept quiet. There have been many meetings held in her office late at night.

I have been coming here for years. First, when I was scavenging her dumpsters for food as a hungry teen for me and my sister. Then when I came with the group of friends, I now consider family, after being hired by Mr. Heart.

O'Brien's Pub is Caelan and Sofia's favorite place. It's *their* spot. Sofia, Antonio's sister, was my first security detail after I was hired. She was young and was being stalked by a madman. Mr. Heart gave me the honor of protecting her. I guarded her with my life. I always will. Sofia and I have a special bond. A life altering situation brought us together. I was sad for her and myself as well when it brought back memories I never wanted to rehash. I saved her life that day, but there were two others I couldn't. I will always harbor that guilt. At the time, Sofia's fiancé and Antonio's best friend, Caelan wasn't okay with Sofia and I being so close, but now that it's been years, we're cool with each other.

"Hi, handsome. What can I do for you today?" Pat embraces me with a warm hug that I return.

I scan the bar area and then the rest of the restaurant. "I stopped by to talk to Isabelle."

"Oh?" Her brows furrow. I've never come in here looking for her before. Pat's confused and concerned curiosity shows. "She's not here. She works a shift at Lenny's Diner a few blocks down before coming here for her night shift."

Instantly, I am furious. No wonder she looks haggard. She works two jobs, has a little girl to take care of, plus she deals with the arrogant prick she was with this morning whether that be her boyfriend or husband.

"Do me a favor, Pat?" I reach into my pocket and pull out the small stuffed animal. "Give this to her. Tell her if she ever needs anything to come see me at the club." She looks at the stuffed animal I'm holding in my hand then back at me. She holds my gaze, and her tongue for a moment, contemplating if she should say what's on the tip of it. Before she can, I explain, "It's for her daughter, Abigail."

Her brows furrow more. I give her a quick chin jerk and head for the door. I won't answer the questions floating around in her head. It's none of her business.

Just as I'm opening the heavy, dark-stained wood door, Pat calls me.

When I turn back only to humor her, she informs me by saying, "She's married."

"To an asshole," I immediately respond, annoyed she felt the need to tell me.

"All the same." She rocks the stuffed lion back and forth in her hand.

"I didn't ask. Give her the stuffed animal, Pat," I order before walking out the door.

Isabelle
CHAPTER FOUR

"Table five needs their home fries, Isabelle."

"Okay." I drag my tired feet across the worn black and white tile. I have an hour left in my shift and then I can check in on my baby girl before heading to my second job. I hand the doe-eyed couple their matching bacon cheeseburgers and head to the kitchen to grab table five's home fries. I lean on the counter and yell for Bobby, the cook. He pops his head around the corner. His smile is big and wide while throwing my order up under the heat lamps.

"Bell, when you going to let me take you out on a date?"

"Never, Bobby. I'm a married woman, remember?"

"I try not to."

"But she is." His voice sounds from behind me. *His* voice.

I turn in hopes I'm imagining it, but there he stands: Tommy, my husband.

"What are you doing here?" I ask, grabbing a stack of napkins before heading in the direction of the table waiting for their food. When I turn back, Tommy is staring me down. I know that look in his eye. It means trouble.

"Get me a cup of coffee," he snaps.

There is no "please" or "thank you" or even a "can you." It's a "get me," like I'm his servant.

I do as he asks to keep the interaction between us calm while we're in public. He was already in a bad mood this morning and right now he looks even more irritated. When I slide the cup over to him, he grabs ahold of my wrist and stops me from pulling away.

"Stop," I grit my teeth and whisper. "You're going to cause a scene." I jerk my arm.

"How long has the cook been hitting on you, *Bell*?" He enunciates the nickname Bobby has given me.

"He's just joking around, being friendly." I try to lighten the situation.

"He has a dick, Isabelle. Men are only friendly for one reason." He tightens his grip on my wrist.

"You're hurting me, Tommy. Let go," I quietly snarl.

He only lets go because he hears Eric, his partner in crime, walk up behind him. I pull my arm away as soon as the tension in his fingers lessen, then give my red wrist a soothing rub.

"We cool here?" Eric asks, watching our exchange with concerned interest.

"I'd be better if my wife stopped entertaining the cook's advances." His upper lip twitches as he glares at me.

"I wasn't," I whisper-rumble, defending myself.

"Put my coffee in a to-go cup, *darling*." He snickers with a saccharine smile and winks at me. "Would you please be so kind?" His syrupy tone fools no one.

I grab his coffee and dump it into one of our Lenny's Diner to-go cups. I smile politely at Eric. "Do you need anything, Eric?"

"Nah. I'm good, Isabelle."

When I hand the cup to Tommy, he pulls me in for what looks like a hug to anyone else, but I know different. "I come first. I will always come first. Got it? The next time I catch you flirting with the cook, he'll find himself face down in the alley." He makes a click clack noise with his mouth. "Bang. Bang, baby."

"Get out," I growl and turn away from him.

Forty-five minutes later, I'm in a cab calling my beautiful baby girl to check up on her while rushing through the city streets heading to my next job.

Flying through the doors of O'Brien's Pub, I hurry through the bar and head straight to the bathroom to clean myself up and change for my evening shift. At the diner, I have to wear an old school uniform. Here at the pub, it's a pair of black jeans and V-neck t-shirt with O'Brien's Pub logo on it.

Tommy hates that I work here. I refuse to quit. It's the one place he has never stepped foot in. It's my place of solitude even with a bar full of drunk patrons. Tommy comes to the diner all the time to check up on me, but he has never stepped foot inside the pub. I have wondered why, but I won't jinx my peace and quiet by asking. The pub is the first *real* job I got when I came to the city. I guess you could say washing dishes at some seedy small restaurant was my first job, but I don't. I didn't even make minimum wage. I got paid cash and most weeks the owner gypped me. It was more of *I'll pay you if you return the favor by sleeping with me.* I always declined. I love Pat, the owner of O'Brien's. She is the sweetest boss. She acts more like a mom than a boss and she always makes sure we go home with money in our pockets.

I brush my hair out and pull it up into a high ponytail. I pinch my dull cheeks and throw on some lip gloss to give them some kind of life. The dark circles under my eyes are like a flashing light in the midnight sky showcasing my lack of sleep. Working two jobs is killing me. I have no time for myself, but more importantly, I barely have any time for my baby girl.

Mother's guilt is a real thing, it weighs heavily on my shoulders. For starters, I gave Abigail a shitty father. Plus, now that I'm working a lot and I hardly get to spend time with her, I feel like I gave her the same life I ran from. In the end, I have to remember I'm working both jobs for her and I. Once I have enough money saved, I'm leaving Tommy for good.

It's what I keep telling myself.

I left him once before, but he pulled me back in with promises I fell for. The last incident between us was the last straw for me. His artwork on my ribs from two weeks ago still lingers with an array of yellows, purples, and blues.

When I met Tommy, I thought he was a good man. He was a good man, at least, I think he was, but maybe he just hid it well. Either way, his true colors came out shortly after we got married. I blamed myself in the beginning. Even now, at times… I still do. It's my fault I'm in this situation. It's my fault my daughter shares the same blood as that man. I should have known better. I should have seen the signs.

I come from a small town out west. I hauled ass from an unhealthy environment when the first opportunity presented itself. My father is a drunk, but a rich one. A powerful man who basically owns the town I grew up in. My neglected mother passed her time and attention projecting her own self-worth onto me. She became the crazy pageant queen Mom. At the time, being I was so young, I barely understood why. I saw her as the overbearing mother, which she was, but now that I am older and have a child with a little bit more life experience under my belt, I see it very differently. Now, after going through what I have with Tommy over these last few years, I totally understand I was my mother's outlet in an unhealthy and unhappy marriage. My mother was lonely and needed something to fill her time while my father was out doing his thing. I became her made-up doll on the weekends and his work horse during the week. The steaming hot two-hour long baths on Friday nights my mother would insist I take to remove the dirt from under my fingernails turned my skin into a dry cracked mess by the time I was a teenager. The ranch I grew up on was breathtaking in its scenery, but ugly in its nature. Every cream my mother could find at the local pharmacy became her new obsession. I had to drench my body in lotions and oils so that I would look the perfect part come the weekend. I had to shine, shine so bright that it would deflect from the darkness that hid behind the closed doors of our home.

I ran when I was seventeen. I remember that night like it was yesterday. I had on an emerald green, floor length satin gown. It went perfectly with my red hair and green eyes. My hair was in an updo with spirals framing my face. My makeup was over the top. My eyes sparkled with glitter on the outside but on the inside, that shine was long gone. When the judges announced my name as the winner, it came with no surprise. My daddy, I'm sure had fixed the pageant. It didn't matter to me. I had won the Miss Sugar Lane County beauty pageant. It was and still is the biggest pageant my home state holds. What mattered to me was the prize. It was two thousand dollars. I remember how I felt inside like it was yesterday. While my momma gushed about our win, I itched to get clean, to take off the over-the-top dress and the caked-on makeup and get into my pajamas. It hit me hard when she squawked on with so much excitement about getting a new dress. I had the money to run. It was right there in her purse. It wasn't enough to last a long time, but it would get me far away from where I was born. The money wasn't in my possession though, and that was the problem. I would have to take it from my mother's purse, and that was stealing. I didn't want to steal from her, but I knew it was my only chance. When we pulled onto our long driveway and made the mile trek to our home, my mind was made up. I was taking the money I had won before my daddy could spend it on booze or my momma could buy me more fancy dresses. And I did just that. I waited until they went to sleep. Then I took the money, and I ran. I hopped on the train, saving the money I had just stolen and made the decision to steal a ride in an open box car filled with cargo. I took it as far as I could go. Then I jumped on a greyhound and found myself in New York City.

I met Tommy when I had just turned twenty. I had been in the city for three years by then. I was such a naïve kid, but I was determined. It wasn't until I met Tommy that I moved from my coworker's couch to Tommy's house. We were only dating for six months before he proposed and two months later, we were married. It was a whirlwind. We had a small ceremony by the justice of the peace with just Tommy's family in attendance. I didn't care, I had no family as far as I was concerned, but I did have Zoey. She was my one and only friend. It was her couch I slept on, but Tommy didn't like her, so, I chose not to ruin our special day by upsetting him with her presence. After we got married, Tommy became my only friend. I had let the friendship between Zoey and I go. Tommy insisted she was a bad influence. I listened to him to a certain extent until I finally relented. He was a good man with a good job. His coworkers held him in such a high regard. They respect him so much that I thought I should at least give him the respect he deserved as my husband and listen to his feelings. I completely severed my friendship with Zoey. At the time, in the beginning, Tommy was all I needed. His family became my family and that was enough for me. Little did I know being married to him would soon make me feel like I stepped in my mother's shoes. I had found myself unhappy in an unhealthy relationship I didn't know how to get out of, just like my mother.

I still miss Zoey. Now that I know what Tommy is like, I mourn the loss of a good friendship.

I thought I had found my prince charming. I was over the moon, living blissfully for the first six months. Then he progressively became the monster he is today. Tommy and I have been married for five years. Abigail, my sweet angel—although she was not planned, and I was on birth control—is the best thing that has come from our marriage. Me working two jobs and taking away our time together is for her. I want her to grow up in a stable home with the unconditional love a parent naturally gives their child. Even if it's just the love from one parent. Tommy wanted me to have an abortion when he found out I was pregnant. He didn't want to have children. Children in his mind would only take the attention he should be getting away from him. We fought. I told him he was a selfish prick. He agreed and made no apologies for it. Then he proceeded to tell me I was the selfish one for not getting the abortion. He said no man should have to raise a child he didn't want. I told him he should have worn a condom then. I was backhanded.

I give myself a once over and make sure I look good enough to go out on the floor. My tips at the diner are good but the tips I get from O'Brien's is the money I live on. I make my way down the hallway and head to the waitress station. I grab my black apron and smile when I see how crowded it is. As tired as I am, I will hustle my butt off to fill my pockets.

I check the seating chart then make my way to my section to make sure everything is in place. I head over to the bar when I see Walter, our resident bar fly's familiar face. Walter is an older gentleman who bellies up to the bar each night until it closes because he doesn't want to go home to a quiet house. His beloved wife died a few years back. They had been happily married for fifty years. He holds pictures of her in his wallet and proudly shows them when he speaks of her and their time together. The twinkle in her eyes the image captures only confirms they were truly a happily married couple.

"Hey there, handsome." I run my hand over his shoulder as I walk behind him.

"Hi, sweetheart. You going to marry me today?" He sips his beer.

"Not today, Walter. Not today," I repeat with a slight affectionate chuckle. I give him a squeeze. He asks me every day he sees me. "How was your day today? Anything new happening?"

"Pruned the Misses rose bushes today. The buds were starting to sprout. She always hated when I waited to do it," he reminisces.

It makes me so sad when I hear him speak of her. Even though his wife has been gone for a few years now, he still makes sure her garden flourishes. "Awww, Walter, I'm sure she is looking down on you with a loving smile."

"She always did have a beautiful smile," he recalls just before taking a sip of his beer.

The tears springing into my eyes makes me squeeze him tighter. "I have to go start my shift, handsome." I make the excuse hurrying away before he sees them.

"You go make that money, sweetheart." He speaks to my back as I'm scurrying away.

Elizabeth, the hostess, sits one of my tables. I head over to greet them and grab their drink order. It's the start of a very busy night. Table after table fill and refill. The night feels endless, but before I know it, my shift is almost done. I drop my tired body onto the empty barstool next to Walter and lean my head on his shoulder.

"You going to have your usual with me?"

I look at my watch. "Still on shift. Give me an hour," I tell him.

"You can indulge now." Pat taps the bar and signals for Josh to give me my usual end-of-the-night shot of tequila. "Long day?"

"Feels more like three days."

Josh slides the shot in front of me with a smile. Pat nods her head giving Josh the go ahead to pour his own. With his shot glass filled and lifted, Josh, Walter, and I tap glasses with a toast to a good night's sleep. Which I need desperately.

"Isabelle, this was left here for you today." Pat sets down a stuffed animal on the bar.

My movements halt. It's not just any stuffed animal. It's the lion that I had to leave behind this morning at the bodega because I didn't have enough money to pay for it. My eyes snap to hers. Then back to the lion. Then back to hers. "Where? How?" I fumble over my words.

"Why we freakin' out over a stuffed lion, tuts?" Josh takes it from Pat. "It's cute. Your kid will love it."

Without answering Josh, I look back to Pat. "How did you get it?"

"Let's just say someone dropped it off for you."

I swallow, and I can feel my breathing pick up a notch. I grab the lion from Josh's hand and stare at it. I roll my lips as the anger builds in my chest. "Was it…" I linger off, not wanting to say his name.

"Yes."

"He brought this here?"

"Yes."

"When?"

"Early this afternoon."

I feel myself huff harshly. He was watching me. After I walked away from him to go pay for my stuff this morning, he was still watching me. He saw me push the toy to the side when I didn't have enough cash. He saw Abigail throw a temper tantrum because I couldn't buy it for her.

He went and bought it after I left.

I'm so angry I could spit nails.

I jump off the barstool in a ball of angry energy. "Pat, I have no more tables. My shift is almost over. Can I leave?"

"No."

My eyes widen. I'm shocked at her refusal. "Fine." I breathe deep. "I'll just wait until my shift is over." I turn to go clean up my station, angry at her for refusing to let me go.

"Don't do anything stupid, Isabelle." She places her hand on my arm, stopping me, trying to calm me in her motherly way. "Take it for what it is. A gift. And leave it at that."

"I can't accept it." I'm furious. How dare he make me feel this way. I couldn't buy it, so he swoops in like a hero and buys it making me feel less than. I'm Abigail's mother. I should have been able to buy it for her. If it wasn't for Tommy being such a dick about me working, I would have had the money. He now insists that I pay for all my own stuff because I have two jobs. Two jobs he doesn't agree with me having.

"Listen to me." She pulls me to the side away from Walter and Josh to get some privacy. "I'm not sure how this came about, but he showed up here with this stuffed animal to give to you for your little girl. He's not a man you want to upset. Just take the toy to your beautiful baby girl and let the situation be."

I hear her, I do, but the warning she's giving me means nothing to me.

I wait the thirty minutes until my shift ends, and I haul ass out of the bar with no goodbyes to anyone.

The cab drives at a steady pace while my heart races. My skin is clammy. The blood boiling in my veins makes my fingers fumble in my lap. I'm damn near strangling this damn stuffed lion. A lion of all things. Just like him. A beast of a man. How dare he? What was he thinking? The situation between Tommy and I this morning was none of his business and then he goes and buys this stupid stuffed lion to what, prove a point that he can? That I'm not a good enough mother to do it?

My heart stammers a few beats when the driver pulls up in front of the most acclaimed night club in Manhattan. It used to be a club called Ice, Fire, and The Devil's Lair but since Antonio Heart, the mafia prince of New York City, opened Temptations, Ice lost its luster. Who wouldn't want the thrill and bragging rights of being in a club owned by a mobster when you're young and stupid?

I grab the door handle without a second thought. I jump out and rush up the sidewalk past the line of waiting patrons. The bouncer sees me coming at a speed that tells him I have an agenda. He gives me a once over. His nose turns up when he sees me in my uniform. Clearly, I am not here to go clubbing for the night. When his hefty arm reaches out to stop me, I dip my small frame, duck under him, and beeline for the door. He starts yelling for me to stop, but by that point, I have pushed past a bunch of drunk people and weaved my way through the bar.

Blue lights turn to red and then to purple encapsulating the massive building. The music is so loud, but the song is a good one. Fire shoots from cannons to the harsh beat of the music. I wish I had a moment to enjoy the hard beats of *Derp* by Bassjackers and MakJ, but I don't. I am on the run from an abnormally large bouncer and running to another abnormally large man. I'm on a mission to get to the man that made me feel like the worst mother in the world.

I dip under the stairs and look up at the balcony. I know behind those shaded glass windows is Antonio Heart's office. It has to be. The question is… how do I get up there? I see an opening to a back hallway and dart across the dance floor. I bounce off sweaty dancers with no apologies spoken. I make it to the other side and hit the elevator button. The doors don't budge. My head swivels on my neck and my feet bounce in anticipation of being caught and thrown out before I can get to him. I hit the button again and shuffle in my spot. The stairs I just left come back into view. I could go up that way, but I know I'll never get past the three bouncers guarding the steps to the VIP area. Out of the corner of my eye I catch a glimpse of a woman I believe is Antonio's wife, Lilah. I saw the two of them in the society pages once. Her beauty is hard to forget. The guard following her is no more than a step behind. She disappears around the corner.

In my head, it's a good idea.

I follow her.

If she is going upstairs, I'll be able to get in the same way she does. When I turn the corner, she is gone. I feel defeated for all of two seconds before I see my opening. A group of men come out of an elevator hidden in the back of the hallway. The men don't pay any attention to me and before the doors can close, I slip in and hit the button for the upper level. I pace from one side of the elevator and back. Before the doors open, I notice the camera in the corner. Without a second thought I throw my middle finger in the air. My heart is pounding so hard, I lose my breath when the doors slide open. The heavy beat of the music doesn't help. It's just as loud up here too. I step out into the empty hallway and see two sets of doors. The music is beating intensely when my hand grabs the handle to the door closest to the dance floor. I fling it open and come face to face with four very scary men, dressed in black with guns pointed at my head.

"What the fuck!" I hear a deep thunder rumble through the space before seeing the only female in the room being shoved behind the only man that is allowed to touch her.

It's only then I realize my hurt ego made me make a lethal mistake.

Giovanni
CHAPTER FIVE

"**W**hat the fuck!" Antonio hollers, pulling his gun right along with the rest of us when the door to his office unexpectedly flies open. He shoves Lilah behind him just as I'm stepping forward to shield both of them, protecting my boss and his wife, ready to murder whoever it is that burst through the door.

That is until I take in who the assailant is. The music is at a deafening beat with the door open. It takes me a stunned minute before I lower my gun and hold my hand up in the air to calm Demetri, Luca, and Antonio down. I take in her tired—but stunning—pissed off look now morphing into a scared face.

"Lower your weapons," I yell over the heavy beat of the music while tucking my gun back into the waistband of my pants. "What the fuck are you doing?" I step in her direction.

"G?" Antonio harshly questions from behind his desk across the room.

"Who is that?" I hear Lilah ask from behind Antonio's broad shoulders.

"No one," he snaps, holding her back with his arm.

"Oh, she's someone, all right," she sarcastically chimes, taking in the angry redhead. "A pissed off redhead is never a good situation, boys."

"Yeah, no shit. Neither is a brunette," Antonio mutters.

"I'll handle it," I firmly thunder.

I know he recognizes who she is. He wouldn't be doing his job if he didn't know who worked in one of his partially owned establishments. My feet move swiftly. I grab her arm and push her out the door, slamming it behind us. I forcefully push her down the hallway to the only other room on this floor. The music is still cranking and it's irritating the hell out of me.

"What the fuck are you thinking?" I slam the door closed and push her up against the wall once we are inside.

"Who the fuck do you think you are?" she screams at me.

I'm taken back at the proximity between us and the heat from her anger. It's a little unnerving. Her question baffles me as her smell floods my senses.

"How fucking stupid can you be?" I slam my hand against the wall next to her head. "You wanna fucking die? Is that it? You must have a death wish. Because what you just stupidly did, that is a sure-fire way for it to come to fruition, Isabelle! *Fuck!* What were you thinking?" I slam my hand twice more against the wall. She flinches and turns away from me. I step back, giving her space that I don't want to give. "Tell me! What were you thinking?" I bellow then watch the resolve move through her body.

"I was thinking you are the biggest dick I have ever met in my life!" She steels her shoulders.

"I highly doubt that after I saw how your *husband* treated you this morning."

"Fuck you!" she screams with passion.

"Been there. Done that. Wanna tell me if you were married when we slept together?"

She's silent.

"That's what I thought. How long have you been married, Isabelle?" I slide both my hands in my pockets and watch her.

"None of your business!"

"Kinda is when I didn't know I should be looking over my fucking shoulder."

"Don't you always have to look over your shoulder, Giovanni?"

"Never from a vengeful husband that I didn't know 'bout." I pull my hands from their confines and place both of them low on my hips and wait for that to sink in.

"He knows nothing."

"Clearly. Neither did I."

She sneers. "Would you have really cared?"

I ignore her question. She doesn't deserve the answer. "Why are you here?"

"Because you bought me this!" She straightens her arm and I see the stuffed lion I bought this morning thrashing in the air by her tense hand.

"You almost died over a stuffed lion? Seriously? You have got to be fucking kidding me."

"No, I almost died because... because... You had no right to buy it!"

"So you almost lost your life tonight because I bought something you think I shouldn't have?"

"You had no right!" she repeats on a furious yell, pushing herself off the wall.

"You are not making any sense, Isabelle. And by the way, it's not for you. It's for your daughter. She is your daughter, right, Isabelle? His daughter, I assume?"

"I should have been the one to buy it and you went and bought it!" She throws the lion at my head.

I catch it mid-air. "Let me get this straight." I step towards her questioning, holding the lion mid-air between us. "You almost died tonight because of your fucking ego?"

"Yes! She is my daughter, Giovanni. I take care of her. I am her mother! Me! I am the only one she needs," she screams with heart-wrenching emotion, her body is riddled with anger and passion. Then I see the shame surge and radiate in her eyes.

"Ahhh." I cup the back of her head and pull her into me. "I won't apologize." I hold her to my chest and whisper into her hair. "I would buy it again." I feel her wince when my other hand slides over her ribs. "Are you hurt?"

"What? No!" She tries to pull out of my arms.

"Isabelle." I turn her with quick precision and pull her shirt up to the point where my hand just slid across. "What. The. Fuck?" I bellow when I see the bruise on her ribs.

"Stop it! Stop it right now!" She struggles, slapping at my hands to get out of my arms. "Stop it!"

I let her go and step back, giving her space. "He did that to you?" I point at her side.

"What? No! I fell." She's quick to make the excuse to cover for him.

"Fucking right. Don't lie for that bastard."

"You don't even know him!"

"You're right. I didn't even know you were married."

"It doesn't matter." She tucks her shirt back in her jeans in a rush.

"It does, baby. It does." I step towards her again.

"Don't call me that. What gives you the right? Why? Because I slept with you?"

"I would have continued, but you cut it off."

"I'm married!"

"I'm guessing it's not a good one or you wouldn't have dropped your panties for me." I turn my back on her and take a few steps away. "Fucking finally," I mutter when the music changes into something less loud, less abrasive to my ears but still intense. "I expect you to give the lion to your daughter. The scum you're married to should have bought it." I eye her. "Tell her it came from you. I don't give a fuck. She was crying. I didn't like seeing her cry. Just like I don't like what I just saw on your body."

"Forget you saw anything. I have it handled."

"Don't you all," I mutter under my breath. "Until he almost kills you."

"What?"

"Give your daughter the stuffed animal, Isabelle. Make the kid happy."

"How dare you! I do make her happy!"

"Correct. You do. Trust me when I say this, you may think she is happy, but living in that atmosphere with a man that can do that to her mother, she isn't. Don't mistake her age as a shield. She knows exactly what is happening to her momma." I step towards her, not able to handle hearing anymore. My initial reaction is to grab her arm and walk her out, but I don't. I won't touch her. "Let's go." I point at the door.

"Wait! This conversation isn't over," she argues.

"It was over before you even decided to come here." I'm so angry right now I need to be away from her.

"Giovanni?" she softly calls to my back as I start to open the door. "Giovanni?" Her hand lays on my back.

"Don't." I shrug her off before pulling the door open with enough force to pull it from it hinges. I step into the hallway and am greeted with Demetri standing guard. I wait for the sound of her footsteps to follow and then I walk her to the back elevator without looking back.

"Please wait, Giovanni."

Isabelle
CHAPTER SIX

The music changes from the harsh intense beat to *Waiting Game* by Banks. "Please wait, Giovanni." I quickly move around to his side.

"It's time to go, Isabelle. You should have never come here to begin with."

"I was mad." I firmly press my hand on his back.

"Clearly." He quickly turns. His hand comes to my face and snatches my jaw in his strong, authoritative yet tender fingers. "Leave him. If he can do that to you, he will have no problem killing you."

"Have you thought of me?" I stupidly ask, ignoring his statement.

He drops his hand. "Time to go."

"Please tell me."

"Yes, I have. You ended it. I moved on. Time to go."

I feel my heart drop. "You're seeing someone?" I ask, even though I know what I did with him is wrong. I have dreamt of the time we shared together. To hear him say he moved on, it bothers me.

"It doesn't matter, does it? You're married."

I step into him. His body is so strong, and his natural body scent mixed with his cologne practically hypnotize me. "If I told you I wish it hadn't, would you look at me differently?"

"Isabelle." He frowns.

"Tell me, Giovanni."

He looks me dead in the eyes. "You're playing with the wrong man, angel."

I inch closer to him, needing him, wanting his strong, unforgiving but gentle touch. I know this is wrong. I know it is. But I still inch closer and closer to him. When I lift to the tips of my toes and he bends slightly to meet my lips, I swallow with a guilty rush of anticipation. Just as I think I am going to feel the soft skin of his lips brush over mine, he pulls away, and I drop to the flat of my heels in disappointment.

Disappointment I have no right feeling.

"I'm sorry." I look up at him in shame.

His eyes soften, if at all possible, coming from such a strong hard man.

A rush of huffed air leaves him. "You're being faithful to a man that is abusing you. Abuse does not equal love, Isabelle. Abuse equals control because he feels out of control and the only person he can control, is you. You are a victim to his weaknesses. The prey he sought out to soothe his inadequacies. Staying with him means you're being unfaithful to yourself." I open my mouth to defend myself, but he cuts me off with a raised hand. "Save it, Isabelle. I've heard it all before." He turns, holds the pad of his thumb over the sleek box to activate the elevator and walks into the cart when the doors slide open. I follow him, speechless. When we reach the back of the building outside, he waves a black town car over, opens the back door, and instructs me to get in. He gives the driver instructions and before he closes my door he leans down and looks at me sitting in the backseat. "You leave him, you let me know. He hurts you and you need me, you come to me, Isabelle. Understood?"

I say nothing. His declaration to help will only lead to tragedy.

"He touches that innocent little girl and I find out, he's a fucking dead man."

"He's never laid a hand on her."

"Yet." He huffs harshly while standing to his full height. "A fucking blessing."

"I'm sorry," I whisper, peering up at him.

"Don't ever be sorry for wanting something better. Just make sure it's something worth it." He tosses the lion on my lap. "Give it to your daughter, Isabelle," he gruffly barks.

"Was I? Worth it?" I rush out, selfishly asking before he closes the door.

I watch his chest expand and with the slightest huff he exudes, he stares at me and slowly shakes his head. Without saying a word, he slams the door shut on me and steps back, effectively ending my tantrum. Two loud thumps from his fist to the roof of the car make me jump. The car pulls out and away from the back of the building and further down the alley. I watch him as he watches the car drive down the street. I keep watching him until the crack between us becomes a crater. When the car makes a right turn on to the main street and I can no longer see his strong stature standing in the middle of the alley, I feel a loss I have no right to feel.

"Where the fuck have you been?" Tommy yells when I walk through the door.

"I worked late. I picked up some extra tables. Where's Abigail?" I lie while dropping my bag on the counter. I grab the lion and turn back towards the opening of the kitchen.

"In bed. Where she belongs. Where was her mother?" he sneers.

"I just told you." I walk away from him and head towards the hallway, waiting for his spiral. I can see it in his eyes. He is not going to let this go. I need to check on my little girl before all hell breaks loose.

"Bitch, I'm not finished with you." He grabs the back of my hair and yanks me back to him. "Don't ever walk away from me again. You will obey me." He yanks me back again.

"Let go of me, Tommy," I grit my teeth and calmly say so Abby doesn't wake up. "I need to check on our daughter."

"She is fine. Daddy spent the whole night watching cartoons with her, while her mommy was out being a whore."

"I was working. Let me go, Tommy."

"Working, huh? I find out you were with someone else, trust me, wifey, you will not like the repercussions."

"I was working, Tommy," I reiterate, hoping if I keep repeating myself, he will be appeased. "Now let me go so I can give Abigail her new toy."

"That's what you work extra shifts for, to buy her some stupid stuffed animal? If you weren't such a terrible wife, I would have bought it for you to give to her."

Anger at how he blatantly disregards my hard work sets me off. I know before the words leave my mouth what is going to transpire, but at that moment I'm not thinking, I am acting on enraged impulse. I want to hurt him with my words just as he has me.

"If you weren't such a shitty father, you would have just bought it for her yourself in the first place, but you didn't. You're nothing but a selfish prick."

As soon as the words are out of my mouth, I know I made a very big mistake. The following few minutes became nothing but a void of blackness and pain.

"Baby, wake up."

I feel the feather light touch of skin on my bruised skin. I roll my head to the side and feel the nausea roll around.

"That's it, baby, wake up. You have been sleeping for a while now."

I moan and uncontrollably shudder with the pain radiating throughout my body. I try to take a deep breath, but when I do the nausea becomes unbearable.

"Sick." I quickly roll to my side and throw up.

"Fuck. You almost got me." I hear him shuffle.

My head is spinning. I'm dizzy and extremely nauseous. I lay back down and try to get my bearings. Abby. Where is Abby? I move to get up and the spinning ceiling forces me to lay back down.

"Tommy... Abby... Where?"

"She's fine."

"Help. I need to make sure."

"I said she is fine. You should be more worried that you just threw up all over the floor. You're going to have a hell of a mess to clean up in the morning."

I lay there and assess my injuries. I can't really move without my whole body hurting, and my left eye won't open. I feel like time is a sledgehammer slamming into me over and over with each tick of the clock. Within a few minutes, darkness is pulling me under. The last thing I feel is Tommy's hand rubbing my arm. With each swipe of his hand all I can think is... I have to get to my baby girl.

Giovanni
CHAPTER SEVEN

The metal clanking with each drop of the steel bar rattles my brain. *Sweet Emotion* by Aerosmith pounds through the speakers adding energy to our late morning workout.

"Come on, fucker. Another one," Antonio antagonizes me.

"Keep it up and I'll accidently drop the bar on your throat when it's your turn," I tell him.

He laughs knowing he's getting to me. "Come on, old man. I know you got more than that in you." He flips his middle and index fingers carelessly, telling me to raise the bar from my chest.

I pump three more out, drop the bar on the rack, and sit up. I grab my hand towel and wipe the sweat from my face. I crane my neck to the side, look at him, and deadpan, "Calling me old is like calling yourself old since I only have two years on you. You realize that, right?"

"Had to get that blood of yours pumping somehow. You're slacking this morning."

"I never slack. I slack on something, mistakes are made. If mistakes are made, we die or even worse, we go to prison." I stand and switch spots with him.

He lays on the bench, grabs the bar and lifts it from the rack, and says, "You want to talk about last night?"

"No."

"G, it was my office she busted into. My wife was in there. Granted she may have not thought her plan out thoroughly before busting through my door, but the fact of the matter is, she did. How long have you been laying her down?"

"I'm not."

"That was not the face of a woman who hasn't been beneath the man she was seeking out in anger."

"Drop it, A."

"Was it casual?" he pushes. "A fling? Or are we talking about something special?"

"She's married."

He drops the bar in the rack and sits up to look at me. "We have enough marks on our backs. We don't need a jealous husband hawking us down."

"I didn't know. And correct me if I am wrong, but I don't remember your dick being active at the same time as mine when I was doing the work. The mark would be on my back, not yours." I grab my water bottle and take a big, frustrated swig.

"You didn't know? My enforcer. The man who checks everyone and every detail, didn't know?" He stands and grabs his hand towel and wipes his face. "I find that hard to believe."

"You question my loyalty and my job to this family again, you and I are going to have a problem." I stare him down.

He glares back at me. The boss in him is raging to retaliate on his employee. He takes a deep breath, and I watch the friend in him come forth. "I wasn't questioning your loyalty to this family or your job. I never have and I never will. I was questioning why you had not vetted her. If you had, you would have known she was married."

"Did you vet every girl whose legs you spread before Lilah came along? As a matter of fact, you didn't even vet Lilah. I did," I argue the fact.

"Exactly, G. This the reason why I am asking the question. I was thinking with my dick. Apparently, you were too."

I drop my shoulders and take a deep breath before I lose my cool. I'm already on edge now, knowing what she is living in. I barely slept last night thinking about it. "It was five months ago. I stopped at O'Brien's one night to have a few drinks. She's cute. I turned on the charm. It worked. I wanted nothing more than an hour. I got more than that. A week later, I showed up there again. She was there. That was the last night. She declined. End of story."

"What happened yesterday to have her come charging into my office?"

"Long story." I walk to the squat machine in my home gym. "Not one I am willing to get into."

"G?"

"Drop it, A."

"All I was going to say was that she is more than cute, brother. She is a fiery redhead with major fucking looks."

"Yeah. No shit. Why do you think I went back again?" I leave that statement hanging in the air.

My afternoon becomes a sequence of events. First, I went to Temptations and fired the bouncer who let Isabelle squeeze through last night. He knew better than to argue the fact. Not just because of who I am or who we are as an organization, but because he knew he messed up when he let a female half his size get around security and make her way to the boss' office. Not for nothing, but Antonio has a long list of former female companions that are not too happy he has chosen his woman to settle down with. Jealousy is a major bitch to the psyche. Especially when it comes to powerful, good-looking men. Had Isabelle been one of his prior lovers and barged into his office, who knows what could have happened.

Second, I checked the security footage from last night. I needed to see how it was that she finagled her way around security inside and made her way all the way up to Antonio's office without being detected. I watched Isabelle, in a uniform no less, maneuvering through the club. She saw every weak spot we had, and she took advantage of it.

I even saw the middle finger she gave the camera while she was in the elevator.

Third agenda for the day; hold an immediate meeting and reassign security to those weak spots. With all that said and done, I finally meet up with Demetri and Luca at the warehouse. I make my way downstairs and watch Demetri do his thing to the guy hanging from his feet. While bleeding out from the two small slits on each side of his neck, I interrupt Demetri's torture tactics with the hope that mine will work better at getting the information I have been waiting for all afternoon. This man is just a pawn. We all know that. He was used to show face but also useless in the future for whoever hired him. Whoever hired him, had hired him to get under our skin and let us know someone is coming for us. Let them come. I will be waiting for each and every one of them.

My only question is… "Did Cillian McKittrick hire you?" I ask the pale man. He has a slight Irish accent my ears honed in on. He tried to disguise it, he did a stellar job too, but I heard it at the base of his throat with each syllable of his words.

"If you let me down, I will tell you everything I know." He grieves his own death with his sobbing tears, praying he won't die today, but knowing he will.

"You have two choices. You can either tell me while you hang upside down and your blood slowly runs dry from your body, or you stay strung upside down and I can slit your throat to the point you bleed out faster. I'll even place a mirror in front of you so you can watch the blood run. Either way…" I bend down, crouching, one knee higher than the other, peering into his bulging eyes. "Either way, you're still going to die today," I confirm his worst fear.

He whimpers on. The snot from his runny nostrils courses its way over the ridge of his broken, split nose to the gaping hole in his forehead. Demetri did his job well. He has been trusted and given the privilege to work over an enemy awhile back. He knows how far he has to go to do his job. There's a fine line just below taking an enemy's life to the point he confesses and truly ending it. We want them sorrowful and half dead, not out of commission; that gets us nowhere. None of us will take this man's life without exhausting all avenues. We will use any means necessary to extract the information, but this guy has been through some torture, and he still hasn't talked. Which tells me, he doesn't know much but the basics.

"Let him down," I instruct our newest recruit in the place we call Purgatory. I'm sure the basement of this warehouse houses many spirits from the lives that have been removed from this earth by my hands. I am the one who stays behind and makes sure there is no evidence left to incriminate any of us. I take a step forward and watch Joseph glance at Demetri in question. Demetri crosses his arms and gives Joseph a nod, knowing he just fucked up. The slight shake of his head confirms it. Joseph is still young, so, for that, I will let the full rage his questioning caused me to settle, but he will be reprimanded, harshly.

When the traitor's body lands on the floor, and only after I direct Joseph to pick him up and place him on the chair, do I start my questioning.

I stand in front of him with my hands in my pockets as I wait for the blood to rush from his head and fill his extremities. I see the moment he becomes lightheaded and then also when he becomes aware again. "I'll give you the privilege of being asked one more time." I let my words register before saying, "Did Cillian McKittrick hire you?"

"I don't know."

"You don't know?"

"I was approached. I took the job and the money." He coughs up thick chunks of bloody liquid.

"What was the name of the man who hired you?" I look down on him.

"I don't know." His eyes roll to the back of his head.

"What was your job?"

"To get inside this warehouse and plant some cameras," he sputters through a coughing fit. "I didn't know the job involved Mr. Heart."

"And did you? Get in here and plant some cameras?"

"I'm sitting here, aren't I?"

"Only after you were outside the gate lingering. Shame, you should have maybe taken up a different profession."

"We can't all be you."

I ignore his backhanded compliment. "How long have you been in this country?"

"My whole fucking life." He goes to wipe his nose on his shoulder than winces at the pain.

"I can hear the Irish accent you're trying to hide."

"Not hiding it. My Ma is born and bred."

"She raise you?"

"Yeah."

"Here in the states?"

"Fuck you. Just kill me already. I won't give you any more information about my Ma." His head falls back, unable to hold it up after the exertion of his outburst.

"It's a sad thing when a mother has to bury her son."

"Spare her, please," he cries.

"It will be the only kindness you will receive from me today."

In the moments after slaughtering a man, with my forearms still tainted with his blood, all I can think about is the fair-skinned redheaded Irish girl with the faint spatter of freckles across her nose and those pouty cherry lips. When I was a kid, I used to play in the yard. It was my only place of solitude. I remember I used to grab the dandelions and blow as hard as I could so the seeds would scatter through the air. Her freckles remind me of those dandelion seeds floating through the air and scattering around carelessly when they land. When she busted through the door last night, and I took in who it really was, I lost my cool. I could have killed her. Anyone of us could have shot her. Now today, I can't get her off my mind. With each swallow of my cinnamon tasting saliva throughout the day there is a deep seed growing in my gut that tells me she is not okay today.

"Joseph!" I snap in anger, my voice thundering through the open space of the warehouse. I'm pissed at myself for not being able to get her out of my thoughts, and I'm furious at him for questioning my authority.

"Yes, sir?" He stands in front of me. His shoulders are raised and tense while his arms hang at their sides.

'Do you know who I am?" I glare at him.

"You are Giovanni Moretti, sir."

"And who is that to this organization?"

"The Fixer, sir."

"Which means what to you?"

"That you take care of things."

"Things, Joseph?" I question taking a step towards him. Hoping he chooses his words wisely.

"You handle delicate situations so that no one is aware that they even happened."

Good job, Joseph.

"Who are the only two men above me in this organization?" My brows collapse as I wait for his answer.

He stutters over his words taking in the full effect of my demeanor. "Mr—Mr. Heart and Mr. Heart—Antonio."

"Correct. Tell me why, when I gave you a direct order, you looked to Demetri for permission?"

"I'm sorry, sir."

"I didn't ask you for an apology. Did I?" I snap.

"No, sir."

"You think it was an intelligent move on your part to question my authority?"

"No, sir, but that wasn't what—"

"It is exactly what you did, Joseph. When you looked to Demetri for direction after I gave you a direct order, you disrespected me."

"I'm sorry, sir. I-I—"

"What do you think happens to men who disrespect me?"

I watch his Adam's apple bob with his nervous swallow.

"Correct, Joseph. Now go home." I glare at him, not needing a verbal answer. "When you get there, ask your father what happens to men who disrespect me. Then report back to me and let me know what he says."

"Yes, sir."

I turn away from him and head for the basement when I see Demetri standing there with a few gallons of bleach.

I grab two just as he says, "You think he's going to cut it in this world?"

"He will."

"How do you know?"

"Because he still has a father in this organization to teach him, and he reminds me of someone I used to know."

"You went light on him."

"I did. His father will be a different story."

48

Pat stares at me, disappointment distorts the fine lines of her mature face while she makes me wait a half a second too long for the answer. The question was an easy one. *Is Isabelle here?* I tilt my head to let her know she's pushing that unspoken fine line.

"No. She called in sick." She rests her weight to one hip and leg.

"Who called in, her or her husband?" I inquire, needing the information in order for me to figure out my next move.

"Her, Giovanni."

"How did she sound?"

"Tired. Exhausted, actually. She's working two jobs, has a husband, and a three-year-old."

I turn on my heel and start to walk away from her without another word, but then I stop and look over my shoulder. "Don't tell her I was here."

"Trust me, I won't."

I turn back, not liking her tone of voice. The few steps I took away from her are now redirected and eating the floor as if they were starved. "Pat, I would advise you to watch how you speak to me. I do not care if you are Mrs. Heart's best friend. Do not put your nose in my business and keep your opinions to yourself. I said *I would* advise you, but I would think you would have known that information already. You can take my words as a friendly bit of advice. Going forward, you should adhere to it. However, in the future if I ask, then you may tell me, but until then, keep it to yourself."

She deflates, taking a step closer. "I apologize, Giovanni." She takes another step closer and reaches for my arm in an apologetic gesture. The feel of her hand on me irritates the hell out of me. No one touches me. "It's just that… That girl has had a hard life. I don't know her whole story, but I know she ran from someone or something. She has been on her own since she was a teen. Like I said, she is working two jobs to pay off some bills. She is married and with you coming in here, looking for her, to me that only equals trouble she doesn't need."

"Understood. I can even respect the fact that you are looking out for her. Just know, I am the man that would never cause her any pain intentionally." I take a few steps towards the door and look back at her one last time. "If she doesn't show up tomorrow, I expect a phone call. If she doesn't show up and you do not call me… Well, then, Pat, you and I are going to have a problem." I walk out, get in my blacked-out SUV, and head to the house that I once dropped her off at. All the while I'm trying to talk myself out of it. What's making me drive there are my instincts. How I'm feeling, and the fact that she called herself out is what is guiding me to where she is. If it had been him that called her out of work, I would be more worried.

I feel like I'm taking on Antonio's tactics as I sit here in my vehicle and watch Isabelle's house for any signs of life. He did the same exact thing with

Lilah except he was in denial about how he felt about her. I am not. There is no denying I would have continued seeing Isabelle had she not ended it. Granted, I've done many stakeouts, but being parked in front of a female's house that I had an interest in, is not one of them.

I parked far enough away so that I won't be noticed, but close enough so that if she looks out the window or opens her front door, I will at least see her stunning face.

An hour passes and there is no sign of her. The house is quiet. The curtains in the front window move a few times but I assumed it was from the wind blowing through the cracked window. I sit there another twenty minutes trying to talk myself into leaving. Something is telling me to knock on the door. I talk myself out of it and after another five minutes, I start my truck and drive away. This situation hits too close to home for me. It's throwing me off my instinctual game.

A survival tactic that needs to be on point.

Isabelle
CHAPTER EIGHT

I lay there with my head resting on the back of the couch. The soft fur blanket wrapped around my sore body brings me no comfort. The tears I shed, the ones that drip from the corners of my eyes while I watch the man I spent some time with through the opaque curtains, drop to the fabric I have pressed against my bruised face. Giovanni watches my house from the front seat of his vehicle. I yearn to open the front door and tell him to come inside. I want him to hold me. I want the strongest arms I have ever been held by to wrap around my battered body. I want him to hold me so tight that life before him was obliterated and the moments we spent together could be frozen in time.

It's not wrong to think or feel the way I do. It took me some time to come to that decision. At first, I thought it was. I struggled with that feeling for weeks but then I asked myself this question: How as a human can one be starved of loving affection and only shown the ugly side of human emotion from a supposed loved one, and not dream of something better?

I fought with myself over the decision I had made after I made it. Not because I felt guilty for cheating or for putting a black mark on my marriage. To be truthful, I see my marriage as nothing but a black abyss I'll never find my way out of. This had more to do with me and how I saw myself as a person, a woman, a mom. What if Abby was old enough to comprehend? How would she see her mother if she could?

A few days after, when the high became the low, I started to beat myself up mentally just as bad as Tommy did physically. I became my own therapist. I talked to the girl staring back at me in the mirror and made sure she answered back and if she didn't have an answer right at that moment, I held her accountable for when she did have one.

I declined Giovanni's offer the second time for a few reasons. First and foremost, something told me the handsome man flirting with me wasn't just a guy looking for a few fun times. It may have been his initial thought, but he didn't seem like that type of guy. He was much older than me, at least a decade, and he held a powerful aura about himself. I saw the way people reacted to him. I watched how they made a wide berth when he walked through the restaurant. When he sat at the bar, the only one that held a relaxed conversation with him was Walter. I was drawn to that kind of man. Through my own self therapy sessions, I came to the conclusion that being the child of a powerful man, even though I hated my father for who he was and what he stood for, is what made me seek men like him as an adult. And then it hit me pretty hard when I realized I ran from it, but then I ran right to it when I met Tommy.

It made no sense to me, but I felt like Giovanni was different. His demeanor was different. The way he touched me was with more care than I had experienced in all the five years with Tommy. I figured it would be a quick one and done, but it wasn't. It was hours of pleasure. The longer it lasted between us, the more he handled me, the more our bodies moved together, I realized my sexual health had also been misused. I was a virgin when I met Tommy. I was naïve to his lack of interest in me as a woman. It wasn't until I was with Giovanni just one time that I realized I was nothing but a vessel for Tommy to satisfy himself.

When Giovanni started flirting with me it felt so good, but it was also such a foreign feeling. More importantly, in those private moments, I felt like he was showing me a part of himself most didn't get to experience. There was a softness to him that I was sure he kept hidden from the rest of the world. I had to ask myself, why did he show me?

I shyly smiled at him first not knowing exactly what to do with myself and then after dropping my head to hide my smile, I glanced up at him, and I half-heartedly flirted back through my lashes. That part of me, the feminine part that is in every woman, was dormant. She had been dead for a long time, and until that moment, I didn't realize how much she had died. Giovanni's grin when I glanced back up made me wrinkle my nose and turn red before turning and running away.

To be wanted by another and shown the affection you have craved for so long is almost like feeling it for the first time with your teenage crush. Those butterflies that dance in the pit of your belly? They took flight. Whether the choices I made were good or bad, and most would see them as bad, they were just that; they were mine, and I don't get to make many of my own.

I want to say at one point, I thought maybe my decision was nothing but rebellion, rage against the evil that coexists within the walls of my house.

Which to some extent it was, but when it comes down to it, I craved a human touch that wasn't abusive.

I have wished and dreamt so many times that I could tell someone and have them take it all away, but the simple fact is, I can't. I know I can't. I'm trapped. As my momma would say with her southern twang, I truly got myself into a pickle. As much as I've wanted to reach out to her over the years, I knew I couldn't. Her advice to me, as far as I knew, would still be the point of view from a battered woman's eyes who was still in denial, because that is what I saw when I left.

Now I realize I have been the spitting image of her for years.

I glance over at my little girl. The tears fall faster as I gaze at her angelic sleeping face. Then I look back out the window and watch Giovanni's truck pull away from the curb and slowly drive past the house and down the street. I could swear he saw me watching him. When he turned the corner and the back of his truck left my blurry view, my battered body deflated at the loss of having him so close, and then not having him near at all. Just knowing he was across the street and a few houses down, made me feel safer.

Initially when I heard the motor of a vehicle turn off outside earlier, I instantly went into panic mode thinking it was Tommy coming home early from work, but then almost as if Giovanni silently commanded it, I immediately calmed down when I saw his truck.

Now that he is gone, I stiffly turn over on the couch that sits in front of the bay window I watched him through. I try to lay in a position that isn't too painful. My head still swims in dizziness, and nausea hits me from one minute to the next when I move too fast. With my hands in a praying position, tucked under my head, and Abby at the end of the couch peacefully napping, I stare at the muted TV screen while her favorite cartoon plays. Then I close my eyes and dream of a different life that her and I will hopefully someday live.

Giovanni
CHAPTER NINE

I crack his jaw one more time. The hit releases some of the energy bristling around inside my tight chest. His sweat sails through the air with each one of my punches. In retaliation, he gets a good shot in on me. I grin, welcoming the sting it brings, and then I immediately throw another punch. A sadist, I am. I tap my jaw twice more telling him to hit me. That I want it. That I need it. I need the rush, for the anger to surge, and then to be released. With a left, right, and another left hook, he has my blood boiling. I feel it, that moment when your insides become numb to the pain, and you rationalize the beating you are going to put on the victim in front of you.

The music plays with the sounds of *The Kill* by Thirty Seconds to Mars as I swing out my frustration. My punches get harder and harder as exhaustion starts to set in. It's a complete enigma to what should be happening to my body.

I couldn't sleep last night. Between the lack of sleep and the anger I feel inside, it makes for a deadly combination. Even the three glasses of the finest scotch I swallowed didn't put me down. Nothing worked. My eyes felt like they had toothpicks holding them open. I willed them to close, but to no avail, I now know every mark on my ceiling.

When the sun started to rise, I decided it was time for me to do the same. There was no use in me lying there any longer. I sat on the edge of my bed with my forearms resting on my knees and I watched the orange glow of the new day rise over the balcony.

I grabbed my phone and sent a message off to Christopher O'Reily, letting him know it was me who was going to be walking through his door in the next thirty minutes. Antonio and I have the keys and security codes to everyone's house.

Usually, Antonio and I work out together in my home gym after he has breakfast with Lilah and Romeo, and I have breakfast with my sister, but this morning was different. I needed to burn some pent-up energy before my day started and the only thing that was going to do that was getting in the ring. When Caelan, Antonio's one day brother-in-law, refurbished the firehouse him and Sofia lived in before gifting it to his brother Chris for him and Nikki to live in, he had a full-blown gym set up in the back, including a boxing ring. It was, and still is, the place we all go to when we need to really let off steam and get our frustrations out.

Me heading out for the day, with this kind of bad energy circulating through my system, is not a good situation for anyone.

I could think of a couple different ways for me to expend that energy, but this one was legal, and the other wasn't a solo act.

Demetri is single, with no significant ties except for who he has to kick out of his bed in the morning. I messaged him at five a.m. and told him to get his ass to Chris' place. He knocked on their back door twenty minutes later. We've been going at it since.

"Dude, I'm about dead." His chest heaves for air.

I let out a gruff chuckle and call him a pussy. I have enough energy to go for hours.

"What did I miss?" Antonio walks into the space. The ring is set up in the back part of the garage. Even with the music blaring, Chris and Nikki won't hear us while they're in bed asleep.

I grunt and Demetri lets out a thankful sigh.

"This fucker has issues." He steps back, reaching out so Antonio can release the laces of his glove. "Your turn, Boss." He pats him on the back before walking to get a hand towel to wipe the blood from his lip and the sweat from his brow.

My boss gives me a stern inquisitive stare down. He grabs the back of his shirt with one hand and pulls it over his head in one go. "Throw me my set of gloves." He holds his hand out to Demetri, still watching me.

With my hands on my hips and the energy of a prowling lion, I pace the ring. *Cryin' Like a Bitch* by Godsmack starts playing. I crack an evil grin and point at Demetri.

Once Demetri has Antonio laced up, he stands in the middle of the ring and waits for me to come tap his gloves. You would think after two hours of Demetri and I beating each other's asses I would be tired. That's not the case. By the feel of the unruly energy coursing through my veins, I'm ready to go another two hours.

I land the first shot. It's a brutal one. Antonio's head snaps back. The fucker grins at me when he brings his chin back down. Like what I just graced his jaw with was nothing more than a five-year-old girls' punch. It pisses me off even more. The next two hits are on me. One to the ribs, the other nails my chin. I welcome the fresh strength behind his punches.

Twenty grueling minutes goes by. He nails me again. Then he sternly looks me in the eyes, and asks, "How much do I have to be worried?"

"You don't. Hit me again, fucker."

He nails me so hard with an uppercut I lose my breath.

"I asked you a question."

Punch.

"I gave you an answer."

Punch.

His head jerks back with a sinister huff. With his fresh strength and me now three hours in, I'm starting to feel it, the draining of the rage. The war inside my body has been exhausted and is now dissipating.

My head jerks back once more with a square hit to my jaw. Before I can center myself, piercing pain radiates through my kidneys.

"You about done?" he questions, raising a brow while waiting for me to shake off the pain in my kidneys.

There comes a point in my line of work with every victim when I know the limits that person can take. I can tell just by looking at them. I know how long it will be before I have to torture them before I get my answers. I also know what tools to bring out to literally scare the piss out of them. Men are not afraid to lose teeth. They'll spit those fuckers to the concrete their blood stains beneath them and then they will grin at you after they do. Fingers are more important, but only the weak one's cry at the first initial finger lost. It's the second and third digit that makes them question their loyalty to their boss. Antonio will never question my loyalty to him or the family I consider mine as well. He knows I can, and will, keep fighting right now, but he also knows whatever emotional bullshit I am trying to evade is just about killing me. He proved that point when I left my kidneys wide open for his brutal shot.

Thanks to my boss and best friend, I will be pissing blood for days.

I step out of the ring and stalk my way to Demetri who is still sitting on the weight bench with a water bottle and towel. I hold out my hand for him to untie my laces then head to the refrigerator and grab two waters. I toss one to Antonio once Demetri has his hands free.

He's silent for a few minutes, letting our bodies calm down and my mind from spinning in circles. He takes the last few sips of his water and wipes down his face before asking, "We talking about this, or are you just going to be a brooding asshole the next few days?"

I lift my bottle, finish off what water is left, and ask, "We going to the diner for breakfast or am I cooking a feast in Nikki's kitchen?"

I. Do. Not. Talk. About. My. Past.

Antonio knows this.

Even though this isn't about my past, seeing Isabelle, knowing what my gut tells me is to be true, it certainly is bringing up some unwanted feelings to resurface from my childhood.

"Fuck," I hear Demetri mutter as I walk out of the room.

The day passes relatively uneventful. Temptations' doors opened thirty minutes ago. The club is packed as usual. *Touch It-remix* by Busta Rhymes and Mary J. Blige cranks through the speakers. Antonio is upstairs in his office with Lilah and Romeo. He makes sure they come in a few times a week so they can have dinner together. I have to say, if there is one girl that was made for Antonio, it is Lilah, through and through.

Demetri is talking to security. Luca, Lilah's bodyguard, is covering the security on Antonio's office door. And I was downstairs enjoying a bourbon at the main bar while waiting to take a meeting with a guy who reached out to do business. I showed him to a private room in the back of the club to discuss.

This guy talks like he has more clout than he does. If he had more, he would be in Antonio's office for the meeting. He's a two-bit wannabe, a bottom feeder soldier who is disposable to his boss. In his boasting about himself, he said something that did catch my attention. We don't normally deal in massive quantities of drugs, but while this guy was puking his speech on how many keys of cocaine his boss needs to offload, he carelessly mentioned a shipment of girls. Who he's working for is unclear at this point, he's just the mule. His boss sent him out to take a meeting with the underboss of an organization to see how much interest said organization has in what they are selling. In this case, he doesn't get that meeting with the underboss, he gets the meeting with his caporegime. Me. The moment I took that honor of being Antonio's capo, I took on having all initial meetings. If the deal sounds lucrative and on the up and up, I will take it to Antonio, but the fact of the matter is we don't work with unknowns and this guy isn't willing to say who he's working for.

However, my lack of conversation has this dude rambling. His nerves are getting the best of him. In this world, less is more. The less I speak, the least amount of charges can be brought against me. While my lack of talking has intimidated him, his nerves just made him mention these girls. If there is one thing the Heart organization does not deal in, it's human trafficking. Yes, we own a few Gentlemen's Clubs, but that is the extent of it and the girls are respected, well taken care of, and come to us for a job. This guy's mention of girls being shipped is the only reason he wasn't shown the door faster. I told him I would be in touch after I spoke to my boss. This is a sticky situation. No organization wants to get involved with another organizations business unless it infringes on our territory, but this... this doesn't sit right with me. And it never will.

I wrap up the meeting and head upstairs. Antonio and Lilah should be finished with dinner by now. After I respectfully knock on the door, and Antonio yells telling me to enter, I head inside.

"Hi, G," Lilah greets me from her seat at the table.

"Hey, Li." I lean over and grab Romeo from her lap when his little hands do the grabby sign that he wants me.

"He loves you," she gushes. "When are you having babies of your own?"

"Not anytime soon."

"Oh, don't tell me you have the same mentality as my husband did, do you?"

"Nope. He was an ass."

"No truer words have been spoken." She cocks a smile at Antonio, challenging him.

"If you two are done," he cocks a retribution brow back at her then gives me his attention, "how did it go?"

At times we do talk business in front of Lilah, but this kind of business is not for a female's ear. Just as my phone rings, I give him a subtle head shake letting him know I can't talk about it in front of her. I look at the number on the screen. I don't recognize it. I hand Romeo to Antonio and take a step off to the side and answer.

"Giovanni?" a female's voice comes through the line asking.

"Speaking."

"It's Pat."

I already know what she is going to say before she says it. Isabelle called out from work.

"She didn't come in for her shift today."

"She didn't show up or she called out?" I gruffly ask.

"Called out."

"Who called her out, herself or her husband?"

"It was her."

"Thanks for the heads up."

"Giovanni?" I hear my name called just as I'm getting ready to hang up.

"Yeah?"

"She called out for tomorrow, too."

Fuck.

I hang up and head straight for the door.

"G, what's going on? You good? Who was that?"

"Talk later. You need me right now?" I grab for the door handle, turning back.

"No. You need me?"

"No." I walk out letting the door close behind me with a bang. I take the elevator downstairs, and while I'm pacing the small square, I call one of the valets to bring my SUV around. I better see some kind of movement in that house, and it better be her small frame I see moving or someone will be paying with their blood, and it won't be her shedding anymore.

Isabelle
CHAPTER TEN

My decision to try and leave Tommy had been a weak one. It was first thing in the morning and Tommy hasn't come home from his night shift yet. I chastised myself the morning after seeing Giovanni while tending to my wounds. I told myself I at least had to make an appointment for a consultation with a lawyer, preferably a female. I don't trust men, rightfully so, but I also felt a man could be corrupted by money more than a female. That's not saying a female couldn't, but I think I have a better chance with a woman. I take pictures of every mark on my body and file them in a password locked folder on my phone. I hope that one day those pictures will help me get free of this situation.

I need to know my options. What the proceedings will be? How long will it take? Will I be able to get a restraining order against him? And if I am granted the order, will that keep him away? I doubt it. I also need to worry about Abby. Will he get partial custody? Or worse, full? Will he claim I am a bad mother? Of course, he will. In my head, no judge will give a man any kind of rights to a child after seeing the pictures of what he did to their mother. But, then again, I am not dealing with a normal situation either.

After calling and begging for an appointment, I sit on the edge of the couch in a panic. I explained my situation to her and that it was dire I come in that day, and I only had a small window of time that I actually could. Her PA heard the distress in my voice, knew the situation after I explained it, and told me to hold on. I sit here, on the edge of the couch in a rocking position when she comes back on the line and tells me she will do a conference video call with me. I am so relieved, I burst into tears, but then fear strikes me so hard, I shake uncontrollably. The meeting would take place while Tommy should be sleeping soundly down the hallway.

He was.

Five minutes before the call, I tiptoe down the hallway and make sure he is asleep. Then with nerves rattling my body with the force of an old unsteady wooden rollercoaster, I quietly guide Abby outside and wait for her call.

When the screen lights up and her face comes across my laptop, a part of me is excited that I actually took the step to see what my options are.

Marietta Hayworth is a well put together woman, is what I think at first glance. She is polite and gets straight to the point after her initial shock at seeing my face through the screen of our Zoom call. When she leans back in her tall office chair and drops her arms to the armrest, it brings tears to my eyes. I have seen myself many times this way but to have another look at me with so much pity, I can't stand it. I almost slap my laptop closed, embarrassed that I let this happen, but then I take a breath and tell myself this isn't my fault. That I am taking the first step in getting back control of my life.

Telling her who I am and who my husband belongs to, she is almost hesitant to take my case. I understand because I was hesitant to tell her who I was married to. I'm not even sure when our call is finished that she will take me on as a client when the time does come.

Going up against power and money is scary for anyone.

When she brings herself back from the devastation on my face, and sits up in her chair, I am told I have to be smart about my next few decisions. She offers to help me get into a woman's shelter, but I decline. I have to, and after me explaining, she agrees. Knowing who Tommy is and what he does, the security they put in place will be just a game to him.

She tells me the best way to go about this sensitive situation is to have all my paperwork and plans in order. Do it all in one shot and be ready to go missing for a few weeks. I am to have no contact with the outside world. She also says I need a new cell phone, one that can't be tracked.

I tell her it will take me a few more weeks before I have enough money for her retainer and even then, I will have to wait to make enough money so that I can find a decent place for Abby and me to live at right away.

Once I leave Tommy, I know he will go crazy. Her suggestion of "going missing" is the best one I have heard. My life at that time will be in even more danger away from him than it will be if I am still with him.

"You will never leave me, Isabelle. And if you try, you won't get far. Trust me, I will always find you."

Just hearing his words in my head, I'm scared for myself. I'm scared for my baby girl. I'm scared for my future, for our future. What if his threats come to fruition and he does kill me? Where would Abby go? To his mother and father? That's almost just as bad, if not worse. They're enablers. They make excuses for their only son's behavior.

"Why do you make him so mad, Isabelle?"

"What did you do this time, Isabelle?"

"Why can't you just do what he asks, Isabelle?"

Those are just some of the accusations they ask when they see the bruises on my body.

I'm not scared to be on my own. I've been there. I've done that. I was a runaway teenager from a small town living in New York City, and I survived just fine. But now it's different, I have Abby, and I certainly can't be bouncing from couch to couch. Abby is my first priority. She needs a stable home. I'm petrified of failing her because when I really think about it, I already have failed at so many things. What if I fail again? I'm petrified that one day she will look at me and tell me what I already know deep down inside. That I'm a terrible mother.

Marietta didn't lie. She told me there would be a lot of downs before there would ever be any ups. She told me I had to be smart and patient. When we are just about to end the call, I thank her for her time and knowledge, and she wishes me peace and safety.

Two aspects of life I know I won't see for a very, very long time.

I cancel out the call and clear my history just in case Tommy uses my laptop or goes searching for information. Just as the top lid hits the bottom, I jump back on the seat of the picnic table from the man standing before me. Tommy hovers. His hair is ruffled from sleep. An unreadable expression is in place, and his arms hang at his sides. They look lax, but I know better. I glance over at Abby playing in her sandbox to make sure she is okay. I throw my legs over the bench seat of the picnic table and stand on the opposite side staring back at him.

"Who were you talking to, Isabelle?" His clipped question sets me on edge.

"What? No one. Why would you think I was talking to someone?"

"Because I heard you." The frown lines around his mouth become deep crevices of disdain.

I need to swallow the lump forming in my throat, but I know I can't. Tommy is an expert at reading me. If I nervously swallow that lump, he will know I am lying.

"You heard me talking to Abby."

"Is that so?"

"Yes. I asked her if she wanted a swing set."

He raises his brow.

"You don't believe me? Then ask her yourself."

And of course, he does.

Without her knowing it, the conversation my daughter and I had as I held her hand walking out to the backyard to take the meeting covered my lie.

After a few moments of his intrusive stare down, I walk around the side of the table and stop in my tracks when I glance down the side of the house to the street. It is only for a split second, but it feels like precious minutes are passing, and I am frozen in that time. I can't move. The shiny black SUV slows down when he spots me. His window lowers halfway. Our eyes lock only for a moment before he keeps driving at a speed as if he was leisurely driving down our street. My heart pounds in my chest. My hand goes to my swollen, bruised face, and I drop my head in shame. I want to stand here and hold that moment in a frame, but reality kicks in and my husband's presence is coming towards me.

"Hey, Abby. You ready for lunch? Momma's gonna make you some SpaghettiOs."

"Spa-get-te-tOOOOOOOOssss," she cheers, jumping from the sandbox. "Momma, will you have some with me?"

"Sure will, baby girl." I hold out my hand and wait for hers.

"No, Abigail, your mother will eat adult food like your father."

I shoot him a narrowed look.

He blows my anger off as if it means nothing to him, which I know it doesn't, and then he snarls an order, "Get your fat ass inside and be a good wife and cook your husband some lunch. I have to leave for work."

"Watch how you talk to me, Tommy."

"Or what?" He steps towards me.

"You just got home a few hours ago?" I change the subject, not wanting Abigail to see us fighting.

"And?"

"Nothing." I shake my head and let it go.

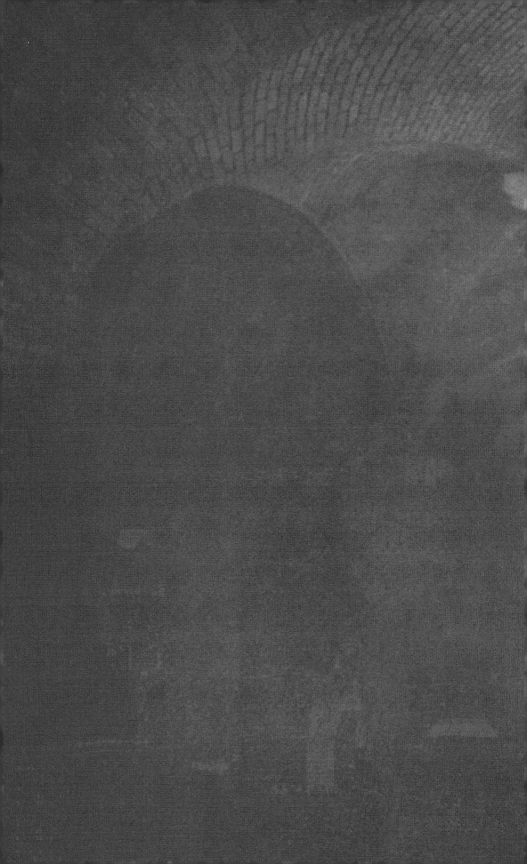

Giovanni
CHAPTER ELEVEN

I waited. I sat in my truck, and I waited to see some kind of life inside their house last night. The blue truck I was sure was his was still there at midnight when I left. Her red jeep was parked in the spot next to his. The lights were on in the house, and I saw his and her shadows moving around. To some extent, that made me feel better and then very quickly jealousy and anger took over. Her abuser was in there with her when I wasn't allowed. He was her husband when I, the man that would give her the world, was denied her company. I felt a part of me slip back to my past when I would, as a child, go inside myself. I was no longer that child anymore. I was no longer the little boy who had to hide behind the door and watch the brutal scene unfold through the cracks of our house.

I was a man.

A Made Man.

A man who people respected, some even worshiped, while others—as they should—feared me. My street cred came from hard work and pushing through horrific memories that plagued me until I was in my late teens. Once I met Mr. Heart and he gave me a chance, I turned my life around. I may be a stone-cold killer, but the depths within the walls of my temple had seen its own pain, pain that I buried a long time ago. Seeing Isabelle sitting at the picnic table, beaten and battered, staring off into space, brings back the times I would see my mom sitting at our kitchen table with a cigarette in her bruised, shaking hand.

When Pat called me last night, I only had one thought; get to where I knew she would be. I almost busted down their door. I talked myself out of it because I knew exactly what would happen. I would go to jail for beating the bastard to death. And I would. I would enjoy watching the life being drained from his body, but my unresolved rage at the situation would make me careless. Being careless is not how I have kept myself out of prison all these years.

I feel like I am caught in a vortex of right or wrong, my past meeting my present, and I question myself to pursue or retreat from the situation. This turmoil I feel is not something I am accustomed to. I have too much life experience to worry about right or wrong. Everything to me is a grey area. I'm too old to have my past brought into my present. Those memories were buried a long time ago. And as for me feeling the pressure and confusion of pursuing or retreating, I never retreat, but I did, for her.

Now, here I sit once again, the next afternoon. I watched his truck pull out and leave a few moments ago. I circle the block to see if she is sitting in the backyard like she was yesterday. When I see her sitting at the picnic table, I pull back around, park, and jump out of my truck. I walk down the side of her house and stop in my tracks when she comes into my view. Even with the discoloration on her face, her beauty is captivating. She is the only woman I have ever been in the company of whose innocent charm seized a part inside of me, a part that I knew from when I was a very small child, was dead

"What are you doing here?" Her shocked voice rises to the point of panic. She jumps up and rushes towards me. Pain at the forefront of each movement.

"Where is your daughter?" I look around the bare yard.

"Sleeping," she exclaims with rushed exasperation.

"Where?" I question, not wanting to move any farther into the yard.

"In her room. Why?" she snaps like she doesn't trust me.

I immediately connect eyes with her and silently chastise her for questioning my loyalty, but I also understand why she did. Her first reaction was to think of her daughter's safety and not hers. "Because I don't want her to see me," I explain, taking a step closer to her.

"I don't want her to see you! Why are you here? You can't be here!" Her arms fly in the air in a mass of anxiety.

I take a step closer and lift my hand. I can't help it. I have to touch her. Calm her. I run the back of my knuckles over her cheek and bring it down to cradle her swollen face in my callused palm. "Little lion…" I breathe in deeply then release the breath I had hoped would calm me. "He did this to you." It's a hazy statement of controlled rage. I don't need to ask, I already know the answer, but my gaze is locked on hers, fully enraptured by her.

"It's none of your business."

"It is now," I simply state. There may have been a point of me wavering back and forth before, but as of this moment, I am no longer.

"Giovanni, please don't do this," she begs. "Please. If he finds out about us…" Her bottom lip quivers so much she has to stop talking. The tears starting to glisten in her emerald green eyes shine with so much sadness.

"Shh." I try to calm her. "He won't find out."

"You don't know him, he will! And it will only be worse for me." She unconsciously steps into me and places her hands on my chest. At first, I think it is to push me away, but now, I don't think she knows she is pressing her palms to my chest in a way that would suggest she is seeking my warmth.

"I know exactly what kind of guy he is." I cradle the back of her head and pull her into me further.

She rests against my chest all of ten seconds and releases a deep breath before she pulls away with energy, and spats, "I don't need you here! I don't want you here! Why are you here?"

"Because I needed to check on you, angel."

She looks confused at my endearment, but she doesn't question it. Her soft feminine side reminds me of a radiant angel soaring through a raging storm with tattered wings that have been clipped or broken one by one.

"What? Now you're watching me? I have enough of that already. You drove past my house twice! Are you crazy?"

"You could say that." I let that sit for a minute. "And no, angel, I am not watching you, I am watching *over* you. It's very different."

"Why? Because we had sex?"

"No, because by the looks of your beating, this was a bad one. His handy work is a few days old. You haven't been to work." I pause a moment. "Which only means they have, and will, continue to get worse and worse each time he puts his hands on you. As much as I want to shove my fist down his throat and rip his asshole out through his larynx, I won't do that. Not right now. I won't for your sake."

"You have to go." She pushes at my chest, forcing me to release her, but I hold on.

With both my hands, I cradle her head and stare into her eyes. "For now, but Isabelle, I will not be far." I free her and reach into my pocket and hand her a burner phone.

"What? What is this?" Her brows furrow, becoming heavy as she looks at the device I just put in her hand.

"Put it somewhere safe. Somewhere he won't find it. It's a burner. The only number programed in there is mine. Use it."

Her eyes become as soft as a newborn baby doe. "Why?"

"Because one day it's going to feel like it's going to be your last. Hopefully you leave him before that happens, but if you don't and that day comes, and it will come, Isabelle, trust me when I say that. It will because it will only get worse and worse as each day passes. I hope you will reach out to me before that happens, but if you don't and that day takes place, get to this phone and call that number."

"Is this… Are you doing this because I slept with you?" Her bottom lip quivers.

A husky noise of irritation leaves my chest. "Don't insult me."

"I wasn't. I-I—" She studders over her words.

"You did. This has nothing to do with what happened between us. Yes, there is no denying I would have enjoyed seeing where we would have gone, but clearly I wasn't aware that wasn't an option."

Guilt floods her soft features. She is quiet a moment while watching me. The questions she wants to ask, read loud and clear in her eyes, but she doesn't ask. She just quietly mutters two words I'm certain she has said more times in her life than any other. "I'm sorry."

"There is nothing to be sorry for. I understand the 'why' more than you will ever know." I lean down and kiss the top of her head. I take in her scent, closing my eyes and savoring it. Then I step back before I can't bring myself to do it. "Use it," I tell her once more, nodding at the phone in her hand. Then I turn and walk away.

I only get halfway down the walkway when she yells with urgency, "Giovanni!" I turn back. She is holding the phone to her chest with both hands. "Thank you." She struggles for her words. "For caring." She nods her head in jerky movements.

She isn't saying yes or agreeing to even using the phone. She is simply realizing that someone cares about her, about what happens to her. That *I care* what happens to her.

"No matter what happens, know I will always be watching over you, angel."

Isabelle
CHAPTER TWELVE

I t's been one week since Giovanni showed up in my backyard. The last words he spoke played on repeat in my head all week. *"No matter what happens, know I will always be watching over you."* It made me feel special, like someone out there cared.

He cares.

If only things were different.

If I had only made different choices in life.

If I had seen through the fake "nice guy" Tommy had portrayed himself to be. What if I had met Giovanni first? How different would my life be right now? I'll never know. As much as I want to go back and change things if I could, I still wouldn't. If I did then I wouldn't have my baby girl.

I have come to the conclusion that life, in and of itself, is one giant school. It's a lesson learned to know what path is right for you. We are all given choices. We either learn from those lessons or we continue to ignore them and make the same vicious loop over and over, effectively staying stagnant in a life where the world around you is continuously moving forward.

I know I don't want to be in the same situation one month from now, let alone three months from now.

It is my first shift back at the diner. Lenny, the owner, called me yesterday and asked if I had quit without telling him. I told him I had the flu and was too sick to come in but that I am better and would be in the next morning if he still wanted me as an employee. My fingers were crossed waiting for his answer. I need that job. I'm still baffled at the fact Tommy isn't putting up more of a fight that I am working there. He hates that I do, but for some reason, he never pushes the issue and I have to wonder why.

My bruises had faded enough for me to cover the yellow discoloration with makeup. When the afternoon came, and the lunch rush cleared, I grab a coffee and sit in the corner booth to count my tips. Working at Lenny's is a pretty good job. The tips are good. Not as good as working at O'Brien's, but still decent.

My first day back after a week of healing and self-pity has a newfound energy for life strumming through my veins. As I sit here dreaming of where the next few months will take me, I hear the bell above the side door chime as a customer enters the diner.

I glance across the space and lock eyes with the most confident man I have ever met. He owns the worn black and white tile beneath his feet as he claims the space with just his presence. With a swagger all his own, that screams, *I am a very important man,* he strides across the diner in my direction.

I watch him as each step brings him closer to where I'm sitting. I can't help but wonder if my attraction to him is because of the power every pore in his body exudes, but then I quickly realize it's not that. He is a very handsome man. His confidence only makes him more alluring.

When I think back to when Tommy and I first met, I thought he had a lot of confidence as well, but almost right after we were married, I realized he didn't have any. It was all show.

I asked myself this past week what it was that he saw in me that he knew I was a person who could be manipulated? My only answer is I somehow showed him my own weaknesses. Tommy is a predator and predators seek weaker people to prey on.

I have to wonder if the man stalking towards me, because that is exactly what he is doing, thinks I'm weak too?

Before I can answer my own question, he throws me a curveball, and he winks at me. My belly does a flip then a flop, and I'm not sure what to do in the moment. The corner of his mouth lifts into a devilish grin from my apparent shock. It makes my heart flutter like never before. My insides turn to teenage girl goo.

I smile at him. It's a small, shy smile, but it's there and it's genuine. My nose crinkles with the shyness I feel, and I shake my head slightly before turning away with an even bigger smile on my face.

His flirting gesture just made me feel something.

Joy.

Giddiness.

Dare I say a small bit of happiness? Especially at the end of a week I didn't think I would survive.

Before I can analyze any of the feelings surging through me, I remember where I am. Picture windows flank across the front of the diner. Tommy could be watching me from anywhere. I have caught him many times before.

I glance over to his favorite spot across the street. It's empty. I let out a breath of relief. I glance back over to the counter where Kellie is waiting on the man that just gave me giant moth-size flutters. She is openly flirting with him. I can't say I blame her. But I also know… I don't like it.

I slide from the booth, telling myself I'm helping him by saving him from her.

That's what I tell myself.

"Hey, Kellie. I'll take care of him. Table five was waving you down," I lie as I round the corner of the counter listening to them.

Although, it was a one-sided conversation. He was completely ignoring her excessive friendliness.

When she struts away, I politely smile, and ask, "What are you doing here?"

"I heard the coffee was good." He smiles. It's a polite smile. One that is as if we don't know each other at all. Quite the opposite of his flirty wink.

"I mean, it doesn't top a Caramel Macchiato latte from the coffee shop around the corner, but then again, you look like you would be the boring black coffee kind of guy, so you would probably appreciate Lenny's coffee more."

The devilish grin is back. "I can assure you; I am not boring." He dips his head, watching me with such a sexy smirk that a zing whips through my dormant loins. "As for my coffee, I like it just like my woman, light and sweet. Very sweet."

Woman. Not women.

And, huh?

"Woman, huh?" I look across the diner at Kellie. "Poor Kellie is going to be devastated."

"Poor Kellie never had a chance. She's cute, but she has nothing on the woman I crave."

That makes me pause. Although it was fun, I should not be flirting with him.

He reaches over the few inches our hands are separated on the counter and places his massive warm palm over the top of mine. "Relax, Isabelle. We are just talking."

I leave my hand there for only one pleasurable second while we have a full conversation through our eyes. I break our connection, and ask, "Really, though, why are you here?"

He watches me for a second. "I told you. I will always be watching over you."

It should scare me. This man half-sitting, half-standing in front of me with his imposing stature should frighten the hell out of me, but he doesn't and that makes me worry. I made the mistake of trusting Tommy and look where that has gotten me. Maybe my instincts have short-circuited, and they need to be rebooted. Maybe I need to do the opposite of what it tells me to do until I can ask and answer every question I have about myself.

"Gio…" I whisper his name, almost in pain.

"Am I interrupting something?" An extremely deep voice penetrates our intense, but now silent conversation.

I instantly jerk my hand away, immediately feeling the loss of energy he filled my veins with, with such a simple touch. Even though I know the voice doesn't belong to Tommy, I feel like I was just caught doing something I shouldn't have been doing. I look to the man that took a seat on the stool next to Giovanni. He's in a black-on-black suit with the top two buttons undone. He has short, black as night hair, perfectly arched eyebrows and a beard and mustache that is kept close to his angled jaw. Then I notice his eyes. One is a deep royal blue with no other color in it and the other is the same royal blue, but it has emerald-green flecks scattered through it. He may have a smile on his face, but it is a wicked one, and there is an undercurrent of danger to him. My gaze flicks back to Giovanni. The two men sitting in front of me scream dangerous. I don't know exactly who Giovanni, or his friend, are, or what they do, but I can tell you that they both command respect. I can also confirm by watching others react to Giovanni, they both get it.

"I'll get your coffee," I mutter, turning away from them both.

"Can you add a double cheeseburger to that coffee, sweetheart," the guy with the crazy eye color asks.

When I turn around to acknowledge his request, Giovanni is shooting him daggers filled with the promise of death.

"Don't do it again." His deep voice penetrates the space between them in a warning.

The guy holds his hands up in a gesture of surrender, but the smirk on his face tells me he did exactly what he wanted to, and that was to intentionally piss Giovanni off. I'm stuck in my spot watching the heated dynamic between the two of them. Their stare off is so long, I start to get anxiety just watching their exchange. I turn around and put in the order for the cheeseburger and then I walk over to the coffee station and make Giovanni's coffee. When I turn back, Giovanni's green eyes are on me again. I slide the cup across the counter to him while holding his gaze. Before I can release the cup, he places his hand over mine. I still, and even though his hand is holding mine in place, his touch is not restrictive. It's a feeling of comfort, a pillar of strength, one that holds you up and doesn't tear you down. The moment feels like it lasts forever, but in reality, it is a timeless moment with so much being said between us without actually saying it.

He's the one that breaks our gaze and proceeds to explain. "The asshole sitting next to me is Demetri. By the end of tonight, he may be a dead Demetri.

Demetri here, is teetering on a very thin line and he knows it. Demetri, this is Isabelle. Isabelle, this obviously is Demetri."

"Hey, Isabelle." He takes two finger and salutes me.

"Hey." We fall silent again and I shift in my space before saying, "I'm just going to go check on your burger." I throw my thumb over my shoulder.

When I turn away, Kellie comes back behind the counter. "What did he say? Did he say anything about me?" she gushes like a love-sick puppy, chattering in my ear while grabbing a stack of napkins.

"What?" I hand her the straws she is reaching for.

"The guy you just gave the coffee to. Did he say anything about me? He was totally flirting with me."

"He was?" I turn, looking over my shoulder at his handsome face. Him and Demetri are deep in a conversation, but then he turns back to me like he could feel my eyes on him. I turn back to Kellie, and tell her, "I-I think he has a girlfriend."

"Really?" She shrugs her shoulder like she doesn't care in the least bit.

"Yeah." My indignant tone makes her shoulders drop.

"Man, I could have sworn he was into me."

I hear the rattle of car keys clank against the yellow-ish Formica counter behind me. I'm throwing napkins and condiments in the bag with Demetri's cheeseburger when I hear someone say, "The customer service around here sucks."

My whole body jerks into a straight position, my spine becoming ramrod straight. My shoulders tense with ligament snapping tension. My limbs start to shake. My toes spread, trying to steady my body. The nervous energy is rushing its way through me and it's starting to take over.

I know I have to turn around and acknowledge him, and soon, because if I don't, he will make a scene. I have Demetri's food bagged up and ready to give it to him, but I'm so damn scared to face Tommy with Giovanni sitting three feet away from him. I know Tommy will notice something is wrong.

When I turn to Kellie to give the bag of food to her, she is standing at the opening between the counters where we come and go. Giovanni is to her left and Tommy is to her right.

I'm stuck.

Stuck in a moment I am not sure how to handle.

When I turn to give Demetri his bag of food, because I have no choice, I notice Giovanni giving Tommy a glacial stare down. He is furious. The same stare Giovanni is giving Tommy, Tommy is giving me, oblivious to the death threat he is receiving from just a few feet away.

Before I can give Demetri his food. I hear Tommy say, "You got a fucking problem?"

My head jerks back to Tommy and then to Giovanni when I realize it is him that Tommy has set his vitriol on.

Giovanni grins, but it isn't a nice one. It's a sneer of contained rage. He stands to his full height and just glares at Tommy while simultaneously pulling way too much money out of his pocket and laying it on the counter. His intimidation factor is not a show of dominance, it is as natural to him as walking. It makes me shake in my shell, but I'm not scared for myself, but for my husband who doesn't realize he has shown his teeth like a big dog, when really, in comparison to Giovanni, he is nothing more than a snarling chihuahua that has bitten off more than he can chew.

"Wrong guy, dude." Demetri stands from the stool and places his hand on Giovanni's shoulder.

"Here you go, sir." I treat them like they are just like any other customer. "Enjoy your lunch." I slide the bag across the counter, connecting pleading eyes with Demetri.

"Do you?" Tommy harshly snaps, twisting his head in a cocky manner. "Because we can take this outside. I should knock you the fuck out for checking out my wife's ass."

Giovanni doesn't say a word. His glare says it all. Demetri looks confused at the fact that Giovanni isn't entertaining Tommy in an argument.

In a hurry, I take the six steps from giving Demetri his food to Tommy. I place my hands on the counter and lean over, pleading with him to stop before he really makes a scene. But he snatches my wrist and yanks me across the counter to him.

"Tommy, let me go. Customers are looking at us," I grind my teeth, growling under my breath.

His nostrils flare. "You like the fact that he was staring at your ass?"

"I can't be held responsible for someone else's actions." I jerk on my arm, hoping because we are in public, he will let me go.

"I advise you to let her go," Giovanni's deep voice instructs Tommy with a calm, assertive, but harsh tone. "Now."

"And what?" Tommy remarks with a condescending tone. "What are you going to do?" He huffs an arrogant laugh, tightening his grip on my wrist. "Do you know who I am?"

"G, we got eyes, man. Lots of them," Demetri calmly murmurs as he steps up next to his side.

Giovanni doesn't flinch at Demetri's warning. He is zeroed in on Tommy's hand gripping my skin. His pupils are expanding at lightning speed.

"I can promise you, if you do not take your hand off this young woman's arm, you and I will be going out back so I can show you what it is like to take a beating."

Tommy releases my arm, shoving it away from him like I have a disease.

I take a step back, holding my arm to my chest. Kellie comes rushing over with a towel filled with ice. Demetri turns his head, leaning into Giovanni and whispers something.

Giovanni hasn't taken his glare off Tommy. He wants to pummel him. I can feel it. He may look the statue of control, but inside, he is raging.

I want to walk away. No, I want to run away, hide myself from the eyes that are intently watching the scene unfold. The embarrassment I feel is far beyond anything I have ever felt. Tommy has never touched me this way in public before. His abuse has always taken place behind closed doors. It's one thing when your spouse is abusive in the privacy of your own home, but it is another when everyone witnesses it happening. The sad fact is both the abuser and the victim need the same thing: control. The abuser needs to control the victim and the victim cowers down to control the situation.

Giovanni finally takes his eyes off Tommy when Demetri leans in once again and mumbles something to him. I have about all I can take. I rush from behind the counter and head to the back of the kitchen where the employee room is located, and I cry with crocodile tears because I have had enough.

Giovanni
CHAPTER THIRTEEN

"I want to know everything, and I mean everything there is to know about that motherfucker," I grit my teeth and order my demand into my phone. "Do you hear me, Freddy? If this guy's dick hangs to the right and he pisses to the left, I want to fucking know. If he taps the tip of his dick with tissue or he fucking shakes his leftover piss, I want to fucking know! I want every detail!" I'm silent, heaving ragged breath through my nostrils while waiting for his confirmation, knowing our tech guy will get me all the facts I furiously seek. It may take a day or two, but by the end of this week, I will know exactly who I am going to be dealing with.

And I will be dealing with him.

I hang up and drop my phone onto the center console. Demetri is silent, but I can feel his attention every few minutes when he corner-eyes me. He's waiting for me to cool down before voicing any kind of opinion. At least he is smart enough to heed his own warning. I am always in control. Right now, there is a storm raging inside my chest. On the inside, I am out of control. On the outside, to anyone who knows me, I am a level above my normal. I will never show the true wrath of what I hold in the cavity of my body. My blood is pumping, the hot liquid banging against the thin walls of my veins forcing the lining to stretch to the point of bursting.

I slam my hand against the window release, letting the fresh air from outside penetrate the inside of the vehicle. The air in the SUV is suffocating. The suit I dressed in this morning is constricting. After a minute, I put the window back up, knowing it was careless and dangerous for me to do. The windows are bulletproof, keeping us safe from our enemies. Rolling down the window all the way, put not only myself at risk but Demetri as well.

I'm tempted to throw the SUV in reverse and drive back to the diner. The desire to make him bleed is more than entertaining, but the need to make sure she is okay is a burning obligation inside my chest. I knew if I had paid her any attention while he was strangling her wrist, constricting it from blood flow, he would have taken more of his anger out on her when they are in private. Had I known he wouldn't, he would have been laying on a stretcher right now being wheeled into an ambulance. I would say consequences be damned, but there would be none. I am too good at what I do. My girl's pain and suffering just saved his ass. Today. It saved his ass, today. I will get him.

Demetri hasn't even touched his burger. I glance over at him and then at his bag. He called her *sweetheart.* It was to piss me off. At the moment, he is lucky I don't take my anger out on him.

"How serious is it?" He breaks the silence as he reaches down by his feet for the bag with his cheeseburger in it.

"What, the fact that you almost died back there?"

"Pretty serious then." He jerks his head before taking a bite of his burger. "I didn't know you were seeing anyone," he noted after swallowing.

I stay quiet, my fingers tapping the top of the steering wheel where my hand rests while waiting for the red light to change.

"She's stunning," he comments his observation.

I slant my eyes and slowly turn my head in his direction.

"Possessive motherfucker, then." He raises a brow. "Takes one to know one, G." He smirks taking another bite of his burger. "Look, clearly there is some sort of triangle going on. That dude her husband? They separated and he can't let go? I definitely saw a ring on her finger."

He says one more thing about that gold band on her finger, I will cut all his fingers off and thoroughly enjoy every second of it. "We're not together. She is just a friend." My teeth grind.

"Yeah, big man, not believing that one at all. You have definitely bedded her a time or two."

"Demetri…" I grind my molars with more force, warning him before taking off when the light changes.

"No disrespect, G, but no man reacts the way you just did because he isn't or hasn't laid her down."

"I'm not. We were together once, months ago."

His eyes expand with shock. "Once? It must have been like eating the most decadent meal at the top of the food chain then."

My fist hurls across the truck and nails him dead center in his chest. The burger he just bit into flies out of his mouth, he starts choking, trying to replenish his lungs with air.

"Fuck, man!" He coughs again, rubbing his chest. "I didn't mean her. I meant the sex in general!"

"Watch what you say." My warning is deep and low.

"All I'm saying is, for as long as I have been in this family, this organization, I have admired the way you handle yourself. You're calm, cool, and collected. Nothing ruffles your feathers."

"I'm not a fucking bird."

"But you are a man, a Made Man, a capo, no less, under one of the most notorious boss and underboss in history. You have that position for a reason. You do not make mistakes. You do not show your cards. To everyone else in that place, you were calm, but I know you, know how you perform. We have worked together in this organization for too long for me not to see you boiling under that suit and tie back there. You were ready to kill that guy. You didn't care there was an audience inside that diner. You could have really fucked up back there, man. You can at least tell me what is going on in case something like this happens again."

"I want her. She's married. End of story," I clip, giving him the answer he seeks.

"That dick was her husband?"

I confirm with a nod.

"You pursuing her?"

"It's complicated."

"Clearly." We both go quiet while I continue to head to the club. After a few minutes of silence he reassures, "You take him out, I got your back. You just tell me when and where."

The music is blaring. I'm still bristling from this afternoon. The drink in my hand is helping to ease the tension, but it may take a few more cocktails to get me back to normal. The vision of his hands on her, it makes me want to torture him for weeks.

I'm sitting in Antonio's private VIP lounge waiting for the underbosses of Brooklyn and the Bronx to show for a meeting. Leo, the underboss of Brooklyn and the son of Alessio Bonetti walks through the door first. Mr. Heart and Alessio go back a long way. While I was being a scavenger in the streets, a starved kid looking for food for me and my sister, Antonio and Leo were being taught how to be underbosses in order to reign over the organization when their fathers/dons finally meet their demise. Both dons leave most of the dealings to their sons now that they are a bit older. Not that Mr. Heart is old. The man is still in his fifty's and looks about forty-five. He, along with Lorenzo, the consigliere of our family, consult with Antonio and me most mornings, leaving us to conduct business throughout the day. Tonight's meeting will just be the underbosses and their lead capos.

Rocco is the son of Santo Ricci. The Bronx is reigned over by a ruthless don. Needless to say, Rocco had it tough with his upbringing, but his upbringing was nowhere near as tough as mine or even Leo's. I watched my mother take on my father's fist my whole life while Leo watched his mother be gunned down in the streets by some low-level junkie gang banger looking to make his mark. Alessio, Leo's father, is a brutal man. Leo is one of the darkest motherfuckers I have ever encountered. I can torture a man for days. It's my job. Leo, with meticulous precision, peels back the skin of each one of his victims over time. And he enjoys it. He gets high off it. His good looks and charm hide the darkness he keeps hidden behind the GQ shell. The only person I have ever seen Leo be genuine with is Antonio. From my understanding, Antonio took Leo under his wing, showing him the ropes when they were kids. To this day, Leo says he owes Antonio, and as dark as he is, he is a man of his word.

Tonight's meeting is about the cargo of humans supposedly being shipped from across seas. From what I understand from the guy I held a meeting with the other night, they are going to be disbursed into some safe houses throughout the Bronx. The sad part, they are not going to be kept safe. They will be used against their will, groomed, and conditioned with heavy drugs to make each victim pliable, forcing them to accept their fate.

It's unacceptable and not a business we have ever been a part of. The Godfather that reigns over the five boroughs does not stand for it. If this is happening in any one of the boroughs, then it damn sure wasn't sanctioned by Robert Heart.

Leo is here because Brooklyn and the Bronx have been doing some business together. Leo and Rocco have been getting closer over the past few months. Antonio knows Leo well. If Rocco is involved in humans being trafficked, then Leo will know about it or at least have some kind of clue about it. When Antonio questions Rocco, it won't be Rocco's reaction we will be watching for, but Leo's.

"A drink, gentlemen?" Antonio offers, holding up a bottle of his finest liquor before starting the meeting. With nods and verbal yeses, he starts pouring. When he turns to the corner of the room and nods is when I notice Joseph in a suit, standing at attention next to Luca. The room is on the darker side, but I can still see the black eye and busted lip Joseph's sporting. He turns away from Luca when he jerks his chin in a gesture to explain what Antonio is asking for. He lowers the music until Luca signals it's enough so we can speak at a normal tone. The road map has been laid for Joseph. He will now learn all that we are willing to let him learn. The rest is up to him on how well he receives those lessons and how well he conducts himself while being a spectator next to us while we are conducting said business.

The privacy glass slides closed, cutting us off from the full atmosphere of the club below just as Antonio starts his speech of fact finding.

"Okay, gentlemen," Antonio begins with a formal business tone demanding all eyes are on him. "It has come to my attention that there may be some illegal activity going on without being sanctioned, much less brought to the table even."

"That's all we deal in is illegal activity, isn't it?" Rocco slides back in his leather seat with his glass of bourbon and a childish grin on his face.

"Do I look like I'm laughing, Rocco?" Antonio pins him with a questioning glare.

"What's going on, A?" Leo chimes in deflating the tension rising between the two.

After a lingering glare at Rocco, Antonio begins. "One of my caporegimes took a meeting the other night. The guy sent was a basement mule. He was sloppy. That only tells me, whoever sent him just wanted to see where I stood on this transaction that is supposedly taking place. Which also means he already knows who I am and where I stand on this situation. "Now," he huffs, taking a sip of his drink before continuing, "the problem with that, is the simple fact that this distributor knows me and my business ethics and chose a mule to bring word about what is going to happen under my nose. *Or* this mule was just too stupid and let this information slip. The fact that he sent a bottom feeder and not even one of his soldiers tells me two things; either his boss is just as stupid, or the boss wanted to see how I would react to what is supposed to be happening right under my nose and didn't care about the guy he sent to relay the message. Either or, his days are numbered."

"What's the transaction?" Leo inquires. His curiosity is now peeked knowing it must be serious for Antonio to call this meeting.

"The promise of an exuberant amount of powder."

"And? Because I know that isn't what you called this meeting for," Leo pushes for more information.

"A cargo full of humans." Antonio's face morphs, dropping the bomb, inspecting Rocco for any kind of reaction.

"What's this got to do with me?" Rocco sits up, the leather of the seat protesting his movement as he realizes this meeting is about him.

"The girls, from what we understand, are being transferred to your territory. Which means either you let down your guard or you are involved. And Rocco," Antonio holds his hand up, stopping Rocco from speaking, ordering him to stay silent while he continues to speak, "if I find out you are involved, I will have this brought before The Commission. I will make sure a punishment is brought down on you that you will not survive."

Rocco's head jerks back, shocked that Antonio would threaten with the severity of all the bosses. The Commission makes up all five heads from New York, plus Buffalo and Chicago. This situation is a New York problem.

The Commission as far as I know, haven't held a meeting in years. The threat was promised so Rocco understands just how serious Antonio is about the situation.

"I'm not involved." His tone is deep. His words adamant.

I watch Leo, judging his reaction to the information. He looks just as shocked.

"For your sake, I hope not, Rocco," Antonio threatens him.

"Give me the details." He sits forward, setting his glass down on the table in front of him, and stands.

Instead of giving him what he asked for, Antonio questions, "Have you been approached by anyone concerning new business ventures?"

"No."

"Do you know a Mr. Cillian McKittrick?"

"Yes, but I have never been in business with him, nor have I done business with him. Why? He got something to do with this?"

"How do you know him?"

"Club. I'm starting to feel like I'm on the chopping block here, Antonio."

"You are," he answers him with a matter-of-fact timbre. "You know where this organization stands on human trafficking. You get greedy, start seeking new business adventures selling humans, I promise you I'll cut your throat myself, slowly. Which club?"

"Don't threaten me." Rocco takes a stance he won't win. "The Bronx is not involved. If there is movement in my territory, I can promise you it is because it is flying under the radar, and I haven't caught word of it yet."

"You better hope so." Antonio's warning words become a threat when he sets his drink down.

Just as the bottom of Antonio's glass connects with the wood of the table, I stand. Leo follows my lead, knowing this may get ugly.

Antonio steps up to Rocco. I know just what the look in his eyes means.

"You misstep and tell me what to do again, Rocco, I can promise you I will handle the situation myself."

Rocco holds a strong stance, but only for a minute before relaxing a bit. Though powerful in reputation and business, he is no Antonio Heart. And he knows it. He apologizes the only way a mobster knows how, by shifting back to business with less tension in his tone.

"I don't like being accused of something I am not involved in, especially a situation like this. Now, if you would give me the details of what you heard, I would appreciate it. I need to take it back home and start figuring out who is running side hustles in my streets without my consent."

Antonio's on the phone putting out some feelers. I'm standing at the glass window watching the crowd below. Our meeting has been over for an hour. The few glasses of liquid relaxer I swallowed to calm my nerves did nothing to quell the tension in my shoulders from this afternoon. The vision of Isabelle's husband's punishing grip on her delicate wrist enrages me. I have to talk myself down each time I think about it. As the night progresses, I'm more apt to drive to the pub to see if she is working and if she is okay. Who knows what happened after I walked out. The guilt I feel, because I did nothing to help her, is starting to eat me up inside. It was the right thing to do. I know it was, but it doesn't make me feel any better. If it had been anyone else, I would have throttled the guy. The fact that he was that aggressive in public makes me worry for her even more. Most cowards hold off their abuse until they are behind closed doors. I know my father did.

Antonio is still talking on the phone. The calmness I always hold close starts to fray at both ends. The need to see her, lay my eyes on her, maybe touch her in a way that gives her some comfort, weighs heavy on me.

I hear Antonio behind me just as he is ending his call with the boss. He shoulders up next to me, hands tucked in his pockets, waiting in silence. The only thing penetrating the space is the remix of *Body* by Loud Luxury, Brando, and Dzeko blaring. We both look out over the crowd. Only he may be checking over the clientele while I am just occupying my time while watching the movement below. I'm ready to bounce and Antonio knows it.

"Not that I am questioning the punishment Joseph is sporting on his face, but I would like to know why he received the beating. All I know is he said he deserved it. That your work?"

"No." I state my one-word answer and stay staring down at the crowd. A minute passes before I explain. "It was the man who gave him life. I left it up to him."

"The reason?"

"He questioned my authority by looking to Demetri when I gave him a direct order."

"His father was there?"

"No." I look over my shoulder at the kid. Even though he's not a kid, but a young man now at twenty, I still call him a kid. I have the right; he is much younger than me and hasn't been primed to the dirtiness of what the deep underground streets has to offer. At his age, I had already lived a lifetime and shed the skin like a snake to live in an even darker one. I witnessed things I should have closed my eyes at. I have done things grown men would need to see their hundred dollar an hour therapist for. "I told him to go home and tell his father. By the looks of his face, he did."

"By the looks of it, he did just that."

A grin pulls at my lips. I'm proud of the kid. He meets my eyes with

91

unsure ones from across the room. "Joseph! Come here," I command, yelling over the music.

"Yes, sir?"

I grab a hold of his jaw and turn his face to the left then to the right. "You gonna live, kid?"

"Yes, sir."

I can see he wants to jerk his face from my grip, hating my inspection, but he won't out of respect. "You going to question me or my orders again?"

"Never, sir."

"Good. Here's another order for you to heed. Never let anyone put their hands on you, including your father, unless it's some little honey and you want her hands on you. Understood?" I let go of his chin, ending my evaluation.

He smirks at my comment. "Yes, sir."

"Go with Luca to pick up Lilah," Antonio orders him, knowing I'm done. When it's just the two of us, Antonio turns to me and questions, "You think he'll make it?"

"He was ordered to tell his father. He did. Would you have?"

"Hell. No." He gruffly laughs.

"Exactly. He'll be just fine. Kid's got balls. I want him to stay under me. He's a good-looking kid. He's smart. He learns fast. We can use him a lot."

"He's not a kid. What were you doing at his age?"

"Learning how to fucking survive."

"Exactly. You were taught by the best."

"Yes, I was." I nod, agreeing that Mr. Heart was the best teacher in a life most don't understand or survive.

We're quiet for a few minutes. While I reflect on the past, I can feel Antonio has something he wants to say.

As the relaxed atmosphere of business dissipates and the strain of my personal life creeps back into the tension of my shoulders, swallowing the air around me, Antonio verbalizes his discomfort in having one of his capos, and friend, bristling next to him and not knowing the exact reason why.

"A blind and deaf man could feel your hostility. What's wrong with you, brother?"

"Nothing."

"Looks like something to me, man. Don't make me pull the boss card on you, Giovanni."

"All due respect, Mr. Heart, this will be the one time I do disrespect you. It's not about business. This conversation is not up for discussion. End of."

"It's like that?"

"It is."

"Well then, I will take that disrespect as a friend, this way I don't have to end you."

"You would never."

"No, I wouldn't. I will tell you this though, this conversation is not over. Something is bothering you. Which means you are not on point. When you are not on point your life is in jeopardy along with mine and everyone else. Not today, maybe not tomorrow, but we will have this conversation over some heavily poured drinks."

"I got work to do." I turn to walk out.

"G? It was you that made me see things more clearly about Lilah."

"Different story. Yours is a children's book compared to mine."

He waits a beat, knowing he isn't going to get far with me, but frustrated that I am walking away from him. "You got something pressing to take care of?"

"I think I do."

"You need me?" He walks to me.

"No. When I do, it will be to bury a body."

"Just let me know when. I already know where." He slaps my shoulder twice before turning away. "Go. Take care of business while I take care of my wife," he yells from over his shoulder as he heads towards his office.

While walking out I think, *maybe one day I can say that.*

Isabelle
CHAPTER FOURTEEN

With a pint glass in my hand, I dip it into the ice, filling it to the brim with the freezing crystals. Pat yells at us girls all the time for putting the glass in the ice and not using the scooper. If the glass breaks, we have to empty the whole ice bin. Tonight, I just don't have it in me to take that extra step. Tonight, I kind of hope it does break so I can hide in the back away from the crowd while I clean out the bin.

I grab one of the cubes and rub it around the red marks left on my wrist from this afternoon. This particular shift feels like it's dragging on, but I'd rather be here then at home. Going home to the unknown is making me drag my feet.

Tommy left the diner a few minutes after Giovanni walked out. His volatile parting words were a promise to come for what he thinks was me disrespecting him. I'm grateful that Giovanni had enough willpower to leave without hitting Tommy. I saw the look in Giovanni's eyes, he wanted to retaliate on my behalf. What a refreshing change it was, to see a man who could control himself.

I'm just glad Tommy is working the night shift tonight. The only bad part, I will have to face is his parents when I pick up Abigail. They watch her on the nights Tommy works. I'd rather not have them watch her, but at this point I have no choice. At least during the day, she is in daycare playing with other children. Tommy's mother is nice, but her baby boy can do no wrong. His father, that man is another story. He is superficial. I have never liked him. Not from the very first time Tommy brought me home to meet his parents. His father gives me the creeps. When Tommy brought me into his father's home office to introduce me to him, he gave me a slow, evaluating once over. It brought goosebumps to my skin. Tommy blew it off when I said something to him later on that night. He thought it was funny his dad had the hots for me. I didn't.

I murmur the lyrics to *Dance With The Devil* by Breaking Benjamin while zoning out. With my back up against the ice machine, I continue rolling the cold square around my wrist. My eyes become blurry while staring at a dirty spot on the tile floor at my feet. Thoughts of today, of yesterday, of last year, of my lifetime flood the blurry scene before me. I'm somewhat relieved that I will have a few hours of peaceful rest before Tommy gets home from his shift, but I know that will end the moment he walks through the door.

I'm in such a deep thought of my future and what it will be like, what I want it to be, that when I feel pressure on my shoulder it startles me so bad, I jump and gasp. The syllables of my name flow through the air, but it sounds like the person is saying it through a megaphone that is a good distance away. My hand involuntarily goes to my chest. It's tight, begging for air. I realize I'm breathing heavy, too heavy if I want to stay standing vertical, and my sight is blurry from the watery sheet of glass covering my pupils. The touch on my shoulder is not a hard touch, but more of a cautious, firm one, alerting me of their presence. It still makes me jump though, and I am instantly afraid at being unaware of anyone being back here with me. I shoot to my feet from my leaning spot, standing straight, waiting for whatever is to come. While I catch my bearings, I take a step back from the large figure standing a foot away from me. When my focus zooms in on the man standing before me, all I can see is the expensive cloth covering his barreled chest. The first two buttons are open on his dark grey dress shirt. The small scattering of manicured dark hair peeks out, but what really gets my body to relax is the lines of his tattoo poking out from each side of his shirt. I know that tattoo. I have pressed my lips against the dark ink saturating the skin. I have sat in his lap, on his strong thighs, with my forehead laying against the colored skin in unnerving but satisfied exhaustion. Some level of comfort hits me with cruelty. I should not feel safe in his arms, but I do. The man I should feel safe with, I don't. It's indisputable, the feelings that surge through me. I'm grateful for what he did today. The realization that he did it for me, hits me square in the gut. My shoulders drop and all I can do is fall into his body and wrap my arms around his waist. It isn't good enough to just have my arms around him over his suit jacket, no, my body needs to be closer to his. I slide my hands under his jacket. I feel the heat from his skin through the cloth of his expensive dress shirt. I spread my fingers and place my palms just beneath his shoulder blades, feeling his back muscles flex. I need him, but I know I can't have him.

He stiffens at the impact of my body hitting his, but then he immediately blankets me with his muscular arms. His hand comes to the back of my head, cradling me, holding me to his chest. The scent of cinnamon and his masculine cologne fill the space.

The moment is silent except for the music playing. I listen to the words. Everything is wrong, but everything at the moment, feels right. My finger's dig into his dress shirt. He feels like my lifeline. My *only* line to a life. Is that wrong? I ask myself. And then I quickly think, I do not care if it is wrong. What is wrong is living the way I have the past five years. What is wrong is being afraid of what is to come every single day of my life. That's wrong. This doesn't feel wrong.

"It's going to be okay, little lion." He rubs his heavy, capable hand up and down my back with gentle caresses.

Will it? Will I ever see my way out of this? Then I realize that no, no I probably never will. Tommy will hunt me down. Even if I do get away from him, the damage he has done to my self-esteem will always haunt me by creeping back up. How long will it take for me to feel safe? How long will it take me to trust again? How long will it be before my destroyed confidence is resurrected to the point I can actually live, not just get by? I feel tarnished, stained by the cruelty of another. A once shining beauty queen now dull from events life has pushed in my path. How do I run off this path and walk down another?

I think all these thoughts, but here I stand in the arms of a man I barely know, and I feel safer than I ever have. Then before I know what is happening, my body stiffens. The shame and embarrassment, it hits me like a ton. I release his strangled dress shirt from my death grip, and I move to take a step back, but I am restrained, held in the same safe place. I don't feel threatened, all I feel is embarrassment. My head drops further down his chest. With his thumb and forefinger, he lifts my chin until my eyes come in direct contact with his.

"Don't do that. You have nothing to be ashamed of."

I'm taken back at how he could possibly know what I am feeling. Are we that in tune with each other? How can that possibly be? We spent a limited amount of time together. Yes, that time was more than I had anticipated. I naively thought it would be a wham-bam thing between us that night, but it wasn't. It started out that way, but it didn't proceed or even end that way. From the very first moment he leaned down and kissed me, we were sexually frantic. I'll say it was more me than him, but my nerves were all over the place. We didn't even make it to a bed. Hell, I thought he was going to take me against the concrete wall in the alley behind the bar, but that wasn't good enough for him. I saw it on his face when he stared down at my display of uncontrollable panting. I thought he was going to stop what was happening between us, but he didn't. After a surveying look around the alley, he swept me off the hard surface my back was pushed against, and he carried me to his SUV. He never even attempted to go to the front seat. I straddled his lap once he adjusted me to what he wanted and then I desperately ground myself against his erection in the backseat. I rode him at free will under his guiding hands firmly gripping my hips. His shirt was unbuttoned, the two halves laying at his sides. When I grasped at my top to take it off, he held it in place. In his words, the bulk of my shirt sitting just above my breasts and flowing down my sides were the picture frame capturing beauty. My heart melted at his sweet words. Words I had never experienced before. When his fingers flicked the button of my jeans, he watched me with a penetrating gaze. I slid my thumbs into the tough material at my hips and wiggled right out of them. When he grabbed for the condom in his wallet, I took it from him and rolled it down his never-ending length with a shaking hand. He was wide and thick, and I gasped while admiring his healthy virility. His slacks sat at mid-thigh, brushing against my bottom. I remember every single detail and the feelings that assaulted me that night. When the tip of his head breached my opening, I shamelessly moaned while my nails dug into his shoulders.

I knew, right there, in the backseat of his black SUV that I would have the best sexual encounter I had ever had.

It took me a minute to adjust to him. I rode him until my thighs burned. At one point I almost cried because I was riding him so long, I thought maybe I couldn't get him off, that I wasn't doing it for him. But that wasn't it. He was waiting for me. He was watching me enjoy myself. Taking what I wanted and needed from him. When I looked up at him with worry, he grinned the most sexual grin and winked at me. It was like he knew a secret I wasn't privy to. He engulfed my mouth with his while he grabbed a hold of my hips at the same time. He adjusted his own and bounced me three times. It was the perfect onslaught of sensation. We both exploded at the same time. The tension between both our sexual muscles too strong. I cried out in a torturous wail. He dropped his head back and uncharacteristically moaned a husky growl. I could tell it wasn't a normal sexual reaction for him because when he lifted his head back up and looked at me, I saw shock on his handsome face. The back of his hand slid from my temple to my chin. The pad of his thumb rubbed at my swollen lips. Without warning, I was lifted off him, the condom removed and thrown to the side, the half seat beside us was released and laid flat and I was swiftly maneuvered to my back and impaled, bare. I didn't care. Consequences be damned. I wanted him. I wanted to feel him. To soak him in. Bathe in him. I wanted to feel every bit of him. And I did. It was reckless and dangerous, but I felt so alive. For two hours in the back of his SUV. We fucked. We fucked hard. But in his eyes, there was always a glint of softness, for me. And even though days later, when all was said and done, and I felt the guilt creeping in for my actions, I still felt him, the imprint he left in me, on me. I held on to that, tightly.

The spicy scent of cinnamon and Giovanni's cologne pull me out of the memory.

"Thank you for... for today. For not saying anything to him. For not taking matters into your own hands," I genuinely tell him.

If my head wasn't laying against his broad chest, I would have thought he didn't hear me. The rumble that vibrated my ear told me he did.

"You're coming home with me, Isabelle."

What?

"You go home tonight, you know exactly what is going to happen to you."

I pull away, my eyes wildly observing him. He's serious. Dead serious. I take a step back.

"I can't."

"You can."

"I can't!" I immediately counter. Is he crazy? I can't just go home and pack up and go stay with him.

"You can and you will."

"No, I won't."

He tilts his head to the side, watching me.

He stares at me for so long, I start to get antsy. I feel like I have to answer him. Like I have no choice.

"I can't! I really can't. I have Abigail. I have to think about my daughter. I can't just pick her up and move her!"

His chin lifts and he calmly points out, "So it's better for her to be there, in that house, than with a stranger who will only show her kindness?"

"Yes! No!" I grip my hair at the anxiety surging through me. "No! No, it's not!"

"When he beats you, when he lays his hands on you, it also touches her. Trust me, she will always remember the screams from her mother being knocked around."

"Fuck you!" I rage against him.

He stays silent at my outburst.

"Fuck you!" I say again, so frustrated at myself because I know he is right.

"Come home with me."

His calm voice makes me want to run to him. Never leave him. Hold on to him for dear life. Can I do this? Should I do this? Would I be making yet another mistake?

I feel my body start to shake. It's too much. Way too much. The pressure of what is right and what is wrong is unbearable. My brain knows what is right and what is wrong, but the dysfunctional normal is all I know. Spots start to form in my vision. I shake out my hands, trying to release the tingles surging through the tips that the tension is causing. I turn my back on him and start to pace. I can't do this. I need to do this on my own. I don't want his help. I may need his help, but I don't want it. I need to do this for Abby and me.

I turn back to face him. There is an undercurrent of anger to him, but the softness he has always shown me sits in the belly of his pupils as he watches me.

"I can't." I shake my head. "I'm sorry. I just can't."

Resignation makes his feet move towards me. He grabs a hold of my face and stares at me so long it's like he is committing every curve, every line, every mark to his memory. I almost feel like this is a goodbye of some sorts. A goodbye to a beginning that never really started. A lump forms in my throat. My hands go to his hips. I sink my thumbs beneath his belt while my fingers wrap around to his back. Kiss me. I want him to kiss me. I want to feel the closeness we shared that night, not the crater I feel fracturing between us in this moment.

My head is tilted back. He is so much taller than me. His thumbs stop the tears from running their course as he takes every bit of me in. His gaze drops to my lips. *Kiss me*, I silently beg, closing my eyes when he drops his face closer to mine. I breathlessly wait until I feel just the slightest brush of his lips over mine. It's a whisper of skin on skin. The warmth of his breath penetrating the walls inside my mouth, replacing my own. The slightest skim of a touch across my lips, it's not a tease but a tortuous want of movement that will never become something more. He lays his forehead against mine for just a moment. The noise of the bar, the music, the people talking about their day, it all fades. It's all white noise until it comes back with screeching volume when he pulls away without pressing his lips against mine. I feel the moment he resigns. His head lifts from mine. The strength of his hands cradling my face leaving cold air in their place. I'm afraid to open my eyes. My bottom lip trembles. I feel like I've just lost something I never rightfully had.

"Open your eyes, little lion."

With a slight flutter to my lifted lashes, I do as he commands and look up into his eyes. He has a small smile on his face.

"If you need me, you have my number. Don't hesitate, Is. I will come for you." He drops his lips to my forehead, kisses me and then turns and walks out, taking my heart with him.

With Abigail all packed up, we stand by the front door saying our thank you's and goodbyes. Tommy's mother is stealing kisses from Abby. She giggles and scrunches up her body with childish laughter, wiggling every which way. It's music to a mother's ears and it makes me smile even though my body is still tense from earlier with Giovanni. She suddenly stops when Tommy's father comes out of his office. She stiffens and saddles up next to my leg, wrapping her little arms around me.

"Say goodbye to grandma, baby girl." I purposely leave Tommy's father out.

He leans down and takes her little hand from my leg. I take a step back. One big enough that Abby's hand is pulled from his. He glances up at me. The anger radiating in his squinted glare gives me chills.

"Miss Abigail! Miss Abigail!" The housemaid comes running from the back of the house. "You forgot your little lion."

My heart gives a thump at her words.

Tommy's father intercepts the hand off and holds it ransom in front of him.

"Well, isn't this cute," he mocks. "Who gave you this?"

"Momma," Abigail shyly tells him, still glued to my leg.

"Do you know what the lion symbolizes?"

"You know she wouldn't know that." I hold out my hand, waiting from him to hand over the stuffed animal Giovanni bought.

"Hmm." He stares at the lion, falsely pondering when I know he already knows what he is going to say. "He's proud. The leader of his pack. He's strong. He's loyal. I wonder if your mommy knew that when she bought it for you?"

"She knows exactly what loyalty is. She also knows what strength is," I deadpan. "But does her grandfather?"

His sneer is disturbing. "Sometimes I wonder if she does." He holds out the lion to Abigail, but instead of just handing it to her, he holds it just out of her reach. Just like his son, he needs the control.

I rip it from his grip and give it to Abby. I give his mother a small smile. Then turn to walk out.

"Oh, and Isabelle…" His revolting voice echoes off the decorative walls in their oversized foyer. His condescending tone makes me what to throttle him. "Do dress appropriately for the fundraiser tomorrow night." I turn and grab the doorknob, ready to bolt from their mansion before I cause a war. The only one that will suffer, will be me. "Also," his elevated higher hand speech makes me turn back once again, "if I were you, I would be on my best behavior as well. I wouldn't want my son to have to put you in check in front of the brotherhood now, would we?"

His threat is received, although I didn't physically show it. I opened the door and leave without voicing my opinion. His son is too much of a coward to do what he does in public. But then again, today happened and that was in public.

The air I suck in once I close the door behind me is refreshing compared to the toxic air inside those walls. My only reprieve is the fact that Tommy's promise of punishment tonight will be put on hold. He won't want anyone to see his handy work on my body tomorrow at the event.

"Momma, I don't like Daddy's daddy. He's a meanie."

I glance down at my daughter. Her little face way too serious for a three-year-old. "You know what, baby girl?" I crouch in front of her. She shakes her head no, her little red ringlets bouncing. "That is the last time you have to go spend time there."

"Can Ms. Melodie come to our house and bake her cookies?"

How do you tell your child that the housemaid is under house arrest by her employers? You don't. You can't. So, I give her a little white lie.

"Of course." I tug on her arm when I stand. Then I feel guilty. "Or we can make up our own special cookies." I widen my eyes, making it seem exciting. "How 'bout that?" I raise my brows and plaster a huge smile on my face making it seem like it something special.

"Yay, Momma."

Isabelle
CHAPTER FIFTEEN

Tommy pushes his chair back and stands. Tom Walker's *Not Giving In* starts to play. I ignore his actions by staring off to the opposite side of the room. I'd rather be anywhere else but here right now, especially with Tommy. The room is beautiful. Elegant, dimly lit, crystal chandeliers sparkle throughout the space. Small, white votive candles flicker on each table. The silver is perfectly placed and polished to the highest shine sitting next to the decorative charger that awaits gourmet food. The fragrant blue flower arrangement sitting in the center of the table give off a fresh, lavish scent. The whole room feels as romantic as it can be with the cause at hand and the three hundred guests mulling around.

Without a parting word, Tommy walks across the room to his father who is schmoozing the governor and the police chief. They greet him with familiarity. I watch their interaction with interest. Tommy is relaxed and his father is disgustingly using his charm. I turn from the nauseating scene to the woman next to me when she places her hand on mine and expresses how lucky I am to have such an attractive, successful husband. If she only knew. I pull my hand out from under hers and reach for my glass of wine. I clear my throat and effectively end the very short one-sided conversation when I turn my head, ignoring her ignorant comment. She turns her attention to the couple on the other side of her, and I thank the Gods for the silence.

If I could be anywhere else but here. Somewhere on a deserted tropical beach would be the dream.

I scan the room and once again find myself watching the interaction between Tommy and the affluent men he is speaking with. Something seems off to me, but then again, I ignore it since I know Tommy has an alter ego. With a glance in one direction, I see high society women chatting in one corner about their manicures, pedicures, and the jewels they wear around their necks. Then a quick glance in the other direction, I see a group of men having what looks like a serious conversation. All I really see is powerful men with puppets for wives.

I can't help but think to myself how out of place I am here. With an edge of uncomfortableness, I readjust in my seat, brush off the invisible crumbs and cradle my hands on my lap like the good girl I'm expected to be. The soft strands of *Poison & Wine* by The Civil Wars plays. I watch as couples dance to the slow song. I'm drawn to one couple in particular. With genuine gazes of love between the two, he moves her around the dance floor flawlessly. He holds her so close their bodies look as one. The sight of them causes a sudden wave of emotion in me. *One day,* I think to myself. *One day.* I just have to get through today.

I glance back over to the group of men who were having an intense conversation just a moment ago. With the power of a lightning bolt, I jerk back in my seat. My heart drops to my stomach and my insides turn to jello. Laser sharp eyes are drilling me from across the room. Not just any eyes, but *his* eyes. I nervously swallow and look for Tommy. When I look back to Giovanni, I realize his face is stone. He looks lethal. The heavy beat from *Seven Devils* by Florence + The Machine add to the ominous feeling exuding from him. I can't help but hold his stare with mine. I'm glued to him, mesmerized by him, entrapped by his being. Is he mad because of last night? How could he be? I may have declined his offer but he's the one that walked away from me without a word. When he left the way he did, it felt like an ending. But then again, he also told me he would come for me if I needed him. I should tell him that every night when I close my eyes, I see him. But that wouldn't be fair. To me or him.

I'm confused as to why he is staring at me with so much disdain. Why is he here? With these people? Is he part of their society? He must be. I can't help but think he could never be, but then again no one would think my husband, of all people, would treat his wife the way he does either.

I squirm under his scrutiny. I nervously pull my eyes off him and grab for my glass of wine. With three large unladylike gulps, I swallow the alcohol and my nerves as I glance back in his direction. My heart instantly thuds in my chest.

He's gone.

Vanished.

Just disappeared.

How did he walk away so fast without me seeing him?

I scan the oversized room.

Nothing.

I turn left.

Nothing.

Then right.

Nothing.

I connect eyes with Tommy who is watching me, questioning me with his glare. I stupidly smile at him. I never smile at him. He squints and twists his head in suspicion at my uncharacteristic gesture. I panic, so I give him a dirty look, but there is too much emphasis behind it. I need to calm down. I need to get control of myself. I try not to glance to the side of the room where Giovanni was just moments ago, but I'm having a hard time refraining. I look back in Tommy's direction to see if he is still watching me. I must have not kept his curiosity long because he is back to speaking with the men he is standing with.

But Giovanni, when I scan the room again, is nowhere to be seen.

I release a nervous but relieved breath. He must have left, not wanting to see me, even be in the same room as me. He must have decided to leave. The sting of what feels like rejection hurts. It's better if he did leave. I don't think I could handle having Tommy and Giovanni in the same room together. The pressure would be too much. But just thinking about him no longer wanting to be here, in the same room as me, it hits me hard with an overwhelming sadness. I don't want him to leave even though I know it's for the best.

I push my chair back, stand, and after grabbing my clutch, I make my way out of the ballroom and head down the hallway to the ladies' room just around the corner. The hallway is filled with guests, most smiling and waving at me as I walk by. I know it is only to be courteous, but I can't stand fake people. After a few waves and some forced smiles, I push the door open and walk inside. I try to pull myself together. There is one other woman reapplying her lipstick in the bathroom. It's a bright shade of pink. Not a color I would have ever picked but I guess it suits her with the pink floor length gown she is wearing. She acknowledges me, but only for a moment. I think I startled her when I walked in because she looked shocked to see me. I give her a quick nod before heading into a stall. When I come out, the woman is gone and I'm grateful to be alone. I take the minute I need, collect myself as best I can and make my way out of the bathroom.

Two steps.

Two steps are all I make before my wrist is grabbed from behind. A hand is placed over my mouth. The last thing I see is the back of a guy standing at the corner before I'm whirled around and yanked into a solid chest. Large, strong hands imprison my face just as lips consume my mouth. Puffs of hot air steam roll through his nostrils hitting my upper lip. I sag into his embrace, lavishing on the stroke of his cinnamon tasting tongue, forgetting all time. He consumes me and leaves me breathless when I hear a man's voice from a few feet away.

"Got company."

Giovanni pulls back. My eyes spin in a dazed shock looking up at him. His hands grip my face with more strength. His thumbs tuck under my jaw and he holds me in place. His deep penetrating gaze makes me freeze in my spot.

"My patience has ended, little lion," he gruffly states, gazing deeply with so much heat into my eyes he's burning the barrier of my protected soul. "I'm done." He slams his mouth against mine then swiftly walks away, leaving me standing there in a state of pure utter shock.

I turn, wanting to call out to him, but the spin was too quick, and I'm instantly hit with dizziness.

A woman rounds the corner just as the man standing there lifts his phone to his ear.

The woman passes him and stops in her tracks when she sees me. My physical state of shock must be glowing like a neon sign because she asks with concern, "Are you okay?"

"Ahh, yeah, yeah," I answer after a few seconds, noticing the man behind her turn his head to listen in on our conversation. That is when I notice it's the same guy with Giovanni from the day before. Demetri listens in on our conversation. "Yes, I'm okay. Just a sudden wave of dizziness." I place my hand against the wall to steady myself.

"Could you be with child? You are flushed, and you have a glow about you."

"Lord, no," I abruptly snap, then realize how harsh it was. "I'm sorry. I have a toddler at home." I make up a shitty excuse.

"Well, that will do it to you." She pats my arm, but her pat is almost patronizing, and it makes me uncomfortable. "Mom and Dad's night out is always a good thing when you have the stresses of a beautiful toddler at home. You and Tommy should take more time to be together."

Her comment takes me back. "I'm sorry, have we met? Do we know each other?" I ask, feeling like this lady knows too much about me when I have never laid eyes on her before.

"Congratulations on your husband's promotion. It's well deserved." She turns and walks into the bathroom leaving me standing there baffled.

My husband's promotion? Tommy got a promotion?

As much as I should be thinking about questioning Tommy, I'm not. I'm enthralled with the memories of the kiss Giovanni just laid on me.

What was that?

Why?

I make my way back to the ballroom. After taking my seat, I realize my wine glass is empty. I probably shouldn't have any more since I've already had three, but I decide against the sensible part of my brain and agree with the nonsensible part telling me I need it to get through this night.

"As much as I don't want to, appearances are necessary." Tommy holds his hand out in front of me. The charming smile he holds is so well rehearsed. I shake my head, only slightly, telling him I don't want to do whatever it is he feels we need to do. He leans down getting so close to my ear I can feel the skin on his venomous lips. "Get up." I narrow my eyes at him. "Before I make you get up. I'm sure you wouldn't want the entire room to see how I reprimand my insubordinate wife, would you?" he taunts, still smiling with a smile that anyone would see as a man who loves his wife.

I slowly stand, lifting my chin. "I'm not a doll, Tommy. Nor am I worried that you would let all your fellow coworkers see what kind of person you really are." I specifically used the word person instead of man because a real man would never do the things he does.

"Ahh, so true, wife. But do you really want to find out?" He turns and walks to the edge of the dance floor and waits.

I should let him stand there by himself and make him wait for me. I should flip the tables on him and let him know I have some control, but then I think better of it. It would only be a false sense of control and short lived at that. Two hours from now, I would pay for it.

I walk through the couples that are dressed to the nines with frustrated steps. Most women are in glamourous floor-length gowns. I would think by the way some are dressed that we were at a Cotillion awaiting the debutantes to be presented and not a fundraiser for human trafficking. The high dollar floating around are all due to my father-in-law's reach. It's the only thing I can say I respect about him. It is him who supports my husband's organization and therefore gives him so much more control. Without their support, my father-in-law would be nothing and wouldn't hold the clout he does.

A wide salacious smile pulls at Tommy's lips. I cringe inside. When his hand slides around my waist, my entire body goes stiff. He pulls me into his chest and rest his head against the side of mine. It may look sweet to everyone in the room, but I know better.

"Loosen the fuck up," he snarls next to my ear.

"How am I supposed to do that while I'm being held in the arms of a man I detest?" My outburst shocks even me.

He pulls back, looks at me through slitted eyes. "You look like a whore in that dress."

Now, I jerk back. "What?" I try to pull from his arms, needing to get away from his vile mouth. With a proud grin he pulls me back into his body, knowing he did exactly what he wanted to do; make me feel uncomfortable. "Maybe you should have thought about that," I snap with my own venom. "You bought me this dress and forced me to wear it tonight."

"Yeah, well, you also got fat. It no longer fits properly." He kisses the side of my head.

I jerk in his hold and push my palms against his chest. I need to get away from him, but his arms instantly become my jail. Even though I know his words are just words to hurt me and make himself feel like he has more power, I now feel uncomfortable, like everyone in the room is looking at me, criticizing me. All I am to him is an object. If I don't fit the mold, I'm no good.

"Let me go, Tommy." I clench my jaw. Three words that hold so much meaning behind them.

"Never." His eyes deadlock with mine, while his fingers grip my waist tighter. "I've told you before, there is only one way you're leaving me."

The tension building between us is unbearable. The more I challenge Tommy by staring him down, the more I will pay for it later when we get home. If I bruise his ego here in front of his colleagues, it will only end up being worse for me.

I look away, only to be zapped by a lightning bolt when I find myself deadlocked with another man's eyes.

I thought he left.

Giovanni's eyes are piercing me, slicing straight through the room of dancing bodies, intensely focused directly on me. His arms are crossed over his barreled chest and his stance is wide. The man next to him, I recognize as Antonio Heart. There was a big write-up with his picture in the entertainment section of the newspaper about his club Temptations. I knew who he was the night I ran through his club looking for Giovanni. Antonio leans over and says something to Giovanni, but Giovanni's glare doesn't move from Tommy and me. The look on his face is frightening. If I saw him in a dark alley late at night with that look on his face, I would recite the Lord's Prayer and cross my heart accepting my fate. It's this moment it hits me. Really hits me. I realize that Giovanni has something to do with Antonio Heart, the underboss in one of the most feared mafia families in New York. I knew where to find Giovanni that night I went searching for him to give back the lion. Why did I never fully comprehend who Giovanni is? Instantly, I become a ball of nervous energy.

I close my eyes and try to inhale a little more than the shallow breaths I've been able to capture just moments before. When I open my eye's again, green inflamed orbs are still laser focused on me. My body sags in Tommy's arms. Not because I want to stay here, even though Tommy takes the gesture as if I have given in to his demands. I haven't, but the look on Giovanni's face is, although scary, pulling me to him. Those thick arms he has wrapped around his chest, I know what those arms feel like when they were wrapped around me. They are way safer than the arms restraining me at the moment and unknowingly holding me back from running to him.

Antonio leans in saying something to Giovanni, but once again he ignores him. Then Antonio follows his line of sight. I can feel him staring at me, but my gaze never leaves Giovanni.

"What the fuck?" he mouths, dropping his arms to his side. Antonio's hand goes to his forearm in warning.

I shake my head, close my eyes, and release a breath. I feel like I'm in a pressure cooker waiting for the explosion to blow any second. I could not have chosen two men any more different from each other.

It's black and white.

Good verses bad.

Innocent and guilty.

Giovanni, I'm assuming is angry I'm dancing with Tommy.

What am I supposed to do?

"That's a good wife." Tommy's bitter voice sounds next to my ear as he rocks me over the parquet floor. *Care for You* by Mario plays, and what makes me sad is it's such a sweet song, but the man I want holding me, moving me across the floor is standing on the edge of the dance floor throwing me daggers. My insides twist from nervousness. I want to run to him, but I know I can't. I turn away, afraid to look back in Giovanni's direction. He doesn't belong in this room with these people. His stature alone makes him stand out. Besides that, I am in the middle of the dance floor surrounded by all of Tommy's coworkers. If one of them sees the two of us staring at each other the way we are, there will be a situation I know will become volatile by the look on Giovanni's face.

I can't have that weight on my shoulders.

The song comes to an end and the acoustic version of *How Did You Love* by Shinedown starts to play. I pull from Tommy's arms with the excuse that I need to use the restroom, but the fact of the matter is, I need air, air away from the same one he is breathing and the burning eyes of another.

I readjust my knee length dress and rush to our table to grab my clutch. Just as I'm turning to leave, I hear, "Dance with me?"

Oh. My. God.

I turn back. "I'm sorry," I start to say, but notice Tommy coming up behind him. "Married," I finish the sentence. "I'm married but thank you for the offer."

"Fucking married." Tommy bursts from behind Giovanni.

I take a step to the side so Tommy can't see my face. "Please don't do this," I mouth.

"My apologies." He turns facing Tommy. "I didn't realize she was married. You're a lucky man. You have a beautiful wife."

"You're fucking right I do," Tommy barks with hostility.

Giovanni smirks. "Your jealousy is unneeded. You act like I fucked your

111

wife. I just asked her for a dance."

I gasp. Throttled by his words.

My insides start to shake.

My knees become weak.

My stomach flips.

I need to end this.

How do I end this?

Both men are in an intense stare-off when Tommy disgustingly says, "She fucks like a champion too."

Giovanni's jaw clenches. The muscles dance beneath his skin. "Ahh, you see, that is where we are different." He looks over at me with a wicked grin. "I wouldn't just fuck a woman like you. You're too special. I would take my time, ravishing that beautiful body of yours over and over and over again." He turns back to Tommy. "That's the difference between a man and a boy." He lets that marinate for a second before saying, "Congratulations on your promotion, Lieutenant. Apparently, your performance at work is stellar compared to your inadequacies in the bedroom in order for you to be able to move up the chain of command so fast." Then he turns and walks away without a glance back at the destruction he left behind.

I'm not sure what to do. I'm stuck in my position, unable to move. I have to take the attention off of the way Giovanni referred to making love to me. Somehow, I have to make it look like I'm disgusted at his words when inside I'm burning with the memory of his touch and how he really did make love to me over and over again that night. "Who the hell was that?" I spit with false disgust. "That was so inappropriate. Not to mention rude."

"You don't remember your boyfriend from yesterday at the diner?"

"Huh?" I act stupid, as if I didn't give yesterday another thought.

"Don't fucking worry about who it was," he snaps in return while shooting daggers in Giovanni's back as he walks across the room.

"Whatever, Tommy. I'm going to the restroom."

"You should. Fix yourself while you are there. You look like a mess."

I tilt my head back and look at the ceiling in frustration. After taking a breath, I lower my head to give Tommy a piece of my mind, but he has already turned his back on me and is halfway across the dance floor heading to the bar.

I shift and turn to walk away myself when a woman says, "Honey, if that man is your husband, I feel sorry for you. He's a real jerk."

"Don't I know it," I immediately spit the truth before stomping my high heeled feet against the intricate royal blue and gold carpet. I pass the ladies' room I used before and practically run to the ladies' room farther down the hallway and around the corner.

The back doors to the alley are just ahead. I want to run. Take off my heels, hit the pavement in bare feet and run until my feet bleed. The rain peltering against the glass is scary. I didn't realize the rain from earlier had turned into a full-blown storm. Deep thunder rolls through the night sky, stopping me in my tracks when I feel the rumble inside the building. My eyes are glued to the back door. The lights flicker and the hall goes dark. In that moment, right before they come back on, I know who I'm going to see when the hall illuminates once again. Giovanni. Lightening cracks, lighting the space behind him like he's a God. Our eyes lock through the flicker of intense light. I throw my hand over my mouth letting out a sob. I can't bear the weight of his fierce, angry, questioning stare.

I turn and rush through the bathroom door. Just as it's closing, I hear my name thunder down the corridor. Just before the door latches, I hear a male's voice calling after him. The tone of it is clear. It's a warning. I don't make it far inside before the door crashes open with a deafening bang as it slams against the tiled wall.

"Giovanni, you can't be in here!" I anxiously gasp out the words.

"A fucking cop, Isabelle?! A cop?! No, excuse me, a fucking Lieutenant!"

"I didn't know." I shake my head and wrap my arms around my middle.

"You didn't know your husband was a cop? I fucking thought he looked familiar."

"I didn't know he got the promotion. I never know anything."

"Fuck, Is."

"I'm sorry."

"For what?" His head twists. "What are you sorry for?"

"I don't know!" I burst with so much energy my stomach twists with nausea. "I don't know anything anymore! For hurting you! For being a terrible person!" I throw my hands in the air on a cry and turn my back on him.

"Do you know who his father is?"

"What?" I turn back and face him head on. "Of course, I do, Giovanni! He's my father-in-law!" I step towards him with exasperation. "Do you now understand why I can't just walk away? They have so much power!"

"You can!" he bellows. "You can!" He pounds his chest. "I will protect you! Fuck him! And fuck his father, the Senator! I will protect you."

"You can't!" I yell back. "You can't protect me from him! From them!" I throw my hand in the air, pointing to the door like they are standing on the other side. "Not even now knowing who you work for. You can't protect me."

He stands to his full height and zeros in on me. "Little lion, do not insult me."

"Insult you? I'm not insulting you. You are a good man. He is a bad man. They both are. I don't want you going to jail. I don't want every cop on the force to come down on you. I would never forgive myself for that." Then I think out loud and question, "Are you in the mafia?"

He steps to me, ignoring everything I just said. "Come with me now. We'll go get Abigail and you will never have to see him again. You don't need anything from that house. Leave it all behind, Is. I will buy you everything you need. Whatever you need."

I throw my hands in my hair and grab at the roots. Wishing I could rip every strand from its follicle so I can feel any other pain then the one that is in my chest. "I can't! Don't you see? If I do that, go with you, he will surely get custody of her. He holds her over my head. I can't lose her. I won't lose her!" I start to become hysterical.

He steps to me. "Shh, little lion, shh." He places his hand on the back of my head and pulls me into his chest. "Is, I promise you, you won't lose her. You just have to trust me." He pulls back and runs the knuckle of his middle finger from my forehead over my temple to my cheek. "Come with me, Isabelle. Trust me when I tell you I can fix this." He leans in and kisses me softly, holding my face with both his hands. When he pulls back his eyes flicker over mine. "I am not a good man, Isabelle. You may think I am, but I'm not. What I can promise you, is that I will be good to you." He lets that rest a second before saying, "Come with me."

It takes me a moment because all I want to do is fall inside him and let him surround me. He's like a bear tucking their baby in the hollow of their center to keep them warm and safe, yet he is still so powerful. I push against his chest. The push is weak, but the movement is there. "I'm sorry. I can't," I whisper with sadness and disappointment in myself for making such a mess of the situation.

"Is," he growls, stepping back from me and dropping his head. He swipes the pad of his thumb over the corner of his lip. "Stop being scared, little lion. I will fix this for you. You have to trust me."

"I'm sorry." I start to cry heavy streams of tears. "I'm so sorry, bear." I look him dead in the eyes. "Just go." I push at his broad chest, trying to get some space between us. This feeling wreaking havoc inside the cavity of my chest is unbearable. "Go!" I scream in pain. "Go!" I scream once again with so much agony the sound of my voice pierces the space between us like a knife.

He doesn't move. His thumbs rub away the rushing river coursing down my cheeks. He leans in, rest his forehead against mine and gently presses his lips to mine. He releases a breath and kisses me once more. It's such a soft kiss, a reverent touch, one that you cherish when those moments are no longer available. It's the memory that you bank for those times when you don't have that special someone's physical touch anymore. For the second night in a row, I feel like he is saying goodbye. It feels like the last kiss, the one you know you will never come back from. The one you remember when you are old and grey and filled with regrets, knowing if you had to do it all over again you would have done it differently. He pulls back, studies my heartbroken face, then leans in slowly and kisses the tip of my nose. He holds the connection a moment before he turns and rushes out of the bathroom.

"You good?" I hear an extremely deep voice ask from outside the heavy door before it closes.

I'm left with my tears in the hollow silence of a sterile, public restroom.

The man who holds me in his arms like a protective grizzly bear is gone.

I release an agonized scream, folding myself in half at the failure I feel I have become, in the situation I have caused, in not being able to make the move to free myself from this spiral staircase down. To the feeling of weakness that has grown inside me for years.

I pace from one side of the bathroom to the other, turn and repeat the pattern once more before stopping in my tracks when I hear a song playing. *I'll Follow You* by Shinedown croons from above. I fumble over my own feet just before the door Giovanni just walked out of. I make a rash decision, but I know it's the right one. No matter how hard the future will be, it has to be better than my past.

I take that song as a sign. I swing the door open, glance both ways and rush down the hallway towards the back exit to the alley. The one I see him leave through. I call after him, but he doesn't hear me. I run as fast as I can in my heels and call for him again, but it's raining so hard, I doubt anyone can hear me. Even with me at a run, he gets farther and farther away until he disappears. I run as fast as my heels will allow. My hand slams against the metal bar with force, releasing the latch with a metallic holler. I fling open the door and run into the middle of the alley. Rain pelts me, penetrating my skin as it pours down on me. I run to the SUV and reach for the backdoor handle. The truck pulls away just as the tips of my fingers touch the slick black paint. I stand there with my arms wrapped around my middle at a loss for what I'm losing. I scream out his name once again, but the thunder and lightning are so loud, all you can feel and hear is the rumble down the narrow path I stand in, losing what I never really had. Or did I? I stand there, shaking, in the middle of the abandoned alleyway, watching him drive farther away, a cavernous amount of space separating us. I drop my head back in resignation, letting out a manic laugh that turns into a hysterical sob, and I let the rain mix with the tears on my face. The summer night sky is dark and moody, mimicking how I feel.

Then I see it.

The illumination of the concrete walls glow red all around me. I drop my head back down and see his break lights glowing in the middle of the alley.

The SUV sits there at idle. I raise both my arms out to the side in offering.

His door is thrown open and he jumps out. "What the fuck are you doing?" he bellows with heat as his heavy footsteps stomp through the broken rubble and puddles of the street.

"I don't kno—" I honestly tell him, barely getting to finish my words before his hands capture my face with force, jerking me forward. "You have to promise me," I cry. "I don't care about myself. You have to promise me, you will never let anything happen to Abby."

"You done with him?"

I can do nothing but stare into the heated slits framing the black depths of his scrutiny.

"Isabelle…" he harshly growls, demanding an answer.

"I'm done, Giovanni. I'm homesick. Not for where I ran from or even running from, but from what I hold myself back from. You. I'm bleeding out. My heart is drained. It barely has anything left. If I give you the small amount that keeps me alive and you hurt me... I will surely shrivel up and die because I will have no home to rest my broken heart in."

His mouth is on mine.

He consumes me.

Devours me.

Obliterates the air from my lungs.

"This is it, little lion. I am not a man who plays nice. I put you in that vehicle with me, life as you knew it will be removed from your existence. I can take you home and give you want you need, but you have to give me what I want in return."

"What's that?" I nervously ask.

"You."

I grip his suit jacket and pull him into me, wanting him to wrap me in his arms so I can climb into the safety of his body.

We're both soaked to the bone, surrounded by God's wrath, and dominated by the chemistry igniting between us.

"Is…" he harshly whispers, pulling back and grabbing me by the waist. I liquify, morphing into every muscular curve of his body. My arms wrap around his thick neck and my head falls perfectly under the crook of his stubbled chin just as he finishes swinging me up into his arms. He grabs the handle to the backdoor and yanks at the heavy metal of the SUV. He sets me inside and climbs in after me, slamming the door shut as he does.

"Hello, Isabelle," an extremely deep-rooted ardent cadence chimes from the passenger seat.

I jump at the unknown voice and the depth of its tone, only having eyes for Giovanni and not paying attention to the fact that we are not alone.

"I need a minute, Demetri," Giovanni states while staring at me.

"I'll go back inside. Listen for your phone."

"Isabelle…" He pulls me onto his lap.

"You kissed me." He lifts a brow, confused at my statement. "It was a goodbye kiss, wasn't it? I don't want you to say goodbye." I shake my head frantically. "I don't want you to say goodbye," I repeat continuing to shake my head.

"I wasn't saying goodbye. I was cherishing what I want and couldn't fully have, yet."

"You have me, Gio. You have me."

"Good. Because I am done playing nice."

Giovanni
CHAPTER SIXTEEN

Isabelle sits in my lap, the inside of her knees hugging my hips, looking like the natural born goddess she is. She's soaked to the bone by the raging storm, but her innocent sex appeal is every teenage boy's wet dream and their father's nightly session in the bathroom. Her perfectly coifed red strands that are pulled into an updo have been destroyed by the weather. The makeup she had covering those small rosy-brown speckles scattered across her nose and flushed cheeks has been washed away. I hold the fiery redhead in my arms. *My* fiery redhead. The word beautiful doesn't come close to being an adequate description to describe her. Her beauty is so breathtaking it manipulates your reasoning, tricking you into believing that the air she sucks from your lungs with her beauty isn't needed to survive.

I reach up and unfasten the clasp holding her hair together. I gaze at the wet ringlets as they fall over her bare back and chest. I hold her gaze for just a moment before looking away and reaching for a wild lock that falls forward. The tip ends just above her cloth covered nipple. I wrap the lock around my index finger, and with an assertive tenderness, I pull her to within a hair's width of my mouth.

"Gio…"

Her arduous, breathless plea bears heavily in my chest. I alter my position beneath her heat, lifting her red dress to her waist as I do. My growing erection presses against its constraints, seeking her warmth and the silk of her excitement. Releasing the ringlet from my grip, I drop my hand and run the back of my knuckle over the white lace concealing her from me. Her back arches at my touch and her eyes flutter closed on a whispered moan. Her arousal discolors the delicate material covering her cunt. She reaches for the button on my slacks. I let her, if only to let my erection free from the pain it's enduring. Her fingers work the buttons of my dress shirt. The sides fall open, exposing the contradicting maniacal tattoo that covers my entire chest and upper abdomen. A lesser woman would run at the sight. Some religious worshipers would debate its statement to the bitter end, but it is my existence on this earth that has groomed me to my beliefs. The tip of her finger traces the outline just as the tip of my finger stimulates her engorged clitoris through the damp lace.

"Isabelle, do you trust me?" She nods with aroused excitement. I reach down to my concealed weapon strapped to my calf. Unsheathing my knife, I bring it between us so she can see what I'm holding. It's a test. To see if she really trusts me. Her body stills, her eyes widen, but she is not scared. She is intrigued, and maybe a little intimidated. "I will never hurt you." I give her my oath. "I will only show you my power and strength, and in doing so, I will rebuild your self-esteem until you become the powerful woman that lies beneath the fractured shell. You have control over everything that happens in your life. You just have to take the reins, little lion. Just like I pledged my honor to the code of Omerta as a soldato; I pledge my honor and loyalty to you as a man." She nods slowly, somewhat confused about some of the words she doesn't understand, but all the same, she understands I just committed myself to her. In time, she will find out who I really am, what I am really capable of, and just how serious my spoken words are.

Her hips jerk seeking stimulation. I steady her, protecting her from the sharp edge of the knife, locking her in place with the grip of my other hand before running the flat of my blade over the lace. From her opening to her mound, I hold the cold steel in place. The exhilaration from the thought of danger gives her different sensations to experience. Her eyes roll to the back of her head just as her palms plant themselves against my chest and curl in. Her chest expands, searching for the air she has just exhausted, and then she releases a deep, bone rattling moan. With slow, strategic ease, I turn the blade and slide the sharp edge down the center of the white triangle keeping her from me. Separating both sides with a controlled tear, I open her to me like the present she is. I watch her plump, pink skin clench with eagerness as she tightens her inner muscles needing me. Her clitoris swells, breaching the safety of its surroundings, seeking the warmth and stimulation of a touch. With two fingers from each hand, I pull the material apart farther, just like I will her. I let the material hang in the creases of her thighs, and I run both pads of my thumbs over the plump skin before gently separating them.

"You ready for me, little lion?" I forcibly pull my gaze from her opening.

"Yes…"

"You sure?"

"I have dreamed of being with you again. So many times, Gio. I am… I'm confused at how I barely know you but how I am so comfortable with you."

"Unzip your dress, angel. Let it fall to your waist. I want to admire those cherry pink buds I had my mouth on months ago."

"Ahh, Gio," she hisses in needy frustrated pain. "I'm not sure I can take much more."

"Lift," I instruct her, giving her outer thigh two pats before shoving my pants down. My movements are quick, effortless, and explicit. I want inside this woman. I want to live inside this woman for hours, days even. With one swoop of my arm around her waist, I lift her, drop my other hand down, and spread her cunt wide open for me. I remember every detail of that one fateful night between us. It was a vivid high-definition video that played on repeat. I also remember the moment I entered her body and realized that with my size, I needed to go slow and work her open, massaging her muscles to the point of relaxation before driving myself to the hilt. Our eyes connect, and I enter her at the same time my mouth sucks her nipple past my lips to the tip of my tongue. She fights hard to keep her love drunk eyes open, but the sensation zinging through her body has now made her strangle the life out of the tip of my dick. She pants and moans readjusting and adjusting to my size as I sink in farther. I sit as still as I can, giving her the moment she needs. With one small rock forward, she hisses and throws herself back.

"Isabelle." It's a warning, telling her I can't hold back much longer. How any man can watch the vision before me and not lose his shit is beyond me.

Her hand drops to her lower belly just as her inner muscles bare down on my shaft. It's like she is grabbing for my length through her skin. She comes with so much energy that I lose the control I have, and I follow her down that dark euphoric tunnel. I don't even finish spitting my seed into her before I slide through her contracting walls and thrust us both through the unbearable tingling and back to the buildup of another orgasm. My hands shake with tension, needing another release. Her chest glistens with sweat. Her breasts bounce and sway. Her nipples are peaks of excitement. The sight of her in this manic state is so damn arousing, I jerk forward and with the flat of my tongue I run it up the middle of her chest and over the curve of her neck to the tip of her chin, and bite just as I pull her down on me.

"Fuck, Isabelle." A husky, dominating, growling groan leaves me while I latch onto her lip with my teeth. "Fuck, you are so fucking mine."

She releases a shattered cry of orgasmic pain and pleasure at the same time I release everything I have left in me into her. She drops her head to my chest, panting, trying to capture the breath I stole from her lungs. My hands run up and down her spine, giving us both the minute we need to come down from a sexual act that was as euphoric as a drug induced hallucination. This woman obliterates time and destroys me every single time I am inside her. I cup the back of her head with my hands. She lifts and looks at me with so much adoration.

"Am I?" she asks in question to my statement as I thrust deeply inside her.

"Unequivocally. You are fucking mine."

Moments pass as we both come down. I have to get us moving. There is an entire city of police officers not one hundred feet away through a concrete wall milling around. I am sure by now Tommy Hunt is looking for his wife.

"Isabelle." I shift her, she is destroyed laying against my chest. "Little lion, we have to get moving. We've been sitting unprotected for too long."

She stirs and lifts her head, a hazy gaze beneath even heavier lids. "I don't want to move from the warmth of you."

"I'm sorry, baby, in order for me to protect you, we have to get moving." She groans when she slides off my still semi-erect cock. She looks down then back up to me. "Neither he nor I are finished with you yet, but I have to get us out of here," I assure her just as my phone rings. I grab for it and see Antonio's name flash across the screen. "Yeah," I answer gruffly, still trying to rejuvenate the energy I just expended.

"I hope to fuck it was worth it, brother. The newly appointed Lieutenant Hunt is tearing through this place like a madman looking for his wife."

"Tell D to catch a ride with you."

"He's already on his way to you."

Just as I ask, "Luca still with you?" A knock raps against the back of the truck alerting me to Demetri's presence. "You good?" I ask Antonio.

"Go do what you gotta do." Just before he hangs up, he says. "I hope to God you know what you're doing."

I shift and refasten my pants. With a quick look over my shoulder, I see Isabelle rushing to get her clothes back on like she is afraid someone is going to open the door. "Relax, Is. Demetri won't come in here until I give him the okay." Once she is covered, I jump from the back of the SUV into the still pouring rain at the same time I'm rebuttoning my dress shirt.

"If we're not out of here in the next two minutes, we're going to run into some issues, G. Hubby's on a war path and it's catching some attention."

"Yeah, I heard. Get in." I nod to the driver's seat, instructing Demetri. Then I open the back door to a frightened face that destroys every ventricle that beats through my heart.

"Where—"

I grab her face and pull her to my lips cutting off the panicked words she was just about to spew. "You still trust me, little lion?"

"He's—"

"Do. You. Trust. Me?" I pronunciate each word with as much stern gentleness as I can knowing she is ready to crawl from within her skin at the thought of his retaliation of her not being at his beck and call.

She rapidly shakes her head in contradiction to her words. "I do."

"G, we gotta go," Demetri's deep voice warns.

"Where's Abigail?"

"She's with Ms. Melodie."

"Who's Ms. Melodie?"

"She's the housekeeper for my in-laws."

Fuck.

"Is she there?"

"No, she is watching her at our house."

"Sit back. Put your seatbelt on. Demetri is going to take you to get Abigail. Then he is going to take you to my place. Where you will stay put. Do you hear me? I will come to you as soon as I can. Do not pack any of your things. Only grab the essentials Abigail can't live without. You will only have five minutes, Is. Five minutes. Do you hear me?"

"I'm scared." She desperately looks me in the eyes, fear being the driving force behind her dilating pupils.

"You know why I call you little lion?"

"G." Demetri's warning is heard but ignored. "Less than a minute and we're going to have company. He's coming through the back corridor."

"Because you are strong, Isabelle. Mighty like a lion. And fuck, if that red main of yours isn't fierce as fuck to go along with your strength, but I call you angel because you have a soft side, one where I see your fragile wings that have been tattered with each beating. I see you. I know you. I will protect you. Go with Demetri. I trust him with my life. You are now a part of my life, which means he will protect yours with his." I pull her to me, crash my lips against hers then slam the door shut with two slaps of my hand against the roof of the SUV, letting him know it's okay to leave.

I turn from the SUV pulling away and start walking towards the back door we both exited over an hour ago. I'm tucking my shirt in my pants and straightening my clothes to look presentable to go back inside to the fundraiser when the door flings open, and Lieutenant Hunt comes flying out on a ravenous mission.

I take a step to the right, so he has to look my way. I don't want him to notice the tail end of the SUV pulling out onto the main street. We stand face to face, assessing one another.

"You lose something, Lieutenant?" I sidestep him, grab the handle and head inside, getting out of the wicked weather.

"What were you doing in the alley, Moretti?" he questions from two steps behind me.

"You got a hard-on for me, officer? Again, you act like I fucked your wife or something by the way you're busting my balls." He stands there stoically, but I can see the anger radiating in his pupils while the lunacy I feel travels through my body. Every single limb I have is displaying aggressive movement beneath my inflamed skin. "What or who, Lieutenant Hunt?" I can't refrain from saying. His facial features are hard when I give him a glance over my shoulder. "I could ask you the same thing. You were just out in the alley as well."

"I'm looking for my bitch of a wife. You seen her?"

I see red, slaughter red, but I hold my anger back. Instead, I antagonize his ego. "Clearly. About an hour ago when I asked her for a dance. She's about five foot six, red hair, green eyes. Those flared hips she has that are the perfect size to grab on to and—"

"Cut the fucking shit, Moretti."

"Tell me, Hunt. How did you ever land a woman like that? And keep her? You must treat her like a princess." That comment burned the mark I wanted to sear into his brain. "Ahh, that's right, you don't. I seem to recall a little incident back in the bodega not too long ago, or yesterday at the diner. I thought I recognized your wife tonight."

"Women need to be put in their place, Moretti. Maybe if you knew that, you would have a woman."

I see myself pulverizing him. Dismembering him limb from limb. In due time. "Ahh." I nod. "Is that right? Then who is the man putting you in your place?" I let that slight simmer for a minute before telling him, "No. I haven't seen your wife." I start to walk away, needing to get as far away from him as I can before I do something right here, but then I turn back and say, "Oh, and Hunt, I have a woman. She has the exact same qualities your beautiful wife has that you dismiss." I leave him with that and head inside before I use the same knife I just used on his wife's panties and decapitate his ass in the alley.

Weaving through the crowd, I spot Antonio and Luca on the other side of the room talking to Senator Hunt. We connect eyes for two seconds. A whole conversation is had in those two seconds before he turns his attention back to the senator. I make my way to the bar, grab a drink, and join the few men gathered.

"Well, my portfolio can only grow if I get the upper hand on the Johansson property. My hundred-thousand-dollar contribution to tonight's event has put a dent in my wallet. With your beautiful wife, Victoria's help, I can secure another facet of income," Senator Hunt schmoozes some guy I have never seen before.

"How about you, Mr. Heart? What was your contribution to this evening's event?"

"That would be none of your fucking business, Hunt."

Antonio's slight has made the group uncomfortably laugh. The Senator knows better than to respond. Antonio has way too much dirt on him. His frequent use of the private lounges in Temptations with multiple women, who are not his wife, would not look so good for his political race, should that information get out. It's one of the reasons why Antonio had the private lounges and back door entrance put in. There is always an eye in the sky watching. Senator Hunt's marriage is a political sham. Now that I know who Isabelle is married to, I'm sure her marriage to the senator's son is the same. Isabelle is young and beautiful. I'm not sure how old she is, but I'm sure when she met Tommy, she was naïve and fell for his charm. Knowing what I do know now, she is just a beautiful decoy like her mother-in-law.

Tommy walks over with an angry expression. One he is trying to conceal but is not doing very well.

"Ahh, there's the new lieutenant." Hunt slaps his son's back like the proud father he portrays to be. "You find that wife of yours, son? You know you have to keep women on a short leash." He laughs like what he just said is a man's right to say.

"Yeah. She messaged me. She went home. Terrible headache. She didn't want to interrupt my conversation with the mayor."

I pull my phone from my pocket and check for any messages. There's nothing. Antonio glances my way. I shoot Demetri a quick text asking if she is okay. Then I tuck my phone back in my pocket and pretend to be interested in the conversation being held around me when all I can think about is getting to her. When Tommy turns to talk to his partner who just approached, I notice the bright pink lipstick on his neck just below his ear. Not only is he abusive, he's also unfaithful.

A woman walks over and slides in next to the guy I don't recognize. He reaches for her and possessively wraps his arm around her waist and pulls her into his side. I'm assuming it's his wife Victoria, but he doesn't introduce her. She gives a shy smile, but her eyes go directly to Tommy. That's when I notice the shade of lipstick freshly smothered across her lips.

My cell phone vibrates. I reach inside my breast pocket and flick the notification for it just as I hear the Senator say something to the woman about the property he was just speaking of.

Demetri: Headed to your place.

Me: She okay?

Demetri: That's for you to decide.

I glance at Antonio. He knows why I'm standing here. Trust me, I would rather be with Isabelle right now, but in order for me to protect her, appearances are necessary. The wife of a newly appointed lieutenant in the

New York City police department is currently MIA. Once he gets home tonight and realizes she isn't there, an all-out war will ensue to find her. She is an object and nothing more to him. When he can't find that object, he will turn the city upside down to find it. It's not that he cares for her in any regard. The first sign of that is the fact that he is standing here next to his father with another woman's lipstick on his neck instead of searching for his wife. The reason why I am standing here with my boss is simple. When he does lose his shit and tears the city apart looking for his wife, he won't come looking for me or my boss because we are standing right here in front of him. Therefore, while I am cleaning up my little lion's mess, the focus will be off me for a bit.

"Gentlemen, I'm going to call it a night," Antonio announces. "Enjoy the rest of your evening."

"Thank you for your anonymous contribution, Heart."

"Mr. Heart," he corrects the senator with a stern glare. "It's a good cause. One I fully support."

Giovanni
CHAPTER SEVENTEEN

The ride between Antonio and I is mostly quiet. Luca's in the back tapping away on his cell phone. The three of us left the fundraiser after making sure we were seen saying our goodbyes. I feel on edge. Something I never feel. She makes that emotion come alive in me. I want to make sure she is okay. What she did tonight wasn't easy. I know it wasn't. I know from experience. I can remember my mother trying to leave my father twice, but her attempts were halfhearted, and our options were limited. My best friend, Kathrine, she lived next door to us, her mother was my mother's only friend. I would say they were friendly, not good friends. It wasn't like my mom, my sister, and I could go stay with them anyway. They were too close to home. How could we hide? Besides, back then, no one wanted to get involved in other people's business.

Antonio breaks the rapid thoughts firing in my head as I drive us through the city to Temptations.

"You know what you're doing?"

I glance in his direction then back to the road. It's just a simple question but bears so much weight to it.

"You know you're going to have a target on your back, right?"

I still don't acknowledge him. If he thinks I don't know the depth of the situation then he doesn't know me at all.

He's tapping something out on his phone when I mention, "I'm going to post Joseph at my place. You got a problem with that?"

"What I have a problem with is my capo not talking to me when I speak to him. I get that you got shit going on, but my concern is for you and this organization."

"Tell me, Antonio, if this was Lilah, wouldn't you do the same thing?"

"Can you tell me that you feel the same thing for this girl that I do for

Lilah?"

"Yeah, I can."

"None of my business, but what about you and Kathrine?"

"You're correct, it is none of your business."

"Who you lay down with is none of my concern, but if you tell me that you feel the same way about this girl that I do about Lilah, then you have some decisions to make."

"I already made them."

I drop the two off them off at the club. Antonio will be in his office all night having a late dinner with Lilah. I gave Luca orders to stay close to him. It's my job to keep Antonio safe, but right now, I need to make sure Isabelle and Abigail are settled.

I park the truck and jump out. I unbutton the jacket of my tux and make my way to the private elevator to my penthouse. When I step inside, I punch in the code just as I'm pulling my tie from around my neck and unbuttoning the top two buttons of my shirt. I'm not sure what I am going to walk in to. Isabelle could be a complete mess. She may not. All I know is that when I left her, she was scared, and I hated seeing that fear in her eyes.

The elevator dings when it reaches my place. The door slides open, and I step into my foyer. Demetri slips his phone into his pocket as he's shifting off the couch to meet me. My eyes go left then right searching for her, but I don't see her and that makes me feel uneasy. I walk to the kitchen island and throw my tie and jacket on the cold surface. "Where is she?" I ask, grabbing my cell phone and wallet from my pants pocket and dropping them on the surface as well.

"Spare room with her daughter."

I stare at the opening to the hallway like I can see through walls. "Thanks, D," I say, still staring in that direction.

I only take a step before his hand lands on my forearm. "You know what you're doing?" He nods in the direction of the spare room. "Her old man is a cop, G. A fucking lieutenant at that. Heads are going to roll when he figures out who she left him for."

"Yes, they will." I wickedly grin my confirmation while pulling my arm from his hold.

He jerks his chin towards the hallway. "We all have our demons, don't we?" he says with such surety. Demetri is one of the coldest, most emotionless man I have ever encountered. We've known each other for a long time. When I was running the fighting ring in the basement of the abandoned stone house I took ownership of, he was there, fighting every weekend. He is a chameleon, one way in public, flirting with women and drowning his emotions between the legs of whoever will open them at the end of each night, and then turns back into the stone-cold machine when they are no longer of use to him. The story behind those hollow dual-colored eyes goes deep. Even though Antonio and I are the only ones who know his story, it is only part of his tragedy. Walking to the elevator, he says over his shoulder, "Call me if you require assistance."

I don't acknowledge him, instead I take the steps needed to get to the spare room. The door is shut. I stay silent and listen for her voice. It's quiet. I turn the handle and crack the door slowly, I don't want to wake her if she is sleeping. The room is dark, but I can see the two forms shaped under the covers. I back out and close the door. Even though Isabelle and I need to talk, it can wait until tomorrow.

I head to the bar and pour myself a stiff thirty-year-old Macallan. Two swallows later, I refill it and head to my home gym. I need to get rid of some of this pent-up energy. I change into some gym shorts and runners, turn on music, and hit the treadmill. The urge to turn on the spare room camera is like an annoying nat. As much as I want to invade her privacy, watch her sleep, I won't. Not right now. But in the future, she will learn that I will always have eyes on her.

I work up a sweat with a twenty-minute high-intensity run. I jump off the treadmill and float on my feet as I walk to the weight machine. Instead of water, I swallow some more scotch before wiping my forehead with my hand towel. I throw it to the floor next to the machine, sit up straight and grab the weigh bar on the Smith machine to do some military shoulder presses. *History of Violence* by Theory of a Deadman starts to play. I rep out a set of ten then take another sip of my scotch. I rest my arms on my thighs and let my head hang while I take a minute to catch my breath. Just as I grab the bar for the next set, her soft voice carries through the room.

"Is this what you do late at night?"

She is standing at the door; her shoulder leaning against the frame and her head is tilted to the side as she nervously watches me. She stands there with her arms cuffed in front of her in one of my white V-neck t-shirts. My eyes go directly to mid-thigh where the material stops and the bare skin of her legs begin.

Fuck, she is stunning.

Swollen eyes and all, this girl will stop traffic with her perfection. I'm sure she has been used by every man in her life.

Her hair is gathered on top of her head, wild loose strands twist with unruly curls as they hang down to her shoulders. Her foot is wrapped around the back of her calf on the other leg. It's so damn sexy. With the glow of the light behind her, she is a vision standing before me.

"This is what I do when I can't sleep," I explain.

We watch each other for a minute. The quiet seconds that pass between us become more intense. I can tell she is unsure. She doesn't know if she is

131

bothering me and should leave when she wants to stay or should she have never found her way down here to begin with. I want her to find her own footing. I will teach her how to take those steps to rebuild her confidence. I grab the hand towel from the floor and give my face another swipe, removing the remaining sweat. I wrap the towel around the back of my neck, hold on to each end, and make eye contact with her again. I hold her gaze with mine. She is in the same position, but her leg has dropped, and her thighs have closed the gap.

"Come here, my angel." I let go of the towel and crook my finger in gesture. My demand is firm, but it accompanies the strong desire I feel for her.

She lifts from the door frame, and with small unsure steps, she walks directly to me. Her fingers dance with each other at her sides as her nerves get the best of her. I spread my legs and pull her between my thighs when she gets close enough.

"Tell me why you are so nervous?" I look up at her as my hands find their way to her hips.

"I don't know," she whispers.

"You do." At least she didn't deny she was nervous. I jerk her hips closer to me. "When I ask you a question, I want the truth, Isabelle. I don't care what the answer is. I can only fix it if I have the truth." She shrugs her shoulder, but it's not in defiance, it's because she is unsure of what she should or shouldn't say. "Did you think I would be mad that you came down here?"

"Yes. I thought I would be bothering you."

"Does it look like I'm mad?" She shakes her head. "I am not him, angel." I pull her deeper into the V of my legs and run my hands up and down the back of her thighs while I gaze up into her glassy eyes. "I'm not him," I reiterate.

"I know." Her voice is quiet.

"Did you need something or were you just wandering through my apartment?"

"I wasn't snooping," she's quick to tell me.

"I didn't say you were."

"I woke up and went to ask Demetri when you would be here, but he was gone. I got scared and was heading back to the room when I heard the music."

"You never have to be scared here. No one can breach my threshold. You are in one of the safest places in New York City. There are only four people who have the code to my private elevator. Those four people I trust with my life, and that code changes weekly," I explain, looking up at her while I continue rubbing my palms up and down the back of her legs.

She's cautious when raising her hands and placing them on my shoulders.

132

Looking down at me with want gleaming in her eyes, she runs the tips of her fingers over the muscle. If she wants this, me, she must make the first move. It's not that I won't but I need her to know she can.

I run my hands up and over the swell of her hips to the narrow of her waist. The cotton of my shirt that adorns her body lays on my wrists. I massage the silky skin of her lower belly with the pads of my thumbs.

"Tell me what you want."

"I want you to kiss me."

"Are you afraid to initiate?"

"What if…" She breaks off, not sure she should finish her sentence.

"Continue." I encourage her. "Tell me what you are thinking."

"What if you don't want me to kiss you?"

"Isabelle, do I look like I don't want you?" I look down at my erection trapped between my thigh and my shorts and look back up at her. I grab a hold of her hand and place it over my length.

Her fingers twitch with anxious anticipation.

She sucks in a rush of air. Her chest expands just as her focus becomes heavy. Her nipples pierce the cloth of my t-shirt she's wearing. I'm madly jealous of an inanimate piece of material that I own. Little does she know, my ownership is not just of my shirt, but of her as well now.

"It's intimidating."

"Angel…" I let that linger in the air before saying, "I have already slipped inside the walls of your body, twice." I slide two fingers over her covered lips. When I get to the hood of her mound and feel her clit, swollen with need, I take the back of my index finger and slide my knuckle back and forth over the nub waiting for attention.

"More than twice." She lets out a small moan.

"Correct." I wink at her with a sinister grin. "Two different occasions."

That first night with her, I couldn't tell you how many times both of us got off. If I had had her in my bed, she wouldn't have gotten away so easy. I would have had her restrained to my bed until the early morning hours.

"I know, but here, in this room, where it is brighter, and I have a hold of you in my palm, I can physically feel how well-endowed you are. It makes my belly flutter with apprehensive knots, but also…" she murmurs. "It makes me clench with the urgency to feel you inside me again too."

Fuck.

"You still trust me?"

"Yes," she timidity whispers, watching me. "I don't know why I do. I shouldn't, I've made so many bad choices, but I do trust you."

I stand and whisk her from her feet, only to turn and tell her to spread her legs so I can place her back down on the bench I just vacated. I turn her so she is facing the machine, the bar just above her head, and tell her to grab a hold of it. I lean down and brush my lips over the shell of her ear. I wait until her eyes close. With a softer commanding voice than I would normally use, I order, "Don't move from this spot." I watch the shudder wrack her body. She is weary but she is also thrilled. I can smell her aroma filtering up from between her thighs. My cock jumps at the thought of being with her again. I grab a hold of myself, give myself a strong, gripping squeeze, encouraging the blood flow to ease, and I take a deep breath trying to sate the pain in my groin.

This woman does something to me no other woman has.

Isabelle is much younger than me. I have, at the very least, ten years on her. Her short adult life has been filled with nothing but pain and suffering. I will show her what living is, because up until this point, I don't think she has lived.

I walk to the other side of the room, grab what I need, and flick on the security camera. When I turn back, I fully anticipate that she has rebelled and dropped her arms, but to my surprise, she is still sitting in the same position.

"Good girl." I lean in and kiss the side of her neck before sitting flush with my chest to her back. The warmth of her body seeps under my sweaty skin. She tilts her head and drops her shoulder giving me more room to worship the tender skin just below her ear. The vessel carrying the blood of her passion through her neck thumps furiously with excitement. I release what's in my hand and let it dangle in front of her face. I don't want her to panic. She was just consumed by a man who gave her no say, no rights. She needs to know she has a voice.

The black boxing wrap I use for my hands unravels in front of her, bringing her attention to the object. She looks up at me then back to the material I have hanging off my first two fingers. I kiss her shoulder and wait for her reaction. As innocent as the material may be to me, to her it is threatening. It's a restraint, that in her mind, will take away her freedom.

I thrive on dominance and control. It's part of my DNA. It's not just in the bedroom, it's a staple in every aspect of my life. It's why I have my personal belongings set in the same place throughout my house. It's why my refrigerator looks like it's on display in a model home. It's for the safety of not only my own life, but the others I have devoted to protecting around me. Consistency is the key to surviving in a life of violence, and multimillion dollar backstabbing fortune five hundred backdoor deals. It's who I was molded to be when I had no control, and only refined when I became part of the famiglia. I won't sugarcoat my desires and what I need. She needs to know this is who I am. In return, she will be given the freedom to let go. Not just in the bedroom but in all aspects of life.

I watch her throat bob. Her gaze comes back up to mine. I can tell she wants to say something, but she stays silent.

"You can say no." She shakes her head, and I'm not sure if she is telling me no, she doesn't want me to immobilize her hands, or she is agreeing. "I need your voice, Isabelle. I need your words, your thoughts, your fears. I need you to speak. Use your voice. I want to hear the quiet husky timbre come from your throat. I want to listen and savor it as the days pass, and you become stronger. If you don't want this, then just say no."

"I do... but... he..."

"What were my words from before?"

"You are not him," her throaty, aroused voice repeats my words.

"I am not him," I reiterate for her. "You have more power than you think in this position. Your words are the end all and be all. If you do not want something to happen, then it doesn't happen. If you do and you're just scared, then express your feelings, and I will take it slower. I am much older than you, more experienced. I will show you that you have nothing to be afraid of. Trust me, my tattered angel, I will release you from the rusted cage with the sealed lock he has put you in, and I will place you in a life of luxury that will set your mind, your body, and your spirit free to fly, if you let me."

"Okay."

"Okay isn't good enough."

"Go ahead." She nods at her hands on the bar. "I want you to."

I lay the wrap over the bar then slide my hands under her shirt. I knead her waist, creeping my way up her torso inch by torturous inch to her ribs. "Lift your arms." My deep voice demands with as much gentleness as I can muster with the surge of blood entering my cock. I linger a moment when I feel the plump swell of the side of her breast. I resume my movement, lifting her shirt up and over her head when she does as I ask by raising her arms. I throw the shirt to the floor and pause my motion when I take in the flesh of her back. The muscles surrounding her bone structure stiffen. I pause, stunned at the sight. The tips of my fingers feel like magnets, a forceful entity that pulls them to her skin. I'm in awe of her. Captivated by her. Totally floored by the similarities of the canvas we both chose to gild our bodies with. Her back. My chest. It's symbolic, a homage to the lives we have both lived.

I'm speechless at the parallelism between my endearment for her and her body of armor she wears on her back like a shield.

Angel wings, from shoulder to waist are inked into her skin. The feathers are light and wispy at the center, but the outer edges are frayed as if they have been beaten down by an unforgiving storm. The pads of my deadly fingers float over the lines with gentleness, pausing at the dark discoloration of healed wounds that are partially cover with ink. I can't believe the similarity between how I see her and what she has displayed on her body.

"Tell me why your whole body just became rigid when I took your shirt off."

When she shrugs her shoulder, it instantly infuriates me. My anger is not at her but for what she has been through. Knowing from my own history, watching my mother not be able to express herself, seeing her torment at denying herself, knowing if she let her voice be heard it would only be silenced in the end with a beating, is the exact reason why my anger surges. My angel doesn't feel like she has a voice, but what she doesn't realize is that the little lion that came bursting into Antonio's office that night, searching for me, ready to destroy me over a stuffed animal, was all power and strength.

She has a voice. I just have to free it for her.

"Use your words. Tell me what you're feeling right now."

"I'm no longer beautiful to look at," she murmurs. "I have scars, bruises, blemishes that will always be a part of me, a reminder." Her chin rest on her shoulder, watching me as she softly confesses her insecurity.

"We have been together before, angel. As recent as just a few hours ago."

"Yes, but I wasn't naked. I'm sitting here an inch from your perfectly formed body with only a pair of very unattractive panties on. I feel exposed, insecure that I am not perfect for you in return. With... *him*, I didn't care. He was the one who put those blemishes on my body. He deserved to see them, to witness what he was doing to me. But you, you are flawless. You don't need to look at another man's marks. You are strong and very physically fit. You should be with someone who has no imperfections." She quiets for a moment. I let her ruminate over it because I can see she has more to purge. "I used to be... I used to be pretty, beautiful even." She quiets once again in thought. "But I can't say I was happy then either. Just... perfect on the outside to the voyeuristic eyes who thought my beauty equaled happiness. Only on the inside, I felt grey, dull, not worthy to shine."

Her words tell me we aren't just talking about the last few years of her life. Those few sentences are filled with a lifetime of emotions, of feeling used and unwanted. I won't take her back there today. I don't want to bring those emotions to a day she has chosen to change her life in such a monumental way.

"Flaws are what make a human beautifully unique, Isabelle. What you see on the outside of me is not what I hold on the inside. Flaws are the art of your soul. The being that resides inside you. The map that chooses your course. They are your marks of life, the uniqueness that makes you, you. No two strokes are the same. No two strokes will bring you to the same ending. It only makes me want you more. My only wish is that they didn't stain the flesh of your body as a reminder you see every day when you look at yourself in the mirror. As for me, I only see you, not your scars. I hate that they are there, because for them to be there, I know you have gone through hell."

She remains quiet. I can see the doubt in her eyes at my words. It bothers me because I know she doesn't believe me. Her chin still sits on her shoulder, but instead of watching me, she now gazes at my shirt on the floor, lost in thought. I kiss her temple, holding my lips in place for a minute. When I pull back from her skin, I whisper my truth next to her ear.

"I don't care who you were in the past. Not before him and certainly not when you were with him. I only want to know the woman who has been trapped inside. The part of you I nicknamed little lion is for the fighter I can see sitting just below the surface, and the softer broken girl that I call angel. I am not perfect, Isabelle, and I don't want perfection to stand by my side. I only want real. The realness that is so ugly, it's raw. And you, my beautiful girl, are real."

She tilts her head back and kisses me. It's soft and tender and nothing like how I feel inside.

"Did you get the ink first or after the beatings started?"

"After." Her chin meets her shoulder once again. Her heavy-lidded gaze locked on me. "Are you repulsed by the scars?"

"Not repulsed." I shake my head. "Angry." I want to explain to her how fucking enraged I am inside, and what exactly I am going to do to him when I get him in my clutches, but I don't. There is a time and a place, plus she doesn't need to know, and I won't let him ruin this moment between us.

"The scars will always be there, angel. They do not define you, but they will guide you with a physical reminder that you need to take it one day at a time to make a better life for yourself. As you do that, the scars will fade. Let them be your pillars, holding you up from a life you had enough courage to leave, a life that didn't break you, a life that led you to me and this moment. From this day forward, we will rebuild you to become the woman you were never allowed to be. Once you do that, the shine you don't think you have on the outside will glow so bright from within, you'll wish you had sunglasses," I joke, laughing, giving some levity to a heavy conversation. "I'll even buy them for you." She chuckles. "Is?"

"Yeah?"

"I can't wait to meet her." I lean forward, kiss her shoulder then press my chest to her back. I reach for the wrap hanging carelessly from the bar, and blanket her delicate wrist on one side, tying a bowline knot. It's the easiest knot to release if she starts to become uncomfortable or panics. I give it a second before throwing the other half over the bar and bringing it around to make a loop. From behind her, I reach in front and hold my hand out and wait for her to place her other hand in my palm. When she does, I wrap the material around her wrist and tie the same knot.

"Do you not want me to touch you?" She leans her head against mine.

"Trust me, that is not the case. With your hands immobilized, you are free to feel. To experience what is happening to your body without the worrying or the pressure of if you should or shouldn't touch me. This is me giving pleasure to you and taking it from you as well."

She pulls on her restraints, testing the durability.

"What if Abigail wakes up?"

I point in the direction of the monitor set up high in the corner of the room. Multiple security screens show each room in the apartment. Abigail is soundly sleeping under a white fluffy comforter. "You just feel and let your inhibitions go while I ravish you. I will listen to the bumps in the night like I'm accustomed to doing." I give her a second to let her brain adjust to the restriction. "You ready for me?" My husky voice batters her shoulder with my heavy breath.

"I think I was born waiting for you."

Isabelle
CHAPTER EIGHTEEN

"I will listen to the bumps in the night like I'm accustomed to doing." Why does he have to listen? What exactly is he listening for?

"Ohh…" He slides his hands around my front, plucking my peaked nipples just as he nips my shoulder. He releases one nipple from the delicious torture and captures my chin with a firm hand. He twists my head towards his and places his mouth over my lips. I open for him, waiting for the slip of his tongue to glide inside and twirl against mine. His kiss is warm, inviting, and intriguing, but there is also an underlying emotion filled with so much fervor that's being denied. I can see it in the swirl of his dilating green eyes. He's holding back the intensity that encapsulates his being. I know he is doing it for me, but with him, I don't need that. His powerful energy is what attracted me to him. From the moment I saw him walk across the bar holding so much confidence behind each weighted step, I was captivated by him. His demeanor is familiar, yet so unfamiliar. He is a paradox to the norm I have experienced in my lifetime. The men I have become accustomed to hold that power and use it against you for their own gain. But the depth behind Giovanni's was enticing and so appealing to me in ways I have never felt before.

He tilts my head back, resting it against his shoulder. His voice is deep, husky, and sexually charged with intensity when he explains, "I am going to devour every bit of your body, Isabelle. I am going to twist and turn your body, manipulate your torso while I thrust inside of you. Giving you pleasure I can guarantee you have never experienced before."

"Okay," is all I can murmur as a thrill of nervous excitement zings through my limbs. I can't seem to form any other words while he's plucking at both my nipples. His ministrations are a touch I have never felt before.

They are forceful, yes, but there is a respectful desire behind the strength of his touch. He has me so aroused by just stroking the peaks to their highest point, I think I may be able to orgasm just by that touch alone.

"Watch what I am doing to you."

The cadence of his husky voice stimulates my senses more. I drop my gaze to my chest and watch the way his large hands surround my full breasts. His fingers manipulate my already cherry red nipples into bloodred crests of arousal. "Ahh..." I close my eyes at the severity of his handling.

"Open those beautiful eyes, angel. Watch how your body blooms with the touch of a man who will cherish you for all the days to come."

"Ahh!" I yank on my restrained hands, aching to touch him so badly. I groan, breathing with exasperation.

A deep-rooted, raspy chuckle sounds behind me. "You want me to release you?" He kisses the shell of my lobe waiting for my answer.

"No. I-I just want to touch you." My breathy pants make my words choppy.

"In time."

I feel his amused smirk against my neck just before he nibbles down. I squeal at the spot he has chosen to titillate with his teeth. I squirm in my spot, unable to move away from him as I giggle, but really what I want to do is turn around and wrap my arms and legs around his torso and hold on tight.

His hand slides down the center of my body and dips under the waistband of my pale blue panties. I should be embarrassed at how soaked I am, but I'm not. When his fingers reach my opening and slip through my arousal, Giovanni groans at how turned on he has made me. I lean back, pressing my tattooed skin to his chest as one of his broad fingers glide its way inside my channel. I bear down, releasing a long, drawn-out moan. A burst of fluid rapidly rushes, coursing down my walls and coats his hand. I watch in awe at how he has made my body respond.

"Fuck yeah, little lion. Give me what you've got."

My head drops back on his shoulder, resting there as I rock it back and forth with each twist and turn of his finger. With the slip of his second finger, the heel of his palm massages against my swollen nub, and his callused palm caresses my lips with each thrust. The metal bar my hands are tied to clanks with my jerky movements. A violent orgasmic scream leaves my inner loins, traveling with force up through my throat and filling the room with my torturous howl.

Never in my life have I felt something so strong. It was deliciously painful, holding me on that razors edge before becoming astoundingly pleasurable.

"That's it, my delicate girl, come on my hand."

I feel a forceful tug at my side. It snaps me out of my shaky haze. The sound of material ripping coincides with my heavy panting. Before I know what is happening, I feel a tug on the other side. The front and back panels of my pale blue panties lifelessly fall to the black, leather bench. I swallow with anticipation as I'm lifted by my waist. He has me hovering in the air, letting my soaked panties drop from my body. I'm not sure when he took off his shorts, but when he places me down on his lap, I feel the full intimidating length of him cradled between my silk slicked folds.

"Lean forward. Ass up. Wrap your fingers around the material restraining your wrists and put your weight into the wrap. Bear down on the bar when I lift you."

I do as he commands. He lifts me with ease, my marred, naked body levitating in the air. My ass is on full display for him. His unforgiving lips and teeth kiss and bite their way down my spine. When he gets to the top of my cheeks, he sinks his teeth into each one then sucks on the soft skin just above the valley of my behind. He licks his way up my spine as both his hands slide under me and press against my hips, lifting me. I let out a shocked moan when I feel his tongue reach my clitoris from behind. I'm quickly shifted and manipulated then set down, but I'm not on the bench, my thighs bracket his face. I glance down and directly into his carnal gaze. His tongue slides inside my opening, the tip swirling with vigor. I pull on the wraps tied around my wrists and groan. My bottom clenches and releases against his bulky chest.

"Gio… Gio…" I drop my head back.

A slap stings my behind. "Look at me when you come on my tongue," he croons.

My thighs clench, shaking with intensity. I have never been in this position on a man before. It's new and exciting but also intimidating. "Gio…" I whine.

"Ride my mouth. Cover me with your juices." He laps at my sensitive skin.

My core bursts into white-hot, tingling heat. I clench, bearing down on him like his tongue is the stick to a ten-speed in a luxury vehicle. I'm no sooner hitting my peak when I'm lifted and once again hovering in the air with Giovanni behind me. He grabs ahold of my chin and pulls me back against his chest. His lips assault mine, encompassing my full mouth. His dark beard and lips glisten with my arousal.

He pulls away and demands, "Run your tongue over my lips. Taste yourself. I want you to taste the ripe deliciousness that just fed my soul."

I do as he says. My deep inner insecurities not giving a damn. I moan and press my lips against his. When he pulls back, I am lifted in the air once again and maneuvered so my core is in direct line of his erection. He drops me down slowly onto his lap. The pressure at my opening thrills and scares me. He is larger, more engorged.

"Lean forward and grab the wraps again. Bear down on the material with your hands. It will alleviate the strain on your wrists."

Inch by inch he enters me as he stands to his full height behind me. Inch by inch I am pulled onto his cock, fully under his control. Inch by delicious inch, I am grasping at his remarkable width and length with impatient need. I release a desire filled whine when he shifts his hips. Then slowly, oh so slowly, he starts rocking my body on his as he shifts his hips back and forth. The feeling he is extracting from my body is extraordinary. What he is making me feel is nothing short of magical. In my euphoric headspace, I feel the air surrounding me swoosh with each push and pull. His hands have a grip on my hips as he thrusts into me over and over. Then I feel myself being lifted higher and flipped around. He places me back down on the bench with my back against the leather this time. He spreads my legs open, studies my most intimate parts and wraps my legs around his waist. Then with unforgiving strength, he plunges back inside me. I release a broken scream, arching my back. The feelings are too intense. He is intense. This whole sexual act is too intense. But I love it. I feel like I'm floating, my mind addicted to the pops of pleasure snapping throughout my body. I drift away on what feels like the fluffiest cloud scattered across the sky. He has taken me to a different kind of heaven. A heaven I never want to come down from.

"Look at me," he groans, ripping himself from my body. His eyes expand and for the briefest moment, he squints with pain as he furiously jerks himself to orgasm before his face slackens and he empties himself all over my lower stomach and throbbing sensitive clit.

I want to touch him so bad. I yank on the wrap with vigor, the bar clanks against the steel hooks welded in place holding it. He leans forward and pulls both dangling ends of the wrap. Instantly freed, my arms fall. A rush of adrenaline surges through me, and I push myself up on his lap and wrap my arms around his neck. A tear slips from the corner of my eye. I'm overwhelmed at what I just experienced. My emotions are raging little tyrants wreaking havoc inside my body.

"Shh, my angel," he hushes me with soothing timbre as he lifts us up from the bench. I'm clenched, wrapped around his body, never wanting to let go. It doesn't matter that he has his arm wrapped around my waist or that his hand from his other arm is holding the back of my head so I'm flush with his. I'm not letting him go. "Shh... You're just coming down from a high you are not used to. It's the adrenaline rush that surged through your body and is now crashing that is making you feel this way."

I shed more tears, not understanding, even with his explanation as to why I'm feeling this way. I just had the best sexual experience of my life. Why am I crying?

He walks us through the gym and down the hall, entering another massive room I'm assuming is his master bedroom. He walks to the other side of the room and enters an equally massive bathroom. With me still clinging to him, he turns on the shower and steps inside. He holds me to him and steps under the warm water. The spray feels good on my aching bones, but the running water gets hotter and stimulates my tender flesh.

"I'm going to set you down, Is, so I can clean us off." I release my legs from around his waist and touch my toes to the stone floor. "Hold onto me until your legs feel strong enough to hold you up."

My palms lay flat against his chest as I look up at him and breathe in astonishment. "That was incredible."

The side of his lip lifts. A smirk. It's not cocky, but it is confident in the fact he knew exactly what he was doing and how high it would take me. He kisses my forehead and promises, "That was only a taste."

Isabelle

CHAPTER NINETEEN

I wake to a dark room. My body feels like I've just slept in a five-star hotel. The darkness of the room tells me I should still be sleeping but my internal alarms tell me it's time to get up. That's the moment I go into straight panic mode. Reality hits me. Hard. I reach for Abigail. She's not there, the sheets beside me are cold. I spring up. Panic seizes me. I reach for my phone and realize there is a table lamp next to the bed. I flick the switch, illuminating the room with light, and fully comprehending that my baby girl isn't anywhere in the room with me.

Then it hits me even harder.

I left my abusive husband last night. I made a decision that will change my life, our life, forever. I was brought to my… I don't know what Giovanni is to me, but I was brought to his penthouse by one of his… men, coworkers, employees? I don't even know. I had the best sex of my life. Fell asleep in Giovanni's arms, in his bed after he showered us both, and now, I wake up in this bed alone without him or my baby girl.

Anxiety guts me to the gills.

I jump from under the sheets and rush to the door. I get halfway down the hallway and that's when I hear it. The joyous sounds of a child's giggle, Abigail's giggle. A sound every mother takes comfort in hearing. Then I hear a deep murmur followed by an even deeper chuckle. I tiptoe my way down the hall and stop just before the opening to the kitchen and listen. Abigail giggles away. I hear the sizzle of food hitting a pan and her giving him direction on how to cook.

"Mister, that doesn't look like a pwincess pancake." She sounds so confused.

"I think it does. Look, her crown is right there." I can hear the levity in Giovanni's voice.

"I don't swee it." Skepticism is clear in my baby girl's voice.

"You can make the next one. Call me Giovanni." I hear the scrape of the spatula hitting the pan.

"I want to make a heawt, Giovonky."

"That's cheating. And let's go with just the first letter of my name. G instead of my full name."

"I don't cheat, mister G. And you can call me Abigail."

I hear Giovanni chuckle at that.

"You gave me the hard one and yourself the easy one, kid."

"A heawt is not easy, mister G. It can break in half. My mommy's heawt is bwoken. She cwies a lot."

My heart sinks when I hear her say that. My poor baby girl has lived the first three years of her life in a volatile home.

"Is that right?" The levity in his voice now gone, turning darker because of the information Abigail just innocently released.

"Yeah, my daddy is mean." It's silent between the two of them for a minute. "Are you mean, mister G?"

"Only to the people who deserve it. Your momma isn't one of them."

"Am I?"

"Never, kid."

"I didn't think so. You're making pancakes with me. My daddy never did that."

"I'll make pancakes with you any time you want."

"Even for dinner?" Her voice rises with her excitement.

"Of course. Maybe your momma wants one too."

"She still sweeping."

"I bet she's not. I bet she's standing behind that corner listening to us talk and make pancakes."

I take the few steps it takes to reveal myself knowing I've been caught eavesdropping. I make my way to the side of the island and say, "I don't know about pancakes for dinner. Only good girls get pancakes for dinner." I shoot Giovanni an inquisitive look. *How did you know I was hiding in the hallway?* He just smirks at me.

"I'm a good girl." Abigail's indignant little voice breaks the silent talk between him and I.

"Did you listen to me when I told you last night not to leave the room this morning without me?"

"No, Momma. I'm sowrry, but he was out here, and I was hungwy. He was cooking yellow icky eggs."

I watch Giovanni pick her up from the chair she was standing on at the stove and set her down on the stool at the island. Her eyes grow big. He slides a plate filled with way too many pancakes in front of her.

"She won't eat all of them," I remark with amusement, watching her.

"She will eat until she is full. We can save the rest for later."

"Pancakes for later?" Abigail squeals getting all excited.

"Do you even eat pancakes?" I ask him with a smile, because quite honestly, his body looks like it hasn't consumed a carb in years.

"Of course, I do." His fake indignant tone, matching my daughters makes me silently laugh.

"I don't think he does, Momma. He was eating the icky eggs."

"I agree." I slide in next to her.

"Would you like some pancakes, Isabelle? I would think you would be famished this morning. I made them with my own hands. Watched them drip into the pan and cooked them until perfection with skill." His voice deepens, dripping with every innuendo an innocent pancake can have.

"I would love to taste your pancakes, Giovanni."

"Momma, they are so good," Abigail groans while chomping on a huge mouthful of starch.

Once she is finished eating, I send Abigail to the room to wash up. She ate one whole pancake, leaving the other five on the plate for later. Giovanni slides a coffee in front of me. I grab for it, saying thank you, but he doesn't let go until I glance up at him.

"Did you sleep well, Isabelle?" His voice is so thick I feel like I just swam in a vat of the most decadent liquid chocolate. It's smooth like warm caramel drizzle. It's sex. The man is sex. All six foot three of him is an illicit seductive carnal beast.

"Like the dead. Not sure how I got back into the room with Abigail though."

"I carried you there." He walks around the island and stands next to me.
Because he didn't want to spend the whole night with me?
I glance down at my plate of food, feeling insecure.

"Stop." One simple word, but it snaps me out of my self-doubt.

"W-What?" I glance up at him.

"I brought you back to the room your daughter was in for no other reason than her mother needed to be next to her side when she woke up this morning."

"I agree," I burst, pushing my plate away, getting heated. Does he think I would have spent the whole night with him? I knew I had to go back to the other room to be with Abigail. I couldn't have her wake up in a stranger's home by herself. However, she did wake up and felt comfortable spending time alone with him, cooking. But then what? If I hadn't left his bed, she would have come looking for me and found me in Giovanni's bed? Naked. That would warrant some questions from my three-year-old. I move to shift off the seat, feeling anxious, like he is questioning my parenting.

"Finish your pancakes." He raises a brow and nods at my plate. I don't know why but I listen to him and sit back down. He slides the plate back in front of me and then leans down and kisses my temple. Before he pulls away, he says, "We will discuss your insecurities when we are alone."

"I—"

"Eat, Isabelle." He cuts me off with such a finality. "You are going to need your strength."

He turns his back on me and starts cleaning up the mess by the stove. I do exactly what he told me to do. I eat. I eat the plate in front of me like it is my last meal and then I pick at Abigail's plate too. I am completely famished or maybe it is the fact that I am mesmerized watching his fine ass move around the kitchen with only a pair of gym shorts on. Okay, maybe it is a little bit of both because all I can envision is how his strong, masculine thighs and butt looked while he was thrusting inside me last night. I release a heavy breath and drop my fork.

"Little lion, those thoughts you're having can wait until we're alone."

"Huh?" I lift my gaze from the area his behind was just in and meet his heated gaze. I clear my throat. "I'm sorry, what?"

His half-lipped grin clues me in on the fact that I was caught red handed. My full embarrassment is saved from being brought to light when an alarm inside the penthouse goes off. I startle, not knowing what is happening and for a brief moment, I fear it's Tommy coming to get me.

"Relax, little lion. It's not him. What did I tell you last night?" He raises his brow.

"No one can get in here," I breathe, releasing some of the anxiety that just volcanoed through my system.

"That's right. No one can get in here," he repeats with a matter-of-fact tone like I need to listen and heed his words because they are facts. He stares at me for a moment. "We'll continue this conversation when we're alone."

"Good morning." A cheerful voice spooks me. "Oh... hi?"

A beautiful woman stands there looking dismayed at my presence. She looks to be younger than Giovanni, but she is definitely older than me. Her stunned reaction makes me feel uncomfortable. I'm not sure what to do with myself so I stand from the stool and greet her as nicely as I can. She glances to Giovanni and then back to me. I have no idea who she is and the tension in the room becomes thick. She could be his girlfriend for all I know. I didn't ask him. I never even thought to ask. What if she is? What if they have an open arrangement and she didn't know he brought me home last night? I can't help all the ridiculous scenarios going on inside my head.

"Umm, if you will both excuse me, I need to go check on Abigail."

I glance at Giovanni and then I turn as quickly as my feet will allow, taking only two steps before I am halted in my spot.

"Where do you think you're going, little lion?" The pressure on my elbow from his touch thrills me.

"I need to check on Abby." I take another step. Only his other arm wraps around my waist, stopping my forward movement.

"For a three-year-old, she is very intelligent. I'm sure she will find her way back out here when she is finished."

"You have no idea," I mutter. I should tell him now that my daughter is not very intelligent, but extremely intelligent.

"I want you to meet someone very special to me. And since your mind ran wild in the two point five seconds after she greeted you, I am going to assume that you thought the worst. Am I correct in my assumption, Isabelle?"

His deep voice makes me shiver. "Maybe." I squeak out the word, feeling like an idiot.

"Isabelle." His husky chastising whisper of my name sends chills down my spine as he pulls me back tighter against his chest. "You have a lot to learn about me." Then he does the unthinkable. With his back to the woman, he runs his hand under the t-shirt I'm wearing and slides it up my stomach. I'm speechless and give a wiggle for him to stop. That is, until he starts to caress my chest. I let out a small moan that's filled with nervousness. He chuckles his manly chuckle and releases me.

"Clearly," I huff.

He kisses the side of my neck and gruffly demands, "Now turn around and say hello to my sister, Hope."

"Sister?" I swallow, curving my neck up to look him in the eyes.

"Sister," he confirms. "The one and only."

"Yup, that's me. Just a sister. Over here feeling awkward as fuck?"

"Watch the language, Hope."

"Okay, Dad," she banters with snark.

I twist out of his arms, pull the t-shirt away from my body, hoping to hide the fact that my nipples are now standing at attention, and I face her. "I'm so sorry. I just thought… I thought… well yeah… okay." I run my hand down my front and give the material a tug away from my body once again.

"It's okay. I was just as shocked to see you too. My brother never brings anyone here. I think I have only seen him with one female. Ever. In this apartment."

Okay, well, that makes me feel better. He's not a manwhore. Or maybe he is, but he doesn't bring them here. I mean… I'm here, so what does that mean? I'm special? Who was the other woman? Someone special too?

"Get out of your head, little lion," Giovanni orders from directly behind me.

"I'm sorry." I snap out of it and wave my hand down the front of me. I'm still braless and in Giovanni's t-shirt. This isn't really the way to greet anyone, let alone a family member.

"No worries." She flips her own hand like it's nothing and sets the bags down on the counter. She slides the newspaper across the island in Giovanni's direction. She continues to unload the grocery bags as he opens the paper. He quickly but meticulously goes through the pages of the paper then closes it, turns, and walks to the fireplace in the living room. He flicks a switch and it burst into flames. His fireplace is not the traditional floor to ceiling fireplace your mom and dad have, no, this is very modern. It's at least six foot long with blue glass rocks on the bottom. The flames flicker off the glass giving it a glamorous vibe. He places the newspaper inside and walks away, leaving the fireplace burning. All the while I stand here, watching everything that is going on around me with my arms crossed over my chest. It's almost as if this is a daily routine for the two of them.

"So, now that you know my name, can I ask what yours is?"

"Oh. Oh, I'm—jeez," I fluster. "I've been so rude this morning."

"Her name is Isabelle," Giovanni informs his sister for me as he's walking towards me.

"Nice to meet you, Isabelle."

"You're a dick." I turn to Giovanni. His brows raise in shock. "You could have at least saved me from looking like an idiot."

"Why?" His wicked smirk says it all. "I like seeing you red flushed and nervous."

"Is my brother flirting right now? Nooo, it can't be. The ever-present stoic man who never breaks his persona is flirting? My, my, you really must be special, Isabelle. Who are you and where did you come from?"

"Enough, Hope."

She lets out a boisterous laugh. It's so loud it's catchy and I start laughing too. She throws an orange at him as she is placing the others in a bowl on the island. He catches it with lightning reflexes, tosses it back to her, grabs me, and sweeps me up into his arms.

"You think that's funny?" His deep raspy voice is filled with promise.

"I think you're very sexy when flustered."

"Isabelle, I never get flustered. I only get even." He quirks a brow and a wicked as sin grin. "Goodbye, Hope," he yells over his shoulder as he starts to walk me backwards out of the kitchen.

"It was nice meeting you," I yell and wave over the same shoulder.

"You, too. I'll see you sooner rather than later since I live a couple floors down," she yells back.

The bell I heard when Hope arrived goes off again. Giovanni stops in his tracks. He lets me go and shoots his sister a look. She steps closer to the kitchen island. The whole exchange between them is peculiar. Demetri walks in. Giovanni steps in front of me, blocking me from Demetri's view.

I hear Hope greet Demetri and then I hear the elevator slide open again as she leaves. I can't see a thing because Giovanni is blocking me. I step around his big body and wave. Demetri says good morning with a mischievous smile.

"Go get dressed, Isabelle. Now." Giovanni's tone is sharp, and although it's an order, the way he says it doesn't make me feel like he is controlling me. "Get dressed then meet me back in the kitchen. We have some things we need to discuss." He turns, gives me a chaste kiss, then waits until I turn around and start to head towards the hallway.

Curiosity forces me to turn around to see if he is still watching me. He is. Once I hit the edge of the hallway where Demetri can't see me, I flip the back of my shirt up in the air and tease Giovanni with my naked butt cheeks.

I don't know what possessed me to do it. A moment of giddiness hits me I guess, but it felt good to actually be able to flirt and know that I wouldn't be called a whore.

When I hear the rush of a bull's snort behind me, a thrill zips through my limbs and with rubber legs I turn, wink at him, then run down the hallway as exhilaration fills my limbs.

I hear ridiculously quick steps sound behind me as I'm running. I halt myself at the door Abby and I are staying in and steady myself as I glance back at him. He stands there, at the end of the hallway with a firm finger pointing directly at me and growls, "Be careful what you wish for, little lion. Teasing me will only bring out the beast I can barely contain inside me when I am around you. As you can tell by your levitating body last night, I am not your typical lover. You tease me… I. Will. Torture. You."

His face is stone, but instead of the ice in his eyes like I have seen in them before, there is warmth. I should be afraid, his statement is a threat, but I'm not. Nothing about him makes me scared. He gives me the courage to admit, "I think I would like to meet him." I wink again and dash inside the door, slamming it behind me.

Giovanni
CHAPTER TWENTY

My heart is slamming into my ribs as I walk back into the kitchen. If Demetri wasn't standing in my kitchen and a three-year-old wasn't in the vicinity, Isabelle would be ass up laid across my fucking kitchen island. She challenged me. I'm proud of her. But she has no idea the beast she just evoked inside me. *Fuck.* She has me worked up. Her tight little ass being on display where Demetri could have seen her stirred something in me.

I walk to the island where Demetri is enjoying some leftover pancakes and start cleaning up. "You want a coffee to go with that, princess?" I only say it because of the sly look on his face.

"Won't be necessary. I thought I may be here a little bit longer since Izzy just tested you."

I freeze in my spot, glaring at him.

"I saw nothing. What I did see is your facial expression drastically morph into something sinister. It takes one dominant to know another, and brother, if you are as bad as me, that girl is in for a world of tortured pleasure. I know I don't have to say this, but I'm going to anyway. She is coming from an abusive relationship. Can she handle what you're going to give her?"

"You will refer to her as Isabelle, and what she can and cannot handle will only be my concern."

With a quick nod in understanding and agreement, he slides a yellow envelope across the counter and informs me of our day. "We have a meeting with Mr. H at the house in ninety minutes."

I grab the envelope. "What's this?" I hold it in my hand.

"The information you demanded two days ago. I saw Freddy this morning. He asked if I would deliver it."

The large nondescript yellow envelope feels like the weight of the world lying in my hands. Do I want to open it? I'm not so sure I do. I demanded the information from Freddy after the incident at the diner, but now she is here, in my home. I'm not sure I want to investigate her through paperwork or hear her personal business through her own lips when she is ready. It's a sixty-forty split for me. Intel is how I work. Intel is how I survive. Intel is what has kept me alive and with an untraceable offshore bank account that has enough money for my children's children to live comfortably after I die. If I don't look at it, I could be caught off guard. Everyone has a past. Some are great, some good, and some that will come back to haunt you *or* me if I don't investigate.

I set the envelope down on the stone counter, giving myself the minute I need to talk myself out of opening it. I turn and throw the dishes in the dishwasher. As I'm turning around, Isabelle comes back into the kitchen. She's a bit hesitant, but when I curve my index finger at her, silently telling her to bring her better-be-covered-bottom over to me, she comes as quick as she can. With one arm wrapped around her waist, I pull her flush with me and lean down to the ear that is farthest away from Demetri.

"You want to show me that ass of yours, you do it when we are alone."

"I'm sorry," she whispers, looking like she was just reprimanded by a parent.

Her apology guts me. We will discuss it later. If she never apologizes in her lifetime again, to anyone, even if she is wrong, it would suit me just fine.

"Your apology is unnecessary. Don't get me wrong, I thoroughly enjoyed the view. I just don't want anyone else to take joy in seeing it either." I grin, hoping that will lighten her mood and let her know it wasn't about what she did, but more about the fact that I'm not willing to let anyone else see what I plan on making mine. Who am I kidding, I already consider her mine. The moment she ran out that backdoor chasing after me, she became mine. We just need to get through some serious obstacles before I can make it official.

I kiss the tip of her nose, releasing her when I feel her body relax. She turns to Demetri and greets him once again. He gives her a platonic smile and nod in return.

She grabs the few dishes left on the counter and brings them to the dishwasher. She turns back to the island with a rag and starts to wipe it off. She grabs the envelope and picks it up to wipe beneath it. I wait for either the recognition, the question, or the inquisitive look. Her name is typed in a small font up in the left-hand corner. Demetri is going through his emails. It's his attempt to ignore the situation. I wait, but she places it back down on the counter and continues cleaning. Nonchalantly, I walk over and pick it up and place it in one of the drawers behind us.

"Where's Abby?" I walk up behind her and wrap my arms around her waist.

"She is thoroughly invested in An Elf's Story." She laces her hands over mine, glancing up at me.

Demetri looks at his watch. The simple gesture is to let me know we need to get going.

"I'll wait for you in the truck." He nods at Isabelle, saying goodbye, and leaves.

"I have to go to work. I have a meeting in an hour. Make yourself at home. When I get back, we need to have a discussion about some things." I feel her stiffen in my arms. "Relax, Is. I won't be gone long. I'll bring back some lunch. We can talk then."

Mr. Heart is in his office waiting on the three of us. We're ten minutes early, but to Robert Heart, we're thirty minutes late.

We each take our usual seats as we say good morning to both Mr. Heart and the family's consigliere, Lorenzo. Mr. Heart slides his desk chair in. Bellying up to his desk he places his elbows on the wood and gives the three of us a once over. He slides the glass of orange juice to the side and shifts the ashtray holding his Cuban from the prior night. In the hour before noon, Mr. Heart has our rapt attention by the serious demeanor he is exuding. Lorenzo sits to the side and waits just like the three of us do. Although Lorenzo already knows why this meeting is being held.

"How did the fundraiser go?" he starts off by asking his son.

"Good. Got some insight on a piece of property that is holding some interest with the senator."

"Do we know the property address?"

"I have Freddy checking into the logistics."

"Good. Good," he repeats, bobbing his head. "Did you get any intel on the shipment?"

"Nothing. The event was on the up and up. I didn't witness any side bidding happening."

"How about you, Giovanni?"

"Nothing. I thought for sure we would have seen some side dealing, but Antonio is correct, there was nothing out of the ordinary." Usually when it comes to transactions as underground and secretive as this, side deals are done out in the open. We thought the fundraiser would have been the perfect cover for bidders to bring forth their offers to the ringleader, but we didn't see anything out of the ordinary. The initial bidding is done on a secret encrypted webpage. The only way to be privy to the website is to be invited. It's a secret society of sick men and women. The problem is, no one knows who the ringleader is, but we thought that maybe we could catch a glimpse of some shady side deals at the fundraiser last night. No better way to hide what you do than to pretend that you are against the act with monitory support.

"It has been brought to my attention the two warehouses that are now a rubble of ashes, were in fact, owned by Senator Hunt. They were documented and registered with the county two years ago under his wife's deceased father's name."

"Huh." Antonio contemplates that information. "Was he alive at the time of purchase?"

"No," Lorenzo's raspy smokers voice confirms.

"He didn't seem too torn up about losing two buildings last night." I bring the fact to light.

"No, he did not," Antonio chimes in. "Why would that be?"

"He's either a great actor or he holds the insurance note," Demetri voices. "What was or wasn't in that warehouse? That's the question."

"Correct," Lorenzo agrees, clearing his throat while shifting in his seat.

"Gentlemen, my gut tells me this is bigger than we think. You need to watch your backs. We are not allies with this group, which means we're a threat to their organization. Our women are at risk. Shadows need to be put in place. The security of our women is top priority. Keep your eyes and ears open. There is no better retaliation to our mission then abducting our women for their cause. I will not lose another one of my family members to the malicious hand of a sick individual who preys on the weaker body to sell for their gain. Do I make myself clear?"

We all nod and hum our agreeance.

"Put a call into Denny Jr. See if he's heard anything. Tell him to keep an ear on the ground for any and all information."

"I'll call him when we are done here. I talked to him last week, but nothing of importance was discussed or brought up."

"What was the call for then?" Mr. Heart holds an inquisitive brow.

"I asked him to get some intel on Cillian McKittrick before we held a meeting with him."

"Anything of importance?"

"Nothing. He's an Irish boss. Has held his position for ten years now. Lethal and extremely ruthless in his dealings. His name holds serious clout in his motherland. Seems to be on the up and up wanting to expand into the states. Denny is still checking some things out, but as of right now, I think a business relationship between us and them could be lucrative."

"When's your meeting with him?"

"Tonight."

Mr. Heart looks to me and Demetri. "You both will be there." It's an order he didn't have to make. We nod to be respectful of our boss's orders, but it is a given. He knows that, but there is a tension in Mr. H today and it's putting me on edge. I'm sure I'm not the only one who can see or feel it. He ends the meeting, dismissing everyone. Lorenzo, as usual, stays seated. He doesn't leave Mr. Heart's side. I go to stand and follow Demetri and Antonio out when he orders me to sit back down. I retake my seat and wait.

"I heard you were distracted last night. Care to explain?"

It sounds like a question, but I know I have no choice but to answer. "Not sure what you mean."

"Don't play stupid with me, son. You're too smart for that. You realize you could not have chosen a worse female to pursue."

"I didn't know who she was when I pursued her," I admit.

"Which makes me concerned. You are not the man who carelessly takes on a lover he knows nothing about."

"Not a lover. It was one night."

"Then how did it turn into last night?"

I openly stare at him. Not with disrespect but with a look that implies that it is personal. I do, however, understand why he is asking. This is not a normal situation, and it is the only reason I explain myself. "We were unexpectantly reacquainted after months of not seeing each other. The situation was not what you would call a good one. I stepped in. I didn't know she was married the night I spent with her, and I damn sure didn't know who she was married to. As a matter of fact, when I saw him that first initial time and even the second time, I knew he looked familiar, but I couldn't place who he was outside of his uniform. I have spoken to her a few times after that morning. She's in a situation that hits to close to home for me. I didn't know until last night exactly who she was married too."

"Is this a knight-in-shining armor complex you feel the need to take on to correct a past you can't fix?"

"No. My past is in my past, but with that being said, when I saw the bruises on her body, it did make me want to commit a capitol murder. However, had she not ended what happen the first night, I would have continued my pursuit of her."

"You're serious then?"

"More than."

"Because this hits close to home?"

"Because she feels like home."

"Well, then, we're in for a battle, aren't we?" He sighs heavily looking over to Lorenzo. "Keep your eyes open and your back against the wall, son. No mistakes. Bring her to a Sunday dinner. And Giovanni, for God's sake, do not let this cloud your judgement."

"No disrespect, boss. The advice is appreciated but is unnecessary. I always have and I always will protect this family with a clear mind. Thank you for inviting her to dinner." I stand, waiting to be dismissed, knowing the meeting has ended. With his confirming nod, I walk out and head to the kitchen where I know both Antonio and Demetri are soaking in Mrs. H's cooking.

I dropped Antonio and Demetri off at Temptations. I told them I would be back later. I'm just about home after stopping to grab some lunch for the three of us when my phone rings. Kathrine, my lifelong best friend's, name flashes across the screen. My thumb hovers over the accept call button. It's a natural reaction to answer for her, but at the moment, I can't bring myself to do it.

Kathrine and I… we're complicated. We have had a long-standing friendship since our childhood. It turned into a relationship at some point in our teenage years and then a tumultuous relationship on and off in our twenties. Things got complicated, but I guess they always were. We have been best friends since we were just small children. There's a closeness between us that no one would understand. She knows things about me I'll never tell anyone. I will always be there for her, and she will always be under my protection. But as we grew, I saw her life going in one direction while mine was going in another.

As we grew into hormonal teenagers and our friendship bloomed into a full-blown relationship, I have held Kathrine up on a pedestal. She was the good equalizing my bad. Two complete opposites. While she lived a normal life next door to us with her mom and dad, I lived in hell with mine. While she held radiant smiles on her beautiful face daily, I held a brooding frown. We couldn't have lived more of an opposite life if we had tried. But I loved her. And she loved me. It was a love of true friendship in the beginning. She stuck by me through all the turmoil that life brought. When her father forbid her from seeing me, I understood why, and to some degree, I agreed with him. I was no good for her. But at the time, she was my girl. My outlet. The person I could talk to when my mom wouldn't listen to me when I begged her to leave. I was no good for Kathrine, I knew that and eventually, I started to push her away, but she fought it. She fought me. We started to sneak out in the middle of the night to see each other. The shed behind her house became "our place." She was the first woman's body I entered. It was teenage heaven and became my outlet.

When I made the rash decision to leave my home, running away, and start living on the streets with my sister, I knew I hurt her. I left without giving her an explanation. I felt shitty for it, but it had to be done in that manner. There was no way she would just let me walk away. It wasn't that I didn't care about her anymore. It was the complete opposite. I did care. She had a life ahead of her and I needed to make one for my sister and me.

It was a rash decision that specific stormy night. I had planned on doing it, I just didn't know the specific date I would leave. I knew I had to save some money before taking my baby sister into the vicious world with me. I was naive though, not realizing how fast our money would be depleted. I had saved for months, stealing tens and twenties from my father's wallet after he passed out for the night. For weeks, I held the secret of leaving while I bed down between Kathrine's legs nightly. We talked about the future, even though I knew she wouldn't be a part of mine, but I entertained her in her dreams of a future. I didn't want to break her heart. She had doe eyes when mine were dead, but in the end, I crushed her.

The last night Kathrine and I were together was one of the worst nights living at 34 Decanter Road. When my father smacked my sister for shedding tears because he was in one of his rages and hit my mother, knocking her across the room, I had made my decision. I no longer wanted to exist, let alone live in my childhood home. I knew I needed out. I knew I didn't want the same thing for Hope that my mother and I had endured. When he brought tears to Hope's eyes and my mother sat there with her own hopeless tears dripping down her bruised cheek, doing nothing, the vacancy I saw in her was so transparent it was scary. I knew I could no longer worry about my mom. She had refused to leave so many times.

I made my decision that night. My baby sister wasn't going to live her teenage years the way I did. She had already seen too much. I hated my mother that night. I hated everything she stood for. I left that night with more bruises on my body than I had ever endured from my father's fists. I attacked him when he smacked Hope. I tackled him to the floor and pummeled him, throwing fist after fist. I grabbed my sister's hand as he laid there soundless, looked at my mother one final time and rushed out the front door with Hope in my hand. Later that night, when my father was passed out on the couch and my mother fell into a fitful sleep, I climbed through the window, grabbed both mine and Hope's trash bags filled with our clothes and left for good.

The only falter in my steps was because of Kathrine. We had planned to meet again that night. We were two horny teenagers who couldn't get enough of each other. As I was creeping down the side of my childhood home with our trash bags in hand, I watched Kathrine slip out her window and run to the shed with a smile on her face. I knew she would wait forever for me. I didn't show. Twenty minutes later, at seventeen years old, I was halfway across town headed to the dilapidated foreclosed building that was once someone's home while Kathrine sat and waited for me to show.

To her, I had vanished into thin air that night.

To me, I had shed my old skin for a new thick layer.

Two years later, Kathrine accidently found me. I didn't want to bring her into the world I had entered on the streets. So many times, I had wanted to hear her sweet, hopeful voice. She was always my comfort when I no longer had any. As much as I wanted to talk to her, I knew I couldn't. Two years had passed. I had changed. I watched her grow into a beautiful woman those few times I made it back across town and waited to catch a glimpse of her. She was going off to college while I had become accustomed to the ruthlessness of the streets. Even as bad as it was living in the filth of the streets, I wouldn't change a thing. It was better than living at home. The streets held an air of darkness, and day by day I was becoming darker inside. I had my father to thank for that. There was a small part that held an emotion I kept safe in the muscle that beat in my chest. It was love, and I held that love I experienced from my mother, sister, and Kathrine like a locked away treasure. It was the only thing that kept me human. Three females who were so significant in my life. My sister looked at me like I was her savior, which, I guess I was. Kathrine and I shared the hormonal teenage love, and my mother, her love was the maternal love that got me through those tough nights until she disintegrated inside, becoming an emotionless shell of herself.

All completely different forms of love.

The building my sister and I lived in was in ruins, but it became ours, our home and the basement became a business. Today, the structure looks nothing like it did that first night we laid or heads down. A few months after being on our own, I turned the basement into an underground fighting ring. Every Saturday night I held matches. Two years after leaving, I watched Kathrine walk through the door with her boyfriend. He had a friend fighting that night. The place was packed, but I watched her from my perch while I took bets. She was nervous. She didn't belong in a place like that. We couldn't have been more different at that point in our lives. When her boyfriend left her standing alone in a packed basement full of unsavory men, I watched her shrivel with fear. She was so beautiful, and in no way did she belong in my basement filled with degenerate, blood thirsty men. I made my way over to her when a guy approached her. Her head swiveled from left to right looking for her boyfriend. I knew exactly where he was and who he was with, and it wasn't with his girlfriend. I warned the guy off that approached her. She held my gaze in shock. She couldn't believe it was me standing before her. But it was, just a different version of me. Without thinking, she threw her arms around my neck. I stiffened at the familiar contact then I pulled her off me. I brought her to a part of the basement no one knew about. The building had tunnels that led nowhere. All dead ends except for one. I knew this place like the back of my hand. I selfishly took her down one that led to another room. When she wrapped her arms round me again, excited to see me, I took advantage of it and plowed myself into my long-lost home.

I impregnated Kathrine that night in my selfish abandon seeking her comfort.

One month later she showed up and told me she was pregnant.

Two months after that, she showed up again and told me she had lost the baby. I was crushed for her but also relieved for myself. That was the last time I saw her. I told her to never come back. I didn't want her to be relevant in the life I had made for myself. Selfishly, I wanted her there, but selflessly I scared her away, showing her the guy I had become. It wasn't until three years later while I was standing guard as Mr. Heart and Antonio conducted business that I saw her in the middle of a dance floor at the night club we were in downtown. She was celebrating. She had graduated college, top of her class. I was so proud of her. I sent her our childhood drink and watched her as she searched the club, seeking out the man who sent her the Shirley Temple. When our eyes connected, I watched her gasp and place her hand to her chest, directly over her heart. I was no longer the boy she knew, but now a man, one who was one step away from being a Made Man. She took the steps to come to me, but I shook my head in a silent order not to. It may have been years later but the life I once lived was not the same. I was in even deeper. When the meeting ended, I made my way to her, showing her to a table in the far corner. We spent the night talking, reminiscing about our time together. It felt good. We were thankful for having each other, but now that we were adults, we realized life had two separate plans for us. She was going to be a therapist, devoting her time to children and young adults who needed help. A part of me was crushed. I knew it was because of me and the life I had lived that made her choose that profession. I realized that night that I loved her for who she was and what she had done for me. She was so kind and loving. I loved her as a teenage boy and a part of me always will hold that love for her, but she wasn't the one for me. Sadly, I knew by the look in Kathrine's eyes that I was the one for her. After all these years, Kathrine and I have held a dear friendship. She has her life and I have mine, but I know, deep down, she is waiting for me. Our lives couldn't be more opposite from each other, but we have held a true friendship and respect for one another throughout the years and I always will.

As hard as it is for me, I hit decline on Kathrine's call. When the screen goes black so does a part of my heart. Because I know, in the near future, I am going to crush my childhood best friend when I tell her about my angel.

The few hours Giovanni has been gone have been tough. I went from an exhilarating high to a bottomless low. At first, I was fine, buoyant on the air I hadn't been able to deeply inhale in so long. Then I took a shower and used all the amenities in the bathroom. I had to pause at the thought behind the products stocked in the en suite bathroom attached to the room Abigail and I are sleeping in. The majority of them were women's products. It made me wonder if my assumption from this morning when Hope stated she has never seen him bring anyone home was wrong. My emotional state was confusing, multifaceted in their emotional layers. Maybe he doesn't bring women home, but more of *a* woman. Then again, that doesn't make sense either, unless… unless he doesn't like the women he beds showering in his personal space? Though, he bathed me in his personal master bathroom last night. I chide myself for overthinking too much. I know it's my insecurities exacerbating the unstable situation I'm in.

Then I think about the night before. It hits me like a brutal punch to the center of my chest. I sit with my back against the headboard, my body deflating against the soft material while Abby watches cartoons. I left her father, my husband, a man I took vows with. A certain part of me feels awful. Not that I want to remain in the marriage with Tommy, I don't. I'm done with him, I'm done with the abuse, but I feel bad, guilt ridden for Abigail. The uncertainty behind Abigail's future relationship with her father is unclear. I hate not knowing. I don't want her to see him at all, but is that fair to her? I'm not sure it isn't. Tommy has never really wanted to be a parent in Abigail's life. She has always been a nuisance to him. Is it better for her to have her neglectful father in her life or not have one at all? I know when the time comes, Tommy will fight for her only because he doesn't like to lose, not because he wants his daughter to share in his life.

Then my thoughts jump to the two of us being here, in Giovanni's two-story grand penthouse, his home. The place is immaculate. Every bit of it shines with an impeccable glow. The modern flair is seductive and sexy, yet the brown-suede half-circled couch adorned with oversized pillows in the middle of the sunken living room is comfy and cozy. His master suite, from what I remember from last night, is the ultimate man's bedroom; it's sexy and seductive, masculine in its décor. Curiosity gets the best of me as I sit here thinking about it. While Abby is watching cartoons, I sneak down the hallway and creep up the open step, glass lined back staircase. Automatic lights lead the way with each pad of my foot that I take to his master. His room is just as my hazy, sex-intoxicated mind remembers. It is dark and mysterious with its matte black walls and illuminated multi-tiered ceiling. The luxury furnishings add to its mystery. I never thought a man like him would have such elegant taste. Or maybe, it was the modern simplicity of it all that he was attracted to.

I take the two steps up to his platform bed and slide my hand across the precisely made bedding. The soft tips of my fingers float over the luxurious material of his white comforter. I think back to his authoritative clutch on my hips while he held me in place as he plunged into my body. It was unforgiving and controlling but also attentive and compassionate. His world is so different than mine. Where mine is chaos, his is controlled. While my house with Tommy was your standard middle-class house, filled with ordinary furnishings, it was never a home. Where Giovanni's house is immaculate, sterile almost, furnished with such high dollar items you would think it would be cold, but it's quite the opposite; it's warm and welcoming.

I lower myself to the edge of his bed and stare up at the intricate ceiling. My own vulnerable image reflects back at me. The mirrors above mimicked a photograph of a lost woman captured in time as I still beneath the reflection. I lay back, letting the supple material caress my skin. It's cool and refreshing, just like its owner. I twist my head to glance at the black velvet tufted wall that his bed is adjacent too. It's exceedingly masculine and intimidating as it towers high above me. The four black ornate hooks almost invisible to the eye anchored high and low on each side, twist knots in my belly. I'm lost in thought thinking back to the night before. I barely know the man behind the expensive suit, but I let him restrain my hands and have control over my body.

I reach over and curiously running the tips of my fingers over the solid, cold circular ring. I'm perplexed but also curious to say the least. Being restrained is something I have never desired. It's a loss of control and I already had enough of that my whole life. I'm assuming that is what they are for since he had me strapped up last night to his weight machine. Even in the beginning stages of Tommy and my relationship, when I did trust him,

I wouldn't allow it. Maybe that was a sign I never paid attention to. Maybe I never really did trust him. Maybe inside I always knew but because of my childhood, watching the dynamic between my mother and father I thought what Tommy and I had was better because to the eye it was until it wasn't. Then I think back to the night before—I let Giovanni have his way with me. I took pleasure in every insecure, uncertain second of his ministrations. I question myself, how that could be? He told me I would feel free from the pressure of having to touch him, and in return I would let go. He was right, I did. I trusted him to take care of me, respect me, and he did. I soared, crowning at a sexual point I had nothing to compare it to except for a majestic mountain at its highest peak. I was high on endorphins and lightheaded at my ability to trust him.

My heart does a little somersault, flipping with excitement. The anticipation of him owning me again brings a torrent of fresh arousal down my walls. I shift my hips giving the fluid room to bleed into my panties as I close my eyes and wrap my fingers around the cold steel. What would it feel like? What exactly would he do if he had me spread across his sheets and I gave him free reign to do what he pleased? The thought is thrilling and terrifying like a ride on an intimidating rollercoaster where your knuckles turn white from the unknown twists and turns. It's potent, this feeling inside me. He is an intoxicating, powerful man. My spine tingles at the thought while my inner walls contract with a need I hadn't felt in so very long.

"Do they frighten you? Or are you intrigued?"

His deep inquisitive voice startles me. I still, almost as if I had been caught doing something I shouldn't have. My only movement is my head when I twist it in his direction. He is standing at the door, his shoulders so wide they almost touch both sides of the frame. The way his chest narrows down to his waist is captivating. His arms hang by their side. His suit jacket is unbuttoned, both halves hanging freely. The top two buttons of his dress shirt are open, displaying the smallest color of his controversial tattoo and smattering of chest hair. He is sex wrapped up in a dangerous package with a black bow. I can't decipher the expression on his face and the scrutiny in the depth of his eyes. He looks tense. I assume he is mad that I am in his room, his personal space. That would make sense after seeing all the female products in his spare room en suite this morning. I move to sit up, feeling uneasy.

"Stay right there."

I freeze at his command. If it were Tommy that ordered me to stay, I would have been up and off the bed, taking the steps to get far away from him. But I don't move. Not one muscle. I stay right where I lay, watching him with rapt attention. "I never meant to disrespect your space," I nervously mutter when he keeps silent. "I was curious as to what your bedroom looked like in the daylight."

"Answer my question, angel."

He shrugs his shoulders, slipping his jacket over the defined ball of his arms and down his torso in controlled confidence. He takes the steps needed to drop it on the edge of his bed. He watches me, waiting for my answer. He starts the process of rolling his sleeve to his elbow. I'm riveted at the thick, swollen muscles lace with protruding veins. Seeing the raised blue cords filled with blood stretching up his arms, twisting and turning with his movement does something to my insides. It surprises me at how much they turn me on. It's straight up arm porn for me. I never thought veins in a man's forearm could be so sexy, but my belly flutters at the sight of them.

"Isabelle..." His low deep voice commands my attention and answer.

He watches me like a vulture getting ready to devour its prey. He pops the cuff link from his other sleeve and rolls that one up to his elbow with precision too. He stands a few feet from me and slides his hands in his pant pockets. I lay on his massive bed, feeling paralyzed by his gaze. The chemistry between us sparks like a live wire ready to explode after a storm. I can feel his sexual heat from just the few feet separating us. My panties are now soaked with my arousal, something I am so unused to.

My breathing becomes heavy, tightening my upper diaphragm.

He strolls with a prowl to a switch on the wall. He flicks it then closes the door before turning back to me and dominantly ordering, "Do not move."

"Giovanni..." My breathy voice calls to him in question to an unsure moment.

"Do not speak."

My heart slams in my chest. His demand is powerful, forceful in its delivery, yet the cadence behind his tone lets me know I am safe with him. I want to get up. I feel the need to move. The restless anxiety surging through me makes my fingers twitch with the need to touch him. I am not afraid of Giovanni, but his intense demeanor does make me nervous in a way I find electrifying.

My hooded gaze slides up and down his body with each confident swaggering step he takes until he stands between my bent legs hanging over the side of his bed. He surveys my body, studying the dip and swell of my chest while staring down at me. I fidget, not moving from my spot. I am breathtakingly hypnotized in the intensity of his energy. The heavy, silver box link chain shines as it rolls down his arm to his bulky wrist when he places his palm on my pliable stomach, effectively halting my eager squirming body. The linked pieces are masculine just like its owner, and the close interlocking metal is somehow symbolic to who he is. He keeps his loved ones close. The bracelet matches the chain around his neck adorned with a Saint Christopher and Archangel Raphael pendant that is now swinging above me because he has leaned down to be parallel with my body. He looms over me as the back of his hand runs gently over my cheek and slides into my hair.

"Answer my question, Isabelle," he orders from a hair's breadth away from my face. He reaches out with his other hand and wraps his fingers around mine still holding the metal ring attached to his headboard.

"Are you upset that I am in your room?"

"No." He firmly closes his fingers around mine, causing me to grip the metal with more strength. "Pull on it." His heavy breath enraptures me, beating against my flustered flesh. "Hard. Test it. See if you have enough strength to dislodge it."

I try. I yank hard, jerking my body beneath his. The clatter is loud with each pull, but it doesn't budge. "I can't." My husky voice shakes.

"You can't," he confirms, agreeing with a smile. "You still trust me?"

"Yes, but the level of your intensity is making me nervous," I answer him with honesty.

"Good girl. I always want you to tell me the truth."

The hand, palm flat on my stomach curls and dips under the waistband of the leggings I'm wearing. His fingers dip, grazing the top of my mound. In all my nervousness I still want him to go lower, but he doesn't. He pulls his hand from inside my pants and grabs both sides, yanking them down my legs in haste. He gazes at my bare bottom, licking his lower lip before swooping me up into his arms only to lay me dead center in the middle of his bed with an order not to move. My heart slams against my ribs. I swallow the large amount of saliva pooling in my mouth. He stands at the foot of the bed, watching me, deliberately teasing me as he unbuttons the third button on his shirt with an unhurried show, exposing more of his chest and provocative tattoo.

His heavy gaze dips to my core. "Open your legs, angel."

My knees tremble. He has so much electric energy running through me I almost feel faint. I open my thighs, but my modesty only allows an inch. His fourth button becomes free when he commands, "Wider."

Fuck. He is challenging me.

My insecurities rage with deceptive warning to hide myself. I have a gorgeous man fully clothed standing before me as I lay here fully exposed from the waist down. My white tank top rides over the pouch of my stomach up to my waist with each wiggle of my body. The rippled skin I have never been able to get rid of after giving birth to Abigail is on full display. It is not dark in his room, nor does it have even the hint of dusk to help my insecurity. No, the sun shines through the skyline as bright as a summers clear day could get. My breath becomes short little burst of self-doubt. I was insecure last night in the soft night light but today, every flaw, every blemish, every single mark on my body I expressed my concerns to him last night will shine. My lack of experience and insecurities shows in my meek confidence.

"Wider, angel." His voice softens as he reaches the fifth button of his shirt. "When I get to the last button and my shirt hits the floor, I want you fully naked, exposed to my eyes, and both hands gripping each handle on the headboard."

The nerves beneath my flawed flesh surge with a viciousness. Every endorphin I have rages. Every emotion that rushes through my limbs plays with my thoughts, waiting for the devil's words to ridicule me in some way.

I want to jump out of my skin and run for the sake of my psyche, saving myself from the emotional abuse I have come to know so well. But then I look up, connecting eyes with the gorgeous man before me. He stands there with desire churning in his eyes. He is a man, a real man, not the devil I have become accustomed to. And that man can read my emotions as if they were his own.

"You don't know how beautiful you are, do you?"

I whimper at his stimulating words.

"Those defining lines marring your stomach, hips, and thighs from the birth of your daughter are artwork I would pay millions for. You see them as flaws. I see them as a one-of-a-kind flawless painting. The art of a genuine, selfless woman who brought a beautiful little girl into this world."

Tears spring to my eyes at his kind words. His knee dips the mattress on the edge of the bed. He points a finger at the hook on the headboard, silently telling me to grab onto them. I take a deep breath, inch my shirt up my body, then toss it over the side of his bed. I lay before him, fully nude with nothing but goose bumps decorating the soft tissue of my aroused flesh.

The clasps clank, groaning with the strength of my finger's squeezing at the metal.

"Do not let go, Isabelle."

My only rational thought brings one word over my lips. "Abigail."

He prowls up the mattress from the end of the bed with his suit jacket in hand and hovers over me. "Lift your bottom." He grins then points to the security screen showing Abby still watching TV. Then he slides his suit jacket under me. His grin becomes devious mischief at my confusion for the need to have his jacket beneath my core. "You just enjoy what your body is going to experience." He kisses the tip of my nose then leans back, places both his hands on my knees, and spreads me wide open. The cool air hits my wet folds before my outer knees touch the silky material of his dress coat. "Do not let go of those hooks, angel," he warns before dipping down, running his nose through my glistening folds, and inhaling my scent. He closes his eyes and releases a manly growl. Then he drops his head lower and with one long swoop of his thick tongue, he has my back arching off his bed. He plunges his tongue through my creases and unearths my clitoris.

The hooks my fingers are gripping clatter against their base as I start to bloom with intense sensation. I struggle to stay still, wanting to thrash my body across his bed, but I won't dare let go. With each swipe, nibble, and arousing bite he graces my core with his talent, I feel something building in my lower stomach. My clitoris becomes painfully engorged with the rush of blood and my insides feel like white hot ice. The next few minutes are the most sensual, unbelievably vulnerable, sexual experience I have ever had. I feel a sensation, a sensation I have never felt before. My eyes spring open wide and through the blurriness of sexual desire, they latch with Giovanni's. His wicked grin alerts me to the fact he knows exactly what he has just manipulated my body to do. The chaotic, unsure moment has me starting to panic.

"Relax, my angel. I know exactly what is going to happen. I'm the one coaxing it from your body. The sensation you are feeling is normal. It's not what you think it is. Now, relax your muscles and give yourself permission to let go," his husky growl orders as two of his fingers stroke my front wall like he is calling to me.

He owns my body and cherishes my raw sexuality in that moment. He makes me feel secure and dare I say... beautiful.

Then he consumes the burst of fluid he charms from my body with his skilled fingers and tongue. I come so hard I lose my breath, dizziness swirls through my head as my hearing rings with a pitch so high, I'm sure only angels can hear the energy behind it. I scream to the heavens above as my stomach coils and my back arches off his bed with a demonic twist. He changes my life in that moment, giving me a piece of freedom, however small it is.

He prowls up the bed and over my body on his knees with a manly gait and devilish smirk, infusing his glistening lips to mine, bonding us. My body jostles a bit when he reaches up, and one by one, he releases each one of my fingers still clutching the metal he ordered me to hold onto. His grin is wicked when he releases my lips to peer down at me. I can feel his erection on my belly. I anxiously wait for his welcoming onslaught, ravishing me, taking his own pleasure, but then he shocks me. He moves off the bed and holds out his hand, waiting for me to take it. I slide my nude, limp body over the edge and stand before his partially clothed one. He pulls me against his body and wraps one arm around my waist as the other slides up my torso between my breast to rest at the bottom of my throat. His thumb forces my chin up to look at him. "Come. I brought home some lunch. Normally, I would tend to you myself, take care of you, but Abigail is on the move."

I quickly try to turn my head to look at the cameras, but I am held in place. My undivided attention is to be on him. Days ago, I would have protested, fought the control of a man. If it were Tommy, I would have struggled and fought for my freedom until I was utterly exhausted and bruised, but here I stand, restricted in this man's unwavering arms, and I accept it willingly with a warm welcoming smile.

"You go take care of yourself and I'll take care of her. Meet me downstairs so I can feed you."

That right there is why I don't fight to be released from his clutches. With Tommy, my motherly instincts would have been on high alert, the wrath of a mother's storm in full bloom. With Giovanni, the man that just made me see stars and wants to put food in mine and my daughter's belly, I become compliant because I know in my heart, he is different.

Now, I just need my head to agree with my heart.

I nod my agreeance, stunned at how easily and comfortably he has made my decision. I go to step back, thinking he will release me, but he doesn't. He holds me tighter and intently gazes down into my eyes. I can still feel his erection on my stomach. I timidly move my hand down and plant my palm over the span of his length and girth. My palm tingles as it kicks beneath my touch. His eyes close just a fraction, then he grabs a hold of my hand possessively and braces it against him, stopping my cautious movement. On a deeply released breath he says, "You were beautiful just now, open to me and willing once you got passed the fear of what was happening to your body. I will never guide you in the wrong direction. This," he rumbles, squeezing my palm braced against his erection. "This will have to wait." He dips down, kisses my forehead, and releases me with an order. "Ten minutes, Is. Then I come looking for you."

I smile at him, confirming I heard his order. I glance at the camera out of habit, checking to make sure my little girl is okay. Then I glance over to where his stained jacket still lays on his bed. Astonished at the amount of fluid he forced from my body. I turn to him with a shy smile and murmur, "I ruined your jacket."

"The jacket is replaceable. You are not."

Giovanni
CHAPTER TWENTY-TWO

I left Isabelle and Abigail curled up on the couch watching a movie with full stomachs. Isabelle brought up her two jobs, how she called in today, but tomorrow she had to go to work. Little does she know… it's not happening. I will discuss it with her tonight when I get back home. Whether she likes it or not, she isn't going back to work. If she thinks for one second that her ex won't show up to either one of her places of employment, she isn't thinking clearly. She is safe at my place, where she will stay for the time being until I can take care of him.

I walk through the back entrance of Temptations. The music is loud, blaring a heavy beat as I walk to the private elevator that will take me to Antonio's office. It's late, later than I would usually be here but after this afternoon's lunch, I wanted to spend some time with the girls. That spent time brought me through dinner too until I really had to leave for work. I would have taken the night off if I could have but tonight is our meeting with Cillian McKittrick.

All meetings are risky, but the ones that are enticed as new business ventures are always the most dangerous. We approach with wide, wise eyes. It could be a set-up, a perspective "new" business partner could have joined forces with an enemy of ours and lined up an ambush. Our heads are always on a swivel. Tonight, all heads and eyes will be on deck, even Joseph will be there to listen, watch, and absorb.

I'm waiting for the elevator doors to open when I hear my phone chime from inside my pocket. I quickly grab it thinking it might be Isabelle. Along with lunch, I brought home a new iPhone for her as well. She had my number in the burner phone I gave her but that was left when she came to my place last night. I told her to call or message me if she needed anything. A sudden wave of unease rips up my spine. I know she is okay. I know no one can enter my home, but the feeling is still there, and I don't like it one bit. An unknown number flashes with a message.

Unknown: *You may think you have won but you have not.*

The elevator door slides open just as my thumb hits *My Angel* on my contact log. My stride is slow as I head down the hallway to Antonio's office. Luca is at the door, which only means Lilah is inside. I give him a trivial nod, acknowledging his presence. In return he gives me an inquisitive regard as the call connects and starts ringing in my ear. I stop in the middle of the hallway and wait for her to answer. With each piercing ring that she doesn't pick up, the more tension fills my spine. The call rings off and the voicemail starts to record. I hang up and do what any man in my position would do. I hit the security app on my phone that connects with all the cameras in my penthouse. The feed pops up with a picture from every single room. I search through each eraser sized image, enlarging them, until I see them. Both my girls are lounging out on the couch, knocked out. Abigail is tucked under her momma's protective arm, curled inside her core.

Two angels.

My two angels.

With a relieved forward step in the direction of Antonio's office, I click off the app and go back to the message. I study it, looking for any clues. The context of which the sentence is said, but there is nothing. It could have come from anyone. It is just a plainly written message typed out by a faceless coward. The fact that it came tonight, the night after Isabelle left her husband and we have a meeting with a new buyer, sends red flags flying high.

Distracted, I grab the handle and stop before opening the door. "They decent?" I look back over my shoulder at Luca waiting for his answer.

"I believe they are just having dinner at the moment."

"Imagine that." I huff with levity. "D, here?"

"He just went downstairs to take care of a situation at the bar."

Just in case, I give the door two raps with my scarred knuckles. Antonio hollers to enter. I open the door to one set of eyes that smile from morning until night and the other blazing fire.

"Why is my number one caporegime late?" Antonio lashes his anger at my tardiness.

I hold his leer in return, giving him no answer before turning to greet his wife. "Hello, Lilah."

She pops out of the chair, gives me a hug and kiss, saying hello in return before turning back to Antonio. "If you're taking Luca from my side then tell me what the plan is?" she asks her husband with a demanding tone.

Inside, I chuckle. I know exactly what she is doing. She and I both know the extent of her husband's wrath and she thinks if she intersects, he will calm down some.

She couldn't be more wrong.

His scowling glare is still on me. A silent lashing before turning to his wife. "Lorenzo will be here in a minute to pick you up. You and Romeo will spend the night at my parents." He pulls her into his arms. "I will join you as soon as I can."

"Maybe if you show up with a better attitude then you had over our dinner date, I would be more inclined to give you some of the dessert you were so eager to have."

"Dolcezza, you will open your legs for me."

"We will see, wolfie."

He growls his displeasure at her challenging retort as he pulls her in closer to his body to say his goodbyes. I give them privacy by walking to the glass wall and peering down at the crowd below. Through the flames of the shooting cannons of fire above the dance floor, something catches my eye, but I can't be sure I saw what I think I saw. The sound of the door opening and closing behind me alerts me that we are now alone. Antonio's footsteps come closer and closer.

"Want to tell me why my top guy was late?" he asks, striding up next to me.

"How long has Hunt been here?" I ignore his demand for an answer.

"Came in a little while ago. Why?"

"Not sure. I think I just saw him talking to the guy I had the meeting with a few weeks back."

"Where?" He leans in examining the crowd below.

"Already gone. Hunt's walking to his private lounge." I jerk my chin at the catwalk across from us.

"You sure?"

"No. Your fucking pyrotechnics distorted my vision." I turn from the glass and with a stiff stride I walk back into the heart of the room. I toss him my phone, showing him the anonymous message.

"That message didn't make you hours late."

"Didn't say it did. I was home with my girls, making sure they were okay. Doing the exact opposite of you when you imprisoned Lilah in your penthouse when you couldn't get your shit together." He doesn't disagree with me, but he isn't happy with my statement. Antonio and I walk that fine line between friend and employer. When him and Lilah were having their problems, I was the one busting his ass to get in gear when it came to their relationship. I didn't appreciate the way he handled her, and I can see now that he doesn't agree with how I am handling my situation.

"Your girls?" he questions, watching me. I let his two-word interrogation sit in the heavy air between us. "Where in the club did you see them?" He changes the direction of his inquiry to business when I don't answer.

"By the back second set of stairs." I'm telling him as I walk behind his desk and wait for him to activate the security feed. "Right there." I point at the screen. "The look between the two. The slight movement of their lips."

"How the fuck did you see that?"

"Because like you said, I am your top capo, and I know how to do my fucking job. Which means when I show up late, you shouldn't question why, rather ask as a friend if there is anything you can do."

"Business first, brother."

"Not between us, it isn't."

The pregnant pause in the room swelters with energy. "You think the message is from the soon-to-be dead ex?" He changes the subject back to personal.

"I have no idea. What I do know is we need to go into the meeting tonight with our eyes wide fucking open."

"Agreed."

The dank air from the wharf side wraps its heavily fogged limbs around my bulky, alert mass. The group, except for Antonio, Demetri, and I, are scattered around the yard in covert positions, waiting for Cillian McKittrick to show his face. Luca is manning security at the front gate. Cillian isn't late, we're just calculatedly early. We sit. We wait. We watch. We stand guard anticipating how many men he will chose to bring in his entourage. Will it be more than a handful? A flashy show, the false sense there is more strength in numbers like parents teach their teenagers. That notion is just a ruse to the inexperienced eye. Three of New York City's deadliest men are standing in a circle waiting to conduct business with a new associate.

As the minutes tick by, I silently stand by listening to Demetri and Antonio talk. It's just gibberish to pass the time and nothing but white noise to my ears.

"What do you plan on doing with the problem you've acquired?" Demetri turns his attention to me.

"Take his last breath and revel in the terror in his eyes as I watch the life drain from his face." My straightforward, emotionally detached statement informs him of my plans for the piece of shit Isabelle married.

"Yeah, figured that was coming." Demetri nods with approval.

"You got a plan?" Antonio chimes. There's an edge to the tone of his voice. It's one I'm not appreciative of. I shoot him a glare telling him so. "How bad was it?" he questions, his voice now less harsh than two seconds ago.

I shoot Antonio an expression that tells him it was bad. No words accompany my dead serious scowl. I'm not willing to give my girl's intimate hardships a life beyond her thick walls. I won't divulge that the dark marks on her fair skinned body may fade with time but will never fully heal. I won't explain how the emotional abuse has destroyed her confidence, or the fact that even in the dim light when she lays before me after I request she remove her clothing, how she squirms like a virgin on prom night because she is so uncomfortable in the skin of her own body. Or how I can see it in her eyes that she loathes the fact that I have become a witness to each and every trauma inflicted. Or the fact that the dark shadows under her eyes, that will someday turn back to the soft pink of her freckled flesh with sleep and healing, will always haunt me.

Marks are milestones.

I have my own countless number.

She has more.

Each beating he has inflicted on her has made her stronger, not weaker. My girl is tough. She just has to believe she is.

"He's here," Antonio alerts us. He holds two fingers up, telling us to be quiet while he listens to Luca through the earpiece.

"How many?" I inquire, adjusting my shoulders while reaching for my piece at my back, getting ready for battle if need be.

"Four."

"Respectable," I murmur, pointing out. Not too showy but has men to watch his back.

"That we know of. Keep your eyes open," Antonio speaks into the late spring air.

The black town car slowly rolls up, the gravel crunching with each roll of the car's tires before stopping a good five feet away from where we hold our position. An SUV parks behind him. A tall man with wavy reddish-brown hair steps out from the town car. He adjusts his open suit jacket, snapping it into place on his shoulders with strength. I size him up from head to toe. His frame is large and by the looks of it he doesn't miss a workout. He holds himself with confidence and it's not a spurious performance. He is that secure in himself. I can see it in the stride of his step and the way he maintains the set of his shoulders.

His men trail when he takes the necessary steps to approach us. He stops halfway to where we are positioned. Without glancing back to look at his loyal employees, he holds his hand in the air ordering them to standdown. He takes the remaining steps until he strategically places himself directly in front of Antonio.

"Mr. Heart, spelled like the muscle in your chest. How poetic." His voice is deeper than I expected, but his eyes are sharp and keen to his surroundings like I assumed they would be.

"You've done your research. Tell me, after learning the spelling of our family name, did you dig further and find out why my father chose to change the spelling?"

"Indeed, I have. It is the reason I have chosen your organization to do business with. Your father has heart. Pun intended." He tilts his head to the side slightly with respect.

"Without a doubt he does. Many who have crossed him don't."

"I have been informed."

"We are the only organization to do business with if you want to do business off this pier or in this state."

"Ahh." He clucks his tongue. "I see we have monopolized."

"It's the only way to do business. Is it not? But you already knew that." Antonio feels him out.

"Agreed." He lets that sit there a minute before raising his hand and greeting, "Cillian McKittrick."

"Antonio Heart, underboss to Robert Heart in the Heart Organization, as you already know. My two caporegime's Giovanni Moretti and Demetri Carbone." Antonio gestures to the both of us. "What kind of business are you interested in conducting, Mr. McKittrick?"

"I want to..." He rocks his head side to side contemplating on how much he wants to disclose. I can see the flicker of something behind his eyes. A hint of something emotional. This is personal for him. "Build an empire like you."

"This your lifelong fantasy you conjured up as a teenage boy while lying in bed jerking off?" Antonio's voice becoming harsh, knowing he's being toyed with. "Being evasive will only get you sent back to your mother country. If you want to conduct business with this organization, you would do well to speak openly about your desires. What's the meaning behind the vague statement, Mr. McKittrick, because I already have the empire, I own this city and my name alone is held in high regard through this country as well as my families mother country. I don't need you. Now, tell me why you need me?"

He grips ahold of his beard, pulling down at the coarse hairs growing from his chin as he contemplates his next words. "We have a common interest. I won't know if I can trust you unless we proceed with a side deal."

"And that would be?"

"Fifty kilos of pure snow. I need it moved, kept for the time being before it is distributed through another region."

"You and I both know that's not a side deal. Enticing me, assuming I am an unintelligent, eager boss trying to prove a point will not bode well for you, Mr. McKittrick. I suggest you reevaluate your strategy."

180

"Surely, you do not want to bypass on the amount of cash I'm willing to give you for your troubles, Mr. Heart. It's five million in green back."

"Which I do not need."

"No one turns down a chance to profit five million for only housing product." Cillian tries to discredit Antonio's morals.

"I just did. I will not give you my bottom line. The money you are offering bears no significance to my bank account compared to life behind bars. Moving fifty kilos would be a gift, a… let's say, show of faith in our stance on how we run our organization. However, games will not be tolerated. Your product will go up in smoke if you are not sincere in your dealings. Do we understand each other?"

"I believe we do."

"We will move your product. It will be kept in a safe house to which you will not know it's location. If you can agree to those terms, we have a deal. If not, you can remove yourself from my state and take your business back to your homeland."

He nods. Aggravation and appreciation at the forefront of his expression.

"How much time do you need before shipping?"

"One week. The shipment can be here as soon as tomorrow."

"Tomorrow then. Midnight. Bring your men. My men will not be doing the off load."

"Understood." Cillian reaches his hand out in a gesture to seal the deal.

Before Antonio will accept his hand, he says, "Mr. McKittrick, be advised that tomorrow at midnight I want the real reason why you are here. If you do not divulge your true purpose, then your product will not be off loaded." He grabs a hold of his hand then throws his other in the air with a whirl signaling to Luca to open the gates. "Enjoy the rest of your evening," Antonio dismisses him.

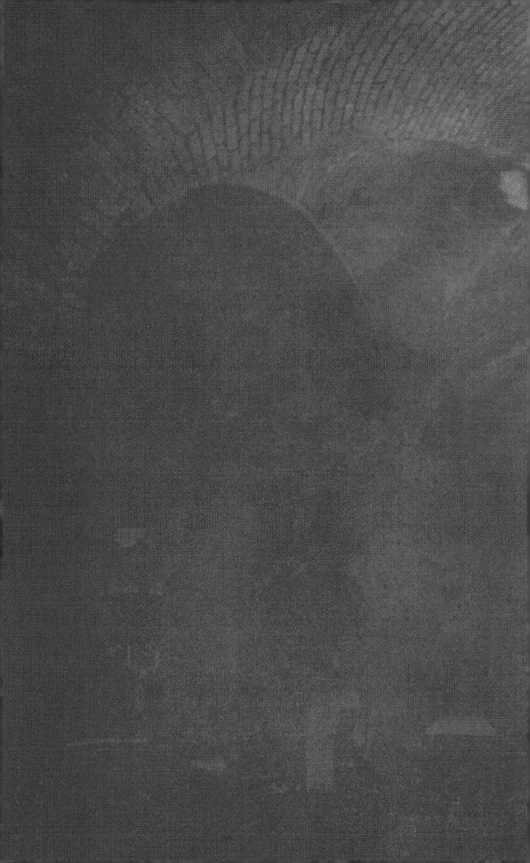

Giovanni
CHAPTER TWENTY-THREE

It's late, well past one in the morning. When the elevator door to my penthouse slides open, I'm assaulted by the sweet smell consuming the air. I glance to the left and see a massive mess strewn across my kitchen island. I take another step into the room and glance over into the living room. Two bodies lay lifeless across the U-shaped sectional, and one is on the floor by the coffee table. I swallow from the sight before me. The television is muted, but I take notice of the movie that is playing. A chick-flick. I wish I could smile at the scene before me but seeing the still bodies in my living room bothers me deeply. My feet move across the room at a pace I don't want to evaluate, but I know in that small, locked box in the back of my head, it's panic from past traumas of seeing a loved one in the same position countless times.

Only this time it's different.

My sight goes directly to Isabelle's chest. The soft flutters of her breathing make her full breasts rise and fall. I glance to Abby and watch how her little mouth sucks on the tip of her thumb. Then I look to my sister, who is sprawled across the area rug like it's the most comfortable place to be.

Sugar comatose.

By the looks of my kitchen island loaded with all the fixings for ice cream sundaes, the three of them are on the downward slope of the sugar rush they rode high on.

"Hey," her sweet soft voice calls my attention from my sister.

"Hey," I return, her sleepy greeting causes me to smile down at her beautiful drowsy face.

"What time is it?"

"Late." I reach down and brush the back of my hand over the small scattering of pale freckles on her cheek.

"We made a mess in your kitchen."

"I can see that." I hold my hand out for her to take.

She shifts, lacing her fingers through mine, pulling herself up with the help of my strength until she is kneeling in front of me. My hands go directly to her face, holding her in place so my lips can lavish on the softness of hers.

"I'll clean it up," she whispers, attempting to shift from my hold.

"It's okay. I'll do it." I hold her in place.

"No. I will. I can see you're not happy."

"I'm fine," I tell her, trying to excuse the uneasiness I feel at my kitchen being destroyed. The chaos of food gives me a sense of lost control. It's something I am going to have to work on. I can't expect Abby or even Isabelle to keep my place as immaculate as I do. The expectation would be unreasonable. "How about you put Abby to bed while I kick my sister out. Meet me in the kitchen." I peck her lips one last time, holding myself back from wanting more of her.

"Deal. Wait for me and I will help you."

I give her one last kiss and watch her shift off the couch. She has a pair of my shorts on. They hang off her body. The red satin material swooshes around her legs like an oversized dress. I can't help but chuckle when I notice she has them banded up at the waist with a rubber band. Even though my shorts are huge on her, when she bends over and embraces Abby, the shorts mold to her perfect ass. An ass I would like to sink my teeth into right now. My hand goes directly to my growing cock. I give myself a stern squeeze, talking myself off the ledge. I wake my sister up and politely kick her ass out. Once the elevator slides shut, I secure it, locking it for the night. With a sexually frustrated, somewhat internal groan, I turn and head towards the kitchen as I watch Isabelle carry Abby through the room. I throw my jacket over one of the barstools and roll my dark sleeves to the crease of my elbows. With a deep inhale, I survey the damage around me. There is caramel, chocolate syrup, napoleon ice cream, cherries, and rainbow sprinkles everywhere. The only thing that isn't smeared across my counter is the can of whipped cream still sitting on the counter, sealed. It shocks me when I chuckle with the thought that they had to have had a food fight. My next thought is I wish I could have seen it, but then almost instantly my stomach twists with uneasiness.

My phone chirps with a message. I pull it from my pocket knowing it's Hope just letting me know she is safe and sound in her apartment, but I need to make sure it's not another message from the unknown number. After confirming it is in fact my sister, I toss my phone to the only clean spot on the counter by the stove. I step into the pantry, unbutton the top two buttons of my shirt to give myself some more air, and grab a roll of paper towels. I walk back into the kitchen and stop short just before the massive mess. A wide grin pulls at my lips. Fuck me, my dick painfully grows with rapid strength at the vision I just had flash through my head. I throw the paper towels to the kitchen counter and walk over to the lights, dimming them. I walk to the opposite side of the kitchen and flick the switch for the security feed. I can see Isabelle walking down the long hallway heading back to the kitchen, to me. I post up against the end of the island facing the opening of the hallway, having every intention of having my vision come true. I cross my arms over my chest and legs at the ankles, and I wait for her beautiful face to come around the corner.

She stops in her tracks when she sees me. Her eyes glance around the kitchen, observing the mess that hasn't been touched yet. She fidgets in her spot, her hands wringing together.

"Isabelle." My deep voice greets her, the tone of it letting her know the next hour or so will be different than what she is expecting.

"I'll… I will clean it." She fumbles over her words, intently watching me.

"Come here." I crook my index finger at her then point at the spot directly in front of me.

With small, unsure steps, she walks directly to me. Even as uncertain as she is—how nervous she is at the moment thinking that I am pissed off about the kitchen—she still trusts me enough to come to me when I command it. She stands directly in front of me. Her green gaze peering up at me with innocent doe eyes. I reach forward and slide both my hands down her sides until I get to the rubber band holding up my oversized shorts. With a tug, I pull the elastic free and let the material fall to the floor. I stuff the rubber band in my pocket then slide my hands over the flare of her bare hips and up her waist, manipulating her t-shirt along with my movement. She lifts her arms over her head then lets them drop in front of her when the shirt hits the floor.

She stands before me completely nude.

"Perfection," I whisper, openly admiring her body. My index finger and thumb brace the point of her chin in my hand, forcing her gaze up to mine. Her hands connect in front of her, her fingers twisting with nervousness. "Release your hands. Let them hang at your sides. Don't hide from me, angel."

"G…" She blinks a few times, watching, waiting for the unexpected.

"Isabelle." Her twisting fingers slide apart at my deep tone and lets them fall to her sides like I asked. "Fucking perfect." I drop, crouching down in front of her and inhaling the scent of her intoxicating cunt. "You shaved." I look up at her, somewhat shocked as I run the back of my knuckle over the soft, clean unblemished skin.

"I wanted…" She looks off to the side before turning back. "I didn't care before. With him. I didn't care what he thought."

"You did this for me? Or for yourself?"

"Both."

"Good girl. You do it for yourself. You do what makes you feel comfortable with your body and what makes you feel sexy. Don't get me wrong, I like the smooth supple skin against my chin, nose, mouth, and tongue. But if you did it for me, as much as I love your smooth skin, I also love the feel of the coarse strip of your hair pressed against me when I thrust into you, and how I can watch the way your fiery flames of red hair absorb and glisten as my cum weaves its way through your curls when I mark you."

"Christ," she breathes heavily, her shoulders and head dropping.

"Angel, when was the last time you said your prayers to the God you believe in?"

"Why?"

"Because I am about to destroy what he perfected."

"W-What?"

"I have been easy on you. You have destroyed my kitchen. I think it's only fair that I get to destroy you."

"When was the last time you prayed?" she questions me, her voice heavy with sexual desire as she cups the side of my jaw.

"I'm kneeling at my alter now, angel. Your sweet tangy taste is like communion on my tongue. I only bow to my God, Isabelle. And he is not the same God you bow down to."

"Then who is your God?" She places both her hands on my shoulders as I grip her hips.

"The only person it can be. Myself. I am judge, jury, and executioner."

"Then you are my God, my hero."

"I am no hero, Isabelle. No bone in my body says I am a hero. I am a villain through and through, but I will always be your villain."

"Sometimes it's better to have the villain then it is to have the hero. I, of all people, know that. But some villains are heroes, and you are mine, Giovanni." She runs the palm of her small hand over my cheek and cups my jaw while gazing down at me with so much admiration in her eyes.

"Can I eat my dessert now, angel?"

"Did you actually just ask?" She giggles like a schoolgirl just before my two thick fingers glide through her folds and enter her. Her shyness reflects in the flush of her cheeks and chest. I pin her with a heated glare as I dip my head, watching her as I drop down farther. "Only if you promise to— oh God." Her head drops back unable to finish her sentence as I swipe my tongue through her plump, flushed folds.

"You were saying?" I pull back looking up at her, grinning.

"Nothing."

"You were saying nothing, angel?" I tease, blowing my warm breath over her eager nub as I continue working her insides.

"I was… Oh, yeah."

"What was that?" I twist my head and quirk a brow.

"Giovanni?"

"Yes, angel?"

"Please stop teasing me."

"Angel?"

"Y-Yes?" she groans with the slide of my finger.

"I have only just begun," I enlighten her. With a torturously slow glide of my tongue over her soft skin, she moans her pleasure in a way I have never heard her before. I suck the meaty tissue of her mound into my mouth, leaving my bruising mark behind, then I sweep her off her feet and place her bare bottom on the cold stone of the island. "Move back a little and open your legs," I order then take a step back and unbutton my shirt, slowly, watching her watch me. I throw my dress shirt over my suit jacket and move to my pants. I unbutton and slide my zipper down, letting the material hang open, giving my painfully engorged erection some freedom. The whole time I'm manipulating my clothing, I eye her arousal seeping from within her body. Her open thighs glisten like the reflection on the ocean's surface when the full moon shines bright at the tick of midnight. Whether she realizes she is doing it or not, her muscles contract and release, impatiently waiting for something to grab a hold of. "Fuck, you are a beautiful sight," I harshly murmur, swallowing the saliva forming in my mouth.

"Gio…" she moans, her voice low and husky and so sexually addicting I should go to an SA meeting. I watch her with rapt attention. Her hand slides down the center line of her body and with two of her fingers, she glides them over my tongue's playground. I'm jealous of those two digits, but she did it all on her own, no coaxing on my behalf, and that makes me proud as hell for her. Watching her pleasure herself turns me on so much, I about come in my boxer briefs.

My girl is getting comfortable.

"Lie back. All the way," I direct her, stepping forward, ready to make a mess of my dessert.

"Umm, there's lots of—"

"Before this night is through, angel, you are going to be at one with that sugary sweetness you three recklessly threw around my kitchen."

I don't give her a chance to dispute her case. I grab the hand rotating in circles and pull it to my mouth, sucking her nectar from the tips. My eyes connect with hers as my tongue weaves through her fingers. Heat flares between the both of us. My chest constricts with emotion. This woman lying bare in front of me doesn't even know how strong her inner strength is. She has been through so much, but yet, here she lays in a mass of sweetness, knowing I'm going to destroy her in the best possible way, and she never batted an eyelash at my statement.

I step up to her spread legs and jerk her hips down so her bottom meets the edge of the counter. My height lines my partially concealed erection up perfectly with her opening, but I don't want that, not yet. I need her open to me with no barriers between us when the urge I can't hold back hits me. I promised her I was going to ruin her, and I will keep my promise.

I reach over and grab the bottle of Smucker's caramel syrup. With a devious smirk, I squeeze the sugary sweetness down the line of her body, ending with a sticky pool dripping from the meat of her hood to her silky lips. I kiss her inner thigh and bite the thickness of her upper thigh before teasing the heart of her core with the tip of my tongue, consuming her and the caramel. Her moan is husky and euphoric, addicting, and contagious. I groan, slipping a finger over her sticky creases before sliding into her channel.

"Giooo…" she howls, not holding back. And fuck if my dick isn't responsive to her heady voice. I grab a hold of myself and give my length an unsatisfied stroke. "Take them off," she begs, observing the cruel grip I have on my groin. I drop my pants and discard them with a kick. "Briefs too," she whispers her demand.

I slide my finger just a fraction back and curl the tip, playing with the spongy tissue that will set her core fluttering with fire. "Are we making demands now, angel?" I tease.

"Mhmmm," her voice rattles. "What are you doing to me?"

I wickedly grin. "Do you want me to stop?"

"N-No. No, don't stop." Her hands clench the side of the counter.

"Tell me what you want, angel?"

"Your pants. I want them off."

"Tell me why?" I manipulate her core, ruthlessly wielding the power the pad of my finger possesses.

"Mmm. Ahhh. Giovanni," she cries out. "I want to feel you." Her chin trembles with the clench of her jaw as her orgasm starts to bloom.

"Later," I clip, pulling my fingers from within her tightening walls, denying her. I grab the melted carton of ice cream and dribble the liquefied pink mess over both nipples. She gasps at the slight chill still lingering as it touches her heated skin. I run my tongue over my bottom lip as I watch her strawberry flesh spike with need. I reach over her body, making sure I rub the head of my cock against her core as I stretch over her and grab the can of whipped cream just above her head. I twist the red cap off and shake it in-between her unguarded thighs, slowly, observing her writhing body. "Let's see how well you can take a mouth full of cream. Because one day soon, it will be me filling that sweet mouth of yours, Isabelle. Open." I hover the can just above her. She runs her tongue along her lips and does as I order, opening her kiss swollen mouth. "Wider." I move the can closer. "Wider, Isabelle. You need to be prepared for the day I thrust my cock through those pretty tempting lips."

"Giovanni…" Her tongue darts out and wets the soft skin.

"Wider," I demand. "You've seen the size of my cock, felt it in your sweet cunt. That innocent opening you have made with those lips won't cut it. Now open wider, Isabelle."

I spray the cream, filling her mouth. When she goes to swallow, I drop the can to the counter and slide two fingers inside her and consume her mouth with mine. Her back arches and her heels dig into the counter at my sides. Her voice is muffled, and her rigid nipples pierce my chest. I pull back and swallow the cream I sucked from her, then I dip down and run my tongue over the peaks of her chest. I play with her. I tease her. I seduce her with my tongue and fingers. I grab the can once again and spray two rows of perfectly whipped peaks over her breasts. Then I grab the rainbow sprinkles and make her a canvas of colorful, edible art.

I hover above her, watching her, licking her, kissing her, and biting every single piece of flesh I have decorated. The caramel bonds our bodies together. I devour her mouth once again as I slide my first two fingers over her caramelized lips. I pull back from the kiss and slide two fingers in her mouth.

"Suck." I feel my pupils expand, dilating from a craving that is borderline psychotic as I watch her suck the sweetness along with her arousal from my fingers. "Harder." My breathing becomes harsh.

Her moans become a full-bodied wail before she's gasping for breath. I take advantage of her enraptured state and jerk her hips further down the stone counter, letting her bottom drop a bit, tilting her pelvis to meet the demands of my groin. I impale her with my now leaking, raging cock. The sight of her blissful figure twisting with desire and the way her walls clamp down around me when I entered her instantly put me on the verge of coming. I need to pull back before I do, but the hunger I feel for her wants me to empty myself into her, on her, all over her, and then fight through the agonizing tickling pleasure as I keep plowing into her, warring for a successive release. But then I take on the painful pleasure in torturing myself and her by holding us both back from orgasming. I inhale a profound breath to control the beast raging within my loins. Then I ravage her body to a sweaty mess until she becomes limp with sated sexual exhaustion while listlessly bathing in sticky sweetness. When I finally let her come, it's with a pleasurable ache that makes tears leak from the corner of her blurry eyes. I unchain the restraint I have on myself and saturate the tender tissue of her insides with a deep harrowing groan, letting every fiber of man and beast residing inside me go. She has just been fully owned by the tainted blood pumping through my engorged veins and speared with what love I hold in my tortured soul.

Entering Isabelle is like the best hospitality at an exclusive luxury hotel. With half lidded eyes and sympathy for my hardening cock, she squeezes with enthusiastic sincerity. She slept peacefully next to my side after I showered away the sticky mess of the sweets and my cum from the night before. I took her once more on my kitchen island. I had an overwhelming need to be inside her. To not sever the connection between us. I showered her, and I would say I fucked her again against the tile wall then carried her to my bed, where she will stay for the rest of her nights, but that is not the case. What happens between Isabelle and I when we are together is not fucking, or even making love, it's exceedingly beyond that. It's consuming, incinerating energy that devours in the most devastatingly exquisite way. It's the hottest flame a fire rages, torching everything around it but keeping the contents nestled safely in the core as it's being licked by flames until the final eruption.

It's the early morning hours before the sun peaks over the city skyline. I rock into her lax body in a slow rhythm. It's selfish of me, I know. The control I pride myself on has vanished and all I want to do is live inside the heart of her body. I want her nipples caressing my tongue and her cunt sucking the life out of my cock. She whimpers through her orgasm as she bites through the flesh on my shoulder. It's the only point of contact she has except for the length of her body flush beneath me and the heels of her feet digging into my lower back since her wrists are trussed up against my headboard. As her peak crests, she jerks at the unforgiving metal while her body spirals.

Stunning.

She is stunning.

The long length of her restrained body is rapidly becoming my addiction.

I collapse my weight on top of her for just a moment then release her hands. I roll to the side and without having to bring her with me, she automatically follows, fitting herself to my side.

"Good morning," her sleepy, sexually slaked voice chimes.

"It is." My own husky voice fills the space between us. Her hand rests on my stomach. The tips of her fingers lackadaisically play with the line of hair leading to my groin while my arm wrapped around her is playing with the soft curve of her hip.

There's a moment, a quiet moment. It's not tense, but more of a heaviness. I know she is thinking. What woman doesn't? She is deep in thought contemplating her life. In one hand, her mind is racing with dozens of thoughts weighing her down, but her body is relaxed lying in the arms of the man she doesn't really know anything about.

A few months ago, she was in turmoil trying to figure out what life would bring her in the future. Then I showed up. Unknowingly, I became her future. We shared a night that was a turning point for both of us. I would love to wipe all her bad memories away. Including the ones from her childhood. I can tell it played a big part in her journey to marrying the man she did. I would replace them with just the ones of her and I.

I wish I could go back and somehow impregnate her and have Abigail be mine.

Ours.

A part of both of us.

The only thing I can do is create new memories for them. By doing that, just maybe I will be able to forget some of my own.

My phone dings from the nightstand. I grab for it, release a heavy breath then duck the call before tossing it back to the smooth surface. It's the third time Kathrine has called. I need to make it a point to call her today and set up a time to meet so we can speak. She needs to know about Isabelle.

The heavy moment between us still lingers, now with even more weight. I'm sure she saw Kathrine's name on my phone.

"Go ahead, angel, say it. I can hear your wheels turning." I kiss the crown of her head, shifting just a bit so I can look down at her.

"I have to get back to work. I—"

"Not happening," I harshly snap, cutting her off, totally taken off guard. That is not what I thought she was going to say. All thoughts of having the talk about Kathrine diminishes rapidly.

She is not going back to work.

"I can't be kept." She goes to move in a huff. I hold her in the crook of my arm. "I won't be." She settles, forgoing the thought that I would let her move away from me. "I need to work, Giovanni."

"You will not be going back."

"Giovanni—"

"Shh," I cut her off. She wiggles from my arm and sits up, staring down at me. "You are not going back to the bar or the diner." She jumps from the bed and stands on the other side. She is hot headed and determined, her temper shooting from her eyes. I release a husky growl at the aggravation of her separating us. I stand from the bed and walk to the end. She follows my movement but stays completely still. "Come here." I stand and wait. "Now."

"No."

"Angel…" My register is so low it's eerie.

"Why? No." I see the determination flicker to fear.

"Come here." I keep my tone low and steady. She walks to me with tentative steps. I slowly raise my hand to cup her jaw. "I will never hurt you. Do you understand me? I am not him. You created a fissure between us by jumping from my arms and putting the bed between us. Don't ever do that again. You didn't like what you heard so you thought you had to separate yourself and fight for it. I will not always agree with you or even agree to some of the things you want to do but if you are going to be with me, you must listen to me, for it will only be me trying to protect you. I know you know who I am, who I work for, but you don't know the dirty part of the world I move around in. I have targets on my back. Antonio, although a friend, is my boss. He runs this city. He, as well as I, have people who want to retaliate for the underhanded affairs we have participated in. You are now with me, Isabelle. Which means you now have a target on your back, too. Am I selfish for bring you into my life? Yes, I am, but I do not regret it one fucking bit, and I *will* protect you with every resource I have. That includes protecting you from your piece of shit husband. If you think for one second, that he is idly sitting by, waiting for you to come home, you're in denial. It is all about control for him and he lost that when you walked out, making him feel inferior."

"I get that but—" she tries to argue.

I won't let her. She needs to know what is in store for her.

"No. He has already showed up at the diner and harassed your old boss. I have put one of our lower ranking soldiers at the diner to keep surveillance. He will stalk the places you frequent on an hourly basis. He knows your routine. He is not alone in his hunt for you. He has help, Isabelle. A whole police force for Christ's sake. I know you know this. He is going to be a problem and I will handle him as I handle all problems." She watches me with wide eyes. "He is also going to use your daughter as a means to get back with you or at you. I will not allow that to happen. I will also not allow you to walk into a trap."

"How do you know all this?" she asks softly. Her gaze follows mine as it fades off to the side thinking about my estranged relationship with my mother. "You speak like you know."

"Because I have to."

Isabelle doesn't need to know about my past. That is for me and only for me to carry. There is no need to go back in time and rehash buried traumas and the heavy emotional baggage I hold towards my mother for not leaving when my sister and I were kids. I'm just grateful Abigail is still so young that she will most likely grow up with only a few fleeting memories. Hopefully, as she gets older, she will hold her mother up on a pedestal for having the courage to walk away if Isabelle ever chooses to tell her the story. Pride, it's feeling I have never been privileged to enjoy. I only got the allowance of getting my hands dirtier. It may become shaky ground between mother and daughter at some point as Abigail grows. When she realizes her father isn't around, she will question Isabelle, but as she gets older, more mature and into adulthood, she will realize what her mother has accomplished.

The strength she had to get out.

The cycle she broke.

Only then will Abigail understand and appreciate the life she was given.

"Go back to sleep. The guys will be here soon for our morning workout. When Abigail wakes up, I will let you know."

"Just like that, huh? Putting an end to the conversation?"

"Yes. We will revisit when I'm not angry about you putting space between us."

"But, G." She takes a step towards me.

"Go back to bed, Isabelle. We'll talk later." I turn from her and head for the bathroom, closing the door after I enter. When I come back out, she has the covers up to her neck and tear stains on her cheeks.

My own fucked up head at not wanting to rehash my past has now effected the woman I adore.

Giovanni
CHAPTER TWENTY-FOUR

"**Y**ou make the call to Luke?" I ask, letting the bar smack against the metal holder.

"Yeah. He and Jess were headed up to the compound for the weekend. Bane, Rocker, and Ronan will accompany him at the safehouse. I gave him an estimated time of two a.m."

"My gut is telling me Mr. McKittrick has his hand in something heavy. Not sure this is a smart move."

"We test the product before it's off loaded. Make sure we aren't being played. If he has no answers for us about his real agenda, then we walk."

"Agreed," Demetri huffs from where he is running on the treadmill. The man is a well-oiled killing machine, sprinting from a past only Mr. Heart, Antonio, and I know about. His secrets are safe with us, but if one day those secrets are brought to life… Let's just say, a blood bath will ensue.

"I've been doing some digging," Antonio breathes, lifting the barbell.

I stare at him, waiting for him to spill what he has been investigating when I already know the answer.

"Lieutenant Hunt has been sniffing around." He huffs out a breath with his rep.

"Tell me something I don't already know." I spot the bar waiting for his return lift to the rack.

"I know my friend is doing this on his own when he doesn't need to."

"You of all people know I am capable of handling things myself."

"Never said you couldn't. It's the reason why you're my top consigliere."

"Then respect me like one." I help him lower the bar and turn my back on him to grab my water from the other weight bench.

"If you didn't have my respect, Giovanni, that beautiful girl of yours would have already disappeared. She comes with a lot of heat, my friend. It is my job to make sure this organization and you come out of this situation unscathed."

I throw my water bottle to the mat, cross my arms, widen my stance, and stare him down. He's pushing it, and he knows it. *Remove my girl?* I don't fucking think so. Although I know he is right. My little redheaded lion does come with an inferno of problems, but I will protect my girl and the organization that has given me a life. Something I feel my mother never did for my sister and me.

I glare at Antonio. From across the room, I hear the treadmill squeal, stopping on a dime. Demetri's feet hit the mat with a single thud. He stands, waits, and watches the both of us. The tension between Antonio and I over the past few weeks has been building. I will never disrespect him as a boss, but as a friend, I will gladly throw him a fist for being an arrogant fuck. His and Lilah's relationship was tumultuous at best. I stood by his side. I was there for him before he even knew he loved her. I was the one that remained by his side when we found out her secrets. Fuck him for questioning my judgment on if I can handle the storm that is coming. I can and will deal with all business that comes our way. I always have and I always will. I am the one that lived on the streets, surviving on my own, taking care of my sister, all before I met Mr. Heart.

I turn my back on Antonio before I charge him.

The gesture is worse than taking him to the mat.

"I'm going to take a fucking shower." I walk from the room without looking back.

My phone rings with a call as I'm walking into my bathroom. With one glance, I throw my phone across the bathroom counter with force. My hope is it will shatter from the brute force of the throw so all the women in my life give me a fucking minute. But then again, I know an hour from now I'll be pissed I need a new phone. And really, it's not *all* women in my life, my little lion and Hope can stay. Kathrine and my mother can go.

The heat from the shower relaxes my muscles to the point I only want to strangle my boss and not maim him. I want to stay under the warm spray longer, but on my pissed off journey through my bedroom to the bathroom I took note that Isabelle was not in my bed where she belonged. I checked the security feed, so I knew where to hunt Isabelle down when I got out. She was alone in the kitchen, making food.

I head to my closet to get dressed for the day when I glance at the monitor once again just to watch her move through my space. She is still in the kitchen, making herself a coffee, but she is no longer alone. I forgo the suit and tie and throw on a pair of shorts and a black muscle shirt when I see

Antonio standing at the kitchen island, talking to her. No fucking way am I going to let him interrogate her. Her secrets are mine. They will die with the both of us.

"What the fuck are you doing?" I turn the corner and throttle him with a look of death.

"Just enjoying a coffee with your girl," he smugly answers before taking a sip.

I glance at Isabelle. She seems fine. I'm not. "Angel, go wait for me in my bedroom."

"Giovanni?" Her brows lower with confusion.

"Now, angel."

She looks between the both of us.

"You plan on interrogating my girl?" I thunder when Isabelle leaves the room.

"Yes," he emphatically admits.

"You know what this means?"

"I do."

I slide my tongue over my upper lip and suck them both in trying to control myself. "You went too far, Antonio. I have never disrespected you by questioning Lilah."

"It would be for your own good. She's a cop's wife, Giovanni. A fucking cop! You put your dick where it didn't belong. You're blinded by that."

Bam!

The skin of my knuckles split with the force of my punch landing against his chin. His head snaps to the side. I brace myself and wait. My anger radiates between the both of us as I wait for his retaliation. I just crossed a line. As did he. I know my fate. I just disrespected a mafia underboss, the son of the Don who took me in and gave me a life by putting my hands on him.

I'm snarling when he turns back to me, but he doesn't make a move to retaliate. He's stock still, surveying me.

"How do you know she wasn't planted with open legs for you all those months ago so we could be brought down? Huh? We run a fucking empire, you and me! I'm protecting you, as well as myself *and* this organization. Dammit, G!"

"I would never jeopardize this organization."

"You did! You didn't even vet the woman you put your dick in!"

"Did you? No, I fucking did it for you. After the fact. That's my job!"

"You're letting your past cloud your judgment, Giovanni. Whether you like it or not, it is my job to make sure she is on the up and up. She is not your mother."

"She is on the up and up." I ignore his comment about the woman who gave birth to me.

"How do you know that? You don't!"

"Because you don't get to experience her quivering innocence beneath you. That's how I fucking know. Think about all the women you have been with, Antonio. You knew the minute you were with Lilah it was different. She was different. You have to trust me on this and if you can't stand at my side, then don't stand by me at all. Our friendship can dissolve, and our relationship will become strictly business."

"You do not want that," he threatens.

"No, I don't, but you're making it really hard to continue this friendship."

"This isn't about friendship. It's business."

"Get the fuck out."

He takes a deep breath, his mouth twists. Our stare-off is interrupted by the slide of the elevator door opening. Neither of us move until Hope comes into our view. Antonio grabs his keys and wallet off the island with a hasty swipe. He nods at Hope with a murmured good morning and heads to the elevator. When he reaches the open door, he turns back and orders, "Be at the club by nine." He steps inside, presses the button but slams his hand against the door, stopping it from closing. "And Giovanni, I will take that punch to my jaw as a friend letting off some steam. Because you know if I don't, I will have to kill you, and I don't want to murder my brother in cold fucking blood." He lifts his hand letting the door slide shut.

"What the fuck just happened?" Hope throws the bags in her arms on the counter in a panic.

"Watch your mouth," I huff, passing her, heading to the sink to wash the blood from my split knuckles.

"Giovanni, this is not good!"

"It's fine," I gruffly try to assure her.

"It's not! You punched him? Seriously, G? You hit him? That's a show of disrespect! You know what the repercussions are for something like that!" She starts to get more hysterical by the second.

"Hope!" I turn and grab her by the shoulders with my wet hands. "Calm down. It's fine."

"It's so not fucking fine!"

"Trust me, it is." I pull her into my arms. "It will be fine." I don't know if I am trying to convince her or me.

"I can't lose you." She starts to cry. "You're all I have."

"You're not going to lose me." I pull her from my chest and bend to her level until I'm eye to eye with her. "Did you hear what he said? He said he will take the punch as a friend letting off steam. Our argument was not over business. It was personal," I lie to calm her. She doesn't need to know that my punch just caused a rift between us. "Okay?" I squeeze her shoulders. She nods her head, but I can see the worry in her eyes. "You okay? I need to go check on Isabelle."

"Go." She wipes her tears away. "Go." She waves her hand.

I enter my room and find it empty. I check the bathroom just to make sure she isn't in there, but I already know she isn't. I make my way down the hall and hear her and Abigail talking. When I enter the room both their backs are facing me. Abigail is sleepily jabbering on about some cartoon and the fact she wants Froot Loops for breakfast. Isabelle is making the bed. She is listening but I can tell she is distracted.

"Giovonky!" Little feet patter across the floor in a rush. Isabelle jerks up, standing straight and watches Abigail run right into my arms. Had I not caught her midair and lifted her up she would have bulldozed me.

"Good morning, squirt." I smile.

"Are you mad? I hear yelling."

"Heard," I correct her. "And no, why? Are you mad? Were you yelling in your sleep?" I try to make a joke. Kids are so perceptive.

"Your body is hot. Do you have Froot Loops?" she rambles.

"I think there may be some in the pantry." I try to keep up with her.

Her eyes grow big. "You eat Froot Loops?" Her voice rises.

"Not really."

"Why? They so colorful. Are you going to be my new daddy?"

And the world come screeching to a halt with the sweet voice of a little girl who deserved so much more in her short life. "I will never be your real daddy but if your momma lets me, maybe someday I can be your step daddy." I watch Isabelle for her reaction.

"Good, 'cause I don't like my daddy very much."

"You and me both," I mumble my truth low enough so she can't hear me. "Hope is in the kitchen, squirt. How about you go find her and ask her to get you a bowl of cereal while I talk to your momma."

"Otay." She is off and running when I set her down. Her little feet slapping the marble floor echoes as she goes.

I turn back to Isabelle and take in her mood. We watch each other for a few minutes before she rounds the bed and walks straight to me with shaky steps.

"Everything okay?"

Not what I thought we were going to discuss. "Everything is fine."

"You punched him?"

I give her and inquisitive look, waiting for her to bring up the daddy discussion her daughter and I just had. "He had no right to question you."

"I heard Hope crying. The situation must be very serious. We were just talking."

"To you it was talking. To him it was fact finding. We are good at what we do, Isabelle."

"Why though? What did he say?"

"Let's go have some breakfast. I have a day planned for you and Abigail."

"But, Giovanni," she stammers. "You're not going to tell me, are you?"

"No." I tug her hand and start to lead her towards the kitchen. "It's business. I won't discuss business with you. It's for your own safety. It will be a big part of our life together. It's something you are going to have to accept."

"Because you don't trust me?"

"No." I stop us halfway down the hallway and face her. "Because the business I deal in is brutal. If you don't know anything then you can't answer questions if you're ever asked. You are going to have to trust me. There is no buts, angel. There is only 'yes, Giovanni, I understand.'"

I watch her pupil's flare. My statement made her mad. It's too bad. I will not waver on this.

"You know, I met Antonio once. You, too. At O'Brien's."

I remember. How could I forget? I thought you were the most beautiful girl.

"There was a group of you having dinner. I was your waitress. I thought Antonio was a very attractive man, but I also knew by looking at him that he was a very dangerous man."

"I am a very dangerous man, angel."

"After what you just told me, I now think he's an attractive dick."

She just inadvertently called me a dick for standing my ground when it comes to business. Touché, little lion. "Don't do that."

"Do what?" The defiance in her eyes shines bright between us.

"I have enough issues with Antonio right now without wanting to end him because you're trying to make me jealous."

She wrinkles her nose. "I thought you were attractive, too. So, I guess, that would make you an attractive dick as well." She winks with an attitude and speed walks past me to the kitchen.

It's the first time she has ever been flippant with me. I give her credit for standing up for herself even if it was in a roundabout way. I watch her ass jiggle as she goes. Groaning, I head in the opposite direction to my bedroom, giving myself a minute to calm down my imperious need to slap some good ol' fashion retaliation to her delectable ass for calling me a dick.

Isabelle
CHAPTER TWENTY-FIVE

I t is by far a fairytale. A dream most little girls lay in bed and envision, but it was never my dream. All I see are dollar signs and someone I have come to trust trying to buy my love. I spin towards Giovanni with a pain in my chest and hurt in my eyes. His stoic expression watches me with a critical eye as my head jerks back to glance around. I'm not sure how to react as my past is recycled and regurgitated to meet my present. I hold a fist over my mouth, speechless in my survey over the exquisite material surrounding me. It isn't until Abigail tugs on my shirt sleeve that I snap out of my panic. I glance down at her but it's only for a fraction of a moment, because I feel like I'm trapped, drowning in a past life while standing in what I thought was a new one.

"Hi. My name is Sofia." The brunette in front of me leans in and gives Giovanni a hug and a kiss before turning her open, outstretched hand in my direction.

I take a step back. It wasn't a planned step but more of an unvoluntary movement of protection. I glance up at Giovanni. Why? Because I trusted his protection of me, of us, but then again, the conflict inside me tells me not to because he brought us here. His bewildered gaze is watching me like a hawk watches his escaping prey. I'm ready to bolt and he knows it. My hand sliding around Abigail's doesn't go unnoticed from his trained eye either. I give the woman in front of me a slight smile and internally start to formulate my excuse to leave when a firm grip to my chin directs my attention to his fierce analyzing examination.

"Give us a minute, Sofia."

"Of course. Can I take your little girl to meet my daughter Lakelynn?" She holds out her hand for Abigail as if I will just willingly let my daughter go with her.

"Yes," Giovanni answers, watching me.

"No," I immediately answer after him.

"Yes, Sofia. You can." His eyelids lower.

I have seen them drop in desire, but this is not that. I've enjoyed his hooded gaze when he is in the midst of coming. Those valued few moments when he loses his domineering restraint is priceless. It's honesty in a vulnerable moment. This reaction is the total opposite. His narrowed eyes are silently evaluating and unknowingly probing with the jagged edge of a serrated knife at a past I have buried. He pinches my jaw in place with his index finger and thumb as he considers his approach. All the while I stand there in front of him, frozen, like I'm the scared little girl from ten years ago.

"Explain." His green eyes flick over mine.

It's not a question. It's a demand. One I know I won't find my way out of. He is too perceptive. "What is this place?"

"I think that answer is clear."

"Why did you bring me here?"

His head dips slightly to the side. "Explain the sudden panic, Isabelle."

I give the elegant boutique a once over. It's absolutely gorgeous and just by one glance, I can tell it is extremely expensive. My mother used to bring me to places like this to find my pageant dresses. I hated it. I hated everything about it. I loathed the fact that she would act as if she had all the money in the world because of who she was married to. In reality, we had no money, because my father pissed it away on women and booze and my mother relied on my winnings to keep them going.

"This is not who I am."

"What is that supposed to mean?"

"The fancy clothes. It's not me. It's not who I am. If this is the kind of woman you want, then you saved the wrong girl. I won't be her again."

"What kind of girl is that?"

"The one that dresses in sparkling fabric to hide the ugly beneath it."

"He bought you nice things?" His head twists, trying to figure out what I'm not saying.

I huff an incredulous laugh. "He never bought me a thing." I huff again at the thought. "Correction, he bought me a few dresses so I could look 'presentable' when I stood next to his side." Then he proceeded to tell me how fat I looked in said dress along with the fact he thought I was a whore.

"Help me understand."

"It's not worth it. Selling my soul to a man. I won't do it. I won't go back there."

"Where is there? Explain."

"Excuse me," the shop owner, Sofia, cautiously interrupts. "I have a comfortable emerald-green velour jogging outfit I think would go with your hair and eyes beautifully. My assistant, Jessica and I both have one. We wear them all the time. Why don't you try one on? Your daughter is in the back playing dress up with my daughter. I have some things for her as well."

"I hate the color emerald green," I snap, then hold up my hand. "I'm sorry…" I linger off as I'm getting ready to decline her offer with more tact so I could leave, but then I fully look at her and it dawns on me. I have met her before. "Sofia? You were the girl in the bathroom at O'Brien's Pub a few years back." I start nodding my head. "Yes. You were the girl in the bathroom throwing up. You were pregnant. No one knew you were pregnant. I told you about saltine crackers and toothpaste."

"Yes! Yes, I remember." Her smile is so bright and friendly it can be nothing else but warm and welcoming. "You told me your sister was really sick when she was pregnant. Those saltine crackers really did work."

From the corner of my eye, I can see Giovanni watching me. He has never heard me mention a sister, and rightfully so, because I don't have one. I had told Sofia back then that it was my sister who was pregnant, but it was me. I just didn't want anyone to know. I was afraid I would lose my job and I desperately needed that job. Tommy kept after me to end the pregnancy and I knew I wasn't going to. I worked all the extra shifts I could to save money so I could afford to leave him. In hindsight, I should have left him then.

"Yes. That's me." I glance in Giovanni's direction. "Your little girl is here? The one that made you so sick?"

"She is. Come on, you can meet her. She's the devil with an angelic face." I chuckle. "Seriously though, ask G-Man." She throws her thumb over her shoulder at Giovanni. "He knows. Then again, she has him and every other male influence around her in the palm of her hand." I glance at Giovanni. He slightly grins at Sofia, ignoring me. "Facts. Right? You know I'm right, G."

His grin gets bigger as she jokes with him.

"You are not wrong." His deep voice rumbles with some humor behind it as we walk towards the back of the boutique.

Once we get to where the girls are in front of an enormous hand carved tri-fold mirror, Sofia and I laugh out loud. I couldn't help it. It's a sight that should bring back so many bad memories, but those memories don't rise because the vision before me is two innocent little girls playing dress up, giggling, and having fun like little girls should.

The way it is supposed to be.

When both girls turn around at their mothers' laughter, we laugh even harder at their appearance.

"I tried to help." A tall, lengthy, handsome male throws his hands in the air flamboyantly. "But they weren't having it. Nope. I got the 'Uncle Swage, I got this attitude.' You know I'm dying right now, right, sugar britches?

These girls got lipstick in places they shouldn't have."

"Momma, Uncle Swag was ready to cwy. I told him no cwying allowed. Uncle G, don't I look pwetty?"

I watch Giovanni crouch down and motion with two fingers for her to come to him. She jumps on his bent knee with excitement.

It melts my heart.

"You are pretty without makeup, LL. But a little bit of lipstick makes you even prettier."

"See, Uncle Swage. I told you." She crinkles her nose in an *I-told-you-so* way.

"How about me?" I hear Abigail chime from in front of the mirror as she fluffs her hair.

Giovanni's finger crooks making the same gesture to her as he did with Lakelynn. It's amazing how he can use those same two fingers in that gesture to summons me, control me, and thoroughly wreck me with just one twitch of two demanding fingers, but the same powerful, controlling movement holds a completely different feel for the girls.

Abby runs as best she can with a pair of too big of high heels on. When she launches herself out of them and onto Giovanni's only available knee, I gasp in panic when I see the red soles. The knot in my throat makes me want to throw up. Those heels cost more than I make in a month. If she ruins them, I will have to work double shifts to pay for them.

"At least they have good taste in shoes," the guy Lakelynn keeps calling Swage mumbles.

"No worries." Sofia leans in when she sees my eyes glued to the shoes. "Those are mine. Lakelynn wears them all the time."

"He's my Uncle G," I hear Lakelynn say as I process the fact that Sofia lets her daughter wear her expensive shoes.

"I don't like my real daddy. Giovonky said he would be my new daddy."

The room goes quiet at Abigail's innocent little girl gibberish. Sofia is watching Giovanni with a look I can't decipher. A small smile pulls at her lips. A joyous gleam shines in her eyes. When Giovanni glances up, the two of them connect. There is a moment. A moment too long for my liking. Something passes between them. A twinge of jealousy works its way up my spine as I watch the two of them hold a silent but undeniably intimate conversation between them.

I clear my throat and turn away, not ready to evaluate the intensity of my jealousy. Life is funny. Had that been Tommy who held a silent conversation with a woman in front of me, I wouldn't care. I would be happy and secretly relieved that maybe he would find me no longer a challenge in his search for power and dominance. There would have been no love lost for me. But this wasn't Tommy. It was Giovanni. And that green running through my veins can only mean one thing. Am I in love with him?

"Chicken nuggets are here." A tall, stunning blonde I remember from the bar walks in yelling as she holds up bags of fast food.

"Chickie nuggies!" Lakelynn jumps off Giovanni's lap after popping a kiss on his cheek. "Colt better not eat all mine!" she yells heading to the back room. "Come on, Abby," she hollers over her shoulder. "We can eat in my momma's office. It's so pwetty."

I glance down only to see a moment between the man I believe I'm in love with and my little girl. It shatters my heart and cements my feelings. Abigail has her little hands holding each side of Giovanni's face. She steadies him then presses her nose to his. When she lays her forehead to rest against his she says, "I be right back. You wait for me, Daddy G? You not leave me?"

I watch Giovanni's Adams apple bob with his swallow. This big, strong, powerful man was just broken by a tiny little girl.

So was her momma.

"I will be right here when you get done. Mommy is going to try on some clothes and I'm pretty sure that Sofia has some outfits for you to try on too."

"I get new clothes too?" Her little voice rises with excitement. "Mommy, I get clothes too!" She lets go of Giovanni's face to look at me.

I'm so conflicted. I feel so much joy watching my daughter be genuinely happy, yet all I feel is sadness at the thought he is trying to dress us up to fit in his world. When I look into my daughter's eyes, all I can do is nod in agreeance.

Sofia immediately takes the lead and guides me to a dressing room. The elegant room is filled with racks of clothes. I feel overwhelmed and unstable. I slowly slide my hand over the hanging garments. All pieces that match my skin and hair color have been chosen for me. I acknowledge the fact that a lot of time and energy has gone in to putting all of this together.

"I have champagne for you if you would like, but Giovanni said you would be more of a diet Pepsi or coffee kind of girl, so I have both for you."

"Thank you." I quietly scan the room, my voice soft and unsure.

"Here's the—"

"Give us a minute." His deep, demanding voice comes from the archway to the room.

With no questions asked, Sofia leaves. Giovanni walks straight to the rack and pulls an emerald-green, thin strap, bodycon dress and a snow white off the shoulder, high-waisted, casual jogging outfit off. He walks to me and throws both outfits on the velour sofa. I watch each one of his actions with hesitant interest. He saunters back over to me, and with the flip of those same two fingers, he demands I lift my arms. My limbs dangle at my sides in refusal.

"Is this how you want to play the game?"

"My life is not a game."

"No, it is not. Your life is now *my* responsibility. I take that very seriously. If I choose to buy you a warehouse full of clothes, I will. If I see jewelry that I think fits you, then I will buy that as well."

"And who do you think I am? That is the true question, Giovanni." My lip flutters at the sudden flip of my shirt snapping over my head. "What are you doing?" I ask in exasperation.

"I believe it is self-explanatory, but I will further explain if you truly need the explanation. When you are naked and beneath me, you are more pliable. I'm not quite sure what happened the moment we stepped in here today, but you went from being carefree to being wound up tighter than a top. I asked you to explain. You declined. You have left me no choice but to strip you naked, little lion."

"Are you crazy?" I gasp as he drops in front of me, my pants sliding down my thighs with his actions. I wiggle, trying to stop the downward course of the cloth covering me, but it only helps him in the action. "Giovanni, we are inside a store dressing room. Stop it." I slap at his hands.

"Boutique. We will be left alone until I permit company."

"You think you can order people around and everyone will listen to you? You can't. You thought bringing me in here and buying me nice clothes was what I wanted? Needed? This is what you need. Not me." My body is jerked around and shoved up against the floor to ceiling mirror. "I'm sorry I don't fit the lifestyle." I continue to run my mouth as my face is plastered against the cool, reflecting glass. "Giovanni!" I stomp my foot before it is kicked to the side, further opening my legs.

"Yes, little lion?" His sadistic smirk and deep cadence lights an unwanted flame inside me.

"You cannot—" The shock at the sound of my panties being ripped from my body fills the air and cuts my words off. "Wha—" The quick metal zing of his zipper makes my eyes widen. "You. I. Giovan—Oh, God." My forehead presses against the mirror as he slides his thick wide length into my body, thrusting his hips powerfully he pins me against the glass.

"Do you still want me to stop?"

"Yes." He grinds against me and shifts his hips as he starts to pull out. I moan. "No, you bastard."

"Am I though? Or are you the one who asked for this since I asked you a question and you refused to tell me what was wrong?" He pulls back further and thrusts back in, pinning me once again. "I can't fix what you're feeling if you don't tell me what spooked you. And, angel, to answer your question, yes, people do listen to my orders. Because they know if they don't, there will be repercussions."

"You can't fix everything."

He huffs a sarcastic chuckle. "You have a lot to learn about me, angel. I can and I will fix it. That is why I respectfully hold the title as The Fixer. Now," he groans, jerking his hips forward with a possessive thrust, "are you going to tell me why you went into silent, rabbit mode, ready to run when I brought you here?" He thrust again, grinding the base of his shaft against my bottom. "Or am I going to have to fuck you raw until you do?"

"If you do, I won't be able to talk," I whimper, pushing back against him, wanting to feel more of him. "This isn't fair," I whine, feeling my arousal seep down his shaft.

"Life isn't fair. You of all people should know that. Life is about taking what we want and making an existence we can live with. Now start talking." He thrusts, pinning his hips against me just as his phone starts ringing.

I close my eyes and whimper once again when I feel him swell within my walls. My fisted hand curls against the mirror. I try to see myself back there, in the small boutique back home with my momma, but it doesn't feel right. It doesn't fit. The past feelings aren't the same as they are with me here, with him, in this boutique today. Giovanni has made me feel more like myself—whoever that is—a woman, an individual who has thoughts and feelings.

On a sputtered breath and a clawed fist on his solid hip with my other hand, I pull him into me as I spew my truth.

"I was a pageant queen back home. You have your dick buried in Miss Sugar Lane. I hate the color emerald green because it is the color of the dress I won the pageant wearing. It went with my red hair. Green is the go-to color for redheads. Since I was a small child, my momma used to parade me around from town to town covering up her truth with my unique beauty. The best deflection for a life of lies is to give it a false façade. I was the structure that keep my parents' reputation. I was used to fit an image that was entirely deceptive to hide the real truth."

"Which was?" He shifts as his hand glides around my hip and slides up my center until his palm lays possessively flat between my breasts, holding my back to his front. My peaked nipples rub against the glass with each one of his thrusts.

"My father was the drunk mayor who ran the town we lived in. He hid his crutch well. If you looked at us from the outside, we had it all. In reality, we were piss poor, living in a nightmare. You see, my momma set the stage for me. I unknowingly learned how to be the dutiful, abused wife from her. The towns people never knew it. What they didn't want to know was that the bruises on my momma that they ignored when they saw her were from him, my daddy. I left when I was seventeen. I had won the grand title of Miss Sugar Lane in a sparkling, emerald green dress. I bailed on my momma that same night after I stole my winnings from her purse. I left her with him to save myself. Only, I ran straight into the arms of a man who is just like him."

I seal my eyes shut as tight as I can to close out the pain.

"Open. Look at the woman in the mirror," Giovanni growls as his palm takes an upward course until it rests at the base of my neck. His fingers grip my jaw, forcing me to look at myself. I should be furious at the way he is handling me, but I'm not. He is domineering in a way that holds my rapt attention. The action may be controlling but the emotion brewing in his eyes is anything but. "Do you know what I see when I look at you?"

I shake my head then answer with a sarcastic rebuke. It's what I'm used to. What I have trained myself to become. "A woman who is making the same mistake again? It's a vicious circle I can't seem to get off of."

"Is that what you think I am? A mistake?" he gruffly asks in anger.

"Isn't it? I fell in love with yet another man who brought me here to dress me up as a doll so he can show me off."

"Not true." He rams himself into me with an angered grunt as he palms my breast with his other hand then tweaks my nipple with a fierce pinch. "I brought you here so that I could shower you with a new wardrobe for your new life. To give you things that will make your transition easier from an abused woman, wife, and mother to a cherished lover and eventually one day after I end your piece of shit husband, my wife. I wanted to show you an existence so very different from the one you were living. There is no endgame to my generosity. The money I spend today has no conditions attached, except that I want to see you in them. Had I been privy to this information you just divulged, I would have known to handle it differently. You denied me that. Now I realize you see my gesture as if it is no different from the life you have only known. If you would have trusted me, and given me the facts of your past, I would have still brought you here, but I would have prepared you for it. Today was supposed to be a good day, a surprise for you, for Abby, and for me."

"I'm not sure what to say," I moan as he drops his hand and viciously manipulates my core. "I-I feel like I should apologize but—" My bottom lip quivers.

"You will not say the words 'I'm sorry' to me. Going forward, you will use that pent up energy to talk to me instead of getting ready to run."

"You're angry." My voice is soft, unsure, not knowing how to handle this moment.

"Fucking furious. You denied me the right to take care of you." He leans in and kisses the back of my head as his palm encases my fist against the mirror. His fingers contract around mine when his phone rings once again. "Push back against me, and Isabelle, I better hear my name drip from your lips when your cunt strangles my cock with the orgasm I also generously give you."

His phone rings once again immediately following the call, but it's a different ring tone. I can only assume it's a text message. My bite back about his cocky attitude is cut off when his teeth sink into the back of my neck. His firm hand holds the flesh of my behind in a bruising grip. He spreads my cheeks wide, sinking himself deeper. I stare into his eyes through the reflection of the mirror when his name drips from my open lips and my body shakes with my release.

I'm mentally exhausted from my admission and physically from the strength of which Giovanni's powerful love making entails.

The sharp ting of his zipper being fastened behind me brings me back to my senses. I turn to grab my shredded, discarded panties on the floor along with my pants when Giovanni's phone rings once again. I glance at the screen held in his hand as he physically beats me to my underwear and stuffs them in his pocket. A female's name flashes across the screen. Someone named Kathrine is calling as the phone rings once again. I watch Giovanni hit decline and I wonder if she is the reason for the previous phone calls while he was thrusting the truth out of my body.

"Who is she?" I fully turn to him. I couldn't stop myself from blurting the question.

"No one you need to worry about."

"A handful of phone calls in the last thirty minutes, as well as this morning," I mutter, raising my brow, assuming they were all from her just now. "Must be really important." I watch him for any kind of reaction as he finishes dressing.

He walks to the sofa and grabs both the dress and the jogging outfit. Holding them up he ignores my comment and spits an agitated statement. "I don't care which one you are more comfortable in. I don't care if you wear sweats every damn day. All these clothes are for you. Pick what you want. Wear them all or wear none. Set fire to all the green if you want. It's your choice. If you see something on the floor you like, tell Sofia. She will pack it up for you." He turns and snatches his dark suit jacket off the sofa after he discards the clothes he was just holding in haste. "Sofia's bodyguard will take you home. Do not, I repeat, Isabelle, do not argue with Sofia or Luca about driving you," he orders when he turns back to me. "I have business I need to attend to. I'll see you at home later."

His chaste kiss leaves me breathlessly startled and thoroughly confused. I turn and look at myself in the mirror once he's left. I look well and truly fucked and carelessly left behind like a used Tinder date. I don't like how he just left. I don't like how it makes me feel. This man has left me feeling disheveled inside and out when he has always handled me with such domineering care.

Sofia buzzes into the room with a quick knock and a cheerful attitude.

"Okay, let's do this." She hands me a small, elegant velvet box. Jessica, the blonde girl I remember from the bar walks in behind Sofia and starts pulling all the emerald green outfits off the rack. Sage knocks and waits all of two seconds before announcing he's coming in. His arms are full of creams, baby blues, and champagne fabric. He starts hanging them and fluffing out any wrinkles he may have caused in the few steps from the front of the store to the dressing room. I stand there in the middle of the flurried action with a box in my hand in confused awe. Sofia catches my attention with the touch of her hand on my arm. "Open the box, you're going to need them. That is, unless you don't mind being naked in front of Jess and me."

I slide the lid off and hunt through the black tissue paper. A pair of exquisite baby blue satin and lace bikini underwear with rhinestone straps lay inside. I drop the box and hold them up. "These are gorgeous," I gush. "The rhinestones make it look so elegant." Ignoring the looks between the three of them at my statement, I turn them over and notice the heart shape stone dangling in the cut out on the back just below my tailbone.

"Firecracker, those are not rhinestones," Sage chirps.

In awe, I play with the smooth glass between the pads of my fingers as his statement sinks in. The prism of reflecting light mesmerizes me. I look up at him and then at both girls. "You mean... Noooo." My voice drops a few decimals in disbelief. "This is... These aren't fake?"

"Honey, if those are counterfeit then I'm not a gay man, and I am definitely a gay man."

"I can't wear these!" I sputter in exasperation, shuffling to put them back in the box.

"If you don't, stud muffin will come right back in here and demand that you do. Now that studly machoism would be something I would want to witness."

"Those were made specifically for you by a La Perla designer." Sofia smiles at me. "They were delivered here last week and kept in the safe in my office."

"I'm ready to throw up," I admit. I'm sure my face is the color of putrid green.

"Just don't do it on the panties, firecracker." Sage quirks his head to the left. "Those things cost more than the average person's yearly salary."

"Okay." Jessica claps her hands. "Let's put the expensive as shit panties on and start this show. I got a date with Luke tonight, and it's been a minute since he has given me any jewelry."

I'm appalled at her statement. All she wants from her man is jewelry? Here I am ready to tuck these panties back in their box because it's too much. I don't want expensive things from Giovanni. I just want him and the safety of his arms and here she is pissed because Luke hasn't bought her any jewelry? That is so selfish. Is she that superficial?

"He's holding out?" Sofia chirps with a slight chuckle.

"You know he loves to torture me." Jessica rolls her eyes.

"Oh, I'm sure it's torture. What did you do that he hasn't given you any?" Sage grabs some nude heels and places them beneath a yellow shift dress while Jessica grabs a cream-colored pantsuit and pairs it with some red heels.

Sofia must see the disgust on my face. As she's removing the box from my hand and gesturing for me to put the panties on, she beckons Jess with the flip of her other hand and says, "Hey, Jess? Why don't you explain to Isabelle why you love when Luke gives you jewelry? I think she may be forming a very bad assumption of you."

"Firecracker, do you want me to leave while you change or are you okay with me being in here? I've seen both their kibbles and bits." Sage addresses me, throwing both thumbs out, gesturing to both girls.

"I, umm… You can stay. I am used to changing in front of a lot of people."

"Former stripper?" he so easily asks.

"Sage!" Sofia scolds with exasperation.

"No, that's not it," he continues, ignoring Sofia shocked expression. "You have a regal look about you." He takes a step towards me, evaluating me. "You hold yourself with pride, your shoulders are straight, and your chin isn't buried in your chest, but that confidence has been smothered by something, knocking you down. Underneath the defeated posture I can see it, you have been bred to hold yourself with the best of the best."

"Sage," Sofia warns. "He will not appreciate you questioning her."

"Beauty queen." I glance at Sofia, confused at her statement. "I have entered so many pageants as a child, I had lost count by the time I was fourteen. My last one was when I was seventeen." It felt good to say that out loud.

"Ahh, yes. Now I see it. And now your confidence is shot to hell because the real world is cruel. Well, most of it isn't but there are some bad ones out there. By the look in your eyes and those marks on your back, you have met one."

"Truth. The real world can be brutally harsh. It's just like a pageant when you're front and center on the stage with Vaseline smeared on your teeth to force your imperfect smile to perfection for people to judge. All looks flawless on the outside but when you step behind the curtain reality hits like an overbearing lover with a slap."

"Or a punch."

"Sage…" Jessica now warns him, her eyes wide.

"Amen to that, firecracker." He ignores Jessica's warning too. "No worries, the attention of the very fine man you caught will be the best thing in your life. This," he says waving his hand around the clothing rack "is appreciation for someone you love. Now, let's get to it, shall we? Jessica needs to get her fill of jewelry sooner rather than later."

I glance at Jessica who is rolling her eyes in humored irritation. "My man has dick piercings," she blurts, laughing.

"Lots of them." Sage winks. "You see, the men in our group like to torture their women in the most delicious of ways."

"And he hasn't given me any in three days," she continues. "Three. Why? Because he asked me not to do something and I did it anyway. Do you know what it is like to go three days without Prince Albert and Jacob rubbing my insides?"

"I thought his name was Luke?"

"Oh, you innocent girl. You have a lot to learn, firecracker."

Giovanni
CHAPTER TWENTY-SIX

"Who the fuck tuned you up, Joseph?" I walk in his direction when I step through the warehouse doors. I see red. I'm already angry with Isabelle, furious at Kathrine because she won't give me a fucking minute, and now, I'm damn near enraged that Joseph would let someone do this to him and even more furious that someone thought that they could do this to him without repercussions. Joseph is one of us. He is under our protection. Fuck, he is under his own protection because he is part of the Heart Organization. Everyone knows that. Whoever dared to lay their hands on him is a dead man.

"Don't worry about it. I can handle it," he says with embarrassment he's trying not to show.

I get it. He is part of an organization that doesn't stand for any disrespect and here he is beat to shit. But what I won't stand for, is his disrespect at not answering my question.

"Before I show you the same disrespect you just showed me by not answering, I suggest you start talking."

"Some guy in the back alley behind the bodega downtown," he explains through a split, now cracked open and bleeding lip. He swipes at the tender skin with his hand and then rubs it on the shoulder of his shirt."

"Has your father seen this?"

"Yes."

"His reaction?"

"I should have been paying more attention to my surroundings."

"Wise words from a man who has succeeded in surviving in the organization for longer than a minute."

"Yes, sir."

"Do you have a name, Joseph?" I twist my head waiting for his answer as red flags start waving before my eyes. "What bodega?"

"No name. It was the bodega by the Chinese restaurant that was closed down by the board of health. The one a few blocks from your place." I already knew this information because said owner of the bodega called to inform me of Joseph's beat down. He saw the incident on his security camera.

"You get a good look at the guy?" He stays silent. "Joseph, I asked you a question. If I have to ask you again your lip will bleed more."

He's hesitant. "It was a cop. He said the store owner told him I stole something."

"Did you?" I'd beat his ass worse if he did. The kid has probably got a couple grand in his pocket.

"No. I was getting in my car, he yanked me back out by my neck. He threw me up against the trunk. I started to fight but then I realized he was a cop, so I stopped. He didn't. He was throwing punches left and right. I got a few in before another cop came out of the building and stopped him. He told me to leave. I left. The cop that hit me was spewing all kinds of shit I couldn't understand. I wasn't going to stick around and ask so they could slap some bullshit charge on me for something I didn't do."

"You did the right thing." I grab my phone and hit a number that has been dial so many times before. "Joseph needs some stitches. We're at the warehouse." I hang up leaving no room for parting words then turn towards Demetri and Antonio walking through the door. I have already informed them both of Joseph's event-filled evening.

"You call Doc?" Antonio questions while giving Joseph a once over.

"Just hung up."

"You let someone do this to you?" he grills Joseph as he ruthlessly grabs a hold of his jaw and twists it back and forth. The grown man we all look at as a kid tries not to grimace, but the slight flicker of his cheek muscles and the squint of his eyes don't go unnoticed. "Toughen up, kid. My wife takes on more pain with my dick inside her." Antonio's nod is sharp, cementing his words for Joseph to toughen his ass up and show no pain or he won't make it in our world. "No one does this to one of us, Joseph. Who was it?" Antonio turns to me then back to Joseph.

"A cop," he informs Antonio.

"A cop?" Antonio repeats, clarifying. "A cop did this to you? Why?"

"Don't know. Told the store owner I stole something. I didn't."

Antonio lets go of Joseph's face and takes a step back. Thick rivulets of blood trickle down his chin. "Go clean up. Doc should be here in a few to stitch you up."

I ignore Demetri's questioning beam on the side of my face. I don't need him to tell me one plus one always equals two.

Antonio steps away to take a call. Demetri takes that opportunity to take a step closer to me.

"You don't have to say it." I grit my teeth.

"I didn't think I did. I'm waiting to hear what we're going to do about it."

I glance over my shoulder at Antonio. "Looks like I am going to have to put my talent of fixing things to good use with this one."

"You going to tell him?" He takes his curiosity over his shoulder to Antonio.

"He already knows." My voice dry, matching my facial expression.

"Motherfucker!" Antonio's Italian leather shoes scuff the floor with determined, furious steps. "Pier forty-two warehouse."

"What about it?" My shoulders stiffen, knowing we have a drop tonight with our new business associate.

"Call Cillian and move the drop to a new location and day. We need to roll." He spins his finger as he's putting the phone to his ear. "Joseph!" Antonio thunders.

"Yes, boss?" Joseph pops his head out from the bathroom.

"Hold on, pop," he utters into the phone before turning to Joseph. "You stay right here until Dr. B stitches you up," he orders. "Then you find your father and help him man the docks."

"What's going on?" Demetri questions as I'm calling Cillian.

"We just had a shipment delivered to the docks. Ten women were inside the hauler. Two weren't so lucky."

I jerk my head in his direction as I hang up the phone. "What?"

"Yeah, brother. You heard me right. We have to clean this up before it becomes what it's meant to be—a full-blown set up."

"Motherfucker."

Isabelle
CHAPTER TWENTY-SEVEN

The ride home was a stifling quiet one. *Home* is the word that lingers in my thoughts. I don't believe I have ever rested my head in a place I felt was a home. When you really think about it, it's a sad concept to accept. Every child should feel like the walls that surround them are a haven, a place that holds security. I have to wonder if Giovanni's penthouse is *my* home now. I know he has referenced it as if it was, but is it really? Do I feel like it is? Because I am the only one that can sense that. Will I even stay here? I haven't given it much thought. Don't I need to live on my own, survive on my own, learning and figuring out who I am before fully sharing my life with someone again? The fact of the matter is, I don't think I ever shared a life with Tommy, and I already feel like I am sharing a life with Giovanni in the short period of time we have been together. I feel a connection with him that I have never felt with anyone I have shared a life with before.

He has taken control of my day to day to alleviate my stress and I have freely let him. I feel like I stepped out of one life and into another without any blow back or repercussions. When I really think about it, I did do exactly just that. I'm not even worried about Tommy finding me. Giovanni has assured me he can't get to me inside the penthouse, and I trust his word. How messed up is that, am I, for having so much faith in a man I hardly know? I already have faith in Giovanni more than I ever did Tommy.

That defining rainy night in the alley, I had made a choice, and I haven't looked back. Strangely, I am at peace here in his bubble. It's a safe place for my daughter and I. Being protected is something I haven't felt in… well, never. Here in his space, in the thick of his intoxicating scent, I feel a stillness, a silence I can easily breathe in. Is that a bad thing, to entrust someone so much after what I have gone through, especially after the way he behaved today? Giovanni was furious with me. I felt his anger. It emanated like a living breathing force of nature off every muscle that flexed in the bulk of his powerful body. I experienced him in a way I hadn't before. It worried me, but even though he was furious, and he expressed that, he still held me with controlled strength and care, showing me how displeased he was with the intensity of his body in a way I felt all the way to the core of my bones. He didn't physically hurt me, but intellectually, he made his feelings well known. His argument was the total opposite of the norm I'm used to. He held me accountable for what he thought were secrets and what I claimed to be mine. My reaction to his generosity hurt him. My withheld truth was almost as if it was a betrayal to him. I should have been more open, but then again, it was mine to keep, and he isn't fully up-front with me either. He himself told me he wouldn't be able to tell me anything about his business, and at times, I would have to do as he says with no explanation, that it would all be for my safety. And really, what does he actually do for the organization? If I ask him, will he tell me? The real question is, do I want to know, or can I keep a blind eye? I know who he works for. I went from being with a man that holds up the law to one I can only assume obliterates it. I think I would rather stay in the dark. But that's not reality, now, is it? I have lived too long in a truth I've had to keep concealed. I want openness between us. As much as he can be with me.

I sit on Giovanni's massive couch with Abigail's head in my lap. My fingers lazily graze through her curls as she sleeps. I'm lost in a fog of conflicting thoughts. Each moment of this afternoon was an eye opener. The day was long, and by the time we finished being pampered, both Abigail and I were exhausted and hungry. I wanted to ask Luca, our driver, to stop for food but I was too uncomfortable. I felt like I should be making small talk, but I had nothing to say, and honestly, what do you say to the bodyguard who protects the wife of a mafia underboss? Besides, I felt like there was tension in the car, like he didn't want to be driving me. I thought maybe it had to do with the fact that he wasn't in his normal element but then I thought more about it. I believe it was because my last name is connected to someone in law enforcement. I chose to keep that to myself because if that was the case, I understood his reluctance. Then I thought, if this is how he feels, then all of them will feel the same. So where do I fit in?

I settle Abigail in the deep corner of the couch where it meets the connecting side. I grab my phone and head down the hallway to Giovanni's bedroom. After stripping down, I dial his number. I feel the overwhelming need to hear his voice. I don't like how we parted today. I feel a separation and I don't know if it's because of him leaving the way he did or because I'm trying to sort through my own feelings. It's most likely both playing on my emotions. My heart sinks when my call is ducked, going straight to voicemail. When I hear his clipped, dry greeting, I can't help but sigh as my sinking heart flutters at hearing his deep baritone. I leave a message telling him I miss him and that we need to talk. That I won't say I'm sorry for today, but I will try to be more open. Then I tell him I don't want to bother him while he is at work, but I need to hear his voice.

Just as I end the call, that little devious devil pops up on my shoulder, making me question so many things. How would I ever know if he really is at work? It's not like he holds down a nine-to-five in an office where I can pop in for lunch. It's after nine o'clock right now, and he is out doing whatever he does. Then I think back to his phone ringing excessively while he had me plastered to the mirror. It was an amount that would heed a warning to something urgent. Or maybe it could have been a female who was pissed at her lover. It was a female who kept calling him, so I have to wonder, right? He did blow it off, telling me not to worry about it when I asked. It's the same thing Tommy used to do, and I'm sure he was cheating on me. I just didn't care.

But Giovanni is not Tommy.

I know this in my heart and soul, but as I sit here stark naked on the end of his bed with my phone twisting around in my nimble fingers and my thoughts rushing through my head, I am worried about it. He's an attractive man. A very powerful, attractive, rich man, at that. That combination is a magnet to every woman out there. He could have any woman he wants. I saw the way women were looking at him the night of the fundraiser. Why would he choose me, the redhead with freckles who has more issues than medusa had snakes slithering around on her head? I jerk myself out of these self-deprecating thoughts because I know it is only my insecurities rearing its ugly self from a lifelong battle of not being good enough.

I decide to change the downward spiral of my thoughts and emotions and make a call I should have made a long time ago.

I wait for the call to connect and take a deep breath. "Hi, Zoey. Remember me? It's, Izzy."

After an hour on the phone talking to the only girlfriend I have ever had, and still have, I hang up feeling good. She made me laugh. She made me cry. She accepted and understood and even yelled at me for not asking for help once I explained what the last few years have been like for me. We made plans to meet up, have lunch and catch up more. She is working for some big wig executive now, and I couldn't be happier for her. She sounded good, happy, and thriving in her journey. She sounded the way I wish I could. I hang up feeling cheerful and also sad for missing those few years of a friendship I think could have been a true sisterhood. Then I think maybe our friendship wasn't meant to be at that time, but I hope it is now.

I make my way to the shower and flip the modern handle, turning on each spray. I stand there waiting for the water to warm up when a thought, a memory, hits me. The first time Giovanni and I were together, that very first night in the back alley in his SUV, he was wearing a chain around his neck with two letters hanging off it. I struggle to remember what initials they were, but I do remember that they were initials. Without turning the shower off, I go in search of the chain. He no longer wears it, so it must be here somewhere. At least, he doesn't wear it when he is with me. My thoughts go back to the other night when he was hovering above me. His chain swung between us, but it was two medals that hung, swinging like a pendulum between our joined bodies.

They were a force of protection.

I make my way into the closet and go straight for his chest of drawers. On top sits a gleaming box I saw him put his watch in once when he was changing. When I lift the lid, I see two Rolex watches, a man's onyx ring with a diamond set in the center, a wad of cash—all hundreds—and a dainty ring with a small diamond in the middle. I pick the ring up and inspect it. It looks like a wedding ring to me. I mean, any ring could be a wedding ring but this ring looking as if it's a genuine wedding ring. That little devil springs back up on my shoulder, but I tamp it back down. I trust Giovanni. He has a past, who doesn't? Jealousy flares when I think of him sharing a life with someone else. Why didn't it last with her? Where is she now? Did she leave or did he leave her? Maybe she couldn't handle the life he lives. Will I be able to handle it? Then I think, hell, I've lived with Tommy's lies, and they were blatant lies. Giovanni has already been up front with me, telling me he couldn't speak of certain things.

I lay the ring down, letting my fingertips roll over the delicate metal as I stare off into an abyss of nothing. I snap out of it when my finger grazes over a felt tab. I pull on it, lifting the top tier from the bottom. I find more neatly stacked money sitting to the side, a few business cards, and a gold chain with two charms. *The* gold chain. The one that captured my attention for only a second as he plunged himself in and out of my body. I take a deep breath and lift the chain in the air. The two charms dangle in front of me like scarlet letters. K & A. The female calling Giovanni this afternoon, the name that flashed across his phone screen, was Kathrine. K & A. Could the second letter just be the second initial in her name? I'm surprisingly interrupted from my thoughts when I hear the doorbell ring and the elevator doors slide open. I'm startled to say the least and a whoosh of worry washes over me. I glance at the CCTV in the corner of Giovanni's bedroom and see Sofia walking through with Sage. They haul racks and racks of clothing into the living room. I quickly grab one of Giovanni's dress shirts and throw it on before running to the shower and turning it off. I'm still buttoning his shirt as I'm rushing down the hallway to greet them and ask why they're here.

I reach the living room and say hello as I wearily glance at the unknown man standing by the elevator. When I receive a warm hug from Sage, I see a flash of recognition in Sofia's eyes. It's the moment I realize I am still holding the necklace in my fisted palm, the charms dangling from my hand at Sage's back. My chest squeezes with brutal strength when Sofia glances at the necklace once again as she walks over to us. The tightness in my chest feels like more of a strangulation. Giovanni and Sofia shared a private moment right in front of my eyes. Maybe he has a whole harem of women. Maybe I am just one of many. And who is the guy standing in the foyer? I glance his way again, inspecting him.

"Stop. I don't know what you are thinking, but I definitely know that look in your eyes. Whatever you're making yourself believe, just stop. It will only make it worse." She pauses following my line of sight. "That's Freddy. He works for the family, for G. I'm guessing you haven't been introduced. Not surprising." She rolls her eyes. "It's for your safety. Just remember, secrets aren't secrets in this family, they are withheld protection."

She formally introduces us, but I find it odd and become uncomfortable when he just stares at my outstretched hand when I greet him after our introduction. At my uneasy reaction, she then goes on the explain that Freddy knows the code to get inside. That only a very few chosen ones have that privilege, and she is not one of them. She seems perfectly okay with that but as I stand there, I become more and more uneasy at the fact that this guy can come and go as he pleases. Abigail and I were here alone for hours today. What if he decided he wanted to come in here? He could just walk right on in. A chill ripples down my now steeled spine, and I take a step back. What if Tommy got his teeth into this guy and bribed him to give him the code so he could get to me? What if he uses his badge to gain entrance? I can't trust that. I don't even know if Tommy knows where I am, but I can't trust that.

Sofia must see my panic staring to rise. She steps forward and lays her hand on my arm. "He didn't shake your hand because he is not allowed to touch you." My eyes flash to hers at her statement. "It is out of respect and also warning from his employer to keep his hands to himself."

I sputter my disbelief, "That is just ridiculous."

"You don't really know the man you're with if you can actually say that. You have a lot to learn about the male that claimed you."

I glance at the man known as Freddy. He stands there stoically, but the small twinkle in his eyes tells me Sofia isn't lying. I am not to be touched by any other man, at the orders of the one I share a bed with. I don't know if I find that infuriating or sexy as hell. It seems the warmth spreading through my chest at the information finds the latter to be more appealing.

I let that information simmer for a moment and then decide to just ask the question that has been burning inside me since she has been so forthright. "Have you and Giovanni... Were you ever lovers? Fuck buddies? Whatever?" I blurt after my initial hesitation.

She laughs with such a boisterous cheer, I'm taken back. "Lord, no!" She cries with laughter, looking to Sage who is laughing as well. "See, I told you whatever you were thinking was only going to be trouble."

Little does she know that that question isn't the only one bothering me. "You two shared a look this afternoon. When my daughter said that one day he would be her father, you two shared a look."

"We have history together," she gently explains. I deflate. "Not *that* kind of history," she corrects, holding up her hands when she sees my reaction. "It's a private matter. I won't be the one to tell you his personal business, but what I will tell you is I think very highly of him, and I don't ever want to see him hurt. If Giovanni wants you to know, he will tell you if you ask."

"Who's Kathrine?" I blurt.

Sage walks back over to the clothing rack and Freddy disappears. "Again, that's a question you will need to direct at him."

"I have. This afternoon before he ran out on me." I throw one hand up and turn away while the other is clutched around the necklace.

"I don't know how much you know about the men in our lives, but they don't hold down regular business hours," she tells me to my back. "They come and go all hours of the day and night. That much I can tell you."

"He left mad. He was furious with me. Because I assumed he was trying to buy me with all of this." I turn and wave my hand towards the racks of clothes.

She laughs once more. "Giovanni will only ever buy you something because he wants to, not because he needs to buy your affections. I must say, you must be worth it in his eyes. He has never done this for anyone else before."

"Who are you to him?"

"The question should be who is he to me? He was once my bodyguard. And he will forever be my friend. If you want to truly know who he is, you need to ask him."

"You are very secretive. I'm not sure if I can trust that," I admit, even though deep down I know I do trust her.

"This family is very secretive. Either get on board or jump off ship if you don't think you have the backbone to handle a family like ours, but then again, he isn't letting you go anywhere."

"And what kind of family is that?"

"One everyone in this city knows not to fuck with. Even your ex."

Sofia and Sage left over an hour ago. I aimlessly walk around the soundless penthouse. The only noise heard is me talking to myself. I feel jittery, on edge, like I need to do something but I have nothing to do. Anything. At least if Abigail was still here, I can pretend I am talking to her instead of the false sense of heavy air weighing me down.

Lakelynn had called to see what time her mom would be home. When Sofia told her she was here delivering all the clothes, she begged for Abigail to sleep over. I immediately said no, not feeling comfortable with Abigail being out of my reach, but then I relented because she had been awake on the couch and overheard us talking. She begged me, and after a few minutes of seeing the little girl sadness in her glistening eyes, I couldn't deny her anymore. I want Abigail to grow and flourish in a different life than I did. I was never allowed to have the typical childhood and I don't want my past to dictate hers. She and Lakelynn had too much fun together this afternoon to prevent her from having a friendship that could last a lifetime if Giovanni and I stay together.

I grab one of the four clothing racks and wheel it down the hallway to Giovanni's bedroom. I organize my clothes to keep some kind of assemblance on my side of the closet that he told me was mine. I grab the next two racks and unload them as well. Just as I'm getting to the last few pieces, I run my hand over the three hanging silk ties I had Sofia add to the order. I liked them, and I thought they would go great with his intense gaze. I turn my focus to his side of the closet and can't help but glance at the regal jewelry box sitting on top of his chest of drawers. The necklace is sitting at the bottom where I replaced it with the notion to ask him about it when he gets home. It burns with worry in my thoughts. I decide I need to give him the benefit of the doubt. I'll ask about it and if he gives me an answer I don't like, then I will deal with it.

I reach for the drawer I have seen him go to for his ties before. He has a whole drawer with individual compartments for each tie. When I go to slide it open it jams a bit, but with some finesse, I wiggle it free. A now crinkled yellow envelope sits on top. I push it to the side, not paying it any mind. That is, until it falls to the floor and I notice my name is written in the upper right-hand corner. Curiosity makes me grab it and unwind the string that secures the seal. I pull the papers out and fall to my knees, letting the pieces to my past flutter to the luxurious carpeted floor in front of me. Everything about me is right there in black and white. My name, my social, my family—living and dead. The few jobs I have held. The only friend I had when I moved to the city. She was marked as a known associate. The town I was born and raised in was typed across the page. My father's and mother's full name—maiden and married—and who my father is. It's all right there at my fingertips. His callused fingertips. He knows everything about me, and I know nothing about him. He even has Abigail's birth certificate. I shove the papers back in the envelope and walk with heavy steps to the kitchen. I pour myself a hearty glass of red wine and swallow a hefty gulp. I pick up my phone and dial his number. The phone rings off after two alerts, going straight to voicemail. He has ducked my call once again. I throw my phone to the counter and grab the bottle of wine. There is a part of me that now feels trapped, kept by a mystery man. This is the same thing Tommy used to do to me. After two years of marriage, he would duck my calls too. My insides feel like burnt ashes just simmering along the delicate lining of my stomach. I twirl the rim of my glass against the stone countertop while lost in thought. So lost that I don't hear the elevator doors slide open or the footsteps that approach the opposite end of the island, or the figure standing there with fury on their face. When I finally do, it's too late.

"We need an extra source of transportation. Has to be something modest. Since we're all going our separate ways, I suggest we have two," I share my thoughts with Antonio as we stand on neutral ground. We're sitting ducks out here. We know it too. We need to get the hauler unloaded and away from the docks.

"Whose trucks can we use that are lowkey?"

"I have a suggestion. You're not going to like it. At this point it's our only option," Demetri chimes in while throwing his half-smoked cigarette to the ground and releasing swirling white plumes through his flared nostrils.

He is correct. Once Demetri voices his thoughts, Antonio immediately shuts him down.

Thirty minutes later, a van pulls into where we stand in a field next to a construction site and a rundown warehouse while waiting to transport. Not two minutes after that, two more vans pull in.

Along with the bodies we were also gifted with twenty kilos of cocaine. Whoever this was, wants us removed. They want our organization not just stunted but obliterated. They were smart, making certain we wouldn't have legs to stand on after we were arrested. Who would be so willing to go the extra mile that they didn't care about the loss they would have capitalized on with the street resale? Not to mention the clout they have to procure women from a ruthless and vile bottom of the barrel organization.

Doors slam shut, interrupting my internal process of seek and destroy. Three men jump out of their vehicles. Greetings and manly back slaps of appreciation can be heard from all around.

"I'm sorry, man." I hear Antonio verbalizes his guilt to my left. "You know I never wanted to get you involved with business. I wouldn't have asked if it wasn't our only option."

"We're cool, A," Caelan assures him while shaking my hand. "What's the plan, brother-in-law?"

"Luca's going to drive you and Luke back," Antonio instructs him. "You know the van will be burned at the end of the night?"

"That's what insurance is for."

"Call it in to the station mid-morning. I'll make sure it is one of the boys that takes the report."

"I'm going with you, A," Luke chimes in, stepping away from the fresh gravel he just stirred up from his drive in. "We'll take the girls up to my compound. My mom and the other women will get them cleaned, fed, and clothed."

"I can't ask you to do that."

"It's done," Luke replies with finality. "Where are you going to do bring them? To the safe house in the city? If the person who set this up doesn't know about the safe house in the city, I would be surprised. It's the first place authorities will look."

"Brother." He turns to Caelan. "You're going home. I don't know what to expect tonight. I damn sure don't want you here if shit goes sideways. I'm going to need my brother-in-law to take care of my son if I hit the ground or worse, go to jai—"

A resounding pop and deadly whistle passes the shell of my ear before Antonio can finish his sentence. Antonio tackles Caelan to the ground, his instincts and years of experience taking over. Both scramble to the side of the truck as Luke and I dive behind the second van. We're taking on heavy fire within seconds. Bullets are flying everywhere. The girls are screaming from inside the walls of the van. I grab for my piece. I hear the faint ringing of my phone through the chaos, but I pay no attention to it because Luca takes a hit and is now lying face down in the middle of the open ground, exposed and ready to be slaughtered. Before I can even think about moving, Luke is sliding across the gravel and grabbing Luca by the clothing on his back. Antonio jumps up and starts shooting at our unknown assailants. I jump to my feet and grab Luca by his lower half, helping Luke pull him to safety while Antonio keeps their gunfire at a stall. Another van comes out of nowhere and skids in sideways, flying debris covers us along with the dust from the unsettled dirt.

Just over the ridge, I see the exploding orange light from the two shooters automatic rifles. Taking advantage of the distraction and the hazy view, I make my way around the side of the truck. The ridge is just a few feet away. I scramble my way behind it and take aim. With a deep controlled breath, I inhale and pull the trigger on my exhale, and nail one of them right between the eyes. His brain matter explodes onto his buddy, distracting him for just a moment. When his thoughts come back to the matter at hand, he changes his trajectory and points his gun in my vicinity. The stillness in my body while under fire is almost an out-of-body experience. The bullets carve divots in the dirt around me. The anarchy outside is controlled inside. I take aim, inhale then exhale and pull the trigger. He goes down. The following silence is the calm before the brewing storm. Lessons all learned from when I was a small child. I know there is more to come. I edge my way around the side of the dirt mound. There he is, the third one just waiting for one of us to make a move.

Not today, motherfucker. Not today. You picked the wrong group of men to take payment on.

Bam!

His body stills and slowly hits the dirt beside his buddy. The incessant ring from my phone irritates me. I don't move, but when I see Rocker, Luke's sergeant-at-arms, come around the back side of the pile of dirt, I grab for my phone knowing our assailants are all dead. The screen lights up with Denny Jr's name.

"Yeah!" I holler, lifting myself from the ground.

"It's a set up! Get out of there! The whole calvary is coming!"

I hang up and run up over the hill with Rocker on my heels. "Get in the trucks!" I yell my order as I come down the hill, hitting the bottom. Antonio is helping Luke put Luca in the back of the van, and when I go to jump in, Caelan is in the driver seat spitting out orders. I turn back and start popping off my own orders. "Load up! Now! It's a sting."

One of the girls slips out from the back of another van. Although she doesn't look like a girl but a young woman. "I can help," she can barely say from the toll her body has taken on through the course of her trip. She's exhausted but willing to help. "I was a nurse back in my country. I can try and keep him stable while you bring him to get him help."

"Why? Why the fuck would you do that?" Antonio shifts all his attention from me to her.

"Because you didn't kidnap us. You saved us. I save him, you send me back home. Deal?"

"Get in the van. And if you try anything, if you're working for them, whoever the fuck this is setting us up, I will put a bullet in your fucking skull." He turns away. "Demetri, follow her." He points at the woman's tattered back. "What?" Antonio turns his sight from Luca's lifeless body and snaps at me.

"Just got word from Denny!" I bellow. "We separate. Watch the burners for instructions." Everyone disperses. I turn back and look at Demetri who's climbing inside the back of the van Luca's in. "He alive?"

"Just."

I jump in the van and tell Demetri to get out and take one of the other vans. I instruct Antonio that I am going to take Luca back into the city so Doc can work on him. Then I realize I can't take him back to the warehouse. It's been compromised. I make a rash decision and tell Antonio I'm taking him back to my place. Dr. B can meet us there. Demetri jumps in the front seat and tells Antonio that it would be better to follow Luke to his compound.

Orders are barked from every direction.

The outcome is the same.

There is a dying man in the back of this van that needs medical attention.

I tell Rocker to get the two deceased women and put them in the back of another van and head to my place upstate. Luke instructs Antonio that his guys will take care of the vans once everything is situated. Our trust in Luke is as if he is one of us, a brother. He is a powerful man who rules over many men. His word is as sacred as his power.

Just as Luke slams the door my phone starts ringing once again. I grind my teeth, but I know I have to answer. I have declined her call one too many times.

"Isabelle," I answer, my breath heavy and gruff from all the adrenaline surging through my body. A moment passes as I wait for her to speak.

The woman in the back starts yelping with a high-pitched moan. I glance in the rearview mirror to see what the hell is going on. Demetri has her by the neck. She holds a knife in her hand. Within seconds the blade clatters to the floor of the van from Demetri's skilled lessons in pressure points.

I glance back to the road with my phone still to my ear knowing he has it handled and demand, "Isabelle, answer me."

All I hear is a sniffle and then silence. I look at my phone to confirm the call ended.

Alarms start going off inside my head. I flick over to the app that has my security cameras. I find her in the kitchen, sitting at the island with a glass of wine and tears in her eyes. But her gaze is on the door. I flick to the camera in the elevator. Nothing is there. I then flick over to the security feed in the lobby. There is nothing out of the ordinary. I flick back to my kitchen. She still sits there but this time her index finger is tapping the stone with rapid speed. She's irritated and it infuriates me that I can't be there to fix it right now.

I make a sharp right turn, alerting Demetri my attention is not on the road.

"Take it easy, brother. Erratic driving will definitely get us pulled over," he states from the back of the van where he sits with Luca, watching the woman.

"Fuck!" I quietly spew knowing he is right. "How's he doing?"

"Still bleeding. Still out. Still alive."

Fuckin' D with his emotional detachment.

"You call Doc B?"

"He'll meet us there."

"What just happened back there?"

"Misunderstanding," his low gruff voice states with malice.

How the hell am I going to explain this to Isabelle? Even though she knows, she doesn't really know who I am, what I do. I have only ever expressed that it is imperative that she listen to my orders because they would be for her safety. When I walk in with a gunshot victim bleeding out, it very well will change the way she sees things about my lifestyle, now her lifestyle. Then it hits me. *Fuck.* I close my eyes. I forgot about Abigail. I can explain this to Isabelle. But Abby? I rush reaching for my phone. I have to get through to Isabelle. Alert her. Tell her to keep Abby occupied in her room.

The call connects but it rings off. I call again and this time it's cut off immediately. She sent me straight to voicemail. *Touché, my angel, but boy oh boy, is your ass going to be red for that rebellious action.* I try once again, and it is the same thing. My little lion is not going to be so happy once I am standing in front of her. Declining a call because I am in the middle of a gun fight is one thing. Her declining because she's pissed at me for doing it as she sits there with a glass of wine in a safe place is a whole different situation. I throw the phone on the dash and concentrate on my driving with the decision that I will give her a few minutes to cool down.

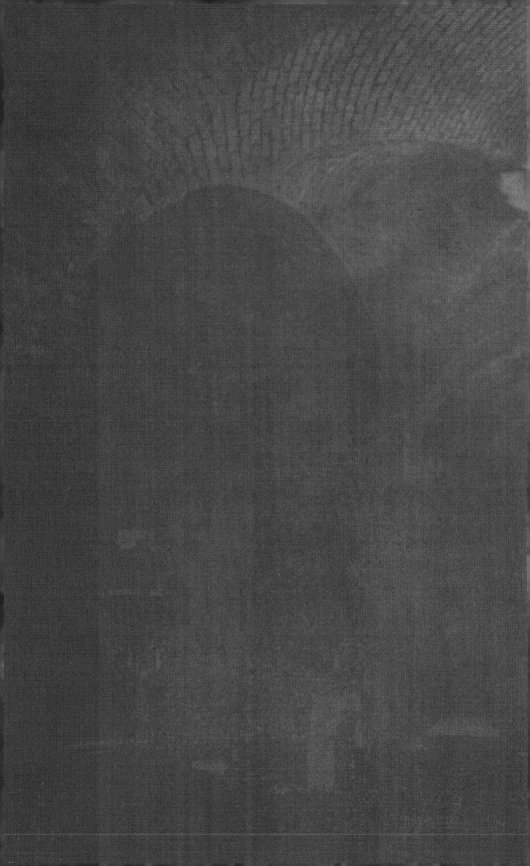

Giovanni
CHAPTER TWENTY-NINE

I burst through the elevator doors in a rushed huff, livid. I scan the room seeking out my angel, but she is nowhere in sight. I have tried her five more times. Each time my call is ducked and sent to voicemail. I rush through every room shouting out her name with dominant force. She is a ghost of my imagination, thinking I will see her around every corner.

Praying that I see her.

Her glass of wine I saw her nursing is still sitting on the kitchen island, only it is tipped onto its side with the remaining red contents spilling over the edge to the floor. That stops me in my tracks for only a heartbeat of a second when my adrenaline kicks back in. I run to our bedroom and search for her in our private space. It's the first place I should have gone to, but my mind is frantic in its search for her, my angel.

I glance to my left and see all the empty racks that held her clothes from the boutique. One rack still housing some of her garments sits in the living room.

What made her stop hanging them?

I step to the opening of the closet and scan the space. I suck in a sharp breath and release a ragged one when I see it.

A cruel feeling hits me square in the chest that I haven't felt since I was a small boy.

Fear.

That fear quickly turns into desperation.

I grab my phone and call her once again, only to be further disturbed at the unknown silence on the other end. When my phone vibrates, I fumble with the device until I put it to my ear and shout her name in so much concerned anger, my throat burns.

"What the fuck, G? We good? He's bleeding out!"

I snap out of my vexed misery. "Yeah! Yeah, we're good. Bring him up." The weight behind my authority overrides the panic I hold in my chest at losing my angel.

I run back to the kitchen and throw the remaining stuff off the island, grab a towel and disinfectant, and start frantically wiping away the germs that have occurred only when two females crashed my place with their messy ways. My stomach clenches at the thought. Just as I'm finishing, the elevator opens, and a bleeding Luca is being dragged in by Demetri and Joseph with the unknown woman from the van and Dr. B in tow.

I rush to them and help them lift Luca onto the island. He's silent and the fact that he is has me planning his funeral. I lean down and bark an order next to his ear. "You wake the fuck up. Your boss needs you to protect his wife." I grab his bare shoulder and grip it hard, wanting him to feel the pain I know is radiating through the tender bruising meat. That pain will let him know he is still alive. I know. It's how I have lived my whole life.

I turn to Dr. B. "Sorry, Doc. This is all I got. The warehouse has been compromised. Don't let him fucking die. The boss won't be too happy his wife's bodyguard isn't around to protect her."

"And what about you?" he sharply asks.

"I protect them. All of them," I snarl back at his nudge to my failure. I take my steps away from him in haste, turn, cross my arms over my chest and watch his every move. If one of my men wasn't dying in my kitchen the good ol' doctor may be working on himself for that comment.

"What the hell is going on with you?" Demetri approaches me as I stand back and watch through slitted eyes. "She's a nurse, Doc. That's what she says, anyway." Demetri turns his attention from me and informs the doctor when the woman from the van tries to help.

"I am. An RN in a surgical unit to be exact," she snips with a frail tone.

Doc gives her a once over, observing what ripped and dirty clothes she has left on her malnourished body. With one more glance, knowing better than to ask, he goes about his business and starts working on our man.

"You going to tell me what the hell is going on with you?"

"She's gone. Both my girls are gone," I growl, shifting from foot to foot.

"Isabelle? She's not here?"

"No."

"You instructed her not to leave the penthouse?" he questions.

I give him a glare that informs him to not ask stupid questions as I'm pulling up the tracker I have implemented on her phone. I'm kicking myself right now for not doing it sooner, but I never thought to since she was here when I checked the cameras.

What happened in the last thirty minutes?

I turn to Demetri to tell him to shout for me if anything changes while I go into my office and check the CCTV recording when the doctor rumbles with frantic breaths.

"He's bleeding out! Get on the counter and put pressure on that hole while I pull the bullet out of this one."

Demetri and I rush to the makeshift operating table. The woman from the van barely has enough energy to lift herself onto the counter but she tries like hell to stop Luca's bleeding chest.

"What do you need us to do?" I shove her out of the way, taking over and pound down on his chest hoping he feels it.

"He needs blood. Do you know what blood type he is?"

"No," Demetri and I both say in unison.

"What a fucking mess." I jump down letting Demetri take over and grab the blood-soaked rags from the floor and throw them in the trash, irritated at my lack of details. How can I fix this if I don't have all the information I need? "Fuck!" I growl my frustration.

"Either of you O negative?" Doc asks.

"No."

"No."

"I am," the woman, profusely sweating with her exertion of just sitting there, mumbles.

"No!" I stop that thought right in its tracks. She may be helping but I have no idea who she is and without any intel on her, she is a threat whether she is helping or not. "I know someone who is." I close my eyes and think twice about it. "*Fuck!*" I bellow, hating myself for making this call, knowing I have no other choice.

"Hey, G. I'm just walking in. I'm sorry I didn't reach out this afternoon. Daniel was a dick. We had a huge fight an—"

"I need you in my penthouse ASAP!" I stop my sisters rant on a dime.

"What's wrong?" She starts to panic. "Oh God. It's Antonio, right? He's retaliated for you punching him, didn't he, G? I told you this was going to happen!"

"Hope," I speak as calmly as I can at the moment while my heart is ready to leap from my rapidly expanding chest. "I need you up here right now," I order her before hanging up, cutting off her worried tirade.

I stride over to the elevator when I hear the call bell. I know I need to meet her and explain before she walks in and sees what is taking place in my kitchen. I may have taken care of Hope most of her life, but I have tried my best to keep her away from the dirty parts of the world I fluidly move through. A bleeding out man is nothing I haven't seen or caused myself before. If it weren't for the ache in my chest over my angel disappearing, I would be as cool as a glacier with the scene happening before me. Nothing gets past the shell that houses the cavern in my chest. That was sealed off when the young child in me turned into a man and distanced myself from the selfish woman I blame my mother to be.

The doors slide open. Hope rushes through in hysterics. I damn near catch her midair. Her mouth falls open at the crimson sea splattered across my kitchen.

"I need you to stay calm." I grab a hold of her shoulders and shake to get her attention off Luca's limp body.

"What—What happened to him?"

"He needs blood. No one knows what blood type he has but your blood is universal."

"Yes! Yes! Here!" she yells as she starts pulling up her sleeve. "You have to save him. You can't let him die. He can't die, Giovanni!" She pulls away and rushes to the doctor's side and slaps the crease of her arm like a junkie. I take pause and with narrowed eyes I try to evaluate her frantic demeanor.

Dr. B looks at me and I nod my agreeance, giving him the order to go ahead with the procedure.

Then I stand back and pull out my phone once again, tapping on the tracker to see where my girl is, but before I can, I hear, "What do you mean I can't! I'm O. I can!"

"You are O positive. You could kill him, Miss Moretti," Dr. B explains to her.

"I thought you were O negative?" I throw my phone to the counter with a thud and step to her.

"No. I'm positive," she shouts. "I can give him blood!"

I close my eyes and lay my hand at the back of my neck and squeeze. My man is going to die because I can't keep my thoughts straight. It's not Hope who has O negative. It's someone else.

Fuck.

I don't want to make this call.

I don't even know if I have enough time to make this call.

I grab my phone from the counter where I threw it and hit the call button. The line picks up on the first ring. An irritated voice I know all too well answers.

My chest fills with heaviness.

I step away from everyone and say, "I need you."

"Where?" There was no hesitation, and the irritation is suddenly gone.

"My penthouse."

The line goes dead at my doing because I can't bear the thought that I needed to make that call.

Less than five minutes later, which baffles me, the bell chimes for the elevator and Kathrine walks through the door. My chest tightens at the site of her and my heart clenches with guilt.

After a silent moment between us, she calmly rasps, "What's happening?"

240

"How did you get here so fast?" I automatically question.

"What's going on?"

I blow off my question not being answered for the simple fact that my man is dying. I look at him and tell her, "We don't know what blood type he is. He needs—"

"O negative. I'm O negative." Her voice drops in disappointment. "That's the only reason you called me." Her displeasure clear as she walks to Luca's lifeless body. She stops, connects eyes with me and pulls up her sleeve in silence, waiting for the doctor to start the transfusion.

I watch her with concern. Her calmness has red flags flying but I can't let myself worry about that right now.

I have a kitchen full of anarchy and people in a space I have always held sacred. All except the one person I want isn't here because of my ignorance.

I step back from the scene in front of me and close my eyes. I fucked up. I should have told Isabelle. I broke her trust. The torture I feel inside for my recklessness subsides when the rage inside me flourishes with a tempestuous blaze. Why didn't she just ask me? She put herself and Abigail in danger being out there on the streets. I know Tommy is searching for her. Because I've had surveillance on him five minutes after I took Isabelle into my arms in that puddle-soaked alley when she finally gave herself to me.

There is a part of me that still can't believe she would leave over finding the report I had Freddy draw up on her. I understand that it's a violation of her privacy, but in my line of work, there is no privacy. It's my job to know everything about everyone. It's how I fix things. Just like her body, I will know every in and out, every crevice that makes up her DNA, and the tortured events of her life that have formed her personality. When she ticks, the way she ticks, it's all for me to know.

"He needs to finish the blood transfusion along with fluids and rest. I don't know what direction this will go. I did my best with what I had. He needs close monitoring. Kathrine is going to need a bed when she is done giving her blood to him. She will need rest."

"For your sake, Luca better come out of this alive. You'll stay here and do just that—keep him alive."

"I'm due in the hospital in a few hours."

"I guess you better pick up your phone and call in sick then, Doc. You're not leaving the premises until I know Luca is going to pull through."

"Mr. Moretti—"

"I advise you to not finish that sentence. That fully padded pocket you have acquired over the last few decades should have warned you of that." I look to Hope. "Show him to the spare room upstairs. Set Luca up in there too. Joseph," I call to the young man quietly standing in the corner watching, learning, and waiting for direction the entire time the chaos was ensuing.

"Stay in that room with them. You keep your eyes on him like it's your mother laying there. Understood?"

"Yes, sir."

"What about her?" Demetri steps up and nods his head in the direction of the woman from the van who is now slouched on the floor in exhaustion with her back up against the cabinets. Her knees are curled up to her chest and her head rests on the hard surface.

"Take her to the room at the end of the hallway. She needs a shower and some food. I'll get Hope to bring her clean clothes. I'll deal with her after I find Isabelle," I tell him as I start to walk towards my office then turn back and inform him, "She'll have information, D. Don't let her out of your sight."

He nods. "And Kathrine?"

That stops me in my tracks. I glance at the group of them moving Luca as one unit. Kathrine's back is to me. A pang of guilt hits my gut. "I'll speak to her." I take two more steps towards my office when my phone rings. As I grab for it, I turn back to him and say, "Let her rest on the couch when she is done with the transfusion."

I turn away, place the phone to my ear, and gruffly answer, "Moretti," to the person calling with the unknown burner number.

"You've got yourself a situation."

Isabelle
CHAPTER THIRTY

I push the sadness I feel to the side, burying it with all the other people and things that have let me down in the past. I take a sip of my third drink and stare at my long-lost friend. She looks good. Better than good. Zoey looks fantastic. Gone is the last crazy hairstyle she had those few years ago. Now she has a medium length pale pink pixie with shaved blonde hair at the sides. She used to have multiple facial piercings but now she has just one. Her radiant olive skin showcases the small, pink diamond stud in her nose.

We chat about nothing and everything. She asks questions about Tommy and scolds me like I am her child for not calling her for help. The vibrancy that glows behind her youthful skin is addicting. I'm more interested about her job and her life, wanting to forget my own, if only for a few hours. I dive into her stories headfirst because I don't want to wallow in my own. She tells me about her boss, who she said is an arrogant ass of a man, but his sexiness and deep voice could make any girl's panties drop. And they do, she goes on to explain. I ask if hers have creeped passed her knees for him. She just smiles demurely and says no. I don't believe her at first but then she goes on to say that they had gone on one date. He took her to this fancy restaurant in the city and they had a beautiful evening together. I ask why it was only one date and she explains that a man like him never wants anything serious and that she does. She wants to settle down and start a family. She is looking for her forever man. The guy who is there through thick and thin. I want to be cynical about her dreams and tell her there is no such thing, but then Giovanni's handsome face pops into my thoughts and it makes me second guess myself.

Up until a few hours ago, I thought I was headed in that same direction. It makes me breathe a sigh of muddied disappointment. In myself and in him. Giovanni knows a lot more about me than I know about him. It wasn't so obvious until tonight. Until his ex, Kathrine, strolled through the elevator doors into his home like she owned it.

He had told me once that only a few select people had the code to enter his private space. It wasn't until after she left her bombshell laying at my feet that I realized she was one of the important ones in his life.

I felt so stupid after her diatribe finally ended and only because I screamed for her to get out. The world I had been existing in for such a short time, that I thought was filled with truth and honesty, was nothing but a case of charity. He felt compelled to help me because of his past. I am that charity case. The helpless woman that can't defend herself. That's a hard pill to swallow. I feel so inadequate. It's the only logical thought I could come up with.

Why wouldn't he tell me about his home life as a child? Why wouldn't he tell me about his mother and what she went through? When I really think about it, he has never mentioned her, and only existing in my own bubble, I had never asked.

Yet Kathrine knew everything about him.

I was too wrapped up in my own worries to realize that he was just being a savior in my misery. That, yes, we may have become close, but he helped me because of his own past trauma. It was a need for him. He found his solace in me while I took from his strength. He's a strong man, but also one with many scars. He couldn't bear to see another woman end up like his mother.

It only dawned on me after she left that the feelings between Giovanni and I are clouded because of the events of our life. If we both stood in front of a mirror and looked at one another we would see one broken boy and one broken girl, who grew into one broken man and one broken woman.

Two people desperate to heal their wounds.

Two separate lives pulled together because of past events.

We could never survive together because of it. Two broken souls equal nothing but shattered glass just waiting for the perfect blow in order to finally fall.

I shouldn't have left the penthouse without speaking to Giovanni. I was safe there, but I wanted to talk to an old soul, someone wiser, someone who had lived life and felt deaths touch and could give me advice. Walter had always been that for me. The old man that bellied up to the bar every night, nursing his beer, mourning the loss of his beloved wife, Edith, was more of a father to me than my own. I had called Zoey to see if she would meet me, knowing what time Walter would be in. It was the same for him. He fed his wife's cat, Marigold, and then ate his frozen dinner before heading to O'Brien's for his liquid dessert and companionship. He was here with me every shift. My only stability in an unstable life.

Zoey left a few minutes ago. We hugged for a long time before I released her with the promised that when I was finally settled and safe, I would contact her again to have dinner. I watched my old friend at the bar playing with the frayed napkin under his beer. I would give quarters I don't have instead of pennies for his thoughts. I turn towards Zoey and watch her walk towards the long hallway that leads to the back door. Then I look to my old friend. Vibrant youth verses wisdom from living a long life. It was the best of both worlds. I want to radiate like Zoey and someday I will, but I also want to grow old with the wisdom of someone who has lived and learned like Walter.

I walk across the bar and smile at Pat as she watches me from the hostess station. I asked her if I could have my job back when I first arrived tonight. After a moment of hesitation, she said she would give me a call next week to set up some shifts.

I need to get back to life.

My life.

Living life.

Being productive instead of sitting stagnant waiting for the unknown. I need to get up in the morning and have a plan, a place to go, a routine to look forward to. I couldn't sit inside his protectant walls for the rest of my life. I need to firmly plant my feet on the ground and do something for myself.

I softy shoulder check Walter and run my hand over his back before plopping down on the seat next to him. "Hey, handsome," I greet him with a small smile.

His return smile is wide and welcoming. A thousand words said with one stretch of his kiss worn lips.

"Hey, sweetheart, how have you been?"

"If I'm being honest, not so good," I admit.

"I can see that. Want to take about it? I have nothing but time." He flicks his finger at Josh, the bartender.

"I would like that." I nibble on my lip. "I think I need some perspective from someone who has lived a life a lot longer than I have," I tell him as Josh sets my double shot of tequila in front of me.

"I feel like that may be a backhanded compliment, sweetheart." His gruff chuckle rumbles in his chest.

"Never. I admire you and would genuinely appreciate the advice you could give me because you have found your way through this journey called life."

"You make me sound like I've lived a life of sainthood. I have not. I am a retired old man who has lived a hard life. On the wrong side of the law, I might add, sweetheart."

"That really doesn't matter, now does it. My soon-to-be ex pledged to uphold the law, yet behind closed doors, he was a villain."

"Some villains have hearts."

"Truer words have never been spoken, but he was not one of them."

"But the one you are with now does," he states. "I have lived hard and loved harder, kiddo. The kind of love that consumes you."

"And I don't think I have truly loved until just recently."

"You think?"

"I was living in my own bubble, being consumed by a man who made me feel when I should have been asking questions. So now I question myself for my choices."

"Ahh, so both yours and his focus were on you and not on him? Let me ask you this, in those moments of being consumed, what did you feel?"

"Yeah, I guess you could say that. I was just told information that made me second guess myself and him and the foundation I thought we were building. It now feels like we're unsteady. I feel unsteady. How did you know I was with someone else?"

"Did you ever think he was protecting you by not telling you? And I can see it in your eyes. My Edith had that same glow. You didn't answer my question, kiddo. How did you feel when he was consuming you?"

"Like he annihilated my weaknesses and infused his strength into me."

I stopped to think about that for a minute. Every time Giovanni and I were together, even though my physical choices were taken away, I still had the power. He made me feel strong. "I do, but I also think he was protecting himself more," I go on to say. "The glow you see is a lightbulb with nothing but question marks floating around in it."

"That's human life, kiddo. We always protect ourselves first. We have to. If we don't, we can't protect others around us. If we're falling apart ourselves, how do we help the falling apart? We can't. We need their strength. When he is ready, he will tell you." He pauses, contemplating. "When my Edith was dying, I shed my tears, many in the dark, but I never cried in front of her. I never showed her my weakness because she needed me to be strong. It wasn't until her final hours that I gave her my strength. It wasn't until we both had no more to give that I held her hand and we cried as I sent her on to a better place where there was no pain or weakness."

"That's really sad, Walter." I blink back tears and reach for my shot to relax my emotion-filled closing throat.

"That's life, kiddo. Life is painful. It's not meant to be easy. It's a lesson. What have you learned through your life? That is the question you should ask yourself. Once you figure that out, your next question should be what do you want for your future."

"I don't even know anymore. I thought I may have been on a recovering path but then I was just hit with some news that derailed my journey. I'm not sure what tomorrow, or even tonight will bring."

"No one knows what the next hour will bring. God willing, I could be holding hands with my Edith in an hour." He takes a sip of his drink.

"Walter, don't say that. I would miss you." I reach out and place my hand on top of his.

"And I would miss you, but I miss my Edith more. The question is, do you miss him more right now than you would miss me?"

"I do. I would."

"Then you should go back to him and ask those questions that are cluttering your head."

"And what if he doesn't answer them?"

"Life is too short to take silence as an answer."

I press my lips to Walter's ruddy cheek with a lingering thank you kiss. I wrap my arms around his shoulders and give him a squeeze.

He pats my arm and kiss the crown of my head. A tear rolls down my cheek. I pull back and swallow the rest of my shot. I take a few steps toward the hallway that leads to the alley and stop when I hear, "Hey, kiddo, when are you going to marry me?"

I turn back and smile so big but my lip quiver along with my flowing tears. "I'm sorry, I can't, Walter. I just promised myself to someone else." I place my hand over my lips and blow him a kiss as the tears spill over my waterline. "Thank you," I whisper.

He winks. "You know where to find me if you need to talk, sweetheart."

Isabelle
CHAPTER THIRTY-ONE

I head into the bathroom so I can wash my hands and throw some cold water on my face to try and settle myself down. I nod at the woman that walks in then I grab my purse and head out the door. I left my Jeep in the alley behind O'Brien's where all the employees park their cars. It felt good to drive. I haven't been behind the wheel in so long, it almost felt odd. Liberating, but odd. It felt great to be able to turn on my tunes and roll down my window to let the fresh air in.

I called Sofia on my way over to O'Brien's to make sure Abigail was okay. Sofia offered to keep her for a few days so Giovanni and I could spend some alone time together. I'm not ready to let my baby girl go for a few days but two nights won't kill me. Then I think twice about it and feel the need to hear her voice again. When I reach for my phone and realize how late it is, I decide against it.

I push on the metal bar, disengaging the lock and shove open the heavy steel door as I hit the call button to a man I should have never sent to voicemail in the first place. I'm grabbing for my keys just as the call connects.

Then I hear his voice.

"You left me?"

In that moment, I knew I made a big mistake.

Startled, I twist in my spot so quickly I lose grip on my phone and drop it. When I hear the plastic clatter to the ground, my heart sinks. My throat closes off my airway when panic starts to set in. We hold each other's tense gaze for a long, silent moment. I open my mouth to say something, but nothing comes out. I feel almost paralyzed. The only noise is my keys rattling from the shake of my hand.

I swallow, then firmly tell myself to turn around and get inside my Jeep, but I can't seem to move. My feet feel like they're stuck in quicksand, and I'm about to be swallowed up by the fear consuming my rational thoughts to move.

"Was that him?" He jerks his chin to my phone on the ground. "You left me for a criminal, Izzy bell." His voice is so soft, almost regretful as he calls me by the nickname he used when we first met.

I finally get myself to turn and put my keys in the door, knowing I need to get out of here while he is still calm, but my hand is shaking so bad, I can't get it in the hole.

"Isabelle, stop. I just want to talk. I won't hurt you, baby."

His hand on my shoulder makes me jerk around in a protective huddle. My keys fall to the ground, landing not too far from my phone.

"Tommy, don't!" I yell.

He drops his hand to his side. "I just want to talk, baby."

"How did you know I was here?" I peek through my protectant arms at him. "You've never come here." I slowly lower my arms when he takes a step back, giving me space.

"Do you know why that is?"

"I don't care why. I just knew that when I came to work, I was free from you, because you wouldn't come here."

"Because this bar is owned by one of the most powerful crime syndicates in the country. Their reach is beyond this country, Isabelle. The place is a cover to launder their money. We're on two different sides of the law. Do you even know who you climbed into bed with?"

"I don't care." I reach down in a stab of strength and grab for my phone because it's closer than my keys. I freeze when I feel his hand on my shoulder once again.

"You should care! You're fucking their hitman, Isabelle! You're so fucking stupid! He's a killer. A ruthless murderer." He runs his hand through his hair. "He kills people for them. Do you get that? Tortures them until they purge their intel, and they get what they want. He's called The Fixer for a reason, Isabelle. He slices their body into bits and pieces and dumps them in the river. Do you know nothing about the man you're spreading your legs for?"

"I don't care," I repeat, grinding my teeth, not wanting to hear it.

"You do. I know you do. You just won't admit your mistakes. Just like you won't admit you were wrong for leaving me." I go to speak my peace, but he cuts me off. "Why do you think I let you work here? I knew you would tell me if you saw or heard anything illegal. You were my mole. You are too much of a goody two-shoes not to tell me anything. I know you, Isabelle. I knew giving you permission to work here would benefit me. We have been investigating them for years, especially him. He is a merciless killer. Bloodshed gets him off."

"So, you used me." My wheels spin listening to his pathetic speech.

"Of course. I'm not fucking stupid."

"Tommy, that's sick. You used me, your wife, to further yourself in your career without my knowledge."

"And he used his mother. His own mother sits in a cement box because of him. Is that the kind of man you want to be with? Raise our daughter with? Because if we are comparing apples to oranges, he is much worse than me furthering my career. He's using you to get to me. Don't you see that?"

Wow. Just wow. He will go to such lows to make himself feel bigger.

There is only one thing that infuriates me out of all his word vomit. He doesn't care about Abby. Never has. Never will.

"Don't you dare pretend like you care about your daughter!" I scream at him.

"I do. I care about you and her. You are my life. Please, Isabelle. Give me another chance."

"Liar!" I shout. "You're a liar!" I screech even louder.

"I'm not. I want you, baby. We're good together. Every couple has fights. We can get through this." He grabs my face with both hands and pushes me up against the door of my Jeep. "I promise it will be different this time," he pleads from a hair's breadth away from me.

His breathing is heavy and harsh, and his eyes are flickering erratically over my face. He steps into my body, pressing himself up against me. I can feel his erection and it does nothing but make me want to vomit.

"No." I shake my head, twisting it to the side so I am not face to face with him. "Let go of me." I grind down on my molars.

"Baby, please. I need you," he begs, placing his lips on my cheek.

With a gruff rasp of frustration, I push at his chest with determination, giving him everything I have. "Get off me!" I push at him even harder. "You don't need me. I was just a trophy you acquired. A political showpiece, a strategic shift on the chess board to make your father happy and your career more stable, therefore advancing you up the career ladder faster, giving your unsatisfied ego the drug it needs to feel important: power. Besides, I really didn't matter anyway since you were sleeping with every woman that would spread their legs for you."

"That's not true. You were different than them."

"The only difference is that I became the punching bag for your weaknesses. Lucky me," I sarcastically spit.

"Izzy, I'm trying to make this right. Why are you trying to provoke me?"

"Provoke you? You've got to be joking me," I incredulously shout. "I never had a voice to provoke you, Tommy. I'm just finally standing up for myself. It's always been about you, Tommy! My voice was silenced by the force of your bare knuckles."

As soon as that statement flows over my lips, it feels like a boulder hit me square in the chest. It's the quintessential difference between both men. Giovanni's every action has always been about me. From day one, his soft but authoritative hands have always held my feelings and thoughts in the softness of his palms. Whereas Tommy is all about himself.

"You're just like your father," I snarl with disgust. "I wish your poor mother would leave that vile man. He sees women as disposable. You have the same mentality." I push him again with a forceful shove. "And thanks for cementing that you're a piece of shit into my box of hate for you by confirming you have never been faithful to me." I laugh, almost in hysterics. "I married a man exactly like my father." I spew my abhorrence out loud but knowing my words were just for my own ears.

"Like father, like daughter, I guess, since you spread those fat thighs of yours for a killer. I guess you just needed time to hone in on your roots."

The impact is hard and penetrable.

Flesh ripples over bone.

The resounding slap can be heard from way beyond our current surroundings as it vibrates over the mortar and brick holding the buildings together, giving us this narrow path with only two outlets. Anger rushes through veins like a raging title wave. I just gave Tommy a taste of his own *discipline*, as he would say after he lost control. I needed to be kept in line. Well, he just learned that the line has been drawn by me standing my ground.

Behind me is the wife he used to abuse, and the woman making a stance in front of him will not lay down again. I know what's coming when his shock wears off. I'm no fool. I may come out of this bloody and bruised, but I am prepared to go down swinging instead of a curled-up protectant ball.

His eyes glow with hatred.

Saliva drips from his snarling mouth.

His arm draws back, the skin across his knuckles stretches, turning white as he makes a fist.

I close my eyes.

And I wait.

I wait for the familiar blow that never comes.

I wait for the impact to spur the disgust I feel for this man and then take my moment and fight back.

When the sting of his skin never breaks against mine, I open my eyes and gasp at the scene before me.

The cold hard steel of a powerful gun is pressing into the side of Tommy's head so hard the tip is invisible. The upper lids shielding Tommy's eyes drop, becoming narrowed paths to the endless black holes of hatred that bleeds like a drug into his heart. I have seen hate in his eyes before, but this version of him, standing in front of me is someone I've never experienced before.

"No!" I shout when I snap out of my shock.

"Were you just going to put your hand on my woman?" Tommy's head jerks back from the force of Giovanni's shove with the gun.

"She's not your woman. She's my wife."

"You lost that privilege the moment you decided that physical abuse was the answer to your weaknesses."

Giovanni's lethal gaze shoots to mine. "Angel. Get in your Jeep and go home."

I stammer over my words, stunned at the man standing before me. His demeanor is far from the gentle manner he uses with me. Absent is the man who held me with calm and commanding hands in his arms the night before as he plunged his body into mine. This man is not the soft-spoken guy with the domineering tone that lights a fire deep in my belly.

This man standing before me is the one people fear.

And I can see why.

His power is intimidating. It's a force. Its own entity.

But he doesn't scare me.

"Baby." I take a step towards him. "P-Please don't." I hold my shaking palm in the air. "I don't want you to get in trouble because of me." I take another step towards him, but he warns me to stay back. "Please, Gio. I don't want this."

"Yeah, Gio," Tommy's snide intonation pisses me off. "Listen to *my* wife. You don't want to do this. You'll spend the rest of *your* life in prison for being a cop killer."

"Did you want to be hit, beaten on, screamed at, or demeaned, angel?" Giovanni's calm and assertive voice asks me, but his glare, it never leaves Tommy's profile, nor does the gun piercing Tommy's temple.

"No. No, I did not," I answer with force behind my words. Then I soften my tone and admit, "But if you do this, if you kill him, I'll lose you." My voice cracks. "I need you, Gio."

"No worries, baby," He turns to me. "I'm good at what I do. Ask your soon-to-be deceased ex. He knows. He thinks he's slick, like we don't know he's been investigating us for a long time, but we do. That's how stupid he is. It's a small world we travel in." He turns back to Tommy. "Isn't that right, Lieutenant?"

"I'm begging you not to do this. Please, Giovanni, for me, I'm begging you. Please, do not do this."

A rumble of disapproval sounds from his chest, vibrating in the narrow, garbage ridden alley with its echo. His jaw muscles pulse with the clench of his teeth. "Little lion, you're killing me." He pauses, then says, "I've asked you this before and I am going to ask you this again. Do you trust me?"

"Wholeheartedly," I answer with no hesitation as a dreaded tear of fear slides down my cheek.

"Then go home."

A defeated whimper leaves my lips. I step back, grab my keys from the ground, and get inside my Jeep. My ears bleed with the howl of Tommy's cries for me to help him as I slide behind the wheel.

The last thing I see, is Tommy's limp body falling to the ground from the brutal blow of Giovanni's pistol in the rearview mirror.

I wipe at the heated tears sliding down my face. I left the penthouse crying and I'm coming back here crying. The only thing, they are for two totally different reasons. When I left, I felt betrayed. As the elevator takes me to the highest floor, I now feel wearily protected. When the doors slide open to what I consider my home, I'm back to feeling betrayed.

I step inside. Three steps are all it takes. My hand flies to my chest as I swallow the iron filled air consuming the space. Demetri stands at the kitchen island, shirtless, with blood-soaked rags in his hands. He slowly walks to the trash can and throws the soiled material in. He reaches over, his gaze never leaving mine, and grabs a clean white hand towel from the counter. His large hands slowly roll around in the soft cotton removing the blood as he watches me with calculated steps in my direction. When I take a step back, he stops. He observes me with the skillful beady eyes of an eagle watching its prey. We view each other for long heavy moments.

"Izzy," he greets in a deep controlled tone. "Where's G?"

"What's all…" I wave my hand with a lack of energy. "What is this?" My frightened gaze frantically takes in all the blood, dismissing his question.

"Izzy, look at me," his rumbling tone commands as he takes a step towards me.

I drop my hand and feel for the wall of cold steel behind me. My body trembles as my hand fumbles for the call button.

"Isabelle, where is Giovanni?"

"He told me to leave. To come home." My words fumble over themselves, shock setting in.

"Where did you leave him?" He takes another step. I press myself up against the metal unsure of how scared I should be at the scene before me.

He throws the now red stained towel to the credenza and takes another calculated step in my direction. The way he speaks is almost hypnotic. It's measured, controlled, and commanding without being aggressive.

"I was at O'Brien's Pub," I mutter through my confusion of if I should run or not. I have been in Demetri's company before. We have had conversations, but this man in front of me is not the guy I have conversed with. "Tommy showed up." I swiftly turn to my right when I hear a noise. I'm shocked to the point of being frozen.

It's her.

The same woman that shattered my bubble just hours ago stands next to the couch I was sleeping on yesterday with a smug look on her face.

"I told you," she utters with potency from just a few feet away.

My insides twist when I notice the shirt she is wearing. It's one of Giovanni's.

My thoughts scatter, blown to bits and pieces before I can collect myself. My face must give away the stampede inside my head.

"Isabelle!" Demetri thunders, stepping towards me. "Don't do it."

Those are the last words I hear over the slap of my hand against the close button before the doors to the elevator slam shut and I'm whisked to what feels like the depths of hell.

"He will always choose me." Her cunning words ring in my head.

When I left the penthouse, it was empty. Kathrine was gone. The air was thick with her vile spoken truth. Her words were delivered in such a way to be painful on impact.

Why did she come back? Why was there so much blood? Who was bleeding? What happened in the time I was gone?

Did Giovanni kill Tommy?

All of it is just too much for me.

The whoosh of the doors when the cart hits the ground floor jolts me back to my senses. In a rush to get out of the confining box as fast as I can, I squeeze through the partially opened door. The piercing sound of material ripping doesn't stop me. I'm on mission and that mission is to get away from everyone and everything right now.

Freddy, the guy who was in the lobby that first night when Demetri brought me here, who I now know works for Giovanni, zeros in on me as he holds his phone to his ear. His focus becomes tunnels of pursuit. My inner voice tells me to run. I burst through the revolving door and wave my hand at the taxi driver as I'm jumping in the back seat. He's alarmed at my frantic behavior, and with a forceful amount of yelling from myself, he speeds off. I don't even look back, because right now, I just need to go forward.

The taxi driver asks where he's going, but I have no clue what to tell him. I didn't think that far. Where do I go? What do I do? I have no place I can go. I could call Zoey, but she just came back into my life. I don't want to bring this chaos into hers. Plus, what would I tell her? My ex showed up in the alley begging me to come back, but then my new boyfriend showed up and sent me away because I'm pretty sure he is going to murder him? Oh, and by the way, my current living space was a blood bath when I got back home and to add the cherry on top, his ex was standing in his living room dressed in his clothing like she owned it.

"Ma'am?"

I stare at his questioning gaze in the rearview mirror, and say, "Take me back."

"Excuse me? You want me to drive you back?"

"That's what I said. Drive me back."

"Where the fuck did she go?" A thunderous roar abuses my ears as the elevator doors open.

"I don't know, man. She booked it when—"

"I trusted you would keep her safe!" Glass shatters.

"I'm right here." I drone out with no strength behind my words while standing there watching Giovanni and Demetri in the kitchen in a faceoff.

"Angel," Giovanni's whispered mutter is so low, it's almost nonexistent, like he can't believe he just heard my voice. His head whips around. He stares at me like I'm a figment of his imagination. Then his gaze comes back into focus and roams my body from head to toe. His steps are quick, influenced by anger with the stride of relief. I'm swaddled up into the heat of his body, suffocated by his concern. "Fuck, angel, you scared the shit out of me." He pulls back and grabs ahold of my face. "Are you okay?" He runs his hands over my arms. "Tell me. Are you hurt?"

"I'm fine," I huff.

"I told you to come home, Isabelle."

"I did."

"You left." He steps back but still has a hold of my upper arms.

"Do you blame me?" I pull my hand away and flip it towards the kitchen. "This is what I came home to?"

He looks back at Demetri, blows out a breath, and turns back to me. "No. No, I don't. I should have explained. I was trying to protect you. I just didn't have a chance. I knew Demetri would explain what he could when you got here."

"Withheld protection," I mutter under my breath.

"What?"

"He didn't have a chance." I look around the open space. Looking for *her*.

"Told you, man. She was like a jack rabbit."

He pulls me back into his arms. "Don't do it again, Isabelle." The warning is there, but it's said in such a way that it isn't threatening. It's coming from a place of distress. "If something were to happen to you..."

"I'm fine." My dry tone makes him focus in on me.

"You almost weren't," he snaps. "If I didn't show up in time—" He clamps his mouth shut and runs his hand through his hair. "He would have put his hands on you once again, and angel, that just isn't sitting right with me in here." He makes a fist and jams it into his chest.

"Is he?"

"Alive." His abhorrence at letting Tommy keep breathing oozes from his voice.

I release a breath of relief.

"For now," he snaps, stepping back, watching my reaction.

I can see the distain in his eyes at my relief for a man who has made my life hell. "Giovanni..." I reach for him because I don't want him to misconstrue my relieved breath.

"What were you thinking, Isabelle?" He pulls back. "He's been watching for you for weeks. Just waiting. Like the predator he is. He knew exactly where you were. He knew he couldn't get to you. He waited for you, and you walked right to him."

My jaw slackens before I inquire, "How? How do you know that?"

He cocks his head to the left. His lips become grim lines of truth. "I've had eyes on him since the night you left him."

"Why didn't you tell me that? Everything is a secret with you!" My anger rises.

"Because I was taking care of you, Isabelle. It's what a real man does. I didn't want you to worry, to be stressed that he would find you. Get to you. I wanted you and Abby to feel safe for once."

Withheld protection.

"Giovanni..." I expel an exhausted breath and look at Demetri, who's now bleaching down the countertops while attempting to mind his own business.

Giovanni blows out a weighted groan. "Look, angel, I'll explain. It just has to be later. Right now, I have to help D get this cleaned up and disposed of."

I watch him for the silent still few moments being forced between us. He's aggravated at me, pissed off even, but there is something else I'm missing. "I'll help." Frustrated, I drop my shoulders and step around him, getting more irritated by the second as I walk towards the kitchen, thinking about his ex showing up here tonight, not once but twice. Adding to my frustration is my ex begging for reconciliation only to transform back into his true self when he knew I wouldn't give in. Last, but definitely not least, I want to know why Giovanni's kitchen looked like a murder scene. What if I was still here? What if Abby was here? Would we have been in danger?

I take only two steps towards the kitchen. He catches my wrist and stops me in my tracks. "It's late," he grumbles from over his shoulder. "Go take a shower. Demetri and I will handle this." He turns to face me. His hand comes to my face and holds my chin in place so that I can't turn away. He wants my undivided attention. He's got it. "Once I get everything settled, I'll be in. We'll talk."

"Yes, we will." I side eye him while easily sliding my wrist and chin from his hands and walk past Demetri. "Good night, Demetri."

"Night, Izzy."

My shower was long and very much needed. I took my time. I had to get my thoughts and emotions together. I wanted answers, not a fight. I thought I had wasted enough time, that by now he would have been in the bedroom with me, but here I sit, alone, with Giovanni's dress shirt draped over my tired body as I lean against his headboard waiting. I decide in that moment I am not going to wait any longer, and I make my way down the long hallway to the kitchen. There he sits, at the island. The space is black. His phone is to his ear and a deep conversation is being held. "Are we sure it's him? I told you I had my suspicions. Where did the intel come from?" He's silent for a minute. "I guess our new business partner just proved his credibility to be partially loyal to the organization. I'll have Freddy pull the feed in the morning. You still have that blackmail we acquired a few months back? Good. Antonio, if this pans out, and I am correct, I will take great pleasure in making him a bloodless man. We have to be vigilant in covering our asses. Understand this though, A. I will use this information to benefit her first." He pauses a beat. "If he doesn't comply? Oh, he'll comply. I owe her at least that much. Yeah, talk tomorrow." He hangs up and drops his phone on the counter. When he reaches for the rocks glass in front of him, I walk up next to him and take it from his parted lips and swallow my own needed sip from the same spot his lips just left an imprint.

"I was tired of waiting." I roll the glass over my bottom lip, sliding the leftover liquid like a gloss.

"Angel," he sighs, then quickly reaches out and wraps his arm around my waist and pulls me between his open thighs, effectively trapping me in-between him and the edge of the island. His fingers curl under my chin while his thumb caresses my lower lip. His line of sight follows his action. "Do you know how scared I was when Demetri told me you left?" His tongue darts out and sucks his bottom lip back in as he watches his manipulation of my plump skin. "He didn't know where you went. All I could do was picture you out there, with your ex watching, waiting for the right moment to grab you again."

"He is many things, Giovanni, but he isn't a kidnapper."

His intense eyes instantly snap up like a shot to mine. "Do not underestimate the man you were married too."

"Still married to," I correct. "I need to call the lawyer I spoke to awhile back and have her draw up divorce papers."

"Don't. Not right now. The timing is wrong." He shakes his head. "You need to listen to me on this, Isabelle."

"Why? I want to move on, start a life without him."

"You need to hold off for a bit. What time will Abby be home from Sofia and Caelan's tomorrow?"

My head jerks back. "How did you know she was there?" I ask, shock filling my voice.

He tilts his head and regards me with a slight smirk, as if to say, *I know everything.*

"You must be exhausted if your wheels are spinning all the time." I observe him, amazed at his tenacity for information.

"Knowledge is power, angel. Power, the right kind of power, is priceless."

"You mean blackmail. I heard you on the phone."

"Protection," he corrects.

"When used in the wrong hands, it's coercion."

"I don't play by the rules, Isabelle. These hands are bloody. You should know this by now."

"I do to some extent, but I'm sleeping with a man I don't know much about except for what's face value."

"Is that all you're doing? Sleeping with me?"

"No. You know that isn't what I meant. But tonight... tonight was a lot. I came face to face with some information that made me want to leave. Leave you." I huff. "I did leave. I don't want to live a life feeling like I'm still in a cage of lies. I want to know you. I want to know your secrets. You know all mine, before I even got to tell you."

His hands drop to my hips. He grips the meaty flesh and pulls me into his tense heat even more. He runs his thumbs over my padded bones while intently gazing at me. "I didn't read your file."

"You didn't?" I jerk back, shocked, my eyes widening. How did he know I knew about the file?

"No, angel, I didn't. I wanted to, but I want this with you. In order for it to be real between us, I needed to get to know you from you, not through emotionless paper with your life scribbled across it."

"And when do I get to know you from you?"

He releases a long breath and drops his forehead to the center of my chest. I let him take his moment and run my fingers through his hair. He's exhausted, I can see the darkness creeping at the corners of his eyes.

When he lifts his head he admits, "It's not pretty, Isabelle."

"Pretty things are overrated, Giovanni."

"Beautiful souls aren't." He leans in and kisses me. "I'm not sure you will be able to handle the tales of Giovanni Moretti's life."

"Tales are childhood stories. I want the raw autobiography told by the man."

"It's ugly."

"Life is ugly, baby." I kiss his lips, slowly, reverently. Then pull back and gently scrub my nails into his scalp while I wait for his next words.

"I desire your beautiful soul as much as your body, Isabelle. You're an addiction of truth for me. A love I never thought I would, or even could, experience. I thought the marred veins running through my heart was beyond the capabilities of pumping the foreign emotion called love through it. There is a part of me that bears the weight of knowing you are the one half of me that I lost at some point through my years."

"A damaged little boy becomes a broken man. A broken little girl becomes a shattered woman. Two unsettled spirits with tormented pasts join together with unknown futures. It's a recipe for more disastrous pain."

"Pain I will endure if I have you by my side. My future is not unknown. I know exactly what I want. The question is, do you?" He squeezes my hips with his steady grip.

"I know what I desire, but I also know life isn't that simple. It never has been. I need answers, Giovanni. The innocent blinders were ripped off a long time ago."

"And I will give them to you. But right now, it's late." He leans in and kisses the crook of my neck. I tilt my head to the side, giving him access. His tongue slides over the swell of my collarbone. "I want nothing more than to slip into the walls of your body and lose myself in my home."

I drop my head back and let the goose flesh run its course over my body. He opens the top two buttons of his dress shirt I'm wearing. His perusal bears weight on my exposed, heavy breasts. His pupils dilate with his touch. His length grows against my core. His hand slides in to one side while his mouth moves to the other. My moan is long and low at the sting of his pinch and the warmth of his touch.

There is one thing between Giovanni and I that can't be fought.

It's a chemically induced desire brewing between us. It drips in lust and love.

There is no denying our bodies were meant for each other.

I reach for his pants, fumbling with fingertips that tingle. The cool metal of his belt hardware sounds with my vigorous tug. I want him to take away my freedom. Dominate me with his manliness and devour me with his tainted love.

"Fuck, angel." He grabs my hand and stops it as he stands. "We have company."

"What?" I look around, nervous. It's three thirty in the morning. Who the hell could be here?

"Trust me." He leans in next to my ear. "I'd take you right here, but I'm not into sharing."

"I am." A deep voice comes from across the open room.

"Say good night to Demetri, Isabelle." He lifts me from the floor. I wrap my arms and legs around his body and stare off into the deep sea of darkness from over his shoulder. In the shadows of the only lights filtering through the room from the city below, I see the outline of a figure on the couch.

"Have fun, Izzy."

"Good night, Demetri."

"She was a good mother, Isabelle. She tried. I'll give her that, but there was and still is a part of me that resents her for what she let happen to her, to our family. Which sounds so fucked up because I know she didn't let it happen to her. She was a prisoner to his abuse, in our home, in a life she never asked for.

"I took my little sister, Hope, from the only home we knew when I was certain my father's reach was going to extend to her. Her innocence was already ruined by the violence and hunger, but I didn't want it to shatter. Broken pieces can be glued back together. Shattered pieces can never be whole again. It's impossible, there are too many small fragments to put back together, to fix. I wasn't going to let my baby sister feel the touch of his wrath.

"When I was a kid, I was helpless to do anything. As I got older, I knew I had to. I took Hope, and I ran. I made a life for us on the streets. I took care of her. I fed her. I protected her. I still do. I gave her the life she deserved."

I lie there in his arms, listening to him tell me about his childhood. While his fingers absentmindedly play with my hair, the tips of my fingers draw circles through the smattering of his chest hair that flows all the way down to his heavy groin.

There is a large part of me that feels like he may have done the same thing with me. He rescued a woman in need. It brings tears to my eyes that I quickly blink away. I can honestly say I am madly in love with this man, but I'm not naïve, I also know that part of that love is because he saved me. How could it not? It is only fitting that he feels some way about saving me too. It's a hardship that stems from rigid handling. A necessity to rescue, has now become a calling, if you will, after being cemented in a child's mind over a lifetime of pain.

That very first night we were together, I felt what kind of man he is. He may be a very bad man, even more than I thought with the recent information that was spewed at me by my ex, but there is a savior inside him too. Whether that is the small child that never leaves any of us, still fighting his way out, or the grown man who plays by his own rules. He is a good man that does bad things. And I am okay with that. The real question is, are his feelings for me misconstrued by his past trauma?

"I begged her, Isabelle. I begged my mother to come with me when I left. She wouldn't. In a twisted way, my mind told me she loved him more than me. I was mad. How could she love him more? I was so fucking mad at her. I convinced myself that was why she stayed, but as I got older, I knew that wasn't the truth either. That anger, it has stayed with me all these years. Fuck, Isabelle. I have to have a piece of cinnamon gum in my mouth every damn day because of the trauma of not having food as a child. It has to be cinnamon too. When we had the luxury of having bread in the house my mom would make us cinnamon toast. Do you know how messed up it is that I need to have a piece of chemically produced rubber in my mouth to make me feel better? It's so fucked up." He takes a deep breath. "Even after realizing she stayed with him to keep us safe, I still hold resentment. She thought if he had her, he wouldn't come for us. It's a selfless act but I'm still pissed about it. I could have taken care of her. For most of my life I have had a lot of misplaced feelings about my mother and my childhood."

"You blame her," I mutter, shifting my weight to curl into him more. "You still do. This wasn't her fault. I can't speak for your mother, but I can speak for the trauma and shame she felt. How she wished she could leave, ask for help, or even help herself by taking a stance. How she would lay her head down at night and dream of a better life, a different future. For me, I was too scared to ask. What if I failed? What if I asked and then caved and went back to him? What if I asked for help and then got it only to crash and burn and have to crawl back to him?"

"Don't say that. You're not weak, Isabelle."

"It's the truth though, baby." I kiss his chest. "Your mom was young. I was young, still am, but the fact of it is age doesn't matter, your mom probably hadn't experienced a 'normal' life yet. What is worse, the unknown world that can be frightening or the world we already know?"

"You were leaving though. You went to see a lawyer for help."

"I did, but it took me a long time to get to that point. For each woman, it is different. Some never leave and some don't make it at all."

We're quiet for a few moments. Lying in the ugly truth of the life we've both been dealt.

"G?" My finger traces the rigid skin around his belly button.

"Yeah," his tired voice answers.

"That first night we were together, did you know who I was? I mean, since the bar is owned by your boss?"

"No."

"So, when we were together, you didn't know who I was?"

"Let me refresh your memory on how I behaved the night at the fundraiser when I found out who you were married to. Did I act like I knew?"

"No."

"What are you getting at, angel?"

"I don't really know," I whisper, letting that sit for a minute while I process my thoughts. "That night was special for me, and I just want to keep it sacred. I need to know that you were with me because you wanted to be with me and not because I was Isabelle, the abused woman who needed to be rescued, and the woman married to the cop who was investigating you. I was just Isabelle. The girl that—"

"Turned my world upside down. That first night was fate, Isabelle. I saw you. Only you. I wanted the fiery redhead that caught my attention. I only saw you, angel."

"And now? Is there a part of you that feels obligated? Maybe a savior's guilt that won't let you let me go?"

His head sharply twists in my direction, turning from the black abyss he stared into above us. He cranes his neck to look down at me. The thick vein in his neck pumps. "You think I'm with you because we share similar stories?"

"A part of you has to. It's only logic that we would connect in a way most normal couples wouldn't. We share a history, even though lived through separately, we know the battles each one has been through."

"Let me be clear, Isabelle. I am not keeping you here because I feel guilty about wanting to let you go because I feel bad for you. I want a life with you. I had thought you wanted the same thing."

"I do," I quickly tell him.

"Then where is this coming from?"

"I don't know," I mutter, but I do know, because Kathrine's voice still fills my ears even hours later about how Giovanni is only with me because he feels bad. That he will always circle back to her because she has always been there for him since they were kids.

"G?"

"Yeah, angel." His uncharacteristic frustrated and tired voice is minutes away from sleep.

"What happened to your mom?" I wait with bated breath.

"She died at the hands of her son."

Isabelle

CHAPTER THIRTY-FOUR

It's a false hope, that it is still the middle of the night. The room is blanketed in darkness, but I know it has to be mid-morning because Giovanni and I didn't fall asleep until after five. I roll to my side and reach for Giovanni's heat but only coldness meets my hand.

"Babe?" I call out. Only to hear silence as my resounding answer.

I roll to my back and push myself up to the lean against the headboard. I grab for my phone and see that it's nine a.m. With a glance at the floor-to-ceiling windows, I see the room darkening drapes have been closed. My only thought is Giovanni wanted me to sleep in and get rest. I'm beyond that. I need answers. Answers to the hurtful words his ex, Kathrine, spewed at me last night. Plus, I need to add to the fact that I am uncomfortable with her having the code to his home, now our home. There is so much that went down yesterday that I know I won't be able to process it all, but at least we discussed the file he had on me. Seeing that file made me feel like I wasn't real to him. Like what we shared meant nothing to him and all I was, was just some information on a piece of paper. I believe in him and that is why I went back instead of running. I'm here to stay, to fight. I just need answers from him. I feel like when it comes to him and his past, his answers will only lead me to have more questions. A pandora box filled with secrets. I need to decipher where the line is drawn for myself. I don't want to toe over and be in his business world. I'm not being naïve either. Giovanni has not tried to put up a pretty picture of who he is. I just know I don't want that part of his life to filter over into our life together. He has given me freedom and peace, and in return, if I can give him the same while we are together, then at least he has a few spared moments outside the dangerous world he navigates through.

I throw my legs over the side of the bed, grab my phone, shoot Sofia a message, then use the bathroom and brush my teeth. When I exit, I hear my phone chime from the top of the dresser where I laid it. The message throws me for second, but then my grin brings me right back to the message.

Me: Good morning. What time is good for me to pick up Abigail today?
Sofia: I'm guessing you haven't talked to G yet. These men, they take over our lives. I told Giovanni earlier when he called that both girls are still sleeping. I'll give you a call later and let you know. Enjoy your morning!

So, he got up this morning and the first thing he did was call Sofia about Abigail? Such a strange turn of events my life has taken. I went from one man who could care less about his blood, to another man who cares almost too much, if that is at all possible. I smile to myself, realizing that Abigail will grow up knowing what honest, genuine love from a male figure in her life feels like. That thought makes me a very happy mother.

I throw my phone on the bed and make my way out of the room. I'm hoping to find Giovanni in the kitchen making breakfast. I purposely left the first four buttons to his dress shirt open, showing the curve of my shoulder and the swell of my breast. I can't seem to get enough of him. Even now, with all these questions in my head, it doesn't stop me from wanting to be with him. He has brought the inner girl inside me to the surface, to the light, instead of hiding in darkness. He makes me feel sexy, but better yet, leaving these buttons open, I make myself feel sexy and that confidence means more to me than anything.

I make my way down the hallway, a certain pep in my step. The smell of food cooking along with the normal sounds of a kitchen make me smile. With hazy eyes, I reach the opening to the kitchen that opens into the living room and stop in my tracks. It's filled with men. Men in suits. Grim expressions hold their faces captive. Giovanni's back is to me for only a second. It's almost as if he can sense the moment I stepped into the open space. With his hands in his pockets, he slowly twists his upper body in my direction. When his gaze drops to my chest, I immediately grab at the two side of material and wrench it closed, covering myself, but I still feel exposed with the shirt only hitting my upper thighs.

And then I see something that throws me into another universe.

Kathrine is standing at the kitchen island. Her hair is a mess, looking like she just woke up. The t-shirt she is wearing is Giovanni's. I know because I have worn it. She also has on a pair of gym shorts that are twice the size of her small frame.

My gaze darts back to him, hurt radiating in my eyes.

Before he can finish saying, "Excuse me, gentleman," I am running back down the hallway.

I sprint into the room like I just ran a marathon. My breathing is heavy and I'm heaving explicit words as I'm ripping off his shirt to change into something more appropriate. I thought we were alone. I mean, I knew Demetri was here last night, but I didn't think he would still be here now, let alone a whole room full of intimidating men in black and *her*.

"What the fuck?" I sputter to the empty room, my stomach flipping.

Then I hear the shift of fabric behind me. I twist in my spot and connect eyes with Giovanni.

"Isabelle." His deep voice penetrates my skin.

"Why is she here?" I grind my teeth.

"Angel."

"Don't *angel* me! Why is she here again?"

His brows furrow. "Angel." He stands in the doorway, watching me.

"Giovanni, I'm so embarrassed. What is going on? Why didn't you tell me there was a room full of very intimidating men here? And why is she here?!" I ramble on, screaming. "I just flashed everyone! I thought we were alone! And why the fuck is she here?" My voice raises with each word.

"Isabelle." His footsteps fall heavy as he gets closer to me.

I turn and face him. He's pissed, and that confuses me. His face is a sheet of ice.

"You're mad?" I sputter.

"Not at you. Although I do not appreciate a room full of men seeing my woman in that manner. I should have told you. I thought you would have slept in since we didn't get much sleep last night."

"You didn't answer my question." I take a step away from him. "Why is she here, Giovanni?" Then I mumble under my breath, "I can't fucking get away from her."

He steps into me and pulls me into his body. "Kathrine is here because she helped me last night. She spent the night in the spare room. A lot of people spent the night here. There was an accident at work last night. Luca was shot. I had to bring him here. Where we normally perform surgeries was compromised. The blood you saw last night was his. He is upstairs with a doctor resting in one of the rooms right now. He needed blood. He'd lost too much to survive. Kathrine's blood type can be used for anyone."

"So you called her for help?" My voice dejected.

"I did. To save my man, I did."

I push from his hold and take a few steps away from him. His ex tormented me last night. I turn my back and rest my hand on my churning stomach. Giovanni doesn't know she was here. He doesn't know she is the reason way I left and went to the pub.

"How do you know Kathrine, angel?" he asks from just over my shoulder, his fingers folding in around my upper arms.

Do I tell him, add to his stress, or handle this on my own?

"Is Luca going to be okay? Not that the guy is my best friend or even a friend at all. I believe he hates me for who I'm married to. That car ride yesterday was dreadfully silent, but I don't want to see harm come to him."

His eyes become slits. "It's touch and go. Now answer my question."

I'm quiet, contemplating what I should do.

"You asked me why she was here. I answered. Now answer my question, Isabelle. How do you know Kathrine and what do you mean you can't get away from her?"

I hesitate for only two seconds because I am not going to play this game. If Giovanni and I are to have an honest and healthy relationship, which is what I want, then open communication is the only way to get that.

"Last night, she is the reason why I left the penthouse. She showed up here, vomited a bunch of lifelong memories about you and her. How you would never leave her for good. That she would always be in your life. That you both had a connection that couldn't be broken. That you were each other's first. Then she said there was a life altering connection that will always bring you together. I assumed it was about a baby. It was then I had remembered your necklace that you wore that first night we were together. I remember it vividly because it swung between our bodies. K and A. Kathrine and the child's initial you had with her. I found the necklace in your jewelry box. Yes, I went searching for it." I reach up and lay my hand flat against the badge of safety he now wears. "Without needing the information, she went on to use the loss of your baby as a weapon to hold on to you. Sad, really, when you think about it." I step back and walk to the closet, needing a moment without his heavy gaze on me. "She was also here when I got back too," I enlighten him from over my shoulder. "That's when I had had enough. I jumped in a taxi and left again." I turn back to face him. "But I came back, Giovanni. I came back. Why? Because I believe in us." I slip a pair of jeans over my hips, knowing he's standing at the door watching me. "Yesterday was a lot for me."

"Come here."

"No." I proceed to button and zip my jeans, ignoring his demand.

"Isabelle." My name a demand rolling off his tongue.

I walk to him and stop a few inches away, facing him. A rumble of displeasure leaves his chest at the distance I left between us. His irritation captured on his handsome face. He reaches out and wraps his hands around my waist and pulls me in.

"I am sorry. I didn't know about Kathrine showing up here. It explains how she got here so quick. She was already in this part of the city. I will handle her. You are my life, my sweet girl. Do not ever doubt that. It is you and only you, along with your beautiful daughter that I want to share my life with. Kathrine is not a vindictive person. She is quite the opposite. This is my fault. I have been declining her calls for weeks. We are friends, yes, but I do know she harbors feelings for me that I don't reciprocate. When I wasn't in a committed relationship, the closeness of our relationship didn't matter. Now it does. I will never disrespect you or what we have." He takes a frustrated breath. "There has to be some boundaries set. Our story is a long one and honestly, I'd prefer and don't think it's important to rehash, but if you are uncertain or uncomfortable and need to know more, I will explain our relationship in further detail."

I'm quiet, not sure what to say. Not sure if I want to know. Not even sure I want to accept the situation. What I do know, is there is a room full of scary men standing in the kitchen and all eyes were on him. He left the room because of me. Giovanni being in here with me doesn't look good to them.

"Those men out there, they're scary."

He nods.

"Why are they here? Are you in trouble or something?"

His grin is cocky. "Angel, I do not get in trouble."

"What's going on then? Why are all those men here?"

"I apologize for not informing you. I also appreciated the view, angel. However I am about to murder fifteen men for seeing my woman in that way." He takes a deep breath. "There is a lot going on. A lot I need to handle. They are here to pay their respects to Luca."

"You said he didn't die?"

"He's a Made Man, Isabelle. He took a bullet. That means something. Besides, we were ambushed last night. Business needs to be conducted."

"You mean retaliation," I drily chirp, suddenly frightened at what that means.

"It's the ways of our world, angel."

Realization hits me. "Which means, Tommy is alive now, but what? Won't be in the future?"

"Is, let's shelf that. Your ex is not good for my blood pressure. I need to get back out there and speak to the men. I'd prefer not to be pissed off when I do it."

I stretch up to my tiptoes and press my lips to his. It's a passive kiss, unsure and uneasy about everything. He grabs a hold of my face and deepens our embrace, moving his lips over mine with intensity. It lasts for more minutes than it should with the tension between us. My hand slides up his body and wraps around his neck at the same time his slides down and grips my behind, pulling my lower half against his. He pulls back from the kiss and uses the pad of his thumb to wipe his bottom lip. A few seconds pass before he reaches up, holds my chin in place, and fiercely holds my gaze captive.

"I love you, Isabelle."

And before I can say it back, he quickly kisses me once more and is already taking the steps to exit the closet before I can reply.

I stand there, awe struck.

I reach my hand out like that will stop him.

He turns around, and says, "Get dressed, angel. Come to me when you are done."

Giovanni

CHAPTER THIRTY-FIVE

T here is no woman on this earth that could ignite the fire in my chest the way Isabelle did when she walked out from the hallway looking the way she did. Fuck, she was sexy. Her long, red hair all mussed up from sleep, looking like I had just had it wrapped around my fist while I took her from behind. She had my shirt draping over her shoulder, showing a hint of her breasts, playing peek-a-boo with her collarbone. She is so damn sexy.

My feet stomping down the hallway was purely led by jealous rage. The green monster inside me couldn't handle the fact that a group of powerful men saw her the way only I should. I excused myself as politely as I could so I could tend to my woman and my feelings.

The discussion I thought we were going to have, turned into an entirely different conversation.

So, Kathrine, my ex from a lifetime ago, showed her jealous colors last night. I'm a bit shocked and sympathetic now that I am feeling my own jealousy. Kathrine's a professional woman who knows how to handle her emotions. I guess I may have dropped the ball on recognizing the extent of her feelings for me. If I didn't need her right now, I would kick her out on her ass for what she pulled with Isabelle. Because no one, and I mean no one, will ever hurt my Isabelle again. The hard part for me right now is that I am stuck in a situation I can't rectify at the moment. I need Kathrine to stick around in case Luca takes a turn and needs more of her blood.

"Gentlemen, I'm sorry for the interruption." I step back into the room, drawing their attention to me.

"It was a pleasant one."

I shoot Leo, the underboss who runs Brooklyn, a look of death for the comment and proceed without a glitch in his verbal speedbump. Leo and

I have hung out a few times at Temptations. Antonio and he were close as kids. As adults they still hang out from time to time. Leo knows me better than to make a remark like that.

"As for last night, it went down in your territory, Santo." I direct my attention to the boss who runs the Bronx. "You have some enemies over there you want to talk about? Maybe our assailants thought we were you?"

"The question is, why were you over in our zip code without a courtesy call?"

"You got the courtesy call, Santo." Mr. Heart steps into the room with Antonio at his side. "I'd advise you not to play games with my consigliere. It won't fair well for you. I almost lost a man last night, still may. You of all people should know how I feel about my men. I'd take that seriously if I were you. Otherwise, I will take it as if it was meant: a slight."

"Rumor has it, his woman is married to a lieutenant. Maybe she is playing both sides of the fence. Maybe you lost your touch, Gio." Santo smirks.

"She's not," I simply state, his first warning set with the tone of my voice.

"Maybe she's suckin' on your cock and going back and telling him your dirty secrets," Rocco, Santo's son speaks up.

"She's not." I grind my molars, trying to hold my temper in its cage.

"How do you know?" he challenges.

"Watch yourself, Rocco, or you will find yourself at the end of my blade." I glare at him through narrowed eyes. "Do not disrespect my woman."

"I think it is I who has reigned over this organization for decades, correct?" Mr. Heart steps up to Rocco interfering before blood is shed. "Son, you have been under your father's thumb your whole life. He has been under mine. He is as ruthless as they come. I, however, am his teacher. Do you think I would allow someone into our organization if I thought they were a threat?" His voice deepens, demanding that his words sink into Rocco's skull before he's crossing a line he can't come back from.

"We have rules. We all do. We abide by them. You—"

"I'm not." My fiery redhead steps out from the mouth of the hallway and respectfully looks at Mr. Heart. Her eyes beg for the floor. He gives it to her with the wave of his hand. I swear I see the corner of his lip quirk up in a smile at her lady balls. It takes a strong person to walk into a room filled with men like us. "I'm not spying for my husband. Soon to be ex-husband."

"Soon to be dead husband," someone mutters in the crowd.

He isn't wrong.

"Isabelle." I step to her, but before I can reach her, she is at my side. I lean down and whisper, "Angel, go back to the room. I don't want you out here with these men."

With a dead stare she admits, "I have been in the presence of worse."

"No, you have not, angel." My hard gaze does nothing to dissuade her.

"You have never met Tommy's father. That man is just plain evil."

Little does she know.

She takes a small step around me with a look of determination. "I have never and will never help the man who has beaten me to within an inch of my life." She reaches out and lays her hand on my arm. "This man right here has my heart and my loyalty. I am forever in his debt for saving me and my daughter. I would give my life for him if I didn't have a child to care for. Even when I was with Tommy, my loyalty wasn't. I know nothing about his job, nor has he ever asked me to help him in anything to do with his work." She glances up at me with so much emotion in her eyes.

The rod of steel in her back rattles with nerves, but her voice is steady. I lean down, place my lips next to her ear and breathe, "I love you, angel. Now please go back to our room until I come for you."

She simply nods, stretches to the tips of her toes, and kisses my cheek before turning and walking away.

When I told her to come find me, I didn't expect everyone to still be here, nonetheless have us be in the middle of discussing business.

"You want to explain why my calls went to voicemail multiple times before you answered, Santo?" Mr. Heart's unforgiving voice demands everyone's attention.

He wanted their focus off Isabelle, and he did just that by the pitch of his voice. The tightening in my chest appreciates it. I don't care if she is around the men of our family but these men standing in my living room are not. As a matter of fact, the only reason they are in my domain is because of the tragedy last night. No one is allowed to break the barrier of my sanctity except for a select few. Kathrine will now be one less. The blood that dripped from my kitchen island last night, except for my own, is a first. The death and destruction I cause in the obscurity of the night is never allowed to taint my home. I made that promise to myself with the memories of my childhood at the forefront of my thoughts.

"I was busy."

"Your mistress could have waited."

"We all can't have what you do."

"Even so, Santo. Do you think it was wise not to answer for the boss?"

"I am a boss. Do not disrespect me."

"And I am *your* boss. Respect is earned when called upon."

"I was entertaining the Senator, if you must know," Santo relents but holds his ground.

"Senator Hunt?" The question hangs in the air.

"I have the opportunity to secure a large parcel of land. Senator Hunt is the only person standing in my way."

"How so?"

"He owns the land adjacent to it. His was the only bid countering mine. I thought maybe if I bought the man a drink and stressed my concern for the only bid holding me back from the purchase, he would relent."

"And?"

"Not even close. He had the expression on his face that told me to fuck off and the cat ate the canary at the same time. Conniving, that fucker is. Total politician. To think he gets to make laws is frightening."

"Why's that? We all knew his goal when he was a prosecutor and played with the legal system. How many of your boys sit in the joint because of trumped up charges?"

"Ain't that the fucking truth," I mutter under my breath.

"You, of all people, know that," Antonio comments, leaning into me.

"You think I'm still wrong about him?" I ask in return.

"I think we need to look a little more in depth about the peoples' choice of politician to run our state before we bring any unnecessary heat onto ourselves."

"You two have something you need to tell me?" Mr. Heart steps up to where Antonio and I stepped away.

"Not yet, Pop."

"This have anything to do with the warehouse fire a few months back?"

Antonio gives a half undecided nod.

"Some of the men that didn't get to pay their respect to Luca went upstairs. The others left. We will conduct business tomorrow before Sunday dinner. Be at the house an hour prior. Don't be late." He turns to me. "Bring, Isabelle." He pauses. "She's got balls, that one. Not many women would step in a room filled with men like us and hold her own. You must be good for her, Gio. Glad to see you have come three quarters of a circle. Now, you just have one more door to close for it to be a full one. Isn't that right?"

My jaw flexes. He's just touched on a nerve, a subject I have shut down since I was a kid just starting out under his thumb, and he knows it too.

"Until tomorrow, gentlemen." He turns and starts to walk away before slowly turning back and saying, "Oh, and, Giovanni, take your girl out tonight. She's been cooped up for far too long."

Antonio holds in his laugh at me being schooled by my boss, but the crack of his smile is there.

"Asshole," I mutter, walking away from him to go find Isabelle.

"Aww, come on. Pop's the man at wooing Mom. Listen to him. Take Isabelle out to dinner. We'll make it a couple's night. I'll send Romeo over to my parents' house and Lilah and I will have dinner with you two."

"Who says she wants to eat a meal with you?" I walk back to him. "Last time you had a conversation with Isabelle, you interrogated her."

"That was then."

"Why now? Because your father is okay with her?"

"G, don't be like this. I have to protect you and this organization. I wouldn't be doing my job if I didn't. You know that. You would have done the same thing."

"Oh yeah? What changed your mind about her then?"

"She left last night when you told her to. She didn't care what happen to her ex in that alley. She left. It shows where her loyalties lie."

I twist and turn my attention to Demetri. He is standing on the other side of the room talking to Leo. Both of their attention is on us. Demetri nods answering my unspoken question, confirming he told Antonio what went down last night.

I turn and walk away when Antonio calls out, "The Surf at seven. Don't be late!"

An uneasy feeling sits in the base of my chest. I can't shake it and I can't figure out what is causing it. My stride down the long hallway to the master bedroom is hard and unforgiving. I need to see my girl. Before I even enter the room, I already know she isn't there. It's a feeling I experience when I am in her vicinity. Knowing she hasn't left because I have been by the only exit, I half jog to the gym knowing she wouldn't be there either. That only leaves me two more places. Abigail's room, or her curiosity got to her, and she went to see Luca.

I check Abigail's room and find nothing, but in my perusal of the room, I tuck a note away to hire an interior designer to redecorate the room into a little girl's fantasy bedroom. I head to the only other place she could be. I pass a couple of the men in the hallway on the way. I say goodbye but don't show them out. Demetri will make sure they leave, then secure the place. I round the corner and hear two voices softly talking.

"I wasn't really a fan of yours. I thought you hated me because of who I am."

I dip my head around the door frame and watch from afar. Isabelle is gently wiping his body down with a washcloth. She dips the cloth into the bowl and slowly brings it down his arm.

"Didn't trust you," his broken words tell her.

"That's okay. I understand. I'll prove my loyalty to you all."

My angel needs to prove her loyalty to no one.

"Jus... just do... don't want G getting burned."

"The person getting burned is me." I still at her comment, confused, worried. "Rug burn. Because your buddy is a machine."

Luca laughs then groans at the pain it caused him.

"Sorry." She smiles her radiate smile. "Relax your hand," she tells him after she requests that the doctor gets her fresh hot water.

"I'm sorry this happened to you. You're going to be okay though." She places her hand on his chest. "Your heartbeat is strong. Giovanni will make sure you're okay. If there is one thing I have learned about that man, is that he is as loyal as they come and as determined as a wild cat looking to devour its prey."

"He's a good man."

"He is." Her head bobs. "The best. It was fate for us to meet. I believe I would be dead right now if it weren't for him. I owe him. I want to spend the rest of my days with him."

"B-But?"

"No buts. Just a little bump in the road before I can fully have a future with him."

"G will take care of him."

"That's what I'm afraid of. I'm scared I'll lose him because of my choices, my mistakes."

He winces when he reaches for her hand. "Let him—"

"Shh. Relax. You need to heal." She places his hand down then runs the washcloth over his chest and around his incisions.

Can't say I'm too happy about the intimacy between the two of them at the moment but I'll rein my jealousy in, just this once for my fallen brother.

I lift off the door frame and make myself known. "You going to be able to get up today and do a workout with me?" I stand by his bedside, joking with him, trying to lighten up the seriousness of his injuries.

Luca turns his head to me. "Fuck." His breathless voice fills the room. "Did we get them?"

I glance up at Isabelle, unsure, but knowing if she is going to live this life with me, she will hear much worse. I return my attention back to Luca after dismissing Dr. B from where he sits in the corner watching over his patient. "We did."

"Who?" His breath comes out with a huff.

"Not sure yet. But I will. You know I will."

"I-I—" He coughs. "I want the person who gave the order."

I nod, already knowing I may have to share my retaliation with him. "You need anything? A hot chick to sit by your side? Give you a different kind of sponge bath? You're not getting one of those from my woman, man."

He huffs a tortured laugh. "Pretty sure my dick isn't getting hard anytime soon." He glances over at Isabelle. "Sorry." He places his hand on hers. "I'm sorry. I should have known better. If he trusts you, I should have too."

"I understand." She glances at me. "I want to protect him too."

"I do not need protecting." My gruff response accompanies my shifting body, knowing her and I will have to have a conversation about not trying to help because helping only makes things worse. "Get rest." I return my attention back to Luca and convey to him, "Your injuries are serious. You almost didn't make it. You will stay here until you are healed. Understood?"

With his nod of agreement, I jerk my head at Isabelle telling her to follow me out. I'm quiet walking her down the hallway with her hand in mine. She follows without saying a word. Just the sight of her with him has my insides raging with fire. Not just because she was touching him but because she was soothing him. She was helping a man I consider family knowing he didn't trust her. She didn't have to do that. It shows her character, who she is deep inside. That part of her turns me the fuck on. I want nothing more than to tear her clothing off and devour her every curve, but the dominant man inside me holds back until I can control myself. Until I can freely take her to the fullest extent of my desire for her without being interrupted.

For now, I push her up against the door to our bedroom and lay a kiss on her that leaves her breathless. My hand slides inside her pants only because I want to feel her heartbeat pulsing the blood of her arousal through her lips. She opens her legs further. I glide my finger through her slickness and enter her, knowing I'll get her off quickly and then end this with a raging erection that I will force myself to ignore, waiting until later when we are alone.

Her head rocks back, her mouth slackens, releasing short puffs of frenzied breaths. The ridged tissue inside her becomes the pad of my finger's best friend. She gasps, her insides tighten, and she releases a moan that I devour and ingest with my mouth. Her body relaxes, sliding down the door a bit while I'm still holding my fingers inside her. Her bottom lip is captured between my teeth and the animalistic urge inside wants me to bite it harder. She lifts her hand and grasps a hold of my furious erection. I want to violently consume her but in the most loving way.

I regretfully brush her hand away, adjust myself, and release my hold on her. I bring my hand to my mouth and greedily suck the slickness of her arousal off. My forehead rests against hers. Our eyes meet. Our mouths open. I lean down and slide the remaining essence of her between our lips. She slides her tongue along the broken seam of my mouth with tiny swirls that send electric shocks right to my fully engorged groin.

"Fuck me," I pant, still resting my head against hers. "Come on." I grab for her hand and step back. "I need to feed you."

"Not that I am complaining, but what was that?"

"That was me, cutting the head of the green monster over you touching another man."

She stops in her tracks. "Wait. You're jealous?" she asks incredulously.

"Jealousy is a kid word for what I feel."

"Seriously?" She cracks a dubious smirk.

"You think this is funny?"

"No. I think this is fantastic!" Her voice elevates ten decimals.

"I definitely do not think you should be so excited over my shortcomings."

"There is nothing short about your comings. I have never had someone be jealous over me. It feels so good." She laughs deeply through her sentence with humorous amazement.

A gruff snort of displeasure leaves me. "Angel, you have no idea." I turn and continue down the hall, releasing her hand when we get to the mouth of the open room. My attention and gaze search for Demetri and Leo where I last saw them standing in the living room as Isabelle makes a right and starts for the kitchen. Demetri's eyes widen with an added head nod in that direction.

"You have got to be fucking kidding me. What the fuck is she doing here? Why is she still here?!"

If I had a minute this morning, just one, I would have talked with Kathrine about last night's events. My concern goes straight to Isabelle. Her eyes are flames of hatred. I understand it. The talk I should have had right away this morning was put off with all the commotion.

Kathrine stands there emotionless, just watching, waiting to see what will happen. What is going to happen will only ever be what happens.

"Isabelle, come here." I step in her direction, wanting to meet her halfway, but she doesn't budge. My girl stands her ground. I'm proud of her for that. "Angel." My call of endearment has Kathrine deflating.

"Does he still need her?" Her foot juts out to the side as her hand goes to her hip.

"I don't know." I continue my steps to her until I am a hair's breadth away. "I don't know," I repeat, placing both my hands on her face, cradling her clench jaw with strength. "I will find out."

"Please do. If she is not needed, I want her gone. If she is, then she can stay in the room until she is."

My girl is pissed, and I understand it.

"I will handle it."

"Yes, you will." She pulls her face from my hands and steps back only to turn around and say, "I'm going to take a shower. If she isn't of use anymore then I want her gone by the time I come back out."

I stand there, holding back my proud emotions. Look at her, giving me orders. Damn, she is feisty. My chest blazes at her newfound comfortable confidence. Self-esteem I gave her the freedom to build. The world better look out, because my Isabelle is going to own it.

I watch Isabelle leave then turn to Kathrine. "My office. Now."

I slam the door shut behind her. "What the fuck were you thinking?" I cross my arms over my chest and wait.

"You're in love with her." A whispered statement she can barely bring herself to say.

"Answer me, Kathrine. What the hell were you thinking?" I bellow with angered force.

She drops into the seat in front of my desk. "I lost you." Another whispered statement.

"You didn't have me, Kathrine. That was dead and buried a long time ago."

"I thought—"

"You thought wrong." My voice dry and cold.

"I just…"

"You just what? Came into my home and threw our history at my woman in hopes to, what? Scare her away? Make her jealous? Claim a man you didn't have? You're better than that."

"I know. I just knew, deep inside, I just knew this time was different. You wouldn't return my calls and when I showed up here to give you a piece of my mind, she was here, without you, in your space. She had a glass of wine. She looked cozy in your kitchen. I knew right then and there that she was different. You weren't here and she was, in your space, without you, Giovanni," she says like she can't fathom it. "Something snapped inside me. I lost a lifelong friend. One I had called when I needed an ear. Someone I have known my whole life was suddenly not available to me. I suddenly missed you and it wasn't even as if time had passed. I just knew you were gone."

"Kathrine."

"I'm sorry, G. I can't say I never meant to hurt her because in that moment, I did. I wanted to hurt her. I wanted her to know about the baby. How we shared precious moment together. I wanted her to know that her short period of time with you couldn't compare to a lifetime of memories. I wanted her to know I had you first and that I still had you."

"But you don't have me, Kathrine. You haven't since we were kids." I walk to the windows and stare out into the unknown.

"I had your friendship."

"Do you know what I would have done to you if you weren't who you are, for doing what you did?"

"G…"

"Don't 'G' me, Kathrine. You are so much better than this." I turn back to face her and walk back to where she still sits. I stop and rest on the side of my desk, looking down at her. She seems so brittle at the moment, so broken, but she isn't my responsibility to fix. She built this up in her head. "Look, part of this is my fault. I knew you had feelings for me since we were kids. While I wasn't attached to anyone it wasn't a problem and maybe that is the problem in itself. I should have been more open about where my feelings lie with you. I apologize for that. It was thoughtless, careless on my part. We share a history together. You got me through some tough times, Kathrine. I will always be there for you if you need me, it just won't be the way it was before."

"I don't think your girlfriend will love hearing you say that."

"Fiancée. She just doesn't know it yet."

"Same ol', G, pushing his way through until he gets what he wants."

"And I want her."

"Ouch." Her lip wobbles.

"It wasn't said to be callus. It was said so you know exactly where I stand."

The moment lingers as she looks off at the open space. "She would have been eighteen. Our daughter would have turned eighteen last month."

"Kathrine…"

"She would have been in her first year of college."

"She would."

"She would have been the only part of you I would always have."

"Kat. Don't do this to yourself." My hardened heart softens for her sadness.

"Do you think about her? If she was still with us, do you think about how crazy our lives would be. What she would look like? Would she be stubborn like her daddy or like to watch tv late at night like me, her mom."

"Kat, don't do this. It was a long time ago. You have to move on."

"That's the thing, Giovanni. To me it was just yesterday."

I lift from my desk and crouch in front of her, placing my hand on her knee. "Then you need to get help for yourself. You are a fantastic therapist, Kathrine. A professional, through and through. You have helped so many people. A woman I consider my best friend being one of them. Sofia would not be where she is emotionally today if it weren't for you. I will always be grateful to you for that, but now it is time for you to help yourself. I'm sorry I've never seen the true sadness you are enduring before this."

"Yeah. I knew if I always had a part of you, I had a part of her too. Now I have lost both."

"You haven't lost me. Things will just be different. I won't let you disrespect, Isabelle."

"I'm sorry, G." She stands and wraps her arms around me when I follow.

For a moment I stiffen, not wanting to lead Kathrine on or disrespect Isabelle's feelings, but then I hold her in my arms. Giving her what she needs to let go of a history we both reflect on differently. I don't let the moment linger for any longer than one needs to say goodbye. Releasing her, I step back, wipe the tears from her cheeks and tell her it's time for her to leave. I can't selfishly keep her here knowing it's going to hurt her. Having her here jeopardizes the stability of my relationship with Isabelle. It's unacceptable and a situation I won't tolerate. I say my goodbyes and part ways, praying Luca won't need another transfusion.

Giovanni
CHAPTER THIRTY-SIX

I hold my palm against the small of her back, leading her through the double glass doors into The Surf. Her gaze searches every inch of the place once inside. She's nervous. My instincts are on high alert. When Isabelle was at home, I had no worries of her ex getting to her. Out here, in the open, he could be anywhere. Men like him, the ones that think they are better, higher up the society ladder even if it's by association, think they can get away with anything. Men like me, do get away with it. We don't ask for permission, nor will we say we're sorry if we are caught. We just do what needs to be done with or without permission or the badge of prestige from a political family name behind us.

We hold the power in a name that runs the city.

"Mr. Moretti," the hostess greets, her smile bright and charming. "It's good to see you again. Miss…" She lingers for a moment not knowing how to greet Isabelle.

"Moretti," I inform her cutting off Isabelle. Her eyes shoot to mine, but instead of correcting me she stays quiet.

"Oh. Congratulations. Welcome, Mrs. Moretti. The table that was requested is ready. Mr. Heart is already seated with his wife."

We follow the long-time hostess to our table. With each step, Isabelle's gaze is burning a hole in the side of my face. I ignore it, knowing this is a conversation we will have to have in private. I know exactly what I want. I would marry her right now if I could. There is one thing I never want to hear again; his last name attached to her.

I lean down and kiss her temple, then linger a moment as I murmur, "It's got a good ring to it, doesn't it?"

She floors me when she says, "It does. Better than the two I've had. How could it not, it's attached to a better man."

I expected somewhat of a push back, rightfully fighting for her independence. What I got was something else altogether and that just made my night so much better.

Antonio stands and greets me with a back slap and hug then turns to Isabelle when her and Lilah are done introducing themselves to each other, and says, "I'm glad you're here. I will admit, I have misjudged you."

"Yeah. My husband has a tendency to go overboard."

"Dolcezza." The warning growl from Antonio bleeds between them.

"Oh, hush, wolfie. If the girl is going to be in this family—and by the way Giovanni is looking at her, she is, because you bastards don't give up—then she needs to get to know who we are as a family."

"My wife, Isabelle." Antonio gestures with his hand in Lilah's direction. "That mouth of hers gets her in trouble all the time." Antonio reaches out, grabs her arm, yanks her body to his, and places a forceful kiss on her lips.

She giggles, giving him a heated look as she pulls away. With a wink and a devious grin, she murmurs, "You like my mouth, wolfie."

When I see the look on Isabelle's face at the forceful intimacy between the two, I lean in and murmur, "Antonio and Lilah have never changed. They are fiercely in love with one another and madly entertained by the challenge of each other."

"That was pure passion between two people. Something I have never been a witness too."

"Would that kind of passion make you uncomfortable?" I ask only because I find myself holding back because of her history.

"No. It is a natural emotion between the two of them." Her head twists as she surveys me. "You have been holding back, haven't you? Because of what I have been through, you aren't showing me your true feelings."

"My feelings? Yes, I have shown you exactly how I feel about you. The magnitude of my attraction to you? Not even close. My sexual desire that I want to experience and share with you, absolutely not. I'm an intense man, angel. My craving for you is beyond the intensity in which I have shown you, but I'm not an asshole, I have compassion for the trauma you have been through."

"Soo..." she draws out in fascinated confusion. "My panties being severed by your knife, or my wrist being captured by restraints, or even the puddle of fluid you persuasively pulled from my body, that's not intense? You have even more elevated sexual acts up that sleeve of yours."

"You have no fucking clue." I imprison her face in the palms of my hands. "We have a lifetime to get there."

She leans up and brushes her lips "Don't hold back, Giovanni. What you have shown me when we are together is only scary because of my inexperience, but I feel exhilarated and free while under your command and in your arms. I want all of you. Every bit of you. Please don't hold back on me."

She leaves me speechless as we take our seats. Without prompt, Lilah and Isabelle hit it off. While Antonio and I talk business as usual, Isabelle and Lilah talk about everything from kids to clothes to jobs. The two of them have so much in common, including just a few years difference in age, yet they have lived two totally different lives.

Isabelle laughs without reserve. I can't help but watch her intently for long periods of time. The beauty she exudes while her inner soul is freely being released is nothing short of spontaneous beauty. She's radiating with a happiness I'm sure she has never felt.

Our meals are served, and while the four of us consume large quantities of food and wine, we still chat about everything and nothing at all between bites.

The night was going perfect until a shadow appears at the side of our table.

I lean in, and whisper to Isabelle, "No matter what happens, know that I will protect you."

The family only ever eats in the back room. It's our room. No one else is ever allowed back there.

Tonight was different.

The Surf is a cover for money laundering. The restaurant, on paper, is owned by a man we all call Uncle Denny, a longtime friend of Mr. Heart's. In our world, this restaurant is owned by the organization, and everyone knows it. In the real world, it is an upscaled five-star Italian restaurant.

The man who had the balls to approach our table knows it.

Antonio and I simultaneously stand. Isabelle gasps at my side. Lilah scoots closer to her then places her hand on top of Isabelle's to comforter her. My hand goes to my back, reaching for my gun, ready for whatever is about to go down. I knew this motherfucker wasn't going to heed the warning I gave him the night before. By the looks of his face, you would have thought he would have. I gave him what he has given Isabelle, a beat down.

He laid there in that alley, unconscious and bleeding from his open wounds. However, no beating will ever give her justice, only his death will.

It will certainly make me feel better.

If I can take out a man whose blood I carry in my veins, then I can for sure remove one from this earth that doesn't. I have countless times before.

Little does Tommy boy know, Antonio and I were ready for this visit.

The text from an associate I hired a few weeks back came through minutes ago. When Johnathan Reznor's name came across my screen, is when my senses went on high alert. The table inside the dining room with the regular patrons was set up an hour prior to our arrival. Otherwise, we would have been in the back private room where the family always has dinner. No one wants to watch their back while they are enjoying a meal. Tommy would have never been able to get to us in there.

Out here, we are in full view of the public. Multiple witnesses to watch his harassment.

He just walked straight into our trap.

Isabelle sits next to me. She is as stiff as a board. The look of fear paralyzes her face. I wish I could have warned her, but it wouldn't have played out the way I wanted it to if I had.

Tommy stands there, his nostrils flared, his fists clenched.

Bring it on.

The ownership he emits over her sinks in the blackness of his eyes, drowning in the belly of hatred he feels for her.

I have all I can do to hold back.

"Officer, can we help you?"

He stands there, voiceless, watching Isabelle. I take a purposeful step closer to her, my thigh brushing her upper arm.

"It looks to me that you may have had a run in with a Mack truck," Antonio remarks, egging him on. "Did that happen on the job or afterhours while conducting extracurricular activities?"

His leer flicks to Antonio and narrows.

"We are simply enjoying a nice night out with our women." Antonio smiles, while casually sliding his hands into his pants pockets.

"Lieutenant," Tommy corrects the slight with a growled response. "This," he points to his face, "is nothing."

"Looks to me like someone worked you over. Who'd you piss off?" Antonio continues his taunts.

"Ask your boy." He turns his attention to me.

"I'm not sure who you're referring to, officer. There are only men on this side of the table. Who exactly would you be speaking of? The pussy on the other side?"

"Maybe when you are sitting inside a six-by-six cell that I put you in, and the block leader takes out trade on your ass, you'll remember."

"I'm sorry, the only recollection I have of last night is when I was buried deep inside my beautiful woman."

"You motherfucker!" He leaps over the table to get to me.

I instantly grab for Isabelle at the same time Antonio grabs Lilah, and Demetri comes from behind Tommy and grabs him.

I lean forward when I knew the girls were secure behind us. "You may want to watch *your* back, officer." I inform him while Demetri holds him back. "I have a few friends inside that owe me favors. You may just share the cell with one of them soon since you don't always uphold the law you took an oath to."

His sight bleeds with murderous intent. He struggles to get out of Demetri's hold. He turns his attention to Isabelle. I'm ready to jump over the table and put a bullet in his head, but I know I have to keep calm.

"Once a whore, always a whore. Too bad you weren't worth it, and I had to go looking elsewhere to get my cock sucked. Maybe I should have broken you in and trained you."

Isabelle physically flinches.

My insides burn with revenge, and before I know what I'm doing, I'm propelling forward in a murderous rage only to be restrained by Antonio.

My planned evening is going to backfire on me because I am going to slaughter this guy right here in front of everyone.

The next thing I know, Isabelle is launching herself over the table and throwing her glass of red wine in his face. The wine saturates his clothing and drips off his face as the glass hits the ground and shatters.

I will end this motherfucker and soon.

I grab for Isabelle's waist. Food is flying in every direction as she's scurrying across the table.

"Is this guy fucking for real?" Lilah yells, cursing like a sailor as she follows Isabelle across the table to get to Tommy.

Antonio releases me, muttering his own explicit words as he's grabbing for his wife. Lilah starts kicking her four-inch, red-soled, stiletto heeled feet at Tommy's torso while Antonio is pulling her back.

Just as Antonio warns Lilah with an order to keep quiet and my hand is latching onto Isabelle's waist, the room is filled with the deafening sound of skin meeting skin.

Fuck.

My heart sinks when I see Isabelle's hand pulling back from Tommy's face. She goes for him once again, her red flames of hair flying as she struggles to get to him.

This is not going how I planned. I am so proud of my girl for standing up to her ex, but she just fucked up, royally.

My plan has gone to shit.

The tables have just been turned.

"D, get him out of here!" I roar with fury. *"Fuck!"* I bellow, grabbing for Isabelle's purse and her hand.

"You will never touch me again!" she screams across the restaurant at Tommy.

Antonio looks at me, knowing we have to leave immediately. He instructs Lilah to get her stuff together then calls his car around to pick us up.

We pile inside the back of his limo. Isabelle is quiet while staring at the hold I have on her hand. Antonio's hand is latched onto the inside of

Lilah's thigh while he is on the phone conducting business, calling in favors, knowing this situation just became a sensitive one. Neither one of the girls know why we are so tense.

"I say we go to the club." Lilah turns to Antonio. "Screw that guy, he's an asshole. Let's not let him ruin our night. Wolfie, let's go to the club and have a good time."

He glances at me. It's a good idea. In fact, it's a great idea. I give a slight nod then wrap my arm around Isabelle and pull her into me and kiss the top of her head.

She peers up at me. "Are you mad? I'm sorry I ruined dinner."

"You didn't!" Lilah sputters with anger. "That guy got what he deserved. Why these two didn't murder him is beyond me."

"Dolcezza, zip the lip for right now, would you."

I turn in to her. "I'm not mad, angel. Not at you."

"Then why are you so quiet?"

"Trying to figure out the next move. I knew Tommy was going to show up tonight. I just didn't take into consideration that it would go down that way."

I shift in my seat and take a deep breath before explaining that we purposely sat in the main dining room so that everyone could witness Tommy harassing us—her. That I didn't say anything to her because I needed her reaction to be real when he showed up. That the cameras were specifically turn towards our table to record every angel of the incident. That it would be Tommy's downfall at being an upstanding law enforcement officer when it showed up on the news from an anonymous person. Then I explained to her that the moment she smacked him, she then became an assailant assaulting a police officer and he has every right to press charges against her.

That's the moment it all sinks in. Tears flood her eyes. She deflates in my arms and releases a heavy breath. "I messed up so bad. I don't know what came over me. I wasn't thinking, I just reacted."

"I will fix this, Isabelle. Antonio is calling in favors right now to make sure no charges are brought against you. You and I are going to go to Temptations and enjoy our evening. Do not let Tommy ruin our night together."

"He already has."

"He only has if you let him. I will not let him spoil the first real date we have."

"I think we are way past dating." Her eyes sparkle up at me with leftover tears.

"You have a lifetime of dates ahead of you, angel. I plan on spoiling you for the rest of our lives."

That brings a smile to her face and a little less heaviness to my chest.

Isabelle

CHAPTER THIRTY-SEVEN

The music is so loud. The beat is deep and bone-rattling. Lights flash with beams of color. Fire shoots with furious force from strategically placed posts. Sparsely dressed men and women dance inside hanging cages. Sweaty bodies move, sliding against each other. I've only ever been to a club one time. It was with Tommy when we first started dating. It was a seedy, dirty place loaded with men that made my skin crawl. It was nothing like this establishment. The night I ran through here, determined to get to Giovanni, I didn't paid attention to the details.

"What do you want to drink, angel?"

"Umm… I don't…" I fumble over my words. "I don't know. I've never really…"

"Get her a Cosmo!" Lilah yells from beside Giovanni. "Jake, make her a Cosmo," she yells over the music to the bartender. "Put it in a tumbler instead of a martini glass because her behind is coming out on the dance floor with me and there is no way we are wasting alcohol with spillage."

"You got it, Mrs. Heart." He smiles, turning to Giovanni. "The usual, Mr. Moretti?"

"Yeah. Antonio's too." He turns back to me and wraps his arm around my waist while we wait for our drinks.

"The bartender calls you mister?"

"Jake has been around a long time. Mr. Heart hired him years ago to work alongside his daughter to keep an eye on her. He has worked for us since then as our eyes and ears in this club. Who better than a bartender who listens to everyone's problems? I've told him continuously to call me by my first name, but out of respect, he won't."

"You work out of this club? Like this is where you are all the time when you say you have to go to work?" I survey the overwhelming amount of sex oozing inside the walls which is hypothetically his office.

"In Antonio's office upstairs." He points to a wall of mirrored glass up high in the second story. He grins. "No worries. I only have eyes for a certain redhead."

I survey our surroundings. "Wow. How did I even make it all the way up there without being caught?"

"You were a determined mother," Lilah remarks with a huge smile. "I get it. Some big bad mother f'er like him giving you a stuffed animal for your daughter. He could have been a creeper."

"I guess I was."

"Come." He jerks his head. "Let's go upstairs to the private lounge."

I follow behind him. I have no choice even if I want one. My hand is clutched in his with a grip that tells me he isn't letting go anytime soon. We enter a room that is luxurious. Giovanni walks behind the bar and pushes a button under the counter. The wall of shaded glass facing the club disappears. The club music fills the room. It's an upbeat song, making my hips move. I wiggle my fingers, silently asking Giovanni to release me.

I walk to where Lilah is leaning against the railing, watching the patrons below.

"Cool, right? Being up here but still able to enjoy the crowd below."

"I wouldn't know." Giovanni steps up next to me, placing his hand on the small of my back. "I've only been to one club. When my ex and I started dating, he brought me to one. It was nothing like this though. Plus, the customers there were not what is down there." I point. "It was a meat market."

"This is a meat market," Giovanni mutters.

"No. No, this place was like women were on display. Like they were there just for the men to view. It was gross. I told my ex to never take me back there again."

"Let's go dance. G, how long will Antonio be?"

"Depends. Few minutes at least," he tells her then turns to me, questioning, "Where was this club he brought you to? In the city?"

"No, it was downtown. I swear it was a strip club, but Tommy assured me it wasn't. Not that I would have minded if it was, but this place was just skeevy."

"Can I take her downstairs?" Lilah throws her arm around my shoulders and waits for Giovanni's permission.

I'm taken back by the question. I don't need his permission to do anything. Out of respect for him, I do as he asks, but to get permission? No. Then I realize I'm not dating a man who has a normal nine-to-five job. Neither is Lilah. She is used to the lifestyle. I am not. I will have some adjusting to do. Giovanni's world and the situations I could potentially face, could be life threatening.

His focus is on me. "Do you want to go down?"

I glance at the crowd below and nod my head, glad that he asked instead of just saying yes or no. I want to experience the energy.

"Yeah!" Lilah exclaims with excitement.

"You coming?" I wait, hoping he says yes.

"You go down with Lilah. I'll be down in a minute. I want to talk to Antonio about something when he comes back." He removes his suit jacket and pulls his phone from his pocket. I give him a kiss and turn to follow her out. "Lilah!" he thunders, twisting his head, giving her a stern look.

"I know! I know! I got this, G!"

"What was that about?" I grab for her arm as we're walking down the back stairs.

"That was your man telling me not to let anyone brush up on you. I'll give him five minutes before he is down here. Right now," she jerks her head up at him, "he is calling security, letting them know we are on our way down. Watch." She points at the security guy standing at the bottom of the far steps. "That's Ricky. Nice guy, but only listens to Antonio and Giovanni. Don't even try to persuade him to do something for you. It won't work. I've tried."

"What about Demetri?"

"Hard ass to the max. He has a sense of humor but behind closed doors..." She shakes her body like she just got the chills. "He's intense...." She lets that linger off too, leaving me curious.

"And Luca?"

"We didn't get along at first. I hated having a bodyguard, but now, now I think of him as a brother. Is he okay? Antonio wouldn't let me go see him this morning."

"Why?" We hit the bottom of the steep steps.

"He said it would be too hard on me. Is he that bad?"

"He's bad. I gave him a sponge bath this morning to remove some of the dried blood."

"Oh, I'm sure Giovanni loved that." She sarcastically laughs.

"He was not happy."

"They are all the same," she yells over the booming music. "I left Antonio one time after having sex with him in the backroom of an exclusive club. He told me he was going to see me home, like he had the upper hand of me, and his word is the only word. I left him standing there, said I needed the restroom and walked out the back door. My best friend, Katie, informed him I left after he stood in the hallway for twenty minutes. Serves him right. I swear he wanted to skin me when I saw him the first time after that." She grins a mischievous grin. "Okay, enough talking. Let's dance!" She throws her hand in the air.

"You love this, huh?" I shout as she pulls me to the middle of the dance floor.

"No, not really. Been there done that. Ya know? But I can see that you haven't experienced any of this and by the little bit I have been told, you need to. You have to live a little since you haven't been able to. I get where you are coming from. Trust me, one day we will have lunch. I'll tell you my story and you can tell me yours." She grabs my hand and starts moving. "Now let's dance!" She starts jumping around. "Us girls have to stick together. Especially in this family. They will be hard on you until they get to know you."

"I met Sofia. She seems nice. I get the inkling that her and Giovanni shared something. When I asked, she was very tight-lipped."

"She is very nice. First time I met her, I made a fool of myself. She just has her guard up because you are new to the family. And yes, her and G are tight. He was her bodyguard for a long time."

I leave it at that and enjoy the atmosphere. I'm having the best time. One song turns into the next. Time almost seems to elapse. My hands are in the air, both of us smiling and singing with the music when Lilah gets a big smirk on her face. Strong hands come around from the back of me, sliding over my waist and resting on my stomach. His body brushes against mine as he manipulates my movements to mimic his. The deep rich scent of his skin wraps around me. I lean my head back against his shoulder and glance up at him. In the blasé moment of joy, something on the second floor catches my eye.

A man standing on the catwalk with three women surrounding him.

Not just any man.

My father-in-law.

"Does he always come here?" I connect eyes with the Senator who's already peering down at me.

"Who?"

"The Senator."

"Where?" His voice is a crack of thunder. His body doesn't stiffen but I feel the moment he is no longer relaxed, the air surrounding us immediately changes. He peers up at him through narrowed eyes like he knew exactly where he would be standing. "He has a private lounge upstairs."

"Like he owns it?"

"He rents the lounge. Some of the private lounges are paid rooms. A yearly membership. His is one of them." His body stopped moving the moment I asked about Tommy's father being here.

"Oh. And the women with him?"

"I don't think I have to answer that question, angel."

"He's scum. You should see the way he treats his wife."

"He's not usually here during the week. Come. Let's go upstairs." His whole demeanor changes, morphing into the man everyone is afraid of as he starts taking steps to exit the dance floor.

That's when it hits me.

Giovanni would have never brought me here if he thought the Senator would be here. Tommy, I'm sure now knows my whereabouts.

"G?" I tug on his hand. Panic starts to set in. He lifts his sight to Antonio's private lounge. The feel-good music from two minutes ago now becomes irritating. Giovanni's face becomes stone.

Lilah and Antonio are standing at the railing watching us. When the two men connect eyes, Antonio narrows his. I watch as Antonio's instincts kick in. He shifts from behind Lilah and places his phone to his ear. His stature stiffens as he yells into the phone. He quickly turns, saying something to Lilah, then they both disappear.

I can't help but glance back at my father-in-law. I just know the next few minutes are going to change my life. A rock sits in the base of my stomach and the sneer of a smirk on the Senator's ruddy face only confirms my night it about to drastically change. He waves at me, but it's not a pleasant hello or goodbye wave, it's slow and methodic, and his facial features switch to something sinister.

My stomach sinks.

His lips moves and it looks like he mouths, "Goodbye."

The next thing I know, my name is being thundered with a certain rage I have experienced too many times before.

It all happens in slow motion.

My arm is ceased. I'm yanked to the railing of the third step. I don't stumble as far as I should have from the force of it because Giovanni has a hold of my waist.

Security from the club swarms in, surrounding us.

Orders are shouted from every direction.

Guns are drawn.

The crowd separates, and in walks my husband. He has handcuffs twirling around his finger like what is about to transpire is a pleasurable joy.

"I'll fucking kill you for this." Giovanni grinds his teeth. "Get your fucking hand off her or I'll break your jaw." He snarls at the uniformed officer holding onto my wrist.

"A threat," Tommy bellows with laughter. "Did you all hear that? This man just threatened a law enforcement officer."

"Shut the fuck up, G." Antonio steps up next to him.

"Release her. Now!" Tommy hollers with force at Giovanni.

The tension in the air is suffocating. Multiple guns are drawn and point at tense bodies.

"Release her or I'll arrest you for obstruction."

Giovanni's head falls back. The bellowing laughter that leaves his body is eerie. When he drops his head back down his fist is already flying through the air. The impact to Tommy's jaw is lethal. Chaos ensues. Men jump on Giovanni. His grip on me loosens in the all-out brawl. My arm is yanked again, only this time it is by a smaller hand. Lilah's voice is screaming next to my ear. She yanks on me once more, snapping me out of my stunned haze.

"Come on!" She turns to run up the stairs.

"Lilah!" Antonio's voice bellows through the chaos. "Take her to our room!"

"Isabelle!" I hear Giovanni roar.

I turn back and witness the scene. It's bedlam. A mayhem of fists being thrown. The dance floor is covered with bleeding bodies.

A shot rings out and screams from every direction pierce the air. Chaos ensues, and I stop dead in my tracks. The pain at what I am going to have to do physically hurts me.

It all happens in slow motion. I release Lilah's hand. I turn back and take a deep breath. Tommy is standing at the bottom of the steps, his arms crossed as if he knows he has already won. The corner of his lip lifts with the first step I take back down the stairs. Two more steps and his smile gets bigger. I hear Lilah calling me from the top of the steps. One more step, and I come face to face with a man I despise.

"That's right. You come to Daddy."

I'm silent as I stand in front of Tommy, but my gaze is looking past him, over his shoulder at the man who is forcefully throwing grown men out of the way to get to me.

I sidestep Tommy. His hand reaches out to grab me, but I yank my arm away.

I stop dead in front of a heavy breathing bull. *My* heavy breathing bull.

"I have to go. He won't stop."

"Absolutely not," Giovanni snarls.

"It will only make things worse if I don't." My voice almost pleading to just let this happen with no more bloodshed.

"Isabelle," he gruffly warns.

"She's right, G." Antonio steps in. "They are wrist slapping charges. Our lawyers will have her out in an hour."

"You're not going with him."

"Baby, listen to me." I place my hand on his chest. "I have to do this. I have no choice. He won't stop. I messed up by letting him get to me. I should have never slapped him."

"Isabelle Hunt, you are under arrest for the assault of a law enforcement officer." Tommy's authoritative voice comes from behind me like black sludge wrapping its filth around me.

Cold metal envelops my wrist from behind me.

"You have the right to remain silent." My body jerks with his force.

I reach to the tips of my toes as my other hand is encased in the adjoining metal.

"You have the right to an attorney."

I place my lips to Giovanni's.

"If you cannot afford an attorney."

He jerks me back from the kiss only to have Giovanni clutch my face in his hands and pull me back to him, laying a searing kiss on me that leaves me delirious and Tommy furious with rage.

Giovanni claimed me right in front of Tommy and I love him even more for it.

"An attorney will be—" He has seen enough and stops reading me my rights.

I'm wrenched away with force. Giovanni thunders with threats. Antonio holds his hand on his chest and Lilah is screaming at Tommy.

I'm forcefully lead away, pushed through the crowd, and shoved through the entrance of the club where Tommy's truck sits at the curb.

The night sky glistens above. With a deep breath, I duck my head and sit in the back seat, knowing that life after tonight will never be the same.

"**G**et him on the fucking phone! Right now! Get McCabe on the fucking phone!" I pace back and forth. "One second of her being with him is too much. Do you know what he could be doing to her right now?"

"You had to let her go. She knew she had to go, G. This isn't your fault."

"Fuck you! You told me there was no report made!" I thunder. "I would have taken her home."

"When I called it in and talked to McCabe, there was no report made of the incident," he calmly explains.

I throw my hand out to the side. "Then tell me what the fuck is going on then."

"I can't. Our lawyers are on their way down there. I should get a call any minute."

"I'm going to end this motherfucker, Antonio. End him! Slice his fucking throat from ear to motherfucking ear." I slice my thumb across my neck.

"In due time, we will handle him. You have to be smart, Giovanni. You let your emotions get out of hand and you will be sitting in jail until death comes knocking with the liquid prick."

I know he's right. My leg starts bouncing. "Motherfucker showed up here with plain-clothed cops," I mumble, ranting with venom.

"It was so security wouldn't alert us. He was smart."

When his phone rings, I drop the rocks glass I was just getting ready to fill. "Tell him he didn't even finish reading her her rights!" Knowing that it's our lawyer calling, I twist in my spot and wait for Antonio to speak.

"Can't be." He looks at his watch. "You positive? It's been over an hour. Stay there. Give me fifteen minutes." He disconnects the call and throws it down to his desk.

I'm hovering, impatiently waiting.

"She's not there," he explains.

"What? What the fuck do you mean she isn't there?"

"He said she hasn't been booked."

"Call McCabe. Get his lying ass on the phone."

Antonio has his ear to the phone within seconds. "McCabe. Yeah. You in the precinct?" I wait for the words of the officer's pockets we pad. "Hunt bring in Giovanni's woman?" He shakes his head at me. "Have you seen him at all tonight?" He shakes his head again. "And there still isn't anything in the computer?" He blows out a huge breath. "Keep your phone close." He hangs up and zeros in on me, asking, "What the plan?"

"He's dead. Everyone is dead. I'll wipe out every single person that had a part in this."

"Stop and think. Where would he take her?"

I turn and pace away from him, my mind racing. "Home. His house is the only place I would know he would bring her." Then it hits me. "Hunt."

"What?"

"Hunt, that son-of-bitch." I take off in a sprint.

My footsteps fall with thuds of vengeance against the metal grates of the catwalk. I round the corner and race to his private lounge with Antonio right on my heels. I bust open the door, grab the slimy fucker by the throat, and throttle him against the wall. I don't even think twice about the fact that some chick's mouth was swallowing his cock.

"Tell me where the fuck he took her." I squeeze his neck. The screaming girls do nothing to stop the brutality in which I hold him by the neck, letting his toes dangle in the air. "If he fucking hurts her, I swear to a God I don't believe in, I will fillet your fucking skin from your body inch by inch and feed you piece by piece to the toxic fucking fish in the Hudson with a smile on my face."

He struggles for air. His eyes bulging from the pressure at his throat. His face is turning redder by the second. I squeeze harder, wanting, craving to hear the cracking sound of his throat being crushed. It would soothe my soul knowing he died at the brutality of my hands. I also know I have to keep him somewhat alive to get answers. I release my hold ever so slightly and let his feet touch the floor. He gasps for air when I relax my grip even more.

"You have a savior complex, Mr. Moretti?"

"No, but shouldn't you have one since you work in public service? Tell me where she is, dead man." His eyes widen, shooting to mine. "If you had a part in this. You will die for it, Senator. I promise you that."

"She's his wife!"

"She was his possession. Father like son, huh, Senator? A woman shoots you down and your ego can't take it?"

"You sanctimonious piece of shit. No gangster treats his woman any better. They are all objects to be used." He shoves at my hands. I constrict my fingers at his words. His eyes go back to bulging and frantic with fear.

"That is where you are dead fucking wrong. Where the fuck did he take her?"

"G, wire," Antonio mutters a truth from behind me that we always have to watch out for.

"You wearing a wire, Senator? Was this little stunt planned out between father and son?" I grip the open V of his shirt and slice the side of my hand down the center, effectively popping every single button, revealing his white ribbed undershirt. Both my hands grip the center of the flimsy material, ripping his shirt to shreds right down the middle.

"I don't need a wire." He shoves at my hands once again finding his balls.

"Tell me where he took her." I slam him against the wall.

"An all-inclusive learning retreat." His smarmy smirk sends me over the edge.

It was only a millisecond of a moment that passed before the syllables of his words ended and my fist connected with his jaw. The second punch is to his gut, forcing what air he had replenished to rush out. I have waited years to do this. Years. Years I have to stand back and wait for the right time. The third punch is my voice bouncing of the inner tubes of his ear canal, letting him know I was onto him. I stare at him, knowing he isn't going to give me any answers, and understanding I have to find her before nightfall.

The explosion of hate inside the barren cavity of my chest begs for a source to unleash its wrath on. The valet already has the doors open and waiting for the three of us to exit Temptations. Antonio, Demetri, and I pile inside. Demetri is at the wheel. I couldn't tell you when he showed up or even when Lilah was sent home. My focus is purely on finding my girl.

"Where to first?" Demetri grips the wheel.

"The house."

The scenery flies past the windows at record speeds. Demetri's can't get us there fast enough. Time is of the essence. Tommy's already had two hours alone with her, enough time to do enough damage she can't come back from. He caught me off guard. I should have known better. He wanted Isabelle and he used his profession to get her.

I know in my gut she is in more danger than before. Tommy's ego is bruised, his manhood humiliated by losing her to another man, but my gut tells me his retaliation is more than that.

Demetri turns the corner, speeding down the street and squealing to a stop in front of her dark house. The front door is ajar. Splatters of blood stain the wood by the handle. I burst through not knowing what to expect. The house is in shambles. A struggle had definitely ensued within these walls. Demetri goes one way, Antonio goes the other, and I charge down the hallway calling out her name. Searching only takes minutes because of the small square footage of the house.

"Giovanni," Antonio hollers from the kitchen.

My feet move on their own accord. I charge through the house, heading in the direction of his voice. I turn the corner, entering the kitchen, and I see the pool of blood and the streak where someone was dragged across the floor. My heart sinks as my rage becomes an inferno, ready to burn the world down to the ground until her screams are the only sound calling me to save her.

My fist slinters the cabinet door. My knuckles throb with the same intensity my chest does.

"Where the fuck is she?!" I bellow with a razor-sharp roar so loud my throat closes up. I instantly go silent. My head drops and when my chin bangs against my chest, it hits me. "The warehouse." I grind my molars lifting my head. "He has her at the warehouse."

Demetri jerks his head in my direction, not understanding.

"Last night's attack. The construction zone. The warehouse just off in the distance. That's the property that is for sale. It's the property Santo was talking about this morning. The only counter bidding was from Senator Hunt. The adjacent property is owned by him. Why doesn't he want to give that up? What's the reason, D?"

"He's hiding something."

"He's hiding something," I reiterate, my feet already headed for the door.

"What about her burner phone? The one Freddy put the tracker in for you?"

"It's in her purse. In Antonio's office."

"Fuck." Demetri blows out a breath, following me out the front door.

"His warehouse at the pier is a rouse. That's why the Senator didn't care that we burned them down. We waited for retaliation, waiting to draw him out, but nothing came of it. Why? I'm telling you, the warehouse on the construction site last night is the one we needed to hit."

"We didn't know about it." Antonio brings to light. "We should have. I should have. We walked right into that last night."

"Exactly. We should have known about it. We're a man down because of it." My snarl is rancid as I jog down the front steps, heading toward the SUV.

"Hey, mister. You looking for the lady that lives there?"

I stop in my tracks and turn, searching for the little voice catching my attention. A small boy sits on the side of his house with a baseball bat. He can't be any more than six years old. "Have you seen her?" I crouch down in front of him. "The woman that lived here."

"She moved away but she came back tonight with the man that lives there. He was not nice to her. I saw them from my bedroom window. I told my mom I was going outside to play ball in the back yard, but I was waiting for them to come back. I was going to hit him with my bat."

"You are very brave, but I think it would be best if you went back inside with your mom. It's late and very dark out here."

"I'm tough. I can handle it."

I huff a confined laugh. The little guy reminds me of myself. "Do you know where they went?"

He shrugs his shoulder assuming he's right. "Doctors. She was bleeding."

I stand to my full height while my stomach curls into a knot. "Okay, little man, get back inside with your mom. I'll handle it from here." I turn and walk towards the SUV. Just before shutting the door, I glance back to see if he listened. He didn't. "Don't make me get back out of this vehicle, little man. Get your ass in the house."

"Yes, sir." He scrambles from the ground and scurries inside.

"We're going to need back up." I turn to Antonio and notice he has his phone already to his ear. "We have no idea what we are walking into."

"If the Senator didn't retaliate, then who sent the cargo box of half dead women?" Demetri thinks out loud.

"Tommy," I answer. "I can almost guarantee the Senator knows nothing about it. Tommy's a scorned man. He lost his wife. He's a loose cannon right now. He wants to bury me. Set me up, send me to prison. That's why the Senator said he was bringing her to 'an all-inclusive learning retreat'. The senator wouldn't allow his side hustle to be jeopardize by Tommy's personal life. I bet he thinks he is bringing her to the club she was talking about tonight."

"What club?" Demetri looks at me and waits for an answer.

"Isabelle said Tommy brought her to a club that was a meat market."

He huffs. "They are all meat markets."

"No. She said she felt like the women were on display for the men to view. I bet that is where they auction off the women."

"What do you think he's holding in the warehouse?" Demetri asks, pulling away from the curb.

"Women. I think Hunt's the negotiator and Tommy's the coyote. I think

Tommy is so far under his Senator father's thumb, he can't see past the nail he put in his own coffin."

"Wait a minute. Didn't Santo say he was entertaining the Senator when Mr. Heart called? I bet the Senator overheard Santo and Mr. Heart's conversation. He knew where we were headed."

"Motherfucker. It was a set up," Antonio mumbles from the back after hanging up the phone.

"Isabelle told me once that Tommy would come and go as he pleased, she never really knew his work hours and that sometimes, he's gone for days."

"That's fucked up. He's the one that held the fundraiser for human trafficking the night Izzy left Tommy to be with you."

"Support the cause, take the focus off yourself. Perfect political play."

The rest of the ride is in silence. The three of us gearing up and anticipating the battle we're headed for.

A few blocks out, we stop and meet up with Luke and his brothers. We sit and watch from the hill behind the building. The dirt still holds the bloodstain from the bodies we dropped the night before.

I was done watching.

The longer I sit here, the more time he has to hurt her.

The building is lifeless. It's so stagnant, I start to second guess myself.

I never second guess myself.

Enough is enough.

The steel door to the warehouse creaks with my manipulation. The building inside is quiet as well. No one has been in, and no one has been out.

I reach for my gun at my lower back and slide inside the building. Except for the natural sounds of a warehouse, the inside is the same as the outside.

Quiet.

Antonio, Luke, and Bane enter from the other side. Rocker and Demetri follow at my back. We left Ronan outside in case we get unexpected company. I wish Joseph and Luca were here, but both would do us no good being beat to shit.

A loud crash rings out. It halts my movement mid-step. That's when I hear it. The shrill bone shaking sounds of her scream. I start to take off, but I am immediately stopped by a meaty hand on my shoulder.

"Be smart about this, G. Your thoughts are running off your emotions. You go busting through here, not know exactly where she is, you could get her killed."

He's right. I know he's right.

A hollow clang rings out. I can't pinpoint the nature of the sound or the exact place it's coming from. It echoes through the space like an evil laugh, mocking me.

My steps only become methodical when her tender scream fills the air once again. Each quivering sound she makes, crying out for help, it lingers like a magnet gravitating towards its partner–my soul.

Tommy hollers words so loud they are undecipherable.

I slip around the corner and spot Antonio through the window on the far side. The only thing separating us are two metal walls and two glass windows with Isabelle and Tommy in the middle.

It's a makeshift office he's holding her in. Isabelle lies lifeless in the middle of the floor on some filthy, threadbare area rug. The woman who burns like an eternal flame inside the loins of my ribs lays there helplessly. I have been on many jobs while being broken into this way of life. I have performed horrific tasks and fixed problems over the years most people would have nightmares even psychiatrist couldn't fix with medicine. This right here, seeing the woman who will forever have my love lying on a grimy rug on a cold concrete floor, with blood dripping from her head, and torn clothing hanging off her body, silent... it makes my knees weak and vomit pool at the base of my throat.

The seconds passing feel like they are on superspeed. Timing is everything since Tommy hovers over her body with a revolver in his hand. The tip of it taps against his thigh while his other hand, holding a small device, runs through his sweaty hair.

I look across the room to Antonio. He is holding up his phone. A sign for me to check mine. I lean back against the steel wall, out of Tommy sight, and grab for my phone.

Antonio: She's awake. I'm not sure if she is playing dead or if she is really hurt and can't move.

Me: I'm not waiting any longer. You distract him from that side, and I will go in on this side.

As soon as I send the message, Tommy paces in my direction. I duck down and wait for the commotion Antonio will cause. Demetri glance over at me, strung high on adrenaline and waiting for the battle ahead. When nothing comes, I grab for my phone again only to see another message.

Luke: We have a basement filled with bodies.

Me: Alive or dead?

Luke: Both.

Me: You do what you have to. We'll handle this up here.

Luke: It's not just the bodies. The place is wired. There are explosives in every corner.

Fuck.

I glance up at Demetri and Rocker. "The place is wired." That's when it hits me. Tommy has the detonator in his hand. I peer back through the window. Tommy is now hunched down next to her body. I slide the window over an inch and listen.

"You're gonna die today, bitch. I gave you a great life. You just had to be selfish and go and fuck someone else."

"Fuck you, Tommy," she yells.

"Nah, you're a nasty bitch now. I wouldn't touch you now that you've opened your legs for him."

"Good, because your touch has always repulsed me," she screams.

He throws his head back and roars with laughter. "That's what your father said about your mother."

I hear Isabelle's small gasp.

"That's right. You think we met by chance? Your father, my father, me, we all run in the same powerful circle."

Demetri's head jerk in my direction. "Did you know they knew each other?" he harshly whispers.

"No." My blunt answer and the fact that I stand to my full height tells him I'm done waiting.

"I can't move! You broke my back!" she squeals out in pain.

My heart sinks. I wait for nothing and no one. I step to the side where the entrance to the room is. I hear a phone ring. Demetri waves his hand at me, gesturing for me to stop. I walk back to the window. Tommy now has his back to Isabelle while he stands at the desk speaking to whoever is on the other end. He drops the detonator to the desk when he yells at whoever in on the line.

I feel stuck. Like I'm watching a movie in slow motion. Isabelle gingerly rises to her feet, swaying. A grimace crosses her beautiful face. She takes four steps. Tommy shouts at whoever is on the other end of the phone. He's more occupied with the argument than he is with Isabelle. She lifts her arm stretching it to the fullest height she can. A letter opener is gripped in her shaking hand. With as much energy as she has, she plunges it into the side of his neck. His back stiffens, stunned, shock setting in as the piercing pain blooms. He drops the phone, twists in his spot with fury as his hand flies to his neck. He eyes her like he can't believe she just stabbed him. Surprised that she finally took her stance and retaliated. He takes two big steps towards her. His arm swings through the air, his fist aiming right for her face. Isabelle jumps back, landing in the soft cradle of my arms. Her body hitting mine stuns me just as much as her. Her tired frame now blocking me from getting to him. She can't believe I'm here, and I don't even realize I moved from outside the room to get to her. I'm on auto pilot. I will die for this woman. Give my life so she can finally live one.

Tommy raises his unsteady hand, pointing a wobbling gun right at us that seconds ago sat on his side. His pupils expand. His skin is becoming paler by the second. His eyes close.

My hand slicing across the air is seconds to late.

Isabelle screams.

Two guns fire back to back.

Blood and tissue matter splatter across both our bodies. Tommy drops to his knees then falls flat onto his face.

Antonio steps out from around the corner.

Demetri comes from the other side.

I take two steps to the desk and listen to whoever is on the other end. It's the Senator yelling for his son.

"Your next, motherfucker." I hang up.

Isabelle starts screaming at the top of her lungs. "I killed him! I killed him!" she hysterically shouts, collapsing into me with debilitating fear as I grab her from Demetri's arms.

I hold her lifeless weight and run my hands over her body, making sure she is okay, relieved that she can stand. My girl lied and told Tommy he broke her back so that he would think she was incapacitated. The pride that fills my chest will go unspoken for the time being. I grab her, shake her, shout her name then shake her again. She has to stop screaming. We don't know if any of Tommy's men are in the building.

"Isabelle. Shh, angel." I hold her against me. She grabs onto my red tie like it's her lifeline. I'm relieved my black shirt hides the flow of Tommy's spreading DNA. "Shh." I try to sooth her. She continues to scream. I pull her face to mine and kiss her with every bit of strength and love I have for her. Her screams slowly dissipate as I move my lips over hers. When she calms and no more distressing sounds come from her tired body, I slowly pull away, watching her with caution.

"I killed him." Her lower lip quivers.

"No, angel. I did."

I wash her hair with gentle strokes. Swirls of red from her ex's blood washes down the drain. I'm waiting for the moment she realizes that when you stand in front of someone and shoot them, their blood and tissue fly away from the force of the bullet and not towards you. If that time ever comes, I will reiterate to her that it wasn't her who killed him, even though he died just before two bullets pierced is body. I will take it to my grave so she doesn't suffer from the aftermath of taking someone's life. I have protected one woman my whole life, now I will shield three from the brutal truth we are handed.

Once I delegated what I wanted done with Tommy's body, and I watched Antonio and Demetri roll his corpse in the threadbare area rug my Isabelle pretended to lay on paralyzed and the one Tommy conveniently collapsed on, I took Isabelle away from the gruesome scene.

I carried her to the SUV and placed her in the front seat, snapped her seatbelt, and reverently kissed her cheek. I held her hand and stroked my thumb over her knuckles in the silent moments between us while I drove. I spoke to her in a calm voice, telling her everything was going to be okay. That she wasn't to blame. That none of this was her fault.

She was speechless the whole ride home.

Even when I carried her up to our penthouse, stripped her bare, and set her in the shower under the warm water to wash away the night, she was mute.

The front of her nude body brushes up against mine while I wash the soap from her hair. Her forehead rests against my chest. I freeze for a moment, not sure if her body brushing up against mine is an accident. Her hands slide around my waist. She holds on to me and releases a yelp of sorrow. Her body shakes, trembling with fear and exhaustion.

I wrap my arms around her and hold her tight. She breaks down in the safe confines of my arms.

"Shh, angel. It's going to be okay. I promise you it will be all right."

"Is this your life?" Her lip quivers. "Your every day? When you leave our home to conduct business, is this it? This is what you do?"

"No."

"No? Then how do you stand there and feel nothing? How did you give orders to everyone in the warehouse with routine ease? How do I get through my days knowing I stabbed and killed a man, and it could come back to haunt me?"

"You will get through it because you didn't kill him. The death he received was too good for him. He deserved something that was so torturous, he screamed for days in agony."

"What if they come for you? What if I lose you? What if they come after me to get to you?"

The panic in her voice twists my insides. The shock of it all weighing her down with frantic worry. "Your value to me is priceless, Isabelle. I will do whatever it takes to make sure you are never hurt because of who I am or what I do. I will give you the life you have always deserved. I just need you to understand, in time, that there are rules you will need to abide by in order for me to keep you and Abigail safe." Is it selfish of me to not let her go? Hell yeah, it is, but when it comes to Isabelle, I will always be the greediest motherfucker there is.

"I'm scared." She gazes up at me, tears flowing from the corners of her eyes.

"Of me?" I ask because the possibility is real that she could be afraid of me. She saw me in a different light tonight. The savage inside the man. The dictator who controls every detail. The ruthless beast that will protect at all costs.

She shakes her head and tightens her arms around my waist.

"There is nothing to be afraid of. I will fix this." I kiss the top of her head. "I promise you, baby, I will protect you."

There is only one situation in my life I haven't been able to rectify. It's been years of an unbearable weight on my shoulders that I can't stomach. But now, now I have the information I need to fix the past too.

I dry Isabelle's body with a warm towel. Then I wrap it around her and carry her to our bed and gently set her down. I crack the seal on the bottle of water that sat on the nightstand next to the two pills I had Dr. B bring down before we even got home.

"Take these." I hand them to her.

"What are they?" she asks, but immediately pops them in her mouth and swallows. It warms a part of me knowing that she trusts me so much that she took them without an explanation.

I have so many details I have to handle but my most important one is the woman lying in front of me. Her eyes glisten with tears and dilate with need when her gaze skims over my still nude body. I won't touch her, not while she is in this headspace.

"Sleeping pills. I got them from Dr. B.," I explain. "You need your rest."

"He's still here?"

"He will be here until I tell him he can leave."

"Does everyone do as you say?"

I nod.

My phone chirps from the dresser. I know who it is and why they are calling. Antonio and Demetri are waiting on me to bury Tommy's body. With instructions to drive to my property upstate and wait until I get there, they will sit for however long it takes for me to take care of Isabelle. Antonio may be my boss, but he is also my friend. Tonight, when he looked to me, waiting for orders on how I wanted the situation to disappear, he was a friend waiting on instructions.

Isabelle's hand brushes over my bare stomach. Her fingers follow the line of dense hair. My dick jumps to life at her touch. She glances up at me with unsure eyes.

"Touch me," she whispers.

I gently shake my head in response.

"I want to touch you."

I step back and open my arms. "Do your worst, angel. You want to take out your fears and worries on me, have at it. I am all yours for the taking."

"Why won't you touch me?"

"Because you are not in the right frame of mind. You're in shock."

She scoots off the bed, determination in her eyes. She drops to her knees in front of me. Her hand reaches out and tentatively reaches for my growing shaft. She watches me as I watch her. Her eyes drop then lazily open. The pills I gave her are kicking in. She leans forward and swipes the tip with her tongue. She glances up at me again with half lidded eyes.

"Giovanni…" Her voice so soft, so tired, so trusting.

I crouch down in front of her and hold her chin with my thumb and forefinger. "Yeah, angel?"

"I'm sorry."

"Nothing to be sorry for." I lift her from the floor and lay her in our bed.

"Will I be asleep for a long time?" I nod. "Good." She sounds so relieved. I kiss her forehead and stand up. "Don't leave me." She reaches out and grabs my arm.

"I'm only going to check on Luca. I'll be right back. Go to sleep, angel."

Before I take two steps away from the bed, she turns on her side, pulls the covers to her chin, and closes her eyes.

My girl will be asleep for hours while I bury her dead husband on the north side of my property.

Giovanni
CHAPTER FORTY

1 Week Later

The finality of the steel bars locking behind me stirs something deep in my soul each and every time the sound echoes through the drab space. The soft soles of my extravagant leather shoes scuff the unforgiving concrete floor, almost as a warning. What you see is definitely not what you get when it comes to me. The rough surface of the floor may eat up the expensive sole of my Italian loafer, but in no way does that soft material represent who I am.

My steps are determined and heavy and my shoulders are square as I am directed to an area I have visited many times before. The odor inside these walls is putrid in its failure, but it also calls to me in a way that hounds me. Each step I take farther inside the sparse room, exacerbates the desperation and depravity I hold close. I am no different than them. I am just better. Where the prisoners here at Irongate Maximum Security Prison may have lost their privileges due to their inability to cover their tracks, I have perfected them. They are just like me, except I have my freedom and will continue to do so. I have been groomed since I was a small child to cover my tracks. It is a part of my DNA just as the man who inadvertently taught me how to. My father. The same man I will despise until my very last breath and beyond. When I see him in hell—and I will—I will make a deal with the devil himself if he obliges my request of torturing the man who destroyed three human lives.

I walk past four round tables with two people sitting at each one. The next four rectangular tables hold broken families of three to five in their seats. It's a sad day when you see a child aching to hold their imprisoned loved one and can't.

My steps falter when I see the lone person sitting at the last table. They was getting the better of me. Our visits were always short, and since the last one, my life on the outside has become even more complicated. It's almost as if someone of a divine entity is bringing my past full circle and is now meeting my present. It was too hard for me to look them in the eye for too long. It's an ongoing agonizing pain that nags my insides. It's not because I am ashamed of who I am, or who they had to become. It's because even after all these years, I am ashamed of myself for not understanding and not forgiving.

I slide into the attached bench seat and smile. It's not a smile of surety. It is the total opposite of that. A wrinkled hand reaches across the table and lays palm up, absolution softens the lines around their eyes. The tattoo inked in beautiful script, reaching up their arm is on full display. *What doesn't kill us only makes us stronger.* No words more fitting. I accept the reaching fingers and my smile becomes more at ease. Harsh words were spewed the last time our eyes met. Forgiveness is held in them now.

"Hello, my boy."

"Hello, Mom."

"I think it's time I tell you a story."

"And I think it's time I give you freedom."

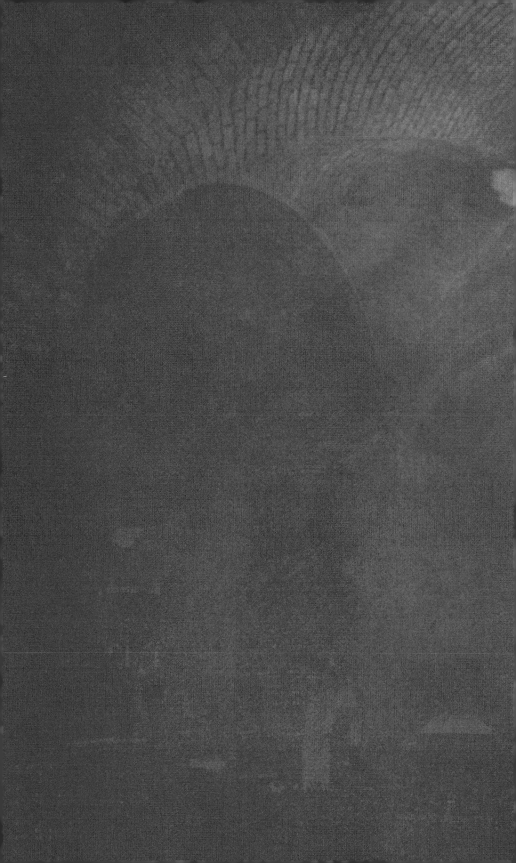

Giovanni
CHAPTER FORTY-ONE

24 Hours Later

I watch him walk out of the government building and collapse with confidence into his chauffeured vehicle. I scan every single one of his movements. Little does he know, the air he easily breathes will be snuffed from his lungs in the next few days.

I follow him through the city as he heads downtown to his mistress's apartment that he keeps for her. It's late, and if I was a nice guy, I would wait and let him get his dick sucked before his life changes forever, but I'm not nice, not to men like him. I give him five minutes to get upstairs and settled before I knock. His mistress opens the door and with a smile he can't see, she widens the entrance and lets me in.

Her pockets have been padded enough to last her a lifetime. Come tomorrow, her apartment will be cleared out and she and her belongs will be settled down on a tropical island.

Senator Hunt stands to his full height when he sees me walk through the door.

Cockiness is replaced with fear.

"What are you doing here?"

"I think you know why I'm here. Let's not start this inevitable conversation off with stupid questions, Senator."

He glances at his mistress with a helpless look. "You're in on this? I have supported you for years!" he sharply hisses at her.

"You're a disgusting man. Had I known all the things you had your hands in, you wouldn't have stepped across my threshold."

"My threshold, bitch. I pay for this space I allow you to live in."

"No worries, Hunt. She has been well compensated for her help."

"You killed my boy." He turns back to me with anger.

"Your boy took his own life with the decisions he made. Worked out to my benefit though. I got the girl."

"What do you want?" He shifts in his spot.

"Oh, I think you know exactly what I want. When I explained to Christy here how your old mistress is rotting away in a prison cell because of your need for revenge and success, she was more than happy to make sure that never happens to her."

"You finally figured it out." His laugh is filled with fake humor.

"That you were the man my mother was having an affair with? I have always known. I've just never been in the position to seal your fate."

"Your mother was the love of my life."

I snort my disgust. "That's why she sits in prison, right? For the murder of a man she didn't commit?"

"She wouldn't leave your father. I begged her to."

"My mother was an abused woman you took advantage of."

"She made her choice."

"So did you. The wrong one. I knew the moment I saw you at the age of thirteen that you were no good. You took advantage of a woman who was trying to feed her family. She may have sought out your touch for what she thought was compassion, but that came back to slap her in the face, didn't it? You took advantage. She needed the groceries you were so willing to bring us. The moment I saw you and my mother together, I knew you were just using her. I knew you would cause more trouble for my family. I knew that someday, I was going to have to come for you, and today is that day."

"Blackmail?"

"Oh, it's more than that, Senator Hunt. I think you know that. You used your position as the prosecutor to sentence a woman to life in prison for a murder she didn't commit. A murder I committed to protect her from my father after he found out about the two of you." What I won't tell, give him the satisfaction of hearing, is that I have lived with this guilt for two decades, thinking if I hadn't killed my father, my mother would still be free. Although, she would never be free because if he was still alive, she would probably still be with my father.

"Even after your piece of shit father was dead, she still wouldn't be with me."

"Because she knew both of you were no good. All she wanted was freedom and you confined her to a prison cell." His eyes narrow. "Yeah, I know why," I inform him. "She found out you were trafficking women. Although I didn't know she knew that until just recently. You sent her to prison in hopes that your orders to have her eliminated was successful and your secret would die with her. It wasn't. She has kept quiet all these years in hopes that it would keep her alive, not knowing it was my protection orders blocking your every attempt at having her murdered."

"Your reach is long. I misjudged your power. No one inside will touch her."

I nod. "No one on the outside will touch her either. My word of protection is to the fullest extreme. You cross that line, hurt someone under my protection, the consequences are brutal before your untimely death. Everyone knows that."

"Tell me what you want."

"Her freedom. I want her exonerated for a crime she didn't commit. In return for her years spent in prison, she will also be compensated with enough money to last her two lifetimes over."

"And why would I do this?" He huffs with a laugh like I'm incompetent and I don't have enough to bury him.

I reach into my back pocket and throw the first set of compromising images at him. They are of him and the women he brings into the club. They were taken months ago by Talia, Temptations club manager.

He looks them over. It affects him. The vein in his neck starts pumping rapidly, but it's not enough to thoroughly scare him into complying. I knew that. All those pictures would prove is he just another politician using his power to act poorly.

"This?" he bellows with a husky laugh. "This is all you got? No chance. Your mother will rot in prison. I will take the heat for some explicit photos." He throws them back at me. "I am a neglected husband. My wife is barren, has no sex drive after her hysterectomy, and she gave me her blessing to discreetly seek out my needs elsewhere. Every male in the country will feel sorry for me. My poll numbers will rise rapidly out of pity."

I stare at him, almost through him, bored, because he should know better. I would never come at him with just those pictures. It's one of the reasons why we have held on to them for so long. It just wasn't enough.

I grab my phone from my pocket and pull up the video Freddy uncovered at the warehouse from the security fed. I won't lie, it was excruciating to watch. The first video was of Isabelle and Tommy. The attack on my Isabelle was brutal. The moment she fought him off when he tried to sear her body with his badge, heated by a torch, to brand her, to prove to her that he owned her, was the moment I pushed stop. The brutality in which he handled her was disturbing to my soul. The man in me wanted to destroy everything and everyone in sight just because. I wanted to bring him back and kill him all over again and again. I was blood thirsty with no one to drink from. Even knowing there was a second video, I set the phone down to the side after hitting stop. I needed a minute of reprieve. I couldn't continue.

Isabelle's emotions have been all over the place, rightfully so. She was almost mute in the days following. It bothered me that she wouldn't or couldn't talk to me, but I also understood it, and in some small way, I was glad. She needed to work it out in her own head before she could express it to me. I understood that from my own past trauma. For as strong as a man as I am, watching the video made me want to vomit, and to a certain extent, feel like a failure for not protecting my woman just like I couldn't protect my mother.

With each day that passes, more and more of my Isabelle shines through. She's a strong woman who brought light into my dark life.

The second video Freddy forwarded to me was Hunt's nail in his coffin.

I flip my phone toward him and hit play with a smile now on my face. It is a video of him standing in the middle of a cement block room, surrounded by half dressed women, dirty, drugged, and abused giving orders on their disbursement.

The ringleader caught in action.

A dead man in waiting.

Isabelle

EPILOGUE

3 Months Later

So many things have happened since the night Tommy kidnapped me. The biggest one was that I shut down for almost three weeks. My words were few and far between. Abigail was my main priority, and we were Giovanni's. I just needed a mental break, a place to rest my head with no worries. That safe place was Giovanni's chest. He has been there for me every step of the way. I had to come to terms with all the emotions flooding through me. I even went as far back as my childhood. I thought about my mother constantly. It was like life was forcing me to think about her. I forgave her for what I thought she had done wrong to me, when only she was trying to protect herself mentally by throwing herself into her child to take away her own reality. I even told Giovanni that one day, no matter how far off it may be, I would like to reach out to her, but that it would have to wait until my father was dead. I never want to see that man again. I just hoped she would outlast him. Now knowing what I do, processing what I could, and the fact that if I stayed with Tommy, Abigail would have probably looked at me the same way. Because each person has their own story and even though Abigail is young, I know in my heart of hearts she didn't go untouched. It's a cycle. One I just broke. I couldn't be prouder of myself.

The biggest and best thing that happened to me—to us—was that Giovanni whisked me away to a tropical Island that Mr. Heart owned. One Sunday night after I started to come around, Giovanni took me to the "family" dinner at Mr. and Mrs. Heart's house. To say I was nervous was an understatement. When I got there, Lilah and Sofia made me feel right at home. I expected men in black suit with guns to be posted at every corner. It was the total opposite. Yes, there were armed guards posted and the mansion was set behind stone walls, but the family—now my family—was dressed down. Jeans and casual shirts were worn by the men. The girls had on comfortable jogging outfits or jeans with their hair in top knots.

The food... oh, the food was the best I had ever tasted. Mrs. Heart knows how to cook, and she put me right to work. I wasn't in the door five minutes when she had me setting the table. Lilah laughed, told me her first time there could have been a disaster but because she is so outspoken, she fell into the family rhythm rather quick.

The kids... they ran that household. There were nine of them running around. Well, seven running and two newborns. Jessica had her baby just before Sofia. River, Caelan and Sofia's son, is adorable, and Ryker, Luke and Jessica's son has eyes like I've never seen before. I never expected to see Mr. Heart sitting on the floor playing tea party with Lakelynn, Gracie, Imogen, and Abigail. Mrs. Heart had the boys in the kitchen helping her cook. She told me to make sure each one had a task, or they would tear up her house. I laughed. She didn't, giving me a stern look. I obeyed. She's a funny, very loving woman with her family, but I feel sorry for the person who thinks they could cross her.

At dinner, Mr. Heart sat at the head of the table. Antonio was to his right and Mrs. Heart was to his left. Giovanni sat next in line after Antonio, and a man named Lorenzo sat next to Mrs. Heart. The kids sat in-between their parents because from what I understand, Lakelynn started a food fight not too long ago. It started with her throwing some mashed potatoes at Jagger. Jagger gave her the stink eye but didn't retaliate, knowing better because he is the oldest. Imogen decided that wasn't good enough and tried to hit Colt with a spoonful. She missed. It hit Mr. Heart in the chest. It wasn't good. Now the kids no longer have the freedom of sitting together at the end of the table until their punishment is over. From what I understand, Mr. Heart laughed his ass off after dinner was over and he was sharing drinks with the men in his office.

During dinner, the conversation flowed like any regular dinner table. "Business," as Giovanni said, was never discussed over Sunday dinner. It was for family time. That confused me a bit because when dessert and espresso came out, Giovanni and Mr. Heart were talking. I heard Mr. Heart ask Giovanni if he had handled a "certain" situation. Giovanni nodded and told him it was done. It sounded like business to me. I ignored it. Then I heard Mr. Heart ask if Giovanni wanted to use his island. My ears perked up, I have always wanted to go to an island. Giovanni said he would be honored.

"What are you waiting for?" Mr. Heart asked.

"Was just giving her some time."

"Was the paperwork filed?"

"Last week."

"I can put in the call to Father John then?"

"Yes, sir."

"When can I tell him we will be flying out?"

"I have to ask first."

"Is one of my toughest men chickening out?" Mr. Heart grinned with a slight laugh.

Giovanni huffed an incredulous chuckle. "Never."

"Now is as good as any." Mr. Heart waved a nonchalant hand and sat back in his chair, as if to give Giovanni the floor.

I was so confused.

"Ask me what?" I turned to look at Giovanni as he is slid his chair back from the table we were all still sitting at. He dropped down to one knee and gave me a cocky smile.

I twisted in my seat to face him. Totally caught off guard, I stared at him in wonder. I knew what is coming and I wanted it more than anything, but I also knew this was not Giovanni. He would never propose to me in front of everyone. Never. He is private. Very private.

I reached for him, cradled my hand against his jaw and leaned in to whisper, "Yes. I will marry you today, right now. The answer will always be yes. But this is not you. You are private. Why are you asking me in front of everyone?"

"Because I love you. These people are my family, now your family. If it weren't for the man sitting at the head of the table, I wouldn't have been here to save you. Yes, I am very private, but my love for you isn't. I want to share it with all of them."

Aww's filled the room while I jumped onto his lap and knocked him over.

"We got a wedding to plan, Ladies," Mrs. Heart cheered, looking to the girls.

The young ones jumped up and down with little hearts floating in their eyes. Our Abigail came running and jumped in between Giovanni and me. She wrapped her little arms around Giovanni's neck and cried. She ripped my heart out and he put it back together when he gave her a kiss on the forehead and then a long hug. When he pulled back, he pulled out the tiniest ring and slid it on her little finger and asked if she would be his daughter forever and ever.

Her eyes sparkled like the purest diamonds.

We had a beautiful wedding on the sands of a topical island, known as Angel Island. I thought that was so poetic since Giovanni always called me his angel. It was an amazing day, filled with so much love. We said I do just as the sun set, and the night following the ceremony was simply magical. There were twinkle lights wrapped around a pergola set just at the shoreline. White candles, and stunning tropical flowers surrounded us. The breeze was perfect and the warm tropical water rushing to touching our bare feet was grounding. I called Zoey and asked if she would stand at my side. She happily agreed with a squeal. Giovanni's best man was a surprise to me. I thought for sure it would have been Antonio, but it wasn't. He asked the man who he claims had given him a life. Mr. Heart stood proudly at Giovanni's side and when the wedding was over, he was the first to pull me into a warm hug and welcome me into the family. It was a beautiful two weeks under the topical sun. The family stayed for the first week to celebrate with us, and then Sofia and Caelan took Abigail so we could have the second week all to ourselves.

One Week Later

The alarm on Giovanni's phone blares through the silent room. I roll into his warmth. The heat from his body makes me want to go right back to sleep, but I can't, not today. Today is my big day. I start my new job. Another first in my new life. I reluctantly gave up the argument when Giovanni told me he didn't want me to go back to the diner or the bar when I stressed that I needed to get a job. He didn't want me to go back to work at all. He told me he wanted to take care of me and for me to be a stay-at-home mom. To enjoy my time with Abigail while she is young. As much as I would have loved that, I needed to have some independence. I had never had that, so I was willing to fight for it if I had to. I told him I needed to make my own money. He was not happy when I told him that. There was almost two hours of silence between us. I hated it. It was torture. Then he took me to bed and showed me his displeasure by showing me pleasure. It was amazing. He is amazing. His skills in the bedroom are far beyond even my dreams. He has taken me to places and has shown me things, pushed my limits and carried me with sure hands through it all. There's this thing between Giovanni and I, a connection I can't explain. It's like we know how each other thinks and what we are feeling.

The argument was tabled until Hope came in for breakfast a few days later with the daily newspaper like she routinely does. Instead of throwing it the fireplace like he usually does, Giovanni left it on the counter when he went to get dressed for the day. My new job was fate intervening. I saw the advertisement for a personal assistant. I quickly wrote down the email and sent in my resume when Giovanni left for work. It wasn't until then that I realized it was O'Reily Construction. It stopped me in my tracks. I almost didn't do it because of who they were and who I was to this family. I didn't want handouts or favors. Then I thought better of it. I went back in and replaced my new married name with my maiden name so they wouldn't know it was me.

What I found out on my interview was that Nikki Heart, Sofia and Antonio's sister is Caelan O'Reily's right hand woman and one day sister-in-law. Apparently, she couldn't find a PA for herself that could keep their eyes and hands off her husband, Chris, Caelan's brother. The ad was to be her personal assistant while she was Caelan's personal assistant. It's confusing, but after my interview with her, I understood. The company had grown to an overwhelming success and Nikki couldn't handle it all. Her overload would become my job.

The greatest part about the job is that they have an in-house daycare. Once Abigail is out of school—the early learning private school Giovanni insisted she go to—she would come here to the office until I was finished with work. It was a dream come true. My baby girl was getting a great education and wouldn't be jostled around anymore while I bounced from job to job.

I roll to my side of the bed to start my day only to be rolled back by a determined hand. Within seconds, I am sitting, thighs spread over Giovanni's bare groin. His hips lift and brush against my center. I moan just from the feel of him, and the residual ache from the night before. Placing my hands on his chest, I close my eyes and rub myself against his growing length. With our clothes still laying at the side of the bed in a heap from the night before, it's almost too easy to be consumed by him once again. My hip is captured as his thumb from his other hand slides over my folds. His deep groan is my undoing. Knowing I bring this man pleasure does amazing things to my insides. I jerk forward, grinding against him as I sleepily gaze down at him. The hand checking to see if I was ready for him clutches the hip he left untouched. I grab for his cock as he lifts me and starts to slide me down his shaft. He seats himself deep inside my core, holding me there with his firm grasp on my hips.

"I hate that you're going to work today." He swivels his hips.

I groan my pleasure and displeasure at his words. "G…"

"I get it, but I don't have to like it, Isabelle." He pumps his hips with a deep jab. "I'll support you any way I can as long as I know you are safe."

"G…" I try to grind down on him, but he restrains my hips, lifting me just a few inches off him, long enough that I open my eyes and gaze down at him.

"Are you going to come already, my angel?"

"If you let me grind against you, I would have already."

"You're torturing me by going to work, so it's my turn to retaliate."

"This is how you're going to get me back? Hmm, I should challenge you more than."

"I see. You think you're slick. I can torture you in many more ways, my angel. You shouldn't poke the king of torture."

"My king of torture."

"That's right, my beautiful wife."

Sometime That First Week

We're settling into our married life. I am the happiest I have ever been. It almost seems surreal, like at any moment, the ball will drop and shatter. I guess it's because our first week back at home, I saw a news article I never in a million years expected to see. Giovanni scans the obituary every day. His reasoning: he needs to know who's alive or dead, so he knows who he has to watch his back for. I hate thinking that everyday could be his last, that one day I will lose his love, but he assures me that he takes every precaution and now that he has Abby and me, he is even more vigilant. If that day ever comes, and I have to stand on my own two feet, the love he has already shown me will last me a lifetime. The article that caught my eye was of a man being gunned down in the back of an exclusive club. A prominent man. There are no suspects and no details leading to his death. It was as clean of a murder as it gets. I read the article twice just to make sure I read it correctly. The article was about my father. He was murdered in cold blood. Giovanni was standing at the counter making his second cup of coffee. His back was to me. I stared at him, watching his movements while he did the simple task. Those hands of his are lethal and loving. I mouthed the words I love you to his back, closed the newspaper and a chapter of my life. Then I walked to the fireplace and tossed it in.

I guess I'm free to go see my momma now.

Giovanni

I sit and watch my angel dress from the bedside. She has a glow about her this morning. A lightness I've yet to see. She has always been beautiful but with this new light, she is simply stunning. I know we still have some battles ahead. Her and I both. We'll get through them together.

"What are you doing today?" she asks while sliding some panties up her legs.

What am I doing today, she asks? This morning, I will stand at the steel fence to Irongate Maximum Security Prison and welcome my mother back into the free world. I have made accommodations for her in an apartment three floors down from Hope. Hope offered her apartment, but our mother declined. She didn't want to intrude on our lives. I didn't agree. I have protected her my whole life and I would continue to. There was no negotiation, she would live in my building under my continued protection. She may be out of prison, but she is yet to be totally free.

"I have to go to the club for a few hours. Take care of security."

"Will you meet me for lunch?"

"Absolutely. What time?"

"I'm not sure. Can I text you and let you know? I'm not sure how the day will go."

She fumbles with a pair of diamond hoop earrings I bought her as a congratulation gift on a job she thinks she got on her own. I will go to my grave knowing that ad for employment was meant for her and that both her maiden and married name to her ex was flagged when her resume came through on O'Reily Construction's end. She wanted to work. I needed her to be protected. We compromised and she doesn't even know it. She thought she was slick using her maiden name. She forgets who she's married to.

"Yeah. Just text me and let me know."

"Will you be home for dinner? Abby wants mac and cheese. I know you won't eat that, but I can stop at the store and get some steaks and a make a nice big salad. Are you okay with that?"

"Perfect."

"Will you be able to stay home with us or do you have to go back to work?" She turns to me, fully dressed and walking in my direction.

"I have to take care of something today."

"Will you be late?"

"Don't wait up for me. It's going to be a long night of torture."

"Literally or figuratively?"

"Politically."

Her brows furrow, confused, but she blows it off, not asking, knowing I won't explain. If she reads the paper or watches the news in the next two days, she'll know.

A long overdue debt will be paid.

I pull her into my arms and kiss the tip of her nose. "We have to get going or you'll be late."

"Okay." She reaches into her pocket and before she can even pull it all the way out, I can smell the spicy scent.

Cinnamon gum.

Two sticks.

One for me.

One for her.

My angel.

Acknowledgements

To My Hubby: Can you believe that this is book #8? You have been my biggest supporter from the moment the words *"I think I'm going to write a book"* flowed across my lips. Thank you isn't enough to the man who has give me so much light in my life. The words I love you will never be able to convey the wealth of feelings I hold in my heart for you. I love you more, baby. No come backs. ;)

To My Girls- Amanda C., Caitlin, Kellie, and the two newest to the team, Amanda F. and Judy. You Girls ROCK! Thank you so much for your support! Your love for these characters and their love story is overwhelming is such a surreal way for me. I knew I loved the Elite Eight, but to have you girls read their stories and love them just as much as I do and want to become beta readers is mind blowing for me. I hope you all love the Bleeding Hearts Series just as much. Thank you from the bottom of my heart.

To Monty Jay– I love our late-night panic writing calls. You are an inspiration, my friend. You deserve the stars.

To My Editor: Thank you so much for polishing my words and for loving Giovanni and Isabelle.

To The Readers: Thank you for reading book 2 of the Bleeding Hearts series. One Fateful Night was a journey for me. A long one. I hope you enjoyed their story as much as I have writing it. Giovanni and Isabelle are two very strong people with hidden weaknesses at no fault of their own. Their story was a tough one, but I had to write what they wanted me to. These two needed to find their way and for them it was better to do it at each other's side. Through this story, even though Giovanni is the strong hero we all crave to read, he still had a heart that was bruised. And Isabelle… she may be a fictional character, but her story is no different than any woman living in the reality of domestic abuse. Stay safe.

There is so much more to come with the Bleeding Hearts Series. As of right now there are two more books floating around in my head. Trust me, these men are bloody gorgeous and alpha 'til the bitter end.

If you enjoyed Smoke and Mirrors or any book from the Heart Series, please take a moment and give a review on amazon and goodreads. Much Love. Until next time…

HEART SERIES

Breathe With Me #1
Breathing Together #2
Breathing On My Own #3
(Caelan & Sofia's story)

Where The Chips May Fall #4
(Luke & Jessica)

Skinny Love #5
(Chris & Nikki)

Anthology

Jingle My Ballz #6
(Luke & Jessica)

BLEEDING HEARTS

Smoke and Mirrors #1
(Antonio & Lilah)

One Fateful Night #2
(Giovanni & Isabelle)

Shattered Diamonds #3
(Demetri & Haven)
Release Date: TBD

Goodreads:
https://tinyurl.com/vr4g2uw

Stalking Is Welcomed!
I love hearing from readers.
www.michelle.b.author@gmail.com

Facebook Readers Group:
Michelle B's Blushing Babes

Instagram: michelle_b_author

Printed in Great Britain
by Amazon

22142044R00200